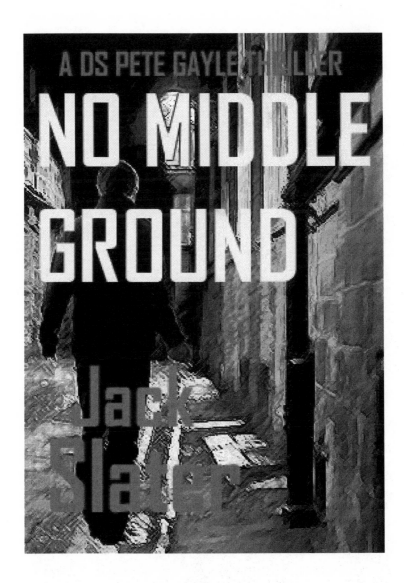

NO MIDDLE GROUND by JACK SLATER

NO MIDDLE GROUND

by

JACK SLATER

A missing father. A desperate daughter. A terrible discovery.

A new case is the last thing DS Pete Gayle needs right now, but when it falls right into his lap, he has no choice. Justice is crying out to be served. With a career-making trial about to begin and his son in imminent danger from a pair of psychopathic brothers, Pete goes on the hunt in what could turn out to be the biggest case of his life.

NO MIDDLE GROUND by JACK SLATER

In memory of my mother Jacqueline who sadly never saw this one completed.

ALSO BY JACK SLATER

The Venus Flaw

Nowhere To Run

No Place To Hide

No Going Back

JACK SLATER

Raised in a farming family in Northamptonshire, England, the author had a varied career before settling in biomedical science. He has worked in farming, forestry, factories and shops as well as spending five years as a service engineer.

Widowed by cancer at 33, he recently remarried in the Channel Islands, where he worked for several months through the summer of 2012.

He has been writing since childhood, in both fiction and non-fiction. *No Middle Ground* is his fifth crime novel in the DS Peter Gayle mystery series.

CHAPTER ONE

'Hello, boss. Nice chat?' DC Dave Miles looked up as Pete returned to his desk from the DI's office at the far end of the squad room.

'What's that doing there?' Pete asked, ignoring the question and nodding at the police radio chattering at Dave's side.

'Grey Man wanted the Archers but the rest of us thought Police Chase would be more fun.'

Grey Man was the station nick-name for the eldest of Pete's team, DS Dick Feeney, who sat next to Pete at their cluster of desks.

'So, who are we chasing?'

'The Southam brothers. Graham spotted 'em on CCTV, phoned Jane once he'd got some bodies in pursuit.' Dave jabbed a thumb at DC Jane Bennett, sitting opposite.

'Why the hell are you all sitting here, then, instead of out there after them?' Pete demanded.

'Waiting for you, boss. We didn't think you'd want to miss out on all the fun.'

Pete grabbed his jacket off the back of his chair. 'If we lose them because you were too busy playing silly buggers to get off your arse, Dave… Where are they?'

'There's three cars on them already, boss.'

The whole team were on their feet, intending to come with him if that's what he wanted.

'And Graham only called up a minute ago. Literally.'

Pete was sorely tempted to tell Dave to stay put and be their ears in the squad room but he was the only one of them who rode a motorbike rather than driving a car. Instead, he pointed at PC Jill Evans, cutting Dave off before he could explain further. 'Jill. Stay here. Keep an ear to the radio. You can guide us in and keep us updated.' He turned to Jane next as he grabbed the door and yanked it open. 'Where are we headed?'

'Graham spotted the elder brother on foot down by the court house, boss.'

She stepped through and Dave grabbed the door so Pete could walk beside her as she explained.

'He guided Sophie Clewes and Mick Douglas in towards him.' Jane took up the explanation. 'When he spotted them, he legged it up towards the shopping centre. They gave chase. He went through onto the High Street. Of course, it's market day. Bloody havoc up there. A pair of PCSO's tried to cut him off but one got a fist in the face for his trouble. He knocked the other one over too and kept running. His brother picked him up in a car down by M&S. Graham said it was a miracle they didn't hit anyone as they turned in off Queen Street.'

By now, they were approaching the custody suite at the back of the station.

'He said their back tyres will have bald spot's bigger'n Bob's, there.' Jane nodded to the uniformed sergeant behind the high desk.

'I heard that. Just 'cause you're not in uniform, DC Bennet, doesn't mean you can disrespect your superiors.'

'Just reporting what I was told, Sarge,' she called back as they headed for the back door.

'So, cutting a long story short,' Pete prompted as he slapped the green button by the back door, releasing it to let them out to the car park behind the station.

'Yeah, they turned right at the bottom. There was a squad car at the second bridge when the shout went up. Tried to cut them off but got rammed for his trouble. There were two by Central Station that joined in and a team had just finished with a domestic on Prince of Wales Road, so they got involved, too.'

Pete took his car key from his pocked and pressed the remote locking button. 'So, after all that, where are they?'

'As we left, they'd just crossed the river towards Foxhayes and turned left, back towards the rugger field.'

'Let's see if we can meet them down there, then, and if not, we can spread out and flood the area. Have Rapid Response been called in?'

'Not that I know of,' Jane replied.

Good, Pete thought. *I want these buggers to myself, if possible.* He ducked into his silver Mondeo and clipped his radio to the holder on the dashboard, switching it on to receive transmissions from the pursuit he was about to join.

Jane's little green Vauxhall was two cars over to his left. Ben and Dick were spreading out across the small car park. As he started the car, he saw Dave step out of the back door, now clad in his black leathers and full-face helmet. By the time Pete had reached the bottom of the drive down the side of the station, Dave was directly behind him on his big, black bike, engine rumbling like a tiger with its eyes on its next meal.

Pete pulled out, turning right towards the ring-road and Dave roared past him, swung left at the roundabout and was gone from sight into the red brick canyon of Western Way.

If they could catch the Southam brothers – or even just one of them – it would be a major weight off his mind after the threats the elder one had made to Tommy which, given their reputation, he knew were all too real. Only the younger of the two had been convicted for child sex offences but they were both known for extreme violence that went far beyond cold-blooded murder. They actively enjoyed making their victims suffer as much as possible. It wasn't just for his own sake and that of his family that Pete wanted them off the streets. It was for the sake of every law-abiding citizen in the land. While they were walking free, anyone and everyone who stood in their way or crossed their path however innocently was at risk.

These two were the very definition of psychopathic.

*

Pete was about to drive off the western end of the downstream one of the pair of big, white suspension bridges that dominated the centre of the city when the radio fixed to his dashboard sparked into life. Traffic was light at this time on a Thursday, the rush-hour long over and the lunch time peak yet to get started.

'Target right, right, right into Fergusson Road.'

A residential street on the far side of the river from the city centre, it went up the steep hill into a huge estate of 1930's housing that looked down towards the river and the city beyond. Notorious as a hotbed of drugs and violence and containing a high proportion of the city's single mothers and benefit recipients, it was the estate where they'd finally arrested Gagik Petrosyan, the Armenian drug lord whose trial was scheduled in another couple of weeks.

Pete had a busy time in court coming up from tomorrow.

The Southam brothers must have crossed at the first bridge they'd come to and cut back south at the far side.

'DC Miles to pursuit. I'll take Davidson Road.'

Davidson ran parallel to Fergusson.

Pete reached for the transmit button. 'DS Gayle. I've got Cowick Street.' He checked his mirrors. 'Dick, you stick with me but hang back, take the first right after the two lanes merge and stop there to box them in.'

'Right, boss.'

'Target left, left, left into Appletree Crescent,' the next report came from the pursuit car.

Pete hit the transmit button again. 'Dave?'

'Two seconds, boss.'

He was almost in place to cut them off.

Pete headed up the westbound section of Cowick, which was divided for several metres after the merger with Alphington by a metal barrier. If they came out this way, planning to head towards Okehampton, he'd have a march on them before they even knew it. He checked his mirrors again. Dick was several yards behind him while Jane and Ben had already gone from sight in the same direction as Dave, planning to block two more of the streets into and out of the estate where the brothers were trying to lose them.

His radio hissed again but nothing came out of it. Then: 'Lost visual. Repeat, lost visual on Appletree.'

He could hear the disappointment and confusion in the voice even through the rough reception.

Pressing transmit again, he said, 'Check the parking area in front of the shops along there.'

'Roger.'

They couldn't have gone far. There were no other turn-offs between the pursuit car and Dave's position.

'Dave?'

'Nothing this end, boss.'

'Well, a two-ton white Audi A5 doesn't vanish into thin air, guys.'

Again, someone hit the transmit button but changed their mind before speaking. Seconds later came the report: 'They're not by the shops. We've lost contact.'

'Shit!' Pete slammed his hands on the steering wheel. An opportunity lost. Where the hell were they? How had they managed to elude a car that was only yards behind them? He hit the button on the radio. 'Find that car, people.'

'Sarge.'

'Shit,' he cursed again.

They'd find the car all right. How could they not? But as for the Southam brothers, that was a different matter. He had no doubt that they'd have ditched it by now. It was just a question of where they'd gone afterwards.

*

'There aren't any side-streets off Appletree, are there? Just the delivery yard behind the shops.'

Pete had pulled over half way up the hill, near the far end of the busy shopping area, before housing took over either side of the road. From here, he could see the last of the exits from the estate where the Southam brothers had gone to ground. He watched the traffic and the pedestrians around him as he spoke into the radio.

'Affirmative, Sarge.'

'And we've got both ends covered so they can't go anywhere without us seeing them so, where are they?' He demanded. 'Find that car.'

A pause.

'Right, Sarge.'

'You hesitated there, car four seven zero. Explain.'

Another brief silence. 'There's one like it in a driveway, Sarge. Third house in on the right. But it's a different reg. We looked and confirmed.'

'Run it anyway. Make sure it's legit.'

'Roger.'

'Dave and Jane, make sure you can see the occupants of any and every vehicle leaving that street.'

15

'Roger.'

'Will do, boss.'

Silence resumed briefly until the radio hissed again. 'It flags as nicked, Sarge. But there's no-one in it. We're on foot to take a closer look. We'll give the house a knock. There's another vehicle beside the Audi on the drive that is legit.'

'These two are known as dangerous. Are either of you armed?'

'No, Sarge. Just batons.'

Pete almost told the two officers to hold off, wait for support, but that would risk losing the Southam brothers. He couldn't bring himself to make that call. There was too much at stake. 'Draw them and use extreme caution.'

'Acknowledged.'

If either of them – or the occupants of the house for that matter – got hurt in the next few minutes, it was Pete's neck on the block, but what else could he do? The two men from Wiltshire were a danger to the public every second they were out of custody. Any opportunity to arrest them or hinder in their escape from justice had to be taken.

He knew what station chief DCI Silverstone's answer to that would be, but he wasn't out here calling the shots. In fact, he rarely stepped out here into the real world of policing. He was too busy trying to keep his own career on-track to bother with the lower echelons of society or the men and women he was in charge of.

The radio sparked again. 'They were here, Sarge. Did a runner through the back. We've found one of the false plates they'd got on the Audi.'

'Are you sure they've gone?'

'Affirmative. They went over the back fence towards the properties fronting Okehampton Road.'

'Received. Ben, have you seen any movement?'

'Nothing yet, boss.'

'OK. Four seven zero, witness statements, evidence collection and get that car picked up. Everyone else, eyes peeled. They've got to come out somewhere.'

He hoped.

If they'd decided to stay put and hide, it would be a matter of more boots on the ground, including armed response, to dig them out. More resources, more time wasted, more arguments with Fast-track Phil, AKA DCI Silverstone, to get it all agreed.

*

As Pete sat at the side of the busy road, eyes peeled for any sign of the two men they were trying to track down, waiting for events to unfold that he was nominally in charge of – at least in DCI Silverstone's eyes – he was all too aware of what lay further up the road, around the bend and beyond the little roundabout just over the brow.

Even as he watched the pedestrians and drivers going about their busy lives, unaware of the drama unfolding around them, he couldn't help picturing the little convenience store where Malcolm Burton had left Tommy as their association ended shortly before his arrest half a year ago.

Half a year! In some ways it had flown by, seeming more like six days than six months. But in others, it had felt endless –

almost as endless as the previous six months while Tommy was missing. His wife Louise had sunk into the depths of a depression that had left her almost incapacitated - to the extent that their ten-year-old daughter Annie had felt the need to take over much of the routine of the house, swapping roles with her mother in many respects.

Pete was still amazed at, and eternally grateful for, the strength of character she'd shown over those awful months of uncertainty and fear.

He used his mobile phone through the vehicle's Bluetooth system. 'Jill. Third house back from the Fergusson Road junction off Okehampton Road. We need occupant details and any vehicles they own.'

'Two secs, boss.'

He heard the tapping of keys and moments later she was back. 'Mr and Mrs Turnbull aged sixty-one and fifty-seven. They've got a 2009 Skoda Roadster, blue in colour.' She read him the registration plate.

Thank God for small mercies, he thought. The Roadster wasn't exactly a boy-racer's vehicle. He'd driven one once. It had a job to do nought to sixty in ten minutes and eighty was physically impossible.

'Thanks, Jill.' He ended the call and keyed the radio.

'All units, suspects have entered the property of Mr and Mrs Turnbull. They own a blue Skoda Roadster, index...'

The radio hissed, breaking over him. 'Boss, its Ben. They just left, heading away from me.'

Dammit! 'Are you sure?'

18

'Positive, boss. I didn't see faces, obviously, but it must have been them.'

'Did you see them enter the vehicle?'

'Negative, the hedge is too high.'

'Check the property. Now. All other units, get after them.'

He released the button on the radio and called Jill again on his mobile. 'Jill, get onto Graham. Get him to find and track that car.'

'Right, boss.'

She broke the connection as Pete switched on the engine, hit the lights and sirens and swung his car around in the busy street to join the chase.

*

'One car for cover, still two-nine miles per hour,' Ben reported over the radio. He was trying to keep the bright blue car in his sights without revealing his presence to its occupants until backup could catch up with him so there were enough bodies to take the brothers without risking harm either to themselves or any members of the public.

'Received.'

His phone rang, jangling through the Bluetooth system.

'Shit.' The last thing he needed now was a distraction. He checked the screen of his ringing phone. The number was vaguely familiar, but he couldn't place it. He hit the green icon. 'PC Myers.'

'Ben, its Sally Hanson. I need to talk to you.'

His eyes flashed wide in shock. He hadn't heard from her in God knew how long and suddenly she was calling him out of the blue. How – or why - had she even still got his number? 'Sally? Jesus! How long's it been? What's up?'

'It's been a while, I know. Too long. I'm sorry. I wouldn't have bothered you now, but it's my dad. He's disappeared. I went round his house earlier and I found something. Something bad.'

'What…? What kind of bad, Sal?' She could hardly have picked a worse time to call, but she sounded desperate. He was reluctant to put her off. Instead, he tried to concentrate on his driving as she hesitated. Coughed.

When she spoke again, her voice sounded strangled. 'I think he might have done some things in the past. Killed some people.'

'*Killed?* Are you…? Based on what?'

'I went to check on him like I said, make sure he was OK or see if he'd left a note to tell me where he'd gone off to. He wasn't there. Nor was his car or a note. But I found some stuff in his loft. I was… I thought, while I was there, I'd see if he had anything about his parents and that. I've never met them and he's never talked about them. Whenever I asked, he just shut me down. But I've been trying to trace our family history, ancestors and that. I saw some suitcases in the loft, thought I'd have a look, see if he'd got anything useful in there. But there was a bunch of other stuff - papers, jewellery, ID's. Stuff he shouldn't… *Couldn't* have if he wasn't involved in... What should I do, Ben?'

'Where are you?'

'Back at home.'

'Stay put. You say he's disappeared? Does he know you've found this stuff?'

20

'No.'

'When did you last see him?'

'It's been three days.'

'I'm in the middle of something now, but give me your number, let me speak to my boss and I'll call you back in five minutes, OK?'

She hesitated.

'Trust me. Five minutes, max. I promise. If anyone can help, it's my boss. He's good folk, Sal.'

He could understand her hesitation. She didn't know Pete Gayle from Adam. But she knew Ben and that she could rely on him. Why else would she have phoned him? Finally, she spoke, decision made. 'OK. Five minutes.' She reeled off her number.

'Got it. Now, lock the doors and stay safe. Five minutes, Sal. Promise.'

'Thanks, Ben,'

CHAPTER TWO

Jesus!

Ben knew Sally wasn't the type to go off the deep end. If she was worried enough to come to him with this, it had to be real. He hit the speed dial for Pete's number while keeping one eye on the road ahead, searching for the bright blue Skoda while at the same time watching for errant pedestrians or other vehicles that might intersect his path as he drove fast towards the edge of the city.

'Ben?'

'Boss, I just had a call from an old girlfriend of mine. And it wasn't a social call. Nothing we can do at this minute, of course, but I said I'd talk to you and call her back.'

'What's the problem?'

'She's in a bit of bother. Her dad's gone missing. Him and her mum divorced years ago, but he stayed local and she stayed in touch with him, though she lived with her mum. Anyway, that's not the point. While she was looking for him she came across some stuff in his loft that points towards him being involved in some murders, way back.'

'Is this for real?'

'She's not the sort to take the piss, boss. And we haven't spoken for years.'

Pete was silent for what felt to Ben like half a minute as he hurtled up the narrow residential road at what would have been dangerous speeds were it not for the lights and sirens that flared and blared from his grille.

Eventually, he could take it no longer.

'Boss, she's come to me because she trusts me. We were close. I can't see her shopping her own dad otherwise.'

Pete sighed on the other end of the line. 'OK, Ben. Tell her to get with some company, just in case, and we'll look into it once we've finished what we're doing. And there are three occupants in the Roadster. Mrs Turnbull and both brothers.'

'Shit.' A hostage situation was the last thing they needed with these two. They were known to be wilfully vicious. 'And thanks, boss. I couldn't have passed it off to anyone else.' Instinctively, he glanced in the mirror, knowing Pete was only a short distance behind him though still out of sight.

'Let's just catch these two buggers first, eh?'

Pete ended the call before Ben could respond. He grinned as he keyed in Sally's home number.

Then jammed on the brakes as he caught a glimpse of bright electric blue from the far side of the car park on his left.

Of course, there were thousands of cars in that colour on the roads, but not so many with that distinctive high roof and boxy shape. He flicked off the lights and sirens, hauled the car round on squealing tyres into the entrance and keyed the radio mike as he let the steering straighten up once he'd made the turn.

'Possible target vehicle, far side of the supermarket car park, Okehampton Road. Checking it out.'

Sally could wait for a few more seconds.

He winced as a dark coloured 4x4 started backing out of a space on his left, just feet away. Reaching for the siren switch, he resisted at the last moment. He didn't want to alert the suspects if they were just a few yards away. The element of surprise was the one thing he had in his favour right now.

Luckily, the big vehicle stopped as the driver spotted him and Ben passed unscathed. Getting closer, he could see that the blue car was indeed the right make and model. He made the last turn and approached cautiously, wishing he had a passenger to provide an extra pair of eyes as he needed both to avoid the shoppers all around him but at the same time needed to read the number plate without making it glaringly obvious.

He saw the last letters first. DFE. Then the numbers. Nine five.

A little white Nissan backed out of a space on the other side of the roadway, just a couple of yards short of the Skoda he was looking at. He stopped to let them out, taking the opportunity they'd inadvertently offered.

Peering at an acute angle at the plate on his left.

WP.

It was them.

He keyed the radio. 'Sighting confirmed. Sighting confirmed. Suspects not visible but it is the vehicle they left in.' He released the radio and swung his car into the space left by the little Nissan.

'Do not approach, Ben,' the response came from Pete. 'Repeat, do not approach. Wait for back-up.'

'Received.'

He wasn't going to waste the next few seconds, though. Keeping his eyes peeled, he picked up his mobile phone and dialled. The call was picked up almost before it connected.

'Ben?'

'Yes. I spoke to my boss. He said to tell you to go somewhere with some company. Ease your mind a bit. We'll look into things as soon as we're done here.'

'Thanks, Ben. You're a star. You really are.'

'And I suppose you're a poet and didn't know it.'

She laughed nervously. 'Yeah, I suppose I am. Where should I go? I've got to pick Jem up from nursery in a bit.'

'Jem?'

'Of course, you haven't met him, have you? My little lad. He's three now. I suppose I could take him round to Mum's. But how long for? Tony'll be coming home and...' She paused. 'Tony's Jem's dad.'

Ben was all too aware of the seconds ticking by.

'Can you call Tony from your mum's get him to meet you there instead? Just go to the nursery a bit early, have a chat with the other mums and that. I can't give you a timescale, Sal. We'll pick it up as soon as we can but we're right in the middle of... Oi!' He frowned sharply at a woman who was clambering awkwardly into the car next to his and had banged the edge of her door into his. 'Gimme your dad's address and we'll be in touch as soon as we can get there, OK?'

'I don't want to...'

The woman glared back at him from the car to his right as her husband started the engine and began to reverse out.

'Never mind that, Sal. It's what we're here for. I remember he used to be up on Wreford's Lane. Is he still?'

'Yes. Number twenty-five.'

'And what does he drive nowadays?'

'A dirty green Peugeot estate car. I don't know the number though. Don't even know my own, if I'm honest.'

'OK, leave it with me. I'll get back to you soon.'

'Thanks, Ben.'

'See you later.' He ended the call as he spotted a patrol car easing up the same roadway he'd used and what he thought was his boss' silver Mondeo on a parallel one to his left. As they both reached the cross-route he was parked on he stepped out of the car, plenty of room around him now as the space next to his had yet to be reoccupied.

He confirmed it was Pete's car approaching from one side while the patrol car came up from the other, swung across the road-way as if it was going to reverse in next to him, then stopped, blocking the route completely. Its blue lights flicked on, silently rotating as the two uniformed officers stepped out and nodded to Ben. As he moved up to meet them a woman with a trolley full of shopping approached the car next to the blue Skoda. Pete crossed quickly towards her, holding out an arm to stop her. She protested briefly but then backed off.

The two patrol officers approached the suspect car cautiously, hands at their belts like a couple of old West gunfighters. Then they looked up and around at Pete.

'Clear, Sarge.'

They'd ditched it.

Had they gone into the store or simply lifted another vehicle and got away?

Ben saw Pete's gaze rise to the lamp posts around the car park as his did the same, looking for security cameras.

'Right. Get the entrance manned. No vehicle leaves without being checked,' Pete said briskly. 'Ben, get onto the others, bring them in here to start a search of the car park then join me inside. We'll go through the camera footage, see if we can spot them.'

'Boss.' Ben ducked back into his car and keyed the radio. He knew enough about the Southam brothers to guess what they would have done. A nice big 4x4, a single woman loading her shopping into the back. They'd have approached her from either side, bundled her in and driven out of here. If she was lucky, she'd survive the experience unharmed, but that was another story. And they had to be sure. Plus, with any luck, the cameras might give them a registration to search for.

'Ben Myers for Dave Miles, Jane Bennett and Dick Feeney. Over.'

*

Pete ran for the store entrance. He met one of the store security guards coming out towards him to see what all the fuss was about in their car park. He lifted his warrant card. 'DS Gayle, Heavitree Road CID. I need your CCTV room. Possible kidnap of one of your customers out there.'

That got his attention.

'Right. Follow me, Sarge.' For a big man, he moved surprisingly fast, heading back towards the store entrance at a brisk pace. Pete didn't recognise him as a retired copper, but he was clearly ex-services of some kind.

Pete followed him into the store and up a narrow staircase to the CCTV room on the first floor. The security man's badge gave them entry to a tiny semi-darkened room. Between the two of them, the bank of screens and another uniformed security man, they pretty much filled it.

'George will give you whatever you need, Sarge,' the big man said. 'I'll get back out there.'

'Thanks.' Pete nodded and turned to the seated man. 'DS Gayle, Heavitree Road.' He accepted the hand-shake the man offered. 'A bright blue Skoda Roadster came into the car park here less than five minutes ago and parked along the back. At least two people got out of it, one of them female. I need to know where they went as quickly as you can. She's a kidnap victim and they may have taken another from here.'

'Shit. Right. OK.' The man spun back to his screens while Pete leaned against the one empty wall – the one that included the door – and watched him work. Keys clicked and tapped in the small, quiet space. The screens flickered. People and cars changed in an instant as the time readouts shifted, then normal service seemed to resume for a second before everything began moving at a rapid pace. Pete had yet to figure out where the guy was looking when he abruptly said, 'There.'

He hit a key and everything stopped as he pointed to the third screen from the left on the top row. Peering closer, Pete could see the blue Skoda angled towards the space it was going to occupy. 'Got it.'

Motion resumed in real time. The car swung into the empty space. Three doors opened. Two men and a woman emerged, the man from the rear getting out behind the woman, boxing her in so she had nowhere to go. He closed his door and grabbed her subtly. The other guy – the larger of the two – pointed and they moved off. Diagonally across from them a woman was loading a stacked trolley of shopping into the back of a black older-model Range Rover. From this distance with her blonde hair pulled into a pony-tail, a blouse and jeans, she looked about Pete's age.

'Have you got a zoom on there?' he asked.

'There's a bit but it's mostly digital. Quality's not good.' The guard grabbed the joystick and demonstrated. The picture hadn't enlarged much when it began to break up.

'OK, that'll do. Maybe they'll get closer to another camera.'

'One of the forecourt cameras catches the exit road.'

'Perfect. Run it on, let's see what they did.' He could have predicted what would happen next, but he still had to see it for himself.

There was a click from the door behind Pete and it opened to admit Ben. 'Boss?'

'We've found them, Ben. Call the others off the search and get ready to move,' he said without taking his eyes off the screen.

'Will do.' Ben stepped out again, the door closing behind him.

The three figures had waited patiently for the woman to finish loading her shopping, return the trolley to a bay a few steps away and come back to her car. Steve Southam kept a tight grip on their female companion all the while, one hand on her upper arm, the other low down, tucked between them.

Pete guessed he had a knife or some other weapon in that hand and he would have enjoyed keeping the woman under tight control as she watched events unfold, unable to do anything about them for fear of her own life.

Then, as the woman returned to her Range Rover, Adrian Southam stepped up quickly behind her. There was no-one else close enough to take any notice as he grabbed her pony-tail with one hand and jabbed her in the spine with the other. Steve brought their original captive across the gangway and they all piled into the 4x4, the woman who owned it in the driver's seat.

Pete could see Southam ordering her to lock them all in before moving quickly around the front to the other passenger door. A quick burst from the exhaust pipe and she reversed out and headed for the entrance, passing Ben's car in the opposite direction as he drove up towards the abandoned Skoda.

'Cheeky bastards,' the security guard muttered.

'You've got no idea, mate. Let's see if we can get a registration number.'

'Right you are.' He hit a key and the motion on the screen sped up until he paused it again, freezing the images and pointing to a different screen. 'That's it, isn't it? Left lane.'

'Yep.' Pete peered closely at the screen he was pointing to.

'Hold on,' the guard said and zoomed the camera in slightly. 'There. Best I can do.'

'It's good enough.' Pete reached for his radio. 'DS Gayle to all units. Suspects are now in a black Range Rover.' He read out the registration. 'They turned left out of the car park three minutes ago, now with two, repeat two, female hostages. Get a registered keeper on that plate and get after them.' He released the transmit button and lowered the radio. 'You know what I'm going to ask for now, don't you?'

'There's already a disc in the drive, Sergeant.'

'Good man.'

Moments later, disc drive humming as it burned a DVD of the footage he needed, Pete's radio hissed. 'Black Range Rover's registered to a Carlton Webber of Cheriton Bishop, boss,' Jane told him.

'Presumably, Mr Webber's married,' he responded. 'And what's the status on our Skoda owner?'

'Mr Turnbull's been taken to the RDE. He was found unconscious on the floor of his sitting room. Looks like one of them used a choke hold on him. Here we go. Carlton Webber married Cathleen Bishop in 2011.'

'There's our second hostage, then.'

The disc stopped whirring and the drive popped open in front of him. The security guard took out the disc and slipped it into a paper sleeve, handing it up to Pete.

'You know we're going to have to hand this off to the double r's, boss.'

The uniformed Rapid Response Unit specialised in pursuit and capture. This was exactly the sort of job they were there for. It felt wrong to hand any job off unfinished and when it involved his own family's safety, every fibre of his being wanted to resist but he knew Jane was right. He had no choice.

'I know, Jane - much as it pains me. Get Dave to give them a shout. We've got something else to do, anyway.' He released the button and thanked the security man.

'What's that, boss?'

'Ask Ben. I'll be there in a minute.'

CHAPTER THREE

As Pete approached Ben's car, the contrasts between the members of his team bunched around the rear of it were starkly obvious in the late spring sunshine. Ben's spiky hair gleamed in the sun between the ginger beacon of Jane's swept back bob on one side and the long, narrow streak of grey that was Dick Feeney on the other. Dave Miles' all-black bulk at Dick's other side was relieved only by the office-pale complexion of his regular features.

Dave's helmet sat on the back of his big black Norton which was parked across the back of Ben's little car. Pete couldn't see either Jane's or Dick's vehicles.

'So, what's the story, Ben?'

'I've known Sally Hanson since we were ten years old, boss. She's solid, despite her circumstances as a kid.' He shrugged. 'Parents divorcing and so on. She called me out of the blue this morning. Hadn't seen her for ages, hadn't spoken to her for longer. But her dad's done a vanishing act. She went round to his house to see what she could see, searched it and found some stuff that she wasn't expecting. She described it as papers, jewellery and ID's related to a number of outstanding cases.'

'Shit,' Jane breathed.

'Did she say how many?' Dave asked.

'No.'

'Have you got his address?' Pete asked.

'He lives up on Wreford's Lane. Been there for years. Ever since the divorce, I think.'

'And Sally's got a key. Where is she?'

'I told her to go somewhere in company like you said, boss. She said she'd got to pick her kid up from nursery and she'd take him to her mum's until her feller gets off work.'

'Mum's it is, then. Let's go.'

*

As Pete turned into the narrow semi-rural lane on the northern edge of the city, Ben in his own car a few yards behind him, he couldn't help but look over at the wide grassy area to his left where, a few months ago, a taxi driver had died horrifically while Pete and several other officers were making arrests at an illegal dog-fight a few hundred yards along the road. His mind pictured the taxi, abandoned near the hedge over there, door hanging open in the moonlight.

Then he was past and away from the scene, back in the present.

Jonas Hanson's house was on the right side of the road, looking over the valley opposite that led down towards the city. There seemed to be two classes of houses along this narrow semi-rural road – well-kept and unkempt. His was of the second variety and his car was still notable by its absence.

Pete parked outside the house and signalled for Ben to pull up onto the short sloping drive that was stained with sand and cement that hadn't been properly washed off. They approached the front door together. Pete knocked loudly. They waited for several seconds but there was no response. Ben produced the key that Sally had given him back at her mother's house.

He inserted the key, turned it and stood back for Pete to push the door open.

'Police. Is anyone in?'

There was no response as they stepped inside, Ben closing the door behind them.

'Hello? Mr Hanson?' Pete called.

Still nothing.

Pete nodded towards the sitting room door as he headed for the kitchen at the rear. He glanced out to the back garden, which was as untidy as the front, then checked the utility and the garage before heading for the drawer Sally had described when they met. Pulling it open, he immediately found the little bundle of keys she'd mentioned and lifted them out, closing the drawer out of habit as he nodded for Ben to lead the way back to the hallway and up the stairs.

As Sally had talked about doing before them, they checked the rooms on the first floor before reaching for the pole to hook the hatch and its telescopic ladder down.

Pete led the way up, found the light switch and flipped it on, revealing a large, nearly empty space with a pale chip-board floor and sloping ceiling. The table and the suit-cases were just as she'd said they'd be. One blue, one burgundy and the third a kind of browny-orange. All it needed was a couple of chairs and they'd be set for the next half-hour or so. He climbed up, couldn't stand up fully in the limited headroom but led the way across to the waiting cases.

'One each or one at a time, boss?' Ben asked.

'A quick glance in each and we'll have them away if she was right,' Pete told him. 'You've got the evidence bags?'

'Yep.'

Pete pulled on a pair of blue nitrile gloves and lifted the blue case aside – Sally had already described its contents to them. 'Here, put that in one, then.'

He went for the next case – burgundy in colour. Assessing the size of the key it would want, he began flicking through the little bundle while Ben unfolded a huge brown paper bag, drew it over the blue case, folded the top shut labelled it.

The third key he tried snicked the lock softly open. He tossed the keys to Ben and nodded at the other case then drew the twin zips apart, ran one of them down the side and pulled a corner of the lid up to peer in under one of the lights.

Just as Sally had said, neatly folded newspapers – whole papers, not just cuttings – half-filled the interior. Among them, at the bottom, he could see the glint of gold and silver. He desperately wanted to pull the case open and see in detail what they'd got, but he knew better. He drew a reluctant breath and pulled the zip back up the side of the case, closing it until they could process it properly.

Ben opened the third of the cases as Pete was pulling an evidence bag over his. Like Pete, he took a careful look inside then glanced up. Their eyes met and Ben nodded slowly. 'Must be about ten in here.'

'Ten?'

'At a guess. I could look closer.'

'No,' Pete said. 'Not until forensics have had a go at them. But we're looking at getting on for thirty cases if that's right.'

'He's been a busy bastard, one way or another, hasn't he?'

'Get a bag on it and let's go,' Pete ordered, not even wanting to speculate about the lives this man had either ruined or ended over the years. And if he hadn't cleared off without warning, they'd never have known. How was that even possible? OK, Sally had said the ones she looked at were from up North, but even so… His lips pressed together as Ben closed the third suitcase and began to pull an evidence bag carefully over it.

This was looking like it could be the biggest case of his career. Of the station's history. And the timing couldn't be worse with the Burton trial starting tomorrow and the Southam brothers out there, intent on causing mayhem. But it was their case. Sally had come specifically to Ben. It was technically possible to hand it over to someone else – Mark or Jim, depending on what else they had on their boards. There was no way he'd give something like this to Simon Phillips. But what kind of message would that send to Sally, to Ben and to the rest of the station? No. He had a good team. They'd just have to work it in his absence and he'd step back in as much as he could until the court was done with him.

Ben finished what he was doing and straightened up.

'Right. You go down, I'll hand them down to you,' Pete told him. 'Two in my car, the other in yours and we'll have forensics meet us at the station to go over them. The sooner we can get into the contents, the better for the victims or their families.'

*

A few minutes later, Pete was knocking on the door of the next house to Jonas Hanson's. There was a car in the driveway beside him, so he hoped that meant someone was in. Ben was on his way back with orders to put an alert out on Hanson's car so that the ANPR system might pick it up, then get onto forensics to meet them back at the station.

He waited for several seconds before a dark shadow moved behind the frosted glass as someone finally approached. The door opened to reveal a man in his forties, dressed in vest and shorts, dark hair curling out of the low neck of his too-tight top and bristling over his shoulders. All he needed was a beer can in his hand to complete the picture, Pete thought.

'Yes?'

Pete lifted his warrant card. 'DS Gayle, Heavitree Road police station. We've had a call to your neighbour's here. I was wondering when you last saw him.'

The man grimaced. 'Don't know. Gotta be a couple of days, I suppose. We don't exactly live in each other's pockets, you know?'

Pete nodded. 'I appreciate that, but anything you can tell me might help. His daughter's quite worried.'

The man grunted. 'I suppose it'd have been Friday afternoon. When he came home from work.'

'And his car. Was it still there Saturday? Sunday?'

'Saturday morning, it was. Don't know about after that.'

'And you haven't heard him or anything?'

'No.'

'OK. Thanks for your help.' Pete stepped away. Had barely turned his back when the door was shut firmly behind him. He shook his head sadly. No questions about what might have happened to the guy. No expression of sympathy. Nothing. This really was a close community – not. He headed for the house on the other side of Hanson's. This was one of the well-kept ones. Two expensive cars sat in the driveway, the curve of garden between them and the road neatly manicured and mulched. The doorbell chimed melodically when he pressed it. A distant, tinny voice came from a speaker somewhere. 'Just a moment.'

When the heavy wooden door swung open it revealed an older lady, stiffly upright in white blouse and dark slacks, her silver hair neatly styled. 'Yes?' she asked.

Pete introduced himself. 'I'm trying to find out about your neighbour. His daughter called this morning and reported him missing so I wondered when you might have seen or heard him last.'

'We don't have a lot to do with him, I must admit. Quiet sort of chap. Keeps himself to himself. He seems to work hard, but you know how it is, officer. We come and go at different times. I last saw his car leave on Sunday, just before lunch. My husband was weeding out here and I called him to eat. We tend to eat early, these days. Better for the digestion you know.'

Pete nodded.

'Just before twelve.'

'OK. And he hasn't been back since?'

'No, but he does go off for days at a time now and then. Working away, you know.'

'Yes, so I understand. Well, thank you for your time, ma'am.'

'Not at all, officer. Glad to help.'

'Oh, one thing…' He took a card from his jacket and handed it to her. 'You couldn't just give me a quick buzz when he turns up again, could you? To save us continuing to search.'

'Of course.'

'Thank you.' Pete nodded and headed for his car. He didn't know what had happened to Hanson or if he would return at some point but, if he did, then he wanted to know about it. As well as stopping the search for the man, he wanted the opportunity to get here as soon as possible and talk to him.

But in the meantime, now he had a timeline, he could go and see Graham in the CCTV room to see if he could provide a direction of travel while they waited for forensics to go over the suitcases.

*

As reluctant as he might be, Pete had concluded by the time he got back to the station that there was only one approach to be taken. He set the last of the bagged suitcases beside his desk, maintaining the chain of custody, and headed straight for DI Colin Underhill's office.

Colin saw him coming and nodded him inside, peering pointedly past him at the three big evidence bags before raising his eyes to meet Pete's gaze without saying a word.

'Evidence,' Pete said. 'Looks like we've picked up another case, whether we like it or not.' He gave a brief explanation of the morning's events.

'So, you're taking on a case on behalf of your team, knowing that you won't be here most of the next few days and that one of your team knows the… suspect, victim, whatever he turns out to be?'

Pete shook his head. 'Ben doesn't know him. He knows his daughter. And what else are we going to do? How would it look to her, having come to Ben – to me – if we go and hand it off to someone else? I've thought it through. You're the boss, obviously, but you know as well as I do, I've got a good team down there. They can handle it whether I'm here to hold their hands or not.'

'His lordship's going to take some convincing. Especially if it turns out to be as big as you think it is.'

Pete sighed. 'Education's a wonderful thing, isn't it? You go out into the world thinking you know everything about everything before you even start work for real. Then if you're humble enough, you learn the truth. If not, you end up like him.'

'And it's mostly those who end up like him that end up in charge, so watch your step, matey.'

'It's a sad old world, isn't it? So, what do you reckon, guv? Do we carry on or what?'

There was a knock on the door behind Pete. He turned as Dick opened it.

'Harold's downstairs, boss. With a team.'

'OK.' Pete turned back to Colin. They both knew who Harold was. Supervising forensic scientist Harold Pointer. Colin thrust his chin at the door. 'Go on. Get on with it.'

'Cheers, guv.'

Pete quickly followed Dick back to his work station. 'Dick, Ben. One each.' He nodded to the big packages. 'We'll see if Bob can give us an interview room to work in.'

'Or two. Or three,' Dick said, picking up one of the cases to follow Pete out of the squad room.

'You'll be lucky.' The station only had three interview rooms. They weren't going to get all of them. This was going to be a long process.

They met the forensics team at the bottom of the stairs. 'Harold,' Pete said. 'Good to see you. I heard a rumour you were planning to retire.'

The chubby, bespectacled man shook his head. 'Not retire, Detective Sergeant, just move to London for a quieter life.'

Pete laughed as he buzzed them through to the back corridor. 'You couldn't. You'd miss us too much.'

'Much as I'd harbour no ill-will towards your offspring, Detective Sergeant, your enforced sabbatical last year did provide a pleasantly quiet interlude, work-wise.'

'You enjoy the challenge. Admit it. You wouldn't be in the job, otherwise. And the public might as well get their money's worth out of you. Wouldn't want you sitting around getting fat, would we?'

'My abdominal diameter is entirely bought and paid for.'

'Yeah, exactly – by the public purse,' Pete retorted as they reached the custody suite. 'Hey, Bob. How many rooms can you give us? We've got some evidence to examine.'

The middle-aged custody sergeant looked up from his keyboard. 'I can give you two right now, but I can't guarantee how long you can keep them both.'

Pete looked back at Harold. 'What do you reckon? Stick to one and take your time?'

Pointer tilted his head. 'Probably best in the wider scheme of things.'

'There you go, Bob. Compromise is key.' He stuck his hand out expectantly.

'Funny bugger. Number three. It's already open.'

Pete nodded the direction. 'After you, Harold.'

The tiny room wasn't anywhere near big enough for an entire forensic team, two police detectives and three suitcases plus their equipment. Harold sent all but two of his team away. Pete sent Dick back upstairs and Ben to the CCTV room to see if he could find any footage of Hanson on Sunday, to gain a clue of the direction he'd taken while Harold opened his aluminium tool case on the floor before lifting the first of the big packages onto the table.

He checked the label before slicing through it.

'We have a brown suitcase,' he announced before cutting the paper bag away carefully with scissors.

'We do,' Pete agreed as he glimpsed the contents of the bag from his position in the corner of the room, arms folded in a newly donned white paper jumpsuit.

They began by brushing finger-print powder thoroughly over the outside of the case. Three sets of prints were found and lifted, one from either side and one from the base of the suitcase. They were large and clearly male but, beyond that, Harold was unwilling to comment. Instead, he ran the zips back and flipped open the lid. Its black interior was taken up with several folded newspapers and a sprinkling of other bits and pieces.

Harold nodded to one of his assistants to begin with the jewellery while he lifted out the first newspaper. Carefully, he placed it on the small paper-covered area of the desk that was not already occupied by the suitcase and unfolded it. Pete saw the Daily Express header.

'June 20th, 2007,' Harold read and carefully opened it up. 'Let's see…'

The paper crackled as he folded back the pages, careful to touch them only at the very corners with his gloved fingers.

'Ah-hah.'

He'd folded back only two pages when he stopped. Pete moved to one side, struggling to see what he'd found past his corpulent white-clad bulk.

Harold stepped to one side, again blocking Pete's view as he turned to face him, hands behind his back. 'Page four, Detective Sergeant. A report of a young woman's body being found in Suffolk. Just outside Lavenham, in fact. Pretty place. Don't know if you've been...?'

'No.'

'Oh, well. You wouldn't like it, I don't suppose. Too peaceful. The victim was found nude and displayed lewdly in the churchyard of a nearby village, it says in the newspaper. She was identified by a police officer from Bury St Edmunds who recognised her as someone he'd previously arrested on several occasions. Drink and drug related charges, none of which resulted in a prison sentence. The report gives her name and age. And here, Detective Sergeant, is her identification which she'd have taken to the local pharmacy for her regular Methadone dosage.' He flourished a small white plastic card which he was holding carefully by its edges.

'So at least four years and two counties. So far,' Pete said. 'And you thought you were busy before, Harold.'

CHAPTER FOUR

'So?'

Colin Underhill looked up from his desk as Pete stepped into his small half-glazed office space at the end of the squad room. It was after four-thirty. Harold and his reduced team had taken more than half a day to go through the three suit-cases.

'It's a complex one.' Pete closed the door behind him and stood facing the big man. 'No prints on the cases except those we expected. The contents, either. There's news reports and trophies from a total of twenty-seven deaths and disappearances from 2003 to 2014, ranging from Yorkshire to Suffolk to Dorset and several points between. But none in Devon.'

'You know what they say about shitting on your own doorstep.' Colin leaned back in his chair, thick fingers intertwining on his belly.

'Yeah, but what does it mean for the case? I mean, it clearly is one case - one suspect - but spread out from here to Timbuktu. I lost count of the different jurisdictions.'

'Well, I don't envy you the writer's cramp or the cauliflower ear from all the time you'll be spending on the phone. But you're going to have to contact each relevant force as well as Missing Persons, get the case notes and go through them, record all the similarities, all the possible links between the locations, the victims and see if your man's kept any paperwork that links him to any of them apart from what you've already got. If he has, fine. If not, you'll need to liaise with the other forces and get them to try and find evidence that he might have been there at the relevant times. You said he's in the building trade?'

'Yes. But what I meant was, is it going to stay our case?'

'You mean as opposed to the NCA's?'

The National Crime Agency, based in London, had been set up with the express purpose of dealing with crimes that crossed multiple jurisdictions, as this one clearly did. But their specialities were in complex and organised crimes like drug dealing, paedophile rings and so on.

'Exactly.'

Colin tipped his head. 'I don't know. That'll be up to his lordship. I'll make the case if you want me to but, right now, I'd have thought something like this was the last thing you need.'

Pete grimaced. 'It is. But there's a responsibility, isn't there? It was brought specifically to us. And it was found on our patch. I'd have thought Fast-track would enjoy the kudos.' *And need it,* he thought. The DCI's reputation was spreading beyond the station – beyond the force, even. And it was not a good one.

Colin pursed his lips. 'You know how thin these bloody walls are, don't you?'

'Slip of the tongue, guv. Sorry.'

Colin sighed. 'You also know he's looking for any excuse to nail your arse to the wall.'

Pete raised an eyebrow. Such frankness in the face of superior ranks wasn't like Colin. 'Another reason for keeping this case. *I* need the kudos from it, too.' He winced. 'That sounded arrogant, but you know what I mean.'

'Hmm. I'll see what I can do. But you'd better solve it. Or your team had. He won't be a happy camper if he sticks his neck out and you don't deliver.'

An image of the DCI clad in black feathers, with his neck sticking out waiting for the fall of an axe popped into Pete's mind and he couldn't stop the beginnings of a grin creeping onto his face. 'Oh, for the opportunity, guv.'

Colin frowned.

'To chop it off.'

'Get out of here before *you* get something chopped off.'

Pete hesitated. The older man's support meant a lot to him and he knew it would to his son, too, as they faced the court proceedings the next day. It felt almost like it was Pete and Tommy who were on trial, as opposed to former teacher Malcolm Burton. Pete wouldn't feel comfortable explaining all that, any more than Colin would, hearing it. 'Thanks, guv,' he said simply.

Colin didn't ask for an explanation. Pete had known he wouldn't. Instead, he just nodded. 'Brief your team and clear off.'

'What about the writer's cramp and cauliflower ear?'

'I'm sure they'll cope.'

'I'll see you in court, then.' Pete turned to leave. He gave the doorframe a double tap as he went through to express his appreciation.

As he got back to his desk five pairs of eyes were fixed expectantly on him.

'For now, at least, the case is ours,' he told them. 'But you know I've got court tomorrow and probably beyond and so's Colin.

So, fingers out of orifices, caffeine on drip-feed and don't let me down. Right?'

'Thanks, boss,' Ben said from beyond Dick Feeney to his left.

'Don't thank me, Ben. You'll be doing the work. And there'll be a hell of a lot of it. We need case notes for every victim to start with. Times and locations. Then we need to try and put Hanson there evidentially or get the relevant forces to. And in the meantime, we need to find him.'

'I put an all-ports out on him,' the spiky-haired PC said.

'Nothing yet on ANPR, though,' Jane added.

Hanson's car would be flagged up as soon as it passed one of the countless automatic number plate recognition cameras positioned in towns and cities throughout the country as well as on the major highways and in many of the police cars that covered them. But ANPR was a present and future system. It didn't look at where he'd been in the past so the fact that they'd got no hits so far could mean anything or nothing.

'Did Graham get anything?'

'Not a peep, boss.'

Pete took a second to absorb that. 'OK. Well, at least that limits which directions he could have taken initially. He's self-employed. He's got to keep seven years' worth of papers related to that. It's the law and, whatever else you do, you don't mess with the tax-man. So, where are they? Spare bedroom? Bottom of his wardrobe? Sitting room sideboard? We need to find them, seize them and go through them. They'll give dates and locations. The other major question is why he stopped – or at least stopped collecting trophies – four years ago. It's highly unusual for someone like him. So, what happened in his life four years ago that was significant enough to put urges as strong as these on hold?' His gaze travelled around his team members.

'We know one thing that happened.'

Pete focussed his gaze on Jane.

She glanced at Ben then switched her green eyes back to Pete. 'His daughter got pregnant.'

'You mean...?' Dave started.

'Ew! That's nasty,' Jill protested. 'Even for you, Dave Miles.'

'And it doesn't need to be true,' Pete pointed out. 'Ben?'

The young PC's expression began to shift.

'When did she take up with her boyfriend? When did they meet and how? That leads you to the question of whether the boy's his. It's a question that needs an answer in the circumstances. Take Jill with you. You can put the lead-up questions; she can step in and ask the big one. Jane and Dick, you go to the house and do the search. Someone will need to get onto the PND in the morning and start downloading all those case files, then chase up anything you need to with missing persons or the SIO's but I'm off. Colin's orders. I've got a trial to prepare for. I'll see you tomorrow, Dave.'

As the actual arresting officer, Dave would be required to testify too.

'Just like these bloody students,' Dick said. 'Cram everything in at the last possible minute.'

'Good luck for tomorrow,' Jane grinned.

Pete's phone buzzed in his pocket. He took it out and checked the screen. Annie. On the mobile he and Louise had bought her a few months ago when it became clear that her safety could be an issue. He tapped the green icon. 'Button? What's...'

'Dad, its Tommy. He's gone.'

CHAPTER FIVE

Pete forced himself not to swear. 'What do you mean, gone?'

'Gone. Walked out. I phoned to wish him well for tomorrow and Nanna said he wasn't in his room, where she thought he was. She checked the bathroom, the back garden, everywhere. She'll probably call you in a minute, herself. She's probably onto the local station now, I expect.'

'When…?' Pete stopped himself. It was no use asking Annie questions that she wouldn't have the answers to and, if she did, they'd be hearsay. 'Never mind. Thanks for calling me, love. You did good. I'll speak to your nan. I'm on the way now anyway. Are you at home?'

If so, Louise would be there too. Otherwise, Annie was still under strict orders to only go home with someone whose parent was there. No exceptions.

'Yes.'

Relief washed over him like a tide. At least he wasn't going to have to be the one to tell Louise. Then guilt followed just as quickly. Annie had obviously had to. 'How's your mum?'

'Frantic, but OK.'

That made sense. It was exactly how he felt.

'He hasn't…? You don't think…?'

'Right now, I don't know what to think, love. But we'll find him. I promise.'

'But…'

'Tell your mum I'm going there myself, right now. Love you.'

As he ended the call he saw that his whole team were staring at him like a set of statues.

'What's up?' Jane asked.

'Tommy. It looks like he may have ducked out.'

'Shit.'

'I'd best tell Colin and then get moving.'

'Go, boss. We can tell the guvnor.'

Pete glanced at the door then over his shoulder at Colin's office and back at the team. 'You sure?'

Dave pushed his chair back. 'I'll tell him. You need to go.'

'Thanks.'

Pete didn't need telling again. He dialled as he was going through the door from the big open-plan squad room and turning towards the stairs. Pushing through the door with its 1970's wired safety glass.

Beep, beep, beep.

Engaged. Annie must have been right: they were talking to the Okehampton police station. There was supposed to have been an officer stationed outside the house for Tommy's safety. Had there been?

Pete thundered down the concrete stairs three at a time.

If so, what the hell was he doing? Sleeping? And if not... Pete grimaced. Either way, he would create merry hell when he got there. There wouldn't be an officer in the station that didn't know exactly what Pete thought of their levels of efficiency and competence, regardless of their rank.

On the plus side, if there was a man on duty there, it limited the options. Whether Tommy had run off or...

Pete swallowed as he ran down the corridor towards the custody suite and the back door. No, the Southam brothers couldn't have taken him. They hadn't had time, surely? And yet, he'd just spent four hours locked up with Harold Pointer and Okehampton was only half an hour away. Of course they'd had time. Especially if they'd been planning it for several days – as they would have.

'You're not helping, Gayle. Get your head out of your arse.'

'Been to see the chief, have you?' Bob asked from the custody desk.

Pete shook his head, not slowing in his flight towards the back door and the car park beyond. Had he really said that out loud? 'Not this time.'

He lifted his ID badge to the sensor, struck the door with the flat of his hand and fresh air hit him in the face like a slap. He shook his head. Was he losing it or what? Muttering to himself as he ran? Jesus! He swapped his ID badge for his car fob. Pressed the button when he was still several yards from the silver Ford. In seconds he was in the car, door slammed, engine running and on the way.

Mid-afternoon, the roads were full of parents fetching kids home from school. He didn't have time for this crap. He hit the blues and twos as he approached the road out front, checked for danger and pulled out, turning right towards the roundabout on Western

Way. It might not be an official shout but there was a boy in imminent danger, he told himself as he accelerated past the queueing traffic. The fact it was his son was beside the point.

And do we know he's in danger? That little voice in his mind was back again. *Or has he just buggered off, of his own accord?*

Pete's parents still lived in the 1930's bungalow he'd grown up in. The plot it sat on would make at least three of the one his own place occupied and even now it was right on the edge of the little market town, backing onto woods that were criss-crossed with a maze of footpaths and bridle ways. Three weeks ago, it would have been a mass of colour in there with the new fronds of ferns uncurling amongst the carpet of bluebells, stitchwort, wood anemones and yellow archangel. The bluebells would be pretty much over by now, but the leaves would be coming out on the trees above them, so it would still be a beautiful place to walk in. He'd spent many hours in there as a kid and he'd made sure to show it to Tommy and Annie when they were younger.

He'd even shown them the old hollow where he and his mates had made a camp with the occasional fire for roasting spuds back in the day and the site of the old ruined cottage, now no more than a foundation pad and a couple of moss-covered stumps of tumble-down wall, where legend had it that an old woodsman had lived right up to the 1940's with no electricity or running water.

Of course, when Pete had first heard the story when he was five or six, his first question was, 'Where did he go to the toilet then?'

His dad had laughed. 'What do you think all these flowers grow on?'

Pete blinked, focussing on the road and the here-and-now. Never mind a five-year-old's sensitivities – what about a fourteen-year-old's? Would he have wandered out there on his own, despite being told specifically not to? Just for a break from being cooped up like a November turkey?

Of course he would. Pete himself would and, after the past year, he didn't doubt that Tommy would want to get out in the fresh air, on his own, just to think – or maybe not to think but just enjoy the outdoors. Specifically not to think, probably – especially about what he was about to be forced to relive in all its gory and perhaps embarrassing detail, under the close and inescapable scrutiny of a court.

If he'd had time, Pete wouldn't have minded doing exactly the same.

As he headed for the edge of the city along a narrow, mostly residential street of old houses and small businesses, his phone rang.

Annie? His dad? Had they found Tommy? He hit the button on the Bluetooth system without even looking at the screen. 'Yes?'

'Boss?' It was Jane. 'Have you got your radio on?'

'No.' The last thing he needed now was music. Then he realised: she meant his police radio. 'Why? What's happened?'

'Mrs Turnbull's been found.'

'Jesus! Where? How is she?'

'She was spotted by a passing motorist, half-in a ditch down the road that leads west out of Cheriton Bishop.'

'And…?' Pete asked when she paused.

'She's alive, but only just. Evidence at the scene suggests they just kicked her out and kept going. We're talking cracked vertebrae, three broken ribs, broken humerus on one side, ulna on the

55

other, cracked hip. She was unconscious when they found her. She's been taken to the RDE.'

'And no sign of the other victim? Cathy Webber?'

'Nothing, boss.'

'So, they dump the old lady and keep the young attractive one. We know one of them's a paedophile. Do we know about the other one? Adrian?'

'There's nothing in his record. Apart from violence and murder.'

'And a jail sentence that ended abruptly, not that long ago.'

'Yeah, I was trying not to think of that, boss.'

'Well, do, Jane. We need all the incentive we can muster. Because whatever she's going through, the sooner we can put an end to it, the better.'

'That much, I was sure of.'

'Is there anything to be gained from me stopping off at the scene?'

'I shouldn't think so, boss. Traffic have got it covered.'

'I'll go straight through to Okehampton, then. Keep me updated.' He switched on his police radio and ended the call with Jane, focussing on the road ahead as he turned onto the main trunk road towards west Devon and Cornwall.

Seconds later, he saw an ambulance speeding past in the opposite direction, lights and sirens blaring. *Mrs Turnbull?* He hoped to God she'd make it. If not, he knew the guilt would eat him

up, rightly or wrongly. He had been in charge of the Southams'
pursuit when they'd gone into her home.

In the meantime, though, there was one thing he knew now
that he hadn't five minutes ago. The Southam brothers were heading
in the same direction he was. Why, he wasn't certain of, but he
didn't like the coincidence - not one bit. The question was, how far
ahead of him were they? There was no way of knowing how long
Mrs Turnbull had lain on that verge before she was found. It could
have been seconds, minutes or hours.

In which case, it was entirely possible that they had taken
Tommy, after all, to stop him testifying in Malcolm Burton's trial.

You don't know that, he told himself firmly. *You can't know
that.* He needed evidence. He needed to be at the scene.

*

His parents lived at the top of a T-shaped cul-de-sac. As he
reached the head of the road and glanced right, towards their house,
he could see a black BMW and three patrol cars parked around the
property. He pulled up several doors down and set off on foot. Had
barely got to within thirty yards of the place when the door of one of
the patrol cars opened and a huge figure in an over-stuffed uniform
emerged, one meaty hand raised to block his path.

'Sorry, sir, you can't…Pete!'

'Dazzer. What's going on?'

Darren "Dazzer" Perkins had been on the force a year longer
than Pete. They had worked together when Pete was in uniform, here
in Okehampton.

'I thought… Sorry, mate, what are you…? Scratch that –
stupid question.'

Pete shook his powerful hand. 'So, which numpty was supposed to be keeping an eye on the place – keeping it safe and secure?'

'Unfair, mate. And no, it wasn't me. But he was on his own out here. You know what staffing levels are like. And you didn't help, buggering off to the big city. They still haven't replaced you, you know.'

'Yeah. Not helpful or relevant when there's a pair of known killers on the loose, wanting to stop my lad from testifying tomorrow.'

'Eh? Bloody hell. Since when? We weren't told that.'

'I spent this morning trying to get them back into custody. And their last known direction of travel was this way. They nearly killed an innocent old lady in the process, back at Cheriton Bishop. So, what's the story here?'

'Scott's been out here since half past eight. All was well at that stage. No unusual activity on the street since.'

'Scott Bishop? How much of that time has he spent awake?' Pete hadn't seen or spoken to Bishop since he transferred to Exeter, but he did remember his inclination to burn the candle at both ends and catch up on his sleep in the middle.

'Needs must, mate. We hadn't got anyone else and we weren't expecting trouble.'

'W...' Pete was incredulous as well as furious. 'What the hell did you think this was all about? If it was just a matter of protocol there wouldn't have been any need to get you lot involved at all, would there? Jesus! Tell me you've searched the woods, at least.'

The big man nodded. 'We have. But there's nothing to see. Spring growth smothers everything. You know that.'

Pete didn't bother to argue. He headed for the break in the row of houses – the footpath that led through and along the backs, between the gardens and the woods – Dazzer following a step behind him. 'The back gate's secure, presumably?'

'Yep.' Relief coloured Dazzer's tone. 'No scuff marks on the gate or the fence. No broken or even open windows.'

'Back door?'

'Unlocked, but he's not a prisoner, is he? He's allowed to play in the garden. Kick a ball about or whatever. And like I said, there's no sign of him going over the fence. Or of anyone else entering that way.'

Who the bloody hell kicks a ball about in the garden, these days? Pete thought. It was a sad reflection on modern life, but accurate nevertheless – kids were more interested in computer games now than real ones. Hence all the fuss about childhood obesity, in his opinion. It was more to do with lack of activity than lemonade and crisps.

The back garden of the house he'd grown up in was surrounded by a six-foot wooden fence. As Dazzer had said, there were no scuff marks or damage to indicate it had been climbed over. He was tempted to reach for the latch on the gate, but resisted. There was one other option, though. If Tommy could get up onto the shed, like Pete used to as a kid, he'd be able to jump over from there.

He walked on another twenty feet to the narrow home-made bridge over the ditch that that people had used since before Pete was born to gain access to the woods. He'd talk to his parents later, see what they thought Tommy had been up to and where. For now, the priority was to find the boy.

As Dazzer had suggested, the spring growth around them as they entered the woodland was profuse, bright and sappy. Grass, ferns and cow-parsley brushed his trousers while hazel and hawthorn sported vivid green leaves and conker trees were festooned with cones of bright white flower while carpets of shiny narrow leaves covered the ground.

Pete scanned the vegetation for any sign of previous clumsy or heavy-footed passage.

'Where are we going?' Dazzer asked from behind him.

'The old cottage.'

'What old cottage?'

'Used to belong to an old coppicer. He made charcoal, hazel rods and so on, back before the war. It's ruined now. Has been for years.'

'I didn't know that.'

'My dad told me about him, I think. Or my grandad. Either way, I know the place and so does Tommy. He could be there. If not, we've got a problem.'

'What do you mean?'

'Well, you're right – I haven't seen any signs he was taken. So, the other choice is, he's done a runner. Again. And the court case starts tomorrow. I thought my DI had convinced him, but...' He shook his head. 'You never know with kids, do you? They seem to spend half their time in a world of their own, swap back and forth between theirs and ours as it suits.'

Dazzer laughed. 'That's what being a kid's all about, isn't it? Imagination. Playing. Learning.'

Pete sighed. 'Yeah. As long as they *do* learn.'

*

'Tommy?'

Pete's voice echoed through the dense woodland.

'Tommy, it's me. Your dad. Are you there, son?'

They'd checked the big hollow first. Nothing. No sign he'd been there. The old ruin was now no more than a hundred yards away, though they still couldn't see it through the densely packed trees and uneven ground.

'You're not in trouble,' he called. 'We just need to know you're safe, that's all.'

There was still no answer.

Ahead, he saw the fork in the path and stopped, pointing it out to Dazzer. 'The old ruin's up the right-hand path. You take the left: it loops round beneath it. The next path on the right cuts back up the hill to approach it from the other side. I'll give you a minute then we'll both close in carefully. Hopefully, he's there, just not answering.'

'Right.'

Dazzer headed off on the downhill path, his long legs carrying him swiftly and surprisingly quietly for such a big man with such a lot of equipment on his belt and vest. In seconds, despite his size, his dark frame was gone from sight. Pete gave him a little longer then took out his phone and checked it was set to vibrate only.

He didn't want it going off at the wrong moment and giving away his presence before he was ready.

He started up the right-hand path, stepping carefully, keeping one eye on the ground to avoid stepping on a twig and cracking it, the other watching his surroundings. He ducked under a low-hanging branch and stepped around a big old oak. Beyond it, another large tree had fallen, some time since he'd last been here. He examined the trunk where it lay across the path. There were no fresh marks where someone might have jumped onto or off it as Tommy would have had to, given his stature.

Pete's lips tightened. Maybe he wasn't up here, then? Or maybe he'd just found another path. He had taken a great interest and pride in woodsmanship, Pete recalled. And he'd spent several weeks, back in the winter, living off the land over towards Plymouth, having broken into a holiday cabin. He would be freshly practiced at all the skills involved.

Pete stepped over the fallen trunk. It wasn't much further now.

When the old ruin came into sight, it was even more moss-covered and broken-down than he remembered, stones scattered here and there around what little remained of the walls. A tree was growing in the one remaining corner of the building. Thin and spindly, it was growing in the very spot that Pete had more than once, as a kid, built a fire to roast chestnuts or even the odd foil-wrapped potato.

As it thickened up with age, the tree would push down most of what was left of the building. By the time Pete retired, there would barely be any sign it had existed. Nature would have completely retaken ownership of the place. He wasn't sure if that was a depressing or a positive thought in the present world situation.

Either way, it didn't alter the one other thing he could see from up here.

There was no sign of Tommy.

Then his eye caught something. The briefest glimpse: movement, beyond the ruined cottage; a shoulder, perhaps, black amongst the bright green of new leaves.

His phone buzzed in his pocket. Instinctively, he reached for it. Took it out, glancing at the screen.

Unknown number.

'Shit,' he hissed softly, taking a backward step to conceal himself behind the dense, dark and jagged leaves of a wild holly bush as he lifted the phone to his ear.

CHAPTER SIX

'Gayle,' Pete murmured, crouching behind the holly bush and peering around it to keep his eyes on the ruin below him.

'Boss?'

Pete's lips tightened. 'This better be bloody important, Dick. Your timing stinks.'

'It is. We just heard on the radio. A car's been found on fire off a back lane just west of Sticklepath. Someone phoned it in: they saw the smoke from about a mile away. Fire brigade got there, but too late. They had to let it burn. It was a Range Rover. The number plates were destroyed, but they found the VIN number. It's the Webbers'.'

The Southam brothers were still heading west, towards Okehampton. 'When was it phoned in?'

'Just under an hour ago.'

'Bodies?'

'No.'

Pete breathed a sigh of relief at that. 'They'll have taken another vehicle from somewhere before they torched that one.'

'Yeah. Nothing reported yet, though.'

'As soon as it is, we need to know about it. The call could come in there or over here. Let the call centre know and the front desk there. I'll talk to the desk at this end.'

He ended the call, still watching the old woodcutter's cottage site and the place beyond it where he was certain he'd spotted movement. There was nothing. He stepped out from behind the big bush and called out, 'Tommy, it's me. Your dad. Come on, son. Enough's enough. You need to come home. You know Adrian Southam's on the loose. And I know he's headed this way. I don't want you getting hurt, son, and you know that's what he'll do if he gets hold of you.'

Movement.

That same figure. Big, bulky and dressed in black from head to toe.

'Dammit!' Pete hissed.

It was Dazzer.

Pete heard the spurt of his former colleague's radio, even over the intervening distance. Dazzer reached for it, bending his head to listen. Then he looked up and shouted.

'Pete, they've got him.'

What the bloody hell's that supposed to mean? 'Hold on, I'm coming down.'

He started down towards the local man.

'Who's got who?' he demanded when they met moments later.

'Tommy. They've got Tommy. Picked him up on Chichacott Road.'

'Who's got him?' At that moment, Pete could happily have strangled Dazzer.

'Eh? Oh. Sorry. A patrol car. They spotted him walking north as they were coming down here to help look for him. They'd got a picture, obviously. Saw him jump into the hedge as they came round a bend and recognised him straight away, so they picked him up. He's not exactly a willing passenger, but...' He shrugged. 'They told him he'd be done for contempt if he didn't come with them. Apparently, he told them, "Fair enough. That's exactly what I feel for the whole sodding business." So, they pretended to arrest him for it.'

'Where is he now?'

'On his way to the nick in town.'

'Thank Christ for that. Let's go, then.'

*

Pete slipped his phone back into his jacket after asking the local police to alert him to any stolen cars that were reported in the next few hours.

That had been his second call. The first had been to Louise, to tell her that Tommy had been found and picked up by the local uniforms. Her relief had choked him up to the extent that he had walked on in silence for several seconds, bringing himself back under control before making the next call.

Dazzer looked sideways at him. 'You know you can't see him, don't you? Tommy.'

They were walking back through the woods towards Pete's parents' house. Had covered maybe half the distance.

'See him?' Pete retorted. 'I'll bloody crown the little sod when I get my hands on him, all the trouble he's caused.'

'Yeah, that's not going to encourage Morris to bend the rules for you.'

'Morris? Isn't he retired by now?' Pete remembered Sergeant Morris Tibbetts from his own days working out of Okehampton nick. He'd been old then and that had been... Pete didn't want to think how many years ago.

'Nah. Silly old fart'll die behind that custody desk.'

'How does he get away with it?'

Dazzer shrugged. 'The cutbacks, I suppose. Saves replacing him, doesn't it? And he hasn't exactly got to get too much exercise in there.'

Pete grunted. 'I know plenty of front-desk officers are retirees who've come back for the purpose, but I didn't know it could be done in the custody suite.'

'I don't know if it can officially, but this ain't exactly the big city, is it? Out of sight, out of mind, eh?'

Pete's frequent run-ins with Exeter station chief DCI Adam Silverstone popped into his mind. 'Yeah, I often think that would have its advantages. But it doesn't alter the fact that Morris is bending the rules just by being there.'

'And that's another reason why he won't bend them any further than he has to for anyone else. There's no point in you stirring it, mate. You won't win and, if you did, all you'd do is put the case Tommy's supposed to be testifying in at risk.'

Pete knew he was right. That didn't make him want to admit it, though. 'Yeah, well... While I'm here, I'd best pop in and say hello to the folks. I expect Tommy will be booked in and interviewed, won't he?'

'Too bloody right he will, after all this bother.'

Pete nodded. 'Good. It might teach him a lesson that I obviously haven't.'

He was about to say more when his phone rang again. He took it out and his eyes widened as he saw the number on the display. He touched the green icon. 'Gayle.'

'Much as I hate to talk out of turn, there's a couple of blokes in here, look like the hooligan twins, and I just overheard them talking about you.' Pete recognised the voice immediately and it did nothing to reduce his surprise. The other Darren in his life. His reluctant CI. The lad almost never called him. Getting information out of him was usually like pulling teeth. 'Not that I've got a problem with that, of course.'

Ah, normal service resumes, Pete thought. But what the hell were the Southam brothers doing back in Exeter? And being so brazen about it?

'But they were talking about your family too. And not in nice terms. So, being a prospective family man myself, I thought I'd give you the heads-up.'

The mention of his family had sent a cold shiver down Pete's spine. If that's what they were back in town for... He had to get off the phone and get back home ASAP. But at the same time, he couldn't just brush Darren off, not when he'd made the effort to call him with this. 'Thanks, Darren. You haven't gone and got some poor girl pregnant, have you?'

Darren sighed. 'I sometimes wonder why I bother. You met her, if you remember.'

A memory clicked into place. A possible witness he and Jane had been visiting when Darren turned up out of the blue. 'I do. Nice girl. Never could figure out what she was doing with the likes of you. But then maybe you've just demonstrated the answer, eh? You're not going make an honest woman of her, too, are you?'

'She always has been honest. One of us has to be. But yes, I am going to marry her, if that's what you mean.'

'Does she know that?'

'Yes.'

'Well, congratulations, mate. I mean it. And thanks for the heads up. Now, best you give it a minute or two and then make yourself scarce for a bit.'

He ended the call and phoned the station. 'Two things,' he said when it was picked up. 'First, I've just received a tip there's an imminent threat against my family. I need someone out to my place right away. And secondly, I've been led to believe that, as we speak, the Southam brothers are in the snooker hall on Front Street. We need to get them arrested as a matter of priority.'

'OK, we're on it.'

'Thanks.' Phone still in hand, Pete ran to his car, consumed by a depth of fear that only a father and husband could feel. Regardless of who else was on the way to his house right now, he needed to get back there as fast as he could. His parents could wait.

CHAPTER SEVEN

Sixteen hours later, Pete knew that Sally Hanson's child was her boyfriend's, not her father's. Her father hadn't been abusing her in that way. But he was no wiser about the whereabouts of the Southam brothers as he sat in the waiting area outside County Court One of Exeter's combined court centre, staring across in silence at his son, twenty feet away on the other side of the wide, bright and modern space. They had left the snooker club by the time officers got there to arrest them and they hadn't shown up at his house. But then, they hadn't really needed to, he realised. All they'd needed to do was sow the seed of the possibility to ruin his night's sleep, making him, and therefore his evidence, more vulnerable to attack by the defence barrister.

Tommy was with his solicitor, the small, ineffectual-looking and grey-suited Clive Davis. His eyes were downcast. He'd glanced at his dad as he entered an hour ago and looked immediately away. They had made no eye contact since, which Pete knew was the way the court usher wanted it to stay. But still, he couldn't help but study the boy. He'd grown over the past year – inevitably, at his age. But more than the couple of inches in height that he'd put on, he had filled out and matured. He was still a boy, but he was beginning to grow into a man.

Despite all he'd done and all he was suspected of, Pete couldn't help the surge of pride that swept through him on seeing the lad.

At Tommy's near side, directly across from the huge modern wood doors that led into the court room, sat Dave Miles. Unusually, he was dressed in a dark grey suit. As he looked at him, Pete couldn't help thinking Dick Feeney would be proud of him, despite Dave's better looks, darker hair and highly polished black shoes. He was even wearing a tie, albeit a police issue one.

Next to him and almost opposite Pete, the Whitlocks sat in silence, parents either side of their daughter, enclosing and shielding her from her surroundings. She had given Pete a timid smile when she saw him, unlike either of her parents, but again, no words were exchanged. Both she and Tommy would testify via video link from a room further along the corridor. Neither would ever enter the court room itself. Their safety was assured – at least from that point of view.

Pete just wished he could say the same about the other point of view – the wider public aspect of their comings and goings and what might happen to them outside this building, especially with the Southam brothers out there, God knew where, plotting God knew what. They could go after either or both of the kids, directly or indirectly, at any point up to and even beyond their testimony.

Pete had ensured that, despite the lack of resources, DCI Silverstone had allocated a team to the Whitlocks 24/7, telling them it was routine in these circumstances. No mention had been made of any direct threats.

Footsteps trudged up the stairs from the ground floor and Pete looked up to see the tweed-suited bulk of Colin Underhill stepping towards them. His eyes went to Tommy, then to Pete as he crossed the polished wood floor to sit down heavily beside him.

'Not late, am I?'

'Nah. You know these judges. Don't believe in nine o'clock starts like the rest of humanity.'

Colin sat down next to Pete and gave Dave a nod. 'Heard anything from in there?'

'Not a peep as yet.' Pete checked his watch. 'Don't suppose it'll be long now, though.'

Colin thrust his chin towards Tommy. 'How is he?'

Pete sighed. 'I don't know. Haven't spoken to him. He seems OK, though.'

'So, what was that all about last night?'

'Again, it's second-hand but he reckoned he just went for a walk to clear his head. Didn't ask permission because he knew they wouldn't like it. Said he intended being back before he was missed.'

Colin raised a thick grey eyebrow. 'Really?'

'That's more or less what I said.'

Colin gave a short laugh. 'I bet. What about Lou? How did she cope?'

Pete pulled in a deep breath. 'Better than I thought – or maybe feared – she might. She was pretty cut up about it all, of course, but by the time I got home, she'd calmed down a bit. Annie was more upset, if anything.'

Both of Colin's eyebrows shot up at that. 'She's OK now though?'

'Yes. Tears before bed time. More of anger than anything, I think. But I took her to school this morning and she was OK.'

Pete had enjoyed the rare opportunity to drop his daughter at school before coming here. She had been a little quieter than usual on the journey, but that was to be expected after last night, he imagined, and she'd seemed happy enough when she kissed him goodbye and ran off through the school gates, disappearing amongst the dozens of other kids.

He'd waited until she'd gone from sight before starting the car and moving off, safe in the knowledge that she was protected and safe for the day until Louise picked her up this afternoon.

'That's one hell of a kid you've got there, mate.'

'I know.' He glanced across at Tommy. 'And you know what? Despite the evidence to the contrary, I suspect she's not the only one.'

'Yeah, well… You're a dad. What else can you think?'

Pete shook his head with a grimace. 'It's not just because I'm his dad. Family or not, you can still tell what a person's like as long as you can admit the truth to yourself. And if you can't do that, you're no use to anybody.'

'Oh, come on. Look at the number of times we've seen mothers in denial about what their kids get up to. Drugs, booze, stealing – all sorts.'

'True, but…' Pete shook his head. 'I just don't see it in Tommy. And nor does Rosie over there, from what she's said. And if anybody knows, it's her.'

Colin blew the air out of his lungs. 'Yeah, I'll give you that. Me, I never thought the boy was guilty anyway, as you well know. But I had to be sure you were still there.'

Pete's phone buzzed in his pocket. He took it out, checked the screen and answered. 'Ben? What's up?'

'Thought you'd want to know, boss. There've been three cars reported stolen in the county last night. One was in Seaton, one was in Exeter but after eleven pm. The third was in North Tawton. Could have been anytime from four o'clock onwards. We've got the details and put it out as a priority with the traffic division.'

North Tawton was several miles north of the road between Okehampton and Exeter but there was a direct route to it from not far east of where the Range Rover had been found. If it was the Southam brothers, they'd gone up there deliberately to try to throw the police off their scent. But they hadn't gone far enough. Not nearly. And the timing was right. 'Well done, Ben. Keep me informed but you know I'll have to switch off at some point.'

'Yeah, we know, boss.'

He put a hand over the phone and looked sideways at Colin. 'They've got a line on the car the Southams are probably in now.'

'Well, that's good news, at least.'

Pete tilted his head and went back to the call. 'So, what about Hanson? Have we got a lead on him yet?'

'Well, that's the weird thing, boss. There's been absolutely nothing. Not a peep. It's like he drove away from that house and straight into another dimension.'

Beyond Colin, the grand double doors of the primary court room in Devon opened and a sonorous voice said, 'Detective Inspector Underhill, please.'

*

The defence barrister went straight for the jugular. No lead-up, no niceties: just straight in like a striking adder.

Pete had tried to relax, waiting outside the court room while first Colin Underhill then Dave Miles were called to testify, but tipping his head back against the wall and closing his eyes just let his brain work overtime. He heard every tiny sound in the cavernous space. The shuffle of feet, the cough of a dry throat, the murmur of low voices, the creak of a seat under a shifting body – even the shuffle of papers. In the end, he gave up, lifted his head, opened his eyes and took out his notebook to read through it again even though he knew exactly what had happened at every stage of the case.

Colin had been in the court room for almost an hour and a half when the doors opened again and that same sonorous voice – which Pete realised this time belonged to the usher standing outside the door rather than anyone from in the court room – called, 'Detective Constable David Miles, please.'

Perhaps predictably, Colin didn't emerge but when Dave did, he gave Pete a grimace on his way past towards the open stairwell. 'He's sharp,' he muttered.

Now, with his testimony for the prosecution over, Pete was faced by the defence. He hadn't seen the man before. He must have come from outside the city. Bristol or London, maybe. Large and bulky, his gown hung over his paunch like a black waterfall, his face florid beneath the powdered white wig. His jowls wobbled above the confinement of his collar as he approached the witness stand, raising a hand to cough politely.

'My learned friend has kindly established that you were the senior investigating officer on this case, Detective Sergeant Gayle. At what stage in the investigation did you realise that your son was involved in the abduction of the latest victim?'

Pete held himself together despite the flare of anger he felt, used to being pressured on the stand. 'Not until after we'd rescued Rosie – the victim you mentioned.'

The barrister tilted his head in acknowledgment. 'Very well. When did you realise there was a connection between Rosie Whitlock and your son?'

Had this tight-arsed son of a bitch got something incriminating? Pete didn't know and he wasn't about to admit to anything until he was absolutely forced to. 'I realised there was a connection between them about three days in when her parents mentioned her swimming practice at Topsham pool on Friday evenings. There was no evidence they actually knew each other, though.'

'But there was, wasn't there, Detective Sergeant?'

Pete frowned. 'No. As I said, there was just the fact that they both attended the pool on the same evenings. I knew nothing more than that and had no evidence to support looking into it further.'

'Because looking into it further would have forced you to recuse yourself from the case – your first since returning to work after compassionate leave due to your son's disappearance. Isn't that correct, Detective Sergeant?'

Pete sighed heavily. 'It was my first case since returning to work, yes. It arose on the day I returned to work. But that had nothing to do with why I didn't look further into the connection between the victim and my son. There was no suspicion that he was, or even could be, involved. She was abducted in a van. My son was thirteen years old. He couldn't be driving, especially as physically small as he was.' He glanced at the jury. 'He couldn't reach the pedals.'

The barrister allowed himself a tight smile. 'Indeed. But there was, in fact, evidence that they knew each other, wasn't there? Knew each other quite intimately, even.'

Pete frowned. He'd got the transcripts, then. The texts that Tommy and Rosie had exchanged, that had been found by the specialists at Middlemoor, the force HQ on the outskirts of the city. Texts that Pete had indeed kept to himself when he was informed of them. 'As it turned out later, yes. We didn't know it at that time, though, and it made no difference to the case - to the fact that he couldn't have driven the van she was picked up in.'

The barrister turned to the bench. 'The defence would like to introduce evidence of texts exchanged between the victim Rosie Whitlock and Thomas James – Tommy – Gayle, My Lord. Texts that show despite their tender ages, they not only knew each other but were more than what most reasonable people would term friends.'

'Objection,' called out the prosecutor. 'Relevance, My Lord.'

'The relevance,' the defence barrister intoned, 'is that, knowing the contents of these messages, Detective Sergeant Gayle continued to pursue the case, thereby jeopardising any hope of conducting a fair and reasonable enquiry.'

'The transcripts will be allowed into evidence,' the judge decided.

The defence barrister inclined his head in thanks and handed over the documents. 'So, as I was saying, Detective Sergeant, despite knowing that your son and the victim were intimate, you continued to pursue the case, am I not correct?'

'Those texts do not show physical intimacy,' Pete argued. 'They show no more than that the two of them were flirting. And again, what possible relevance could that have had to her abduction?'

'The relevance was not for you to decide, Detective Sergeant. It was for your superiors, who you withheld it from. And said relevance was, while we're on the subject, motive. The motive of your son to attain the physical intimacy suggested by the texts they had exchanged.'

'Objection,' cried the prosecutor. 'Badgering the witness, plus where's the question in there? The defence is grandstanding: making statements of his own that he has no direct knowledge of the truth of.'

'Sustained,' said the judge. 'The jury will disregard the defence's statement. And Mr Montague, you will defer your statements for closing arguments. In the meantime, please confine yourself to asking the witnesses for the relevant facts.'

That told him, Pete thought. But as for the jury disregarding what he'd said – there was little chance of that. He'd said it. They'd heard it. It would, at the very least, be in the backs of their minds as they continued through the case. Which was exactly why he'd said it.

The defence barrister bowed. 'Very well, My Lord. Perhaps if I put it another way…' He turned back to face Pete. 'Did you or did you not run your investigation of this case in a manner designed to exonerate your son at any cost and thereby to heap blame on my client that did not belong to him, Detective Sergeant?'

Pete fought down the righteous indignation that boiled up inside him. He drew a long, slow breath. 'I conducted my investigation in the same way as I've conducted every investigation in my entire career,' he said slowly and clearly. 'In a manner designed to discover the truth, regardless of what that truth may be and regardless of the personal cost to myself or my family. And what I discovered during that investigation led to …'

'Thank you, Detective,' the barrister cut in quickly. 'You've answered the question.'

'Oh, no I haven't,' Pete replied. 'Not nearly. And you asked it, so you'll listen to the answer unless the judge says otherwise. Yes, I discovered that my son knew the victim. That's not the same as discovering he was involved in a crime against her and it's not the same as discovering that he's suddenly grown the foot or so that he'd need to be able to drive the van she was abducted in. So, no, there was no need to recuse myself from the case and no need to be distracted by what turned out in the end to be irrelevant and unrelated facts. *That's* the answer to your question, Mr Montague.'

The barrister, meanwhile, had become steadily redder in the face until his mouth started to open and close like a fish out of water. Now he snapped his jaw closed with an audible clack of teeth and drew himself up to his full height. 'I see. So, you set yourself up to be the all-knowing arbiter of justice.'

'Objection,' said the prosecutor. 'We're not here to insult witnesses, My Lord, but to question them regarding the facts of the case.'

'Withdrawn,' Montague said quickly. 'My point was…'

'Objection. Statements rather than questions when the leaned gentleman's already been warned.'

'Sustained,' the judge said heavily. 'Mr Montague, be very careful to ask questions, not make statements in this court.'

'My Lord.' He bowed once more. 'I was merely trying to ascertain whether or not my client was investigated, and therefore charged, fairly and squarely.'

'He was,' Pete said. 'There's no doubt of his guilt here.' *If it's good enough for one side, it's good enough for the other,* he thought as Montague's eyebrows shot up.

'Objection. The witness is making unrequested pronouncements of an opinion that he has no right to. This is exactly the attitude I was attempting to demonstrate.'

'Sustained. Detective Sergeant, you will restrict yourself to answering the questions asked while on the witness stand.'

'My Lord,' Pete nodded. 'Sorry, I thought he was asking a question as you'd instructed him to.'

'Do not be disingenuous, Detective Sergeant Gayle.'

Pete winced inwardly. Had he gone too far? If so it wouldn't be the first time, though it would in these circumstances. 'Sir.'

Montague saw his opening and took it like a fencer with a needle-sharp rapier in hand. 'I put it to you, Detective Sergeant, that you fixated on my client's alleged guilt to the exclusion of all other possibilities and fitted the supposed evidence to your theory.'

'The evidence is real, not supposed, and that's not the way I work. Never has been and never will be, regardless of the circumstances.'

'Is that so?'

'Would you like me to provide character witnesses? I can, from both sides of the law.'

'That won't be necessary, Detective Sergeant. We're not questioning your integrity here, today.'

'Well, it sounds like that's exactly what you're doing,' Pete retorted.

'Detective Sergeant Gayle, you will confine yourself to answering questions put by learned council while in the witness stand,' the judge repeated. 'Otherwise you will be charged with being in contempt of this court.'

'Sorry, My Lord. That's the last thing I am.'

'My suggestion is that you're simply guilty of being a good father, Detective Sergeant,' the defence barrister said mildly. 'However, I also put it to you that my client is guilty of nothing more than playing host to a cuckoo in the form of your son.'

'Objection,' protested the prosecutor. 'Again, making declarations instead of asking questions. How long are we to put up with this flagrant abuse of the witness and this court by the defence council?'

'Sustained. And the answer is no longer. Once more, Mr Montague, and you will also be held in contempt.'

'My sincere apologies, My Lord.' He turned back to Pete. 'Do you have any forensic evidence whatsoever against my client, Detective Sergeant?'

'We have reams of evidence against your client.'

'I asked if you have any forensic evidence against him, Detective Sergeant. Any at all.'

'Technically, no. But what we do have...'

'Thank you,' Montague pounced, cutting him off. 'Yet there is forensic evidence against your son, am I not correct?'

Pete froze.

'You did discover considerable forensic evidence against your son, did you not, Detective Sergeant? On the persons of both the surviving victim, Rosie Whitlock, and at least one other victim.'

Given the few seconds it took the defence barrister to reiterate his question, Pete managed to collect and compose himself, pushing his horror and anger down deep within himself. 'The evidence against my son was refuted by the surviving victim you mentioned,' he said. 'And that on the body of the other victim...'

'Answer the question please, Detective Sergeant. Did you or did you not discover forensic evidence against your son but none against my client?'

Pete drew a breath, the muscles in the sides of his face bunching in frustration. The barrister had managed to back him into a corner with no escape route. There was only one answer he could give. 'Yes.'

CHAPTER EIGHT

'The prosecution calls Thomas James Gayle, My Lord.'

Pete shifted in his seat, a few rows down from the back of the court room. Tension and anticipation battled within him as the large screen on the wall behind the witness stand was switched on. He had only left the witness stand seconds ago. Just a couple more questions had followed his confession to the existence of forensic evidence against Tommy before the defence had announced that they had no more questions for him. They had made their point.

'Due to his age and vulnerability, My Lord, with your indulgence, the witness will testify via video link from a secure position.'

The screen was lit up with an image of a cream-coloured wall, the top couple of inches of a witness stand across the bottom of the screen.

'For continuity, the witness stand on the screen is the same as the one in the court room here,' the prosecutor announced.

Then Tommy moved into shot. He climbed up onto the witness stand and was sworn in before taking his seat, looking tiny behind the wooden frontage of the enclosure.

The prosecutor stood up, adjusting his robes as he gazed at Tommy with a benign, almost fatherly expression. 'Can you see and hear us clearly, Thomas?'

'Yes, sir.'

'How old are you, Thomas?'

'Fourteen, sir.'

Even Tommy's voice was small and deferential.

'As of when?'

'Second of May, sir.'

'So, only just fourteen, then. Which means you were thirteen when the offences we're here to consider were committed, correct?'

'Yes, sir.'

'And you are how tall?'

'Four foot nine, sir.'

'Is that not small for your age?'

'Yes, sir.'

'In fact, the average height of a thirteen-year-old male in the UK is five feet six inches, am I not correct?'

'Objection, My Lord,' intoned the defence solicitor. 'Calling for an answer the witness could only guess at.'

'I know the average height of boys my age,' Tommy argued. 'I should do: I get told it often enough at school.'

'Overruled,' the judge proclaimed. 'The witness may answer the question.'

The prosecutor nodded to Tommy.

'Yes, you're correct, sir.'

'And yet the jury is being asked by the defence to consider the supposition that a boy of your size and weight overpowered girls, at least some of whom where larger than you, and abducted them. Did you, Tommy?'

Pete noticed the switch from 'Thomas' to the diminutive, 'Tommy,' and was sure the jury would have, too.

'No, sir. I couldn't.'

'You couldn't. Do you mean physically or emotionally, Tommy?'

'Both. I know you're planning to call Rosie Whitlock. She's six inches taller than me and a regional tennis player and swimmer. There's no way I'm stronger than she is.'

'Objection, My Lord. Are we going to start conducting arm-wrestling in court to substantiate these claims?' demanded the defence.

'Sustained,' the judge intoned. 'The prosecution will confine themselves to questions which are factually sustainable.'

The prosecutor nodded deferentially to the bench. 'My apologies, My Lord. But, with the court's indulgence, it is documented that girls of eleven to fourteen years are, on average, stronger than their male counterparts. And we have established both that Tommy, here, is small for his age and that, by his testimony, Rosie Whitlock is a champion tennis player and swimmer in her age group and therefore strong for her age, making it highly unlikely that Tommy could have abducted her. And, as the witness suggested, we will be calling on Miss Whitlock herself in due course.'

'Very well, Mr Abercrombie. Continue.'

'My Lord.' He turned back to the screen showing Tommy, who had sat quietly observing the exchange. 'Tommy, were you or were you not involved in the abduction of Rosie Whitlock?'

'Yes, sir, but not willingly. I only participated under threat from Mr Burton.'

'Threat of what, Tommy?'

'The defendant. Look at him. He's twice my size and he's a teacher. He knows how to intimidate kids. He's trained for it. He said he'd hurt me. Did it more than once, too. And he said...' Tommy took a shuddering breath and dropped his gaze, looking young and vulnerable.

'He said what, Tommy?' the prosecutor encouraged.

'He said he'd...' Tommy swallowed audibly. 'He said he'd take my little sister and do stuff to her. Rape her and stuff.'

Pete had heard this before, but still he gasped at the horror of it, dimly aware that he was far from the only one in the court room to do so.

The prosecutor allowed a few seconds for Tommy's words to sink in with the jury. 'I'm sorry, Tommy, but you need to be specific here. "And stuff," is not sufficient, I'm afraid.'

Tommy looked fiercely into the camera. 'He said he'd rape her, torture her, make me watch, then kill her.'

Pete swallowed the bile that had risen suddenly in his throat, a strangled sound emerging from him. He felt a hand on his shoulder and glanced at Colin Underhill, beside him.

'Sorry, Pete,' Colin muttered. 'But...' He shrugged.

'And this is your sister we're talking about?' the prosecutor clarified. 'Who was ten years old at the time, am I correct?'

'Yes.'

'Now, Tommy, my learned colleague on the defence team brought something else up during previous testimony. He pointed out that there was forensic evidence from you found on two of the victims – specifically, the body of Lauren Carter which was found in the river not far from here and on the surviving victim, Rosie Whitlock. Can you explain those discoveries for us, please?'

'My handprints were on Lauren Carter's neck,' Tommy said quietly.

'I'm sorry, Tommy, I'm going to have to ask you to speak up for the jury.'

'My handprints were on Lauren's neck,' Tommy repeated. 'As if I'd strangled her. The reason for that was that Mr... The defendant made me put them there, then put his over them to strangle her.'

'Objection, My Lord,' the defence barrister said, standing quickly. 'There is no evidence of this.'

'Overruled. Sit down, please, Mr Montague. The witness is here to provide testimony that is, in itself, evidence, as you well know.'

Montague sat down heavily, shaking his head.

'Continue, please, Tommy,' the prosecutor encouraged.

Tommy clenched his jaw, drawing a deep breath through his nose. 'There was evidence found on Lauren of... Intimate contact between us.' His eyes widened abruptly. 'You've got to understand, that's what I was there for. That's why he wanted me – to film us together, me and the girls. Some sick fantasy that he sold on-line.'

'He sold on-line? In what form, Tommy?'

'Films,' Tommy repeated as if the man was stupid. 'Videos. I said – he filmed us.'

'And how did he sell these films?'

'On-line. Through some dark-web site. I don't know. I just know he made me take them and post them. He'd know if I didn't because the customers would contact him to ask where they'd got to. I tried it once. Dumped a bundle of them in a skip. He found out and beat the sh… Hell out of me. We couldn't work for ten days after because of the bruises.'

'When you say work, Tommy, what exactly do you mean by that?'

'Film. He couldn't film me because the bruises would show up and it would look like I was being forced into it. Like I wasn't willing.'

Pete knew that several stills from these movies – the less graphic scenes – had been provided for evidence. He hoped to God the prosecutor wouldn't bring them to attention now.

'They would demonstrate that you were acting under duress.'

'That's right.'

'Objection,' the defence barrister announced. 'No man or boy can achieve erection without being willing to do so, My Lord.'

The prosecutor turned quickly towards the defence table. 'The defence council should stick to facts he knows about, My Lord. We will demonstrate in due course that it is indeed possible for a male to achieve erection unwillingly. Have you never had an impromptu erection, Mr Montague?'

Sniggers sounded around the big room.

'Mr Abercrombie,' the judge warned. 'You will refrain from such childish and personal comments to the opposition bench or be held in contempt.'

The prosecutor dipped his head deferentially. 'My Lord. I merely intended to remind my learned colleague that few men have not experienced feelings of arousal at inappropriate or inopportune moments, on occasion. Especially in their youth.'

The judge stared at him for what seemed like a long moment. 'Objection overruled,' he said at last. 'Continue, Mr Abercrombie, but without the personal remarks, please.'

'My Lord.' He turned back to the witness stand and the screen behind it. 'Moving on to other matters for now, we have established that there were at least two victims, one of whom did not survive her ordeal. How many others were there, Tommy?'

Tommy blinked. 'As far as I'm aware, three.'

'Three others, apart from the two we've discussed?'

'That's right.'

'Tell us about them. Who were they, what happened to them and when?'

Tommy drew a deep breath. 'There was a gypsy girl. She was the first I knew of. Not long after I... After I was... With Mr Burton. She was bathing in a stream. We saw her, Mr Burton saw a chance and took it. Took her. She was... He kept her in the barn for about a month. I don't know what happened to her after that. She just suddenly wasn't there anymore. Her name was Abby. I don't know her surname. Then there was another one. I think she was from Bristol. Another man brought her.'

'Another man?' the prosecutor interrupted. 'So Mr Burton wasn't working alone? He was part of an organisation, is that what you're telling us, Tommy?'

Tommy nodded. 'Yeah. Yes sir.'

'And do you know who this other man was?'

'I... I can't say, sir.'

'Can't or won't, Tommy?' The prosecutor's expression was abruptly stern.

'He made threats when he...' Tommy stopped.

'When he what, Tommy?'

'He came to see me in the children's home when I was in there. Conned his way in, pretending to be part of my legal team.'

'At this point, My Lord, the prosecution would like to admit into evidence video footage of that visit to Archways Secure Children's Home, here in Exeter, along with photographs taken from it.' He held up a DVD which the court usher took from him along with a file of photographs and placed them before the judge. The red-robed and wigged judge glanced at the photographs and nodded.

'So admitted.'

'Pages twenty-four and twenty-five in the evidence files,' the judge informed the jury.

The prosecutor turned back to Tommy's image on the screen to the right of the judge. 'And why were you in a secure children's home, Tommy?'

Good, Pete thought. The prosecutor was bringing this out in a benign way rather than letting the defence attack him with it.

'I was… I was afraid after I got away from Mr Burton, sir. Afraid that I'd be in trouble, arrested for attacking the girls. So I ran away, sir. Went into hiding. Then, in the spring, I got a job on a fairground and got arrested for carrying the knife I used on the fair.'

'You ran away after you escaped from the defendant and got a job in the spring,' the prosecutor repeated. 'That's a period of six months that you were – what? Living rough?'

'Effectively, yes, sir. I spent some time in a holiday cottage. They tend to be closed up over winter. But I had to move on a few times to avoid getting caught.'

'And all this time you were fearful of being arrested and charged with the crimes that the defendant had forced you into committing?'

Tommy nodded. 'And of…'

'Of what, Tommy? Or whom?'

Tommy pressed his lips together as if refusing to let the words out.

'The witness will answer the question,' the judge intoned.

Tommy blinked. 'Mr… Burton said his name was Adrian Southam,' he said rapidly.

'This was the man you were afraid of? The man who came to the children's home? Why did he come to see you, Tommy?'

'To warn me.'

'Of what?'

'To keep quiet. Say nothing or he'd…'

'He'd what, Tommy?'

'He'd harm my family. All of them.'

'Thank you, Tommy. I think we all appreciate how brave it was of you to admit that to the court.'

'Objection, My Lord. Where's the question?' the defence piped up.

'Apologies, My Lord,' the prosecutor acknowledged quickly. 'But we are all human here, are we not? We have families we'd do anything to protect.'

Pete saw the defence barrister twitch as if he was going to react to that, but he refrained – as he was required to do by court etiquette.

'Nevertheless, Mr Abercrombie, this court has rules that must be obeyed. Objection sustained.'

The prosecutor nodded. 'My Lord.' He turned back to Tommy on the screen in front of them. 'Now, where were we?' He consulted his notes. 'Ah, yes. A girl from Bristol. What can you tell us about her?'

CHAPTER NINE

Abercrombie paced up and down the area between the council's tables and the judge's bench for several seconds, thumbs hooked in the copious arm-holes of his black robe, head bowed, grimacing and sucking his teeth as if cross-examining a young boy was the last thing in the world he wanted to do. Then he stopped and faced the screen behind the witness box.

'Thomas, I am the council for the defence. You know what that means, don't you?'

'You're there to make sure he gets away with what he did.'

He shook his head slowly. 'On the contrary, Thomas, I'm here to ensure that my client doesn't get convicted of what he didn't do.'

'Which ain't much,' Tommy shot back.

'So you claim. But I put it to you, Thomas, that my client didn't do most of what he's charged with in this court today. That, in fact, you did.'

'You can put what you like but you weren't there, so you don't know what he put those girls and me through.'

'And that why I'm here, Thomas. To determine exactly what my client's role was in what happened.'

'What, you want me to believe that?' Tommy demanded.

Abercrombie's cheek twitched. Pete saw it as he felt a swell of pride in his son's composure and dexterity in answering the defence barrister's claim.

'It was your finger prints on the neck of the girl who was found dead in the river here in Exeter last November, wasn't it? Not Mr Burton's.'

'Objection,' the prosecutor declared. 'The witness has already answered and explained that point, My Lord.'

'Sustained. Get to the point, Mr Abercrombie, if you have one.'

'My Lord,' Abercrombie nodded. 'Thomas, did you or did you not participate in the abduction of the last and surviving victim, Rosie Whitlock, whose testimony we will hear later?'

Pete tensed and felt Colin's meaty hand clamp heavily on his shoulder.

'Unwillingly, yes, I did.'

Abercrombie nodded. 'You did. And what part, exactly, did you play in that abduction?'

Tommy pressed his lips together as his chin began to wobble. A single tear escaped his left eye as he choked, 'I... I distracted her so Mr Burton could drag her into the back of his van.'

'You stepped out of the van and spoke to her, correct?'

'Yes,' he whispered.

'Knowing that my client was about to grab her off the street and take her away.'

'Yes.'

'So, you are as guilty as my client of this crime.'

Pete growled deep in his throat, straining to get out of his chair as Colin's hand clamped even tighter on his shoulder, holding him down.

'No,' Tommy argued. 'I did it because he made me. I didn't want to - at all, but especially when I saw who he intended to snatch.'

'A girl who you knew.'

'Yes.'

'Who you'd chatted with, become friendly with over several months.'

'Yes,' Tommy whispered

'Who, in fact, you'd swum with.'

'Yes.' More loudly this time.

'Who, in other words, you'd spent considerable time with, semi-clad.'

'Objection, My Lord. The defence is badgering this witness.'

'Sustained. Mr Abercrombie, you are fully aware of the protocols regarding interviewing minors in court and you will comply with them.'

Abercrombie bowed. 'Of course, My Lord.' He turned back to the witness box and the large screen behind it. 'Thomas, I suggest that over the months that you'd got to know Rosie Whitlock, you'd in fact fantasised about her in the lewd way that teenage boys will and that you fully intended to act out those fantasies. That, in fact, it was your plan, not my client's, deliberately to target that particular victim.'

'Objection!' the prosecutor shouted, drowning out Pete's muttered, 'Son of a bitch.'

'The defence is blatantly ignoring your previous intervention, My Lord,' the prosecutor continued, 'and abusing the witness in a manner clearly in breach of the rules regarding under-age witnesses.'

'Sustained. Mr Abercrombie, you have already been warned. It will not happen again.'

'My humblest apologies, My Lord. I'm merely attempting to pursue the truth of this matter.'

'Then you will do so in a manner befitting the circumstances of this court, Mr Abercrombie.'

He bowed once more. 'Indeed, My Lord. I apologise deeply for the tone I used but, was I not correct in my assertions. Thomas?'

Tommy stared him down. 'I thought you were here to ask questions, not make up stories.'

'Thomas,' the judge warned. 'This is a court, not a playground. You will answer the questions asked of you and not argue with council.'

Pete saw the flash of contempt on Tommy's face that came and went in an instant before he said stiffly, 'Sir.' He couldn't help recalling himself in the station chief's office on more than one occasion.

'Like father, like son,' Colin rumbled softly beside him.

Pete grunted as the defence barrister focussed once more on the judge's bench.

'I'm sorry, My Lord, but I really need an answer to this question.'

'Then ask it in a manner befitting this court, Mr Abercrombie'

He nodded. 'Thomas, did you fully and deliberately intend to abduct and abuse the victim, Rosie Whitlock, as you waited outside Risingbrook School that morning?'

'No,' Tommy said loudly. 'It was pure chance that she turned up when she did - at least as far as I knew.'

'Very well. Moving on, then. Although, as you've testified, my client was a teacher by profession, he was never your teacher, was he?'

'No.'

'So, how did you become involved with him?'

'Met him in the park one day. He was perving out of his van with a long camera lens at some girls on the play stuff. The slide and merry-go-round and that. I saw him. Challenged him.'

'When you say, "some girls," can you expand on that?'

'Young girls. Eight, nine, ten years old.'

'How the hell did he get to be a teacher?' Colin muttered.

'And he was pointing a camera lens at them from a distance?'

'That's right.'

'CRB checks don't come with house searches,' Pete pointed out quietly.

'Taking pictures or just looking? Did you hear the shutter going off?'

'The windows were up. I couldn't hear. But I saw the shots after. He showed me.'

'But you couldn't be sure at the time that he was actually taking pictures? Or even that he was looking at the girls rather than, for example, looking for his dog?'

'He didn't have a dog,' Tommy sneered. 'A boner, maybe...'

A gasp sounded from several points in the court, including the jury box. *Steady, son,* Pete thought.

'There's no need for crudity, Master Gayle,' the judge said gravely.

'Sorry, sir.' Tommy looked briefly incredulous. 'But this trial is about sex crimes isn't it?'

'You know what I meant, and you will contain yourself.'

'Sir.'

Again, Pete's mind took him back to DCI Silverstone's office and his own responses to the station chief.

'My point is that you didn't know he had no dog when you claim to have challenged him, Thomas. Did you?'

'I didn't need to hear the shutter clicking to know what he was doing. I could see his hands.'

'His hands. And what were they doing?'

'Operating the camera. It wasn't a modern digital. It was manual. He had to focus it, press the button and wind it on.'

'Very well. So, you challenged him about what he was photographing. What form did that challenge take?'

'I opened the door behind him, called him a sicko and told him I'd report him.'

As a smile tweaked the corners of Pete's mouth, he glanced at the jury and saw the same response from some of them.

'And that was it, was it?' the defence barrister asked. 'You didn't expand on that?'

Pete frowned as a nervous flutter disturbed his stomach. *Where's he going now?*

'Next thing I knew, he'd grabbed hold of me and pulled me into the cab,' Tommy told him.

'And then?'

The defence barrister was being persistent with this. What was he up to, Pete wondered.

'He twisted my arm round in a straight lock like they do on the wrestling, told me to shut the door and started the engine.'

'But you hadn't said anything else to him in the meantime?'

Tommy frowned. 'Told him to get off me, let me go.'

'You didn't, for example, add that you'd report him *unless* he did something for you?'

Pete froze.

'Like what?' Tommy asked.

'Objection, My Lord,' the prosecutor protested, too late. 'The defence is going around in circles. This argument has already been answered.'

'Overruled. But be careful, Mr Abercrombie,' warned the judge.

'My Lord,' he acknowledged before turning back to Tommy. 'That's what I'm asking you, Thomas. What, if anything, did you demand of my client in order to prevent you from going to the authorities with your discovery?'

'I didn't demand anything. How could I? I wasn't in a position to, was I?'

'So, you're denying that you suggested teaming up? That you suggested that he put you up in exchange not only for your silence, but for your co-operation in a much more lurid method of gaining his pleasure than he'd been able to achieve thus far?'

'I...?' Tommy shook his head in confusion. '*I* suggested to *him*? Are you serious?'

'We do not jest about such matters – or about anything else – in court, Thomas. I put it to you that my client was quite content with his remote voyeurism, however distasteful that may be, until you came along. That, in fact, it was not my client but you who was the instigator and main force behind these abductions. That he went along unwillingly with you, rather than vice versa, Master Gayle.'

Tommy's lips tightened. 'Then where did Adrian Southam come from?'

'Answer the question, please, Thomas,' the defence barrister insisted.

'I don't know how you could even ask it,' Tommy declared. 'I was thirteen years old. He was a grown man. A voyeur into young kids. Seriously, how likely was I to have even dreamed up a plan like that? And even if I had, like I said, where did Adrian Southam come from? How could I have known him?'

'I ask the questions here, Thomas. You answer them. And you're obfuscating. Please answer the question I've put to you. A yes or no will suffice. To repeat: were you in fact the instigator of the situation that led ultimately to Rosie Whitlock's abduction?'

'No.'

'Did you intend her to be abducted?'

'No.'

'And did you or did you not strangle Lauren Carter?'

'I said before: he made me put my hands round her neck and then squeezed over them. So, no, I didn't kill her.'

'But you did have sexual intercourse with both girls as well as the other victims, correct?'

'Objection. Already answered.'

'Sustained,' said the judge. 'Move on, Mr Abercrombie, if you have any new questions to ask the witness.'

'Just one, My Lord.' He turned back to Tommy. 'Thomas, you are the only witness who has mentioned this Adrian Southam person in this courtroom, and that only as an avoidance of your own culpability. Therefore, my question to you is, is he real or a creation of your own imagination?'

Pete saw frustration and outrage twist Tommy's features as the same emotions surged through every atom of his own body. He was on his feet before he knew what was happening. 'He's all too real,' he shouted. 'We're chasing him down right now.'

'Order,' the judge shouted, slamming a hand on the bench in front of him. 'Sit down this instant, Mr Gayle, or you will be removed from this court.'

Pete felt himself being pulled down by his jacket as a fist slammed into the back of his thigh. *Colin.* He dropped back into his seat, still enraged by the defence barrister's insinuation. For a moment, he struggled to get back up again, but Colin held him down firmly.

'Stay still and stay quiet,' he snapped, his voice low and determined.

'How the fu... How can he get away with shit like that?'

'It's his job.'

The prosecutor turned in his seat to stare at Pete, who mouthed, 'Call me back,' as he jabbed a thumb at his own chest then pointed to the witness stand.

'That bloody well isn't,' Pete said to Colin. 'It's defamation, plain and simple.'

'Outside this room, it would be, but not here and you know it.'

CHAPTER TEN

The fire alarm jangled before Tommy could respond to Abercrombie's accusation, making Pete and several others jump. Gasps and cries of shock sounded around the packed court room, a blue light flashing from above the big double doors as they opened abruptly and the usher's deep voice called, 'Everyone please leave your seats in a calm and orderly manner and make your way down the stairs.'

A glance over his shoulder showed Pete several people moving along the hallway outside towards the stairs. The judge left his seat, heading for the side door at the corner of the room that led out to his chambers while the jury filed out through a door in the opposite corner.

The big screen behind the witness stand had already gone black.

Pete stood, joining the steady press of bodies towards the door. He was aware of Colin moving behind him. At the door, he stepped out of the flow, squeezing against the door jamb.

'What's going on?' he asked the usher, having to speak up over the hum of raised voices.

'All I know, sir, is it's not a drill.' He raised a hand. 'If you'd make your way toward the stairs...'

'Where's my son? He was testifying on-camera when the alarm sounded.'

'He'll be on his way out, sir.'

'Where was he, then? I'd like to make sure.'

'He'd have been in camera room one, third door along on the right.' He pointed in the opposite direction to the stairs.

'Thank you.' Pete headed that way. There were only a handful of people coming towards him now. The door the usher had described stood open. Pete checked inside anyway. It was a small room, not much more than a cupboard. Magnolia walls surrounded a mock-up of the witness stand, a video camera on a tripod, a couple of lights on stands and a chair for the camera operator. A screen behind the camera was still on, showing just the front portion of an empty court room: the position where the questioning barrister would stand.

With a sigh of relief, Pete turned away, heading back towards the stairs. He'd see Tommy outside with his chaperone. He joined the throng moving steadily down the wide stairs. Behind him, the big doors of the main court room closed and the usher's leather-soled shoes tap-tapped after him. Ahead, through the enormous window that constituted the central section of the front of the white rendered art-deco style building, he could see the car park filling with people. They seemed to be milling around randomly like froth below a weir on the river. How was he going to find Tommy amongst that lot?

Of course, legally, he shouldn't be finding Tommy. The boy was still under oath, having yet to complete his testimony, and Pete was another witness in the same case. They should have no contact. But that didn't take into account that they were father and son. He needed to know the boy was safe, at least, if only by seeing him from a distance. But he couldn't make him out from here. Perhaps he was at the rear of the building, where the legal teams, judge, jury and ancillary staff would congregate away from the public throng.

'Sir.' The usher put a hand to his shoulder as he stood at the railing, searching the crowd outside from the half-landing.

Pete flinched and released a breath before turning reluctantly away from the big windows to go with the black suited and white gloved man.

In the foyer, the revolving door had been stopped and folded open, the auxiliary doors to either side of it also standing open to allow the noisy crowd to exit as quickly as possible. The limited space outside seemed packed already. Pete couldn't see Colin among the milling crowd so, once outside, he pushed through towards the main road, hopped up onto the low wall of a raised bed of shrubs and flowers and turned to look back at the building. Smoke billowed high and black from the far corner, the alarms still jangling inside as he heard sirens closing fast from his right.

Where was Colin? Then he saw him coming around the far corner of the big white building, his stride brisk and purposeful, eyes roaming the crowd until they alighted on Pete, head and shoulders above the crowd as he stood on the wall. As Colin changed direction towards him, Pete jumped down and moved through the muttering crowd to meet him.

'Have you seen Tommy?' he asked as they came together.

'No. The judge isn't round there, either.'

A cold feeling of dread gripped Pete's stomach, climbing quickly up his neck to surround his head with a chill as if it was suddenly December again instead of late May.

Something was wrong. He knew it.

He heard the sirens stop at the far side of the court house. The fire brigade had arrived.

'You're...' He stopped. Colin wasn't the type to say anything he wasn't sure of.

The older man nodded sombrely. 'I'm sure. They're not there, either of them. The jury, stenographer, solicitors and barristers... Burton's in cuffs with two guards. But no judge and no Tommy.'

Pete's eyes closed briefly. 'Something's up. It has to be.'

Colin nodded again. 'But we can't go in and check until the fire boys say so.'

'Where is the fire?'

'Records room in the far corner, second floor.'

There would be more paper in there than anywhere else in the building apart from the legal library below it. This could be an accident, but... He shook his head and met Colin's gaze.

'I know what you're thinking, but we don't know anything at this stage.'

'It's bloody suspicious, though.' Pete tried to think of any street cameras in the area but wasn't aware of any. Some of the old buildings up Southernhay Gardens might have private ones. Most were business now, rather than the grand homes they'd been built as. The other direction led towards the shopping areas around the High Street. There would be cameras there but a fast getaway would require a vehicle. He took out his phone and dialled.

'Police. CCTV room.'

'Graham, what have you got in the way of cameras around the court building?'

'Not a lot.'

106

'Anything?'

'The nearest is on the main road in front of it. Hang on.'

'That's no good,' Pete said, but there was no response. Then Graham was back.

'What's going on down there?'

'A fire in the records room, apparently.'

'Jesus. No, the main road's the closest.'

'I need something from behind it.'

'We've got nothing, mate. Even the court house itself hasn't, as far as I know.'

'What, nothing covering the back entrance?' This was where suspects would be brought in from the prison, across the city.

'They might have, but...'

'They bloody well should have. I'll check. Thanks, mate.' Pete ended the call. 'We'll need to find a staff member here,' he told Colin. 'See if they've got their own CCTV.'

His phone rang in his hand. He checked the screen. *Unknown number.* He didn't have time for this now. He pressed the green button, intending to tell whoever it was to call back.

He didn't get the chance. As he put it to his ear, a voice said, 'If you want to see your son alive again, you'll stop that trial.'

West-country accent but harsher, more rural than his own local one. Further east or north. Wiltshire. His fears were realised.

'Southam, I'm...'

Click. A dead line.

'…coming for you,' he muttered.

Colin was watching him carefully. 'Southam, as in Adrian Southam?'

Pete's lip curled, his jaw clamped shut. He nodded slowly. 'He's got Tommy.'

'How? Why?'

'To try to stop this trial.'

'How does he expect that to work?' Colin demanded, but Pete was already lifting his phone to his ear again when it rang again.

He checked the screen. 'Jane.'

'Boss. Are you OK? We just heard there's a fire down there.'

'We're fine, Jane. But I need you and Dick down here ASAP, if not before, plus half a dozen uniforms to canvas Southernhay Gardens for witnesses and CCTV.'

'What, you think it was deliberate?'

'I know it was. Southam just called me.'

'How the hell did he get your number?'

'I don't know. Did anyone there give it him?'

'None of us, that's for sure. I can ask around.'

'Get Dave to do that. And get Ben to see if he can trace the last call to this phone. You get down here.'

'Will do. But that's not why I called. A body's been found in the river, up by Cross Weir. Female. Blonde. Thirties. Stabbed in the chest. We haven't got a firm ID yet, but I'm thinking...'

'Cathleen Webber,' he finished for her.

'Yes. And she was near-naked, so they'd at least sexually abused her, probably raped her before they killed her.'

The intensity of Pete's rage ratcheted up even further at the thought. These two psychos had to be stopped before they claimed any more innocent victims.

*

Dick Feeney's silver Mondeo pulled into the already crowded area in front of the court house with blue lights flashing in the grille. He stopped the car and he and Jane stepped out.

Jane glanced from one to the other. 'Boss. Guv...'

'What happened?' Dick asked.

Pete started to tell them what he knew, sketchy as it was.

'I'll go and check on the fire crew,' said Colin.

'We need to keep this place closed until we've been inside and checked for evidence,' Pete said quickly. 'Especially if the judge is still AWOL.'

'Yeah, I'll deal with that, too.'

'The judge?' Jane demanded. 'What happened to him?'

'That's what we need to find out,' Pete told her. 'Seems like he didn't come out of there when he should have.'

'You don't think he's involved, do you?' Dick asked. 'Part of the ring?'

Pete hadn't thought of that until Dick suggested it. 'I don't know,' he said. 'We'll have to see what we find when we get in there.'

'So, how did they get Tommy? He'd have been chaperoned, wouldn't he?'

'He was. But there was no sign of anyone in the camera room, so we thought they'd taken him out the back until Colin went round there and couldn't find him or the judge. Then I got the call from Southam.'

'Saying they've got Tommy,' Jane added.

'Did he give you any proof of that?' Dick asked.

'No.'

'Then we don't know it for sure.'

'No, but we've got act like it's true.'

Dick nodded. 'I'm just saying there's a chance, that's all. I mean, it'd take some balls to come into a court house and abduct a judge and a witness in the middle of a trial, wouldn't it? And what for?'

'To stop the trial,' Pete told him.

'Yes, but evidence is already given and on record so, again, why? What do they hope to gain?'

'Where was the fire?' Jane asked.

'The records room.'

'Well, there you go, then,' she said to Dick.

'Yeah, but… What about the evidence? The trial can always be started again and it's not like they took the defendant, is it?'

'He was guarded,' Pete pointed out.

'Exactly. So the trial can be restarted, even if it needs a new judge.'

'And, even if this one wasn't part of their ring, the new one might be,' Jane added.

'It's no good speculating,' Pete said as Colin came back into view around the corner of the court house and waved them over. 'Come on.' He started across the crowded space, pushing through the throng with Jane and Dick following in his wake.

By the time they reached the still-closed doors of the court house, Colin had already spoken to the usher and he led the way inside, reporting what he'd discovered at the back of the building as they mounted the stairs.

'It's safe in here now, but I asked them to give us time to examine the scene before letting people in to potentially contaminate it. The fire didn't spread beyond the records room. Whoever set it shut the door behind them so, with the windows closed and the air-con working, the fire ran out of oxygen. The bad news is there's still no sign of Tommy, his chaperone or the judge out there.'

I thought we knew who set it, Guv?' asked Jane as they reached the first floor and started towards the court room.

'We don't know until we find some evidence.'

'Right, Guv.'

Colin opened the big doors and they entered the court room. The big space was eerily empty. It didn't take long for Jane to spot the one thing out of place in there. 'Hey, boss. Guv.' She pointed out the remains of the stenographer's machine scattered across the floor around where she had been seated to one side of the judge's bench.

Court cases were not recorded on video or audio tape. The stenographer's transcript was the only record that existed apart from any notes that the judge or the journalists in the press gallery might have made.

'That supports what we were saying outside,' Dick pointed out.

'Unlikely to be any finger-prints on it, though,' Colin argued. 'That was done with a tool of some kind.' He led the way towards the door to the judge's chambers. It gave into an old-fashioned wood-panelled corridor with portraits of men in red robes and wigs hanging at intervals and several doors leading off. Secretaries, clerks and other back-office staff had offices back here as well as the judge. All the doors stood open, Pete saw as he entered the corridor. The smell of smoke was strong.

He knew from experience where the judge's office and changing room were, as did Colin. They headed straight for them.

Colin stopped abruptly in the doorway, one hand going up to halt the others. 'Get forensics here.'

'Guv?' Jane checked.

'He's dead. I can see that from here. Don't know how yet. There's no blood. But the pathologist will explain that.'

'You sure, Guv?' Dick asked as Jane turned away to make the call.

Colin turned his head. 'About the pathologist?'

'About the judge. Being dead.'

'His ribs aren't moving and I don't fancy having my neck at that angle.'

Pete looked past the senior man's bulky frame. The judge was on the floor of his office, head tilted up sharply as it rested against the old-fashioned cast-iron radiator between two tall windows that overlooked the narrow street down the side of the courthouse. 'They didn't even hide him.'

'No need,' Colin replied. 'Everybody hurrying out of here, concerned with their own safety.'

Pete grimaced. 'I suppose. But what does this mean for Tommy? Or his chaperone?'

Colin met his gaze. 'Let's not speculate, eh?' He reached for the door to close it but stopped himself just in time. The scene needed recording as it was, preferably without his finger prints to contaminate it. They headed back through the court room out to the public space beyond, turning right towards the little room where Tommy had been testifying when the alarm sounded.

'Pathologist and forensics are on the way,' Jane reported as they once more stopped at the door.

Colin nodded, peering in. 'No signs of a struggle. They must have been blitzed.' He stepped back and Pete saw something he had missed before.

'Is that blood?'

'Where?'

'The edge of the witness box, to the right of the camera stand.'

Colin looked closer, still staying outside the doorway to the room. 'Could be.'

'That's it, then,' Dick said. 'Step in, slam the camera man's head down on there to knock him out, then snatch the boy and out. Somebody the size of Adrian Southam could pick Tommy up one-handed. He's got the other hand free, then, to clap over his mouth, stop him yelling for help.'

'He'd fight, though,' Pete said. 'Kick the bejesus out of him if he couldn't do anything else. And he's not one to fight fair.'

'So, if Adrian picked Tommy up while his brother dealt with the judge and destroyed the stenograph, which way would they have gone out of here?' Jane asked.

'Down the judge's stairs, I expect,' Colin said. 'There wasn't another option and they'd have had to move quick.'

'Or stay put,' Pete pointed out. 'Hide inside until everyone's back in, out of the way, *then* go out the back way.'

'Bit of a risk isn't it, with a fire going in the building?' asked Dick.

'Not if that door was shut deliberately,' Pete countered.

'You reckon they're still here, then?' asked Jane.

Pete tilted his head. 'Makes more sense than risking being seen.'

'We're going to need more bodies,' Colin said. 'A thorough search of this place is going to take a while.'

NO MIDDLE GROUND by JACK SLATER

CHAPTER ELVEN

'Can I have everyone's attention, please?' Pete stood in the rear doorway of the combined court house, overlooking the small crowd of officials, jury members and judiciary as the last of the fire crews packed up their gear to his left.

Quiet descended until someone asked, 'When are we going back inside?'

'I'll answer that in a moment. First, has anyone seen two men leaving with a boy about so high.' He raised his hand to roughly Tommy's height. 'For those of you who were in court one, he was testifying when the alarm went off.'

Heads shook.

'They could have been in a car or on foot. They'd have been big, bulky men, last seen with short-cropped hair. Look like a pair of bouncers.'

'He's your son,' someone called out.

'Correct, but irrelevant. We think he may have been abducted by the men I described. No-one saw them leave?'

More head-shaking.

'When are we going back in?'

'That depends on finding the two men I described. They're dangerous and presumed armed. My colleague is checking at the front of the building but if they weren't seen leaving, then they must still be inside, hiding until the coast is clear, so to speak. In which case, we'll need to search the building for them, so it'll be a while.'

'Courts are in session in this building, Detective Sergeant, and not only courts. We can't be left out here indefinitely.' The speaker was a grey-haired man still wearing the red robes of his office.

'It won't be indefinitely, sir. Just until we've cleared the building – as I said, if they weren't seen going out the front, which seems unlikely even for someone as brazen as these two.'

'So, who are they?' someone asked.

'I'm sorry, I can't answer that at this stage for legal reasons.' This being a court house, they ought to be able to appreciate that, he thought as he took out his phone and turned away to call Colin Underhill, who would have been asking the same questions out front of the building.

'Yes?'

'It's Pete. Anything?'

'No.'

'So they're inside.'

'Seems that way.'

'So, if we start at the bottom and work up, floor by floor, we'll have them trapped rather than letting them slip away during a top-down search,' Pete said.

'We'll wait for the uniforms and do just that. They're on the way. Meantime, guard that entrance and I'll stay here. Feeney can go down to the underground car park and keep an eye there. Jane can watch where the prison vans come and go.'

Blimey, Pete thought, trying to recall the last time he'd heard Colin say that much all in one go. 'Right, I'll tell them.'

'Eyes peeled and be careful,' Colin said and hung up.

Pete called up Jane's number on his speed dial. 'Jane. I just spoke to Colin. No sign of them leaving so he said you should keep an eye at the suspects' entrance and Dick should go down to the underground car park, keep watch there. Dick's with you, is he?'

'Yes. I'll tell him.'

'And be careful, both of you. These two are unpredictable at best, bloody dangerous at worst. And cornered, they'll be at their worst.'

'Right, boss.'

Pete put his phone away and stepped back inside to prevent the distraction of answering questions from the assembled crowd.

Minutes later, Colin called him back. 'The uniforms are here. I'll send one each to the exits and the rest can help us search the place.'

'OK, Guv. Dick will certainly need help with the car park.'

Colin cut the connection without further comment but Pete knew he would have taken the observation on-board. The underground car park was single storey, just for the use of staff and legal counsel, but it would still take a while to search effectively.

Pete waited for a constable to approach his position.

When a knock sounded on the door behind him, he thought it must be a member of the crowd waiting outside. He turned, ready to tell them they'd have to wait and, instead, saw a dark uniform and a face he recognised. He opened the door. 'Mick. You on guard duty today, then?'

'Seems that way.'

'Baton out and stay alert then. The suspects we're looking for are at least as dangerous as Zivan Millocovic was,' he said, referring to a huge Polish drug pusher they'd had dealings with the year before, until he was killed in a car crash. 'And there's two of them.'

'Oh, cheers for that.'

Pete clapped him on the shoulder. 'I know you can cope, mate. Anyway, with any luck we'll be driving them up, away from you.'

'Well, that's something, I suppose. What have they done?'

'Abducted Tommy and killed a judge. Today.'

'Jesus, you weren't kidding, were you?'

'Not even slightly. Eyes peeled, Constable. Ears, too. And that lot out there are not coming in until we've cleared the place, no matter what they say.'

'So I've got potential trouble from both sides. Great. Thanks.'

Pete chuckled. 'I know you love it.' He took out his phone and hit Jane's speed dial again.

'Boss?'

'When your cover gets there, clear that yard before you come in, OK?'

'Will do.'

'And be careful,' he reminded her.

'Always, boss. You know me.'

He did. Which was why he'd said it. 'And you know who we're looking for and what they're capable of.'

'Yeah,' she breathed. 'See you later.'

'You'd better,' he replied and broke the connection. 'Right, I'm off,' he told Mick.

'Like you said – be careful.'

Pete grunted. 'And as Jane just said – always.'

There was a corridor leading from the rear door straight back into what seemed like the bowels of the building. It dead-ended at a point Pete guessed to be somewhere near the centre of the ground floor but before that there were doors for the lift, the stairs and several rooms that Pete didn't know the purpose of. Before heading up to the next floor, he would search them all. He walked past the stairs and lift to the first door on the right. With his collapsible truncheon ready in his hand, he tried the handle. It opened onto a tiny room, undecorated and empty apart from two meter-boxes set into the wall, labelled 'Gas' and 'Electricity'. The next door opened on the boiler room which was quiet at this time of year. Then came what appeared to be a cleaning closet. Shelves covered all three walls apart from the one with the door in.

The one after that was locked. The handle went down at his touch, but the door refused to budge. He'd come back to it. Next was another service room, this one housing stationery stores. Shelves of paper, pens, pencils, and essential supplies. Again, nowhere to hide and no-one in there. He closed the door and moved on. Three rooms searched, five to go. His plan was to work his way down one side and back along the other before checking any locked ones. He'd already clarified with Colin that they would check every room, locked or not. Repairs could be dealt with later.

By the time he'd completed the task, clearing every room along the corridor one by one and returning to the stairs, his shoulder was sore from barging two locked doors, the sweat of tension was running uncomfortably down his back and his brain was so wound up, the slightest shock would have tipped him into immediate violence.

He lifted his radio and keyed the mike. 'Jane. Progress report?'

'Nearly done with the bottom floor, boss.'

'Dick?'

'Waiting on assistance, boss.'

'Guv?'

'Ready when you are.'

'Up we go, then.' He pressed the button to call the lift, waited for it to arrive and checked inside as the doors slid open, reaching in to hit the emergency button, blocking its further use before he turned to the stairs.

He was about to emerge onto the first floor when his radio crackled.

'PC 1642 French. Canvas completed, Southernhay Gardens. No witnesses and no CCTV of the suspects.'

'Received,' Colin answered her. 'Come down to the court house and help DC Feeney search the car park, both of you.'

'Roger.'

Pete muted his radio and stepped out through the fire door.

*

The building had three floors above the parking basement. Smaller civil courts and arbitration services were on the ground floor, crown courts on the next with ancillary staff and the records room at the top. There were three crown courts, each with their own judge's chamber, secretarial and runner's offices.

Pete ignored the fact that they had already been in the back rooms of court one. They hadn't covered the whole area and people could move while there was no-one to see them. Forensics and the pathologist had yet to arrive, he saw when he began a second, complete sweep of the section. With the court in session, none of these rooms were locked so it didn't take long, even though there were secondary nooks and crannies like a bathroom off the judges' chamber, separate store cupboards and toilet facilities. Still, he'd worked his way through to the main court room by the time his phone buzzed in his pocket. He took it out and checked the caller ID.

Colin.

He picked up, speaking quietly. 'Guv?'

'Have you got your radio turned off?'

'Yes, why?'

'The pathologist's here.'

He would want access to the body, but Pete hadn't fully cleared the court room yet. 'Give me a minute and I'll be ready for him.'

Colin ended the call without replying. Pete put his phone away. It wasn't a question of his boss being rude. It was just Colin.

122

He didn't waste words. It could be frustrating at times, but there were a lot of worse bosses he could be working for.

He crossed to the jury's entrance. Beyond it, the jury room, a break room and toilet facilities opened off a corridor that led along the back of the court towards the stairs he'd come up a few minutes before. He checked the meeting room first, crouching to see under the big table that took up the centre. Then he moved on to the toilets, checking both the male and female. All the stalls were empty and open. The break room was also unoccupied.

He moved back to the court room with its teak furniture that always seemed slightly cheap and down-market, compared with the mahogany grandeur you expected in such places. The public gallery on the mezzanine above the back, separated from the press gallery by a five-foot gap above the main doors, would have to be checked carefully from the next floor up, but the main room itself was empty.

Pete took out his phone and dialled.

It was picked up on the first ring, as if he'd had it in his hand already. Which he probably had. 'Guv, where are you?'

'Court two.'

'Can someone check the court galleries while we stay put?'

'Yep'

Again, Colin ended the call abruptly. Pete's radio sounded faintly but he couldn't make out what was being said. Didn't need to. It would be Colin sending someone upstairs to do as he'd suggested.

Moments later that was confirmed when the door at the rear of the public gallery opened and Dick Feeney stepped through.

'Hey, boss,' he nodded and checked to either side. From there, he could see across into the press gallery too. 'All clear.'

'Check the others then stay put in the corridor there until we come up,' Pete told him.

'Right.' Dick backed out, closing the doors behind him. Pete heard the click of the lock being turned up there as he took out his radio. He turned up the volume and pressed the call button. 'All clear for the pathologist.'

Pete waited where he was. It took only moments for the pathologist to enter the building and climb the single flight of stairs. One of the big doors in front of Pete opened and the small, silver-haired man stepped through, his customary battered black leather case in one hand.

'Hello, Doc,' Pete said

'Peter. How are you?'

'Tense,' Pete admitted. 'Worried sick, actually. They've left at least one body behind for you and taken Tommy with them.'

'Oh, my God. I didn't realise. I'm so sorry.' Doc Chambers clapped him gently on the shoulder. 'Where are we going?'

'Judges chamber.'

Tony Chambers' eyes widened. 'Not…'

Pete nodded. 'Yep.'

'Good Lord,' the Doc breathed. 'They must be desperate or truly psychopathic.'

'Trust me, it's the latter. So lock yourself in, at least until forensics arrive. We've got one more floor to check, then I'll be back.'

'Right. Lead on,' the older man nodded.

Pete turned back towards the left-hand access door and opened it. 'First on the right,' he said. The pathologist went past him, stopped at the open door to put down his case and open it. He withdrew a white overall and blue plastic shoe covers and pulled them on. There was no need to ask whether anything had been touched in the room. They'd known each other for too long. Pete waited until Chambers had gloved up and stepped inside, closing the door behind him. He heard the latch click and turned away.

Colin and Jane were waiting in the wide corridor outside the court rooms. 'Back rooms are clear,' Colin said.

'So, where's the chaperone?' Pete couldn't see even one of the Southam brothers being able to control both Tommy and the man with him.

Colin shrugged.

'Maybe he went with them' Jane suggested. 'Tommy's his charge for the day. A sense of responsibility comes with that, I expect. If they threatened Tommy's safety unless he followed orders...'

'I hope you're right,' Pete said. The alternative was that there was another body somewhere. Or at least a man who needed medical attention.

'Let's get upstairs and make sure,' Colin said.

PC's Nikki French and Sophie Clewes of the uniformed branch, both of whom Pete had worked with before, came up the front stairs towards them.

Colin turned to meet them. 'You two stay on this floor and check the rooms along there.' He pointed towards the rear of the building, beyond the small room where Tommy had been testifying. 'And between you, make sure you don't miss anyone dodging from one hiding place to another.'

Damn, Pete thought. He hadn't thought of that until now, but the Southam brothers were more than bold enough to stay hidden by swapping locations during the search. 'We'll have to work our way back down in pairs, to make sure we haven't missed anything,' he said as the four of them headed for the main stairway.

Colin nodded. 'It was a question of manpower until the car park was cleared.'

At the front of the building on the top floor was a canteen with attached kitchen which was used by staff, jury members, solicitors and barristers as well as witnesses, if accompanied by a staff member. Across the corridor, which was narrower on this floor, was the arbitration department and next to it, according to the signage, access to the public and press galleries of crown court one, then more toilets and the records library while across from them were the galleries for court two, the stenography department and finally, the court three galleries.

Pete took one side while Colin would check the other, leaving Jane at the top of the stairs to watch for surreptitious movement. Despite the size of the space, it took only moments to check the canteen, glancing under the tables and over the counter. He was heading for the door through to the kitchens when he heard Jane's shout. He turned instantly and ran for the door, snatching it open and launching himself through.

'Jane?'

'Nick and Sophie have found something, boss.'

A feeling of dread swooped deep into Pete's gut as the door opposite opened and Colin appeared. Pete ignored the senior man. 'Found what?'

'A body. In a store cupboard next to the interview room.'

CHAPTER TWELVE

'Who?' Pete demanded before she had chance to continue.

'They don't know. Might be the chaperone who was with Tommy.'

Relief flooded Pete's soul, followed almost as powerfully by guilt. How could he be relieved that another human being was dead, regardless of who it was? But when the alternative was his own son...

'Tell them to continue the search,' Colin said, taking out his phone. He dialled slowly, one finger stabbing at the screen. When it connected, he raised it to his ear and waited a few seconds. 'Doctor, Colin Underhill. Seems like we've got another one when you've finished with the judge. Coming out through the court room, the second door on your right.'

He paused, listening, then nodded. 'He's not going anywhere.' He ended the call and looked across at Pete. 'Carry on.'

Pete turned back into the canteen and headed for the kitchen door, checking behind the counter again as he passed. Reaching for the single wooden door with its long, narrow glazed panel, he pushed it open and stepped through.

The door slammed back at him. His head bounced off the frame hard enough that he saw stars as the door squeezed his ribcage so powerfully it felt like at least a couple of ribs were cracked. Pete gasped, shook his head and immediately regretted it. He winced at the added discomfort, heaving back against the man he could now see on the far side of the door. Not much less than his own height but probably half as heavy again and all of it solid muscle, his bull neck and short-cut sandy hair combined with the smart suit he was wearing to make him look like a bouncer. But Pete knew he was anything but that.

He was on the other side of the law completely.

Pete pushed back as hard as he could against the pressure Adrian Southam was maintaining on the door. Finally, he managed to slip his body out from between the door and the frame, but he wasn't fast enough to get his right leg out of there. The door slammed shut again on his thigh. He heaved and pushed but could only gain limited purchase. What was Southam trying to prove here? Or to do? Was this a question of hurting Pete as much as he could, either just for the sake of it or to slow his pursuit - either to allow his brother time to get away with Tommy or to impede Pete in a chase when he finally let go? Or was he just enjoying it?

Rage lent Pete extra strength. He set his free foot on the lino floor, face twisting into a snarl as he heaved for all his was worth. He gained maybe half an inch. Still not enough to free his trapped leg but enough to be able to twist it so he could set his foot against the door frame and push with that one as well.

A movement sounded from beyond Southam. A shout.

Pete recognised Colin Underhill's voice. He saw Southam's head snap around. Then a large aluminium saucepan winged its way past Southam's head to crash against the wall. He ducked and Pete used the distraction to push against the door again as Southam laughed.

'Come on, old man. That's a woman's trick.'

'So long as it works,' Colin replied and threw another.

His aim was better, but still Southam batted it aside with one hand while the other kept the pressure on the door, Pete gaining nothing against him.

Then Colin threw two almost at once. Southam batted the first one away but the second hit him squarely in the chest. Pete heaved again and gained a fraction of ground but Southam had his foot firmly against the base of the door, his soles gripping the floor as if they were glued down. But more saucepans came at him fast and hard. One, two, three in rapid succession. The first one he avoided, the second hit him on the shoulder. Colin's aim was improving. His arm came up to bat the third one away but wasn't quick enough. He ducked, and Pete managed finally to force the door open enough to dart through before he could recover. But he was wrong-footed to attack the big man before he could dodge away.

He swung a fist at Pete, connecting hard as Pete stepped into its arc. The impact knocked Pete's skull back. He went down on one knee and Southam stepped in to deliver the final blow, but Colin was on him, saucepan in one hand, a big knife in the other. Pete saw him swing the saucepan even as the shock of seeing him with the kitchen knife jolted through him.

If he connected with that it could finish his career and put him in jail.

'No, Colin,' he shouted, lunging up, shoulder slamming into Southam's unprotected side.

Southam's raised arm was jolted out of position so the big pan hit him a glancing blow on the side of his head. He grunted, staggering sideways. He was a big man but two police officers with anger driving them past what would normally be expected was too much. He stepped in on Colin, one arm going for the knife while the other fist bunched and drove at his face.

130

Colin ducked to one side but a shove from Southam sent him sprawling across the steel-topped counter to his left and Southam went past him, heading for the far door with a speed that was shocking for a man of his size.

Pete gained his feet and reached out to Colin, who dropped the knife and straightened as the door at the far end of the room was batted aside and Southam was out and gone.

'Shit,' Colin grunted.

'Are you all right?' Pete asked.

Colin nodded.

'You were going to…?'

'For Tommy, not you.'

Pete couldn't stop the grin from crossing his face. He set off running after Southam. He wouldn't catch him, but he could help Mick tackle him downstairs. As he ran for the door, he reached for his radio. 'Mick, be ready. Incoming. I'm on his tail, but I'm too far back to catch him.'

There was no response, but Pete didn't really expect one, apart from the possible 'Roger.' He must be otherwise occupied, he guessed as he reached the back stairs. He hit the door hard and went through, jumping down the stairs three and four at a time, no thought of safety as he made what time he could, bouncing off the wall at the half-landing with a raised hand to launch himself down the next short flight. His feet touched ground just once before he reached the bottom and turned again.

At the ground floor, he stuck his landing leg out almost rigid to stop himself and yank the door open, surging through into the corridor, hand slapping the wall as he turned fast towards the distant back door. Beyond it, he could see the milling, impatient crowd. On this side of the glass, Mick was on the floor, Southam stamping on his torso as he reached for the door release and took off into the narrow street beyond, turning left away from the crowd, shoving aside a black-robed man who fell into the crowd, knocking several more over like skittles in an alley.

Pete saw Mick stir as if he was going to rise. The last thing he needed was a tangle in this narrow space.

'Stay down,' he yelled.

Mick blinked and did as he was told as Pete leapt over him, slamming his hand on the door release and hoping it worked as quickly as it should. He raised his free hand to the door, still moving fast. It opened and he was through. Now he could hear the protests of the crowd as they struggled to untangle themselves and gain their feet again. He ignored them, setting off after the fleeing man. But Southam was already out of sight. Just beyond the far end of the court building, the narrow street dead-ended at a T junction. One side led back towards the ring-road, he knew, while the other joined a narrow access road that headed into the shopping centre from further up Southernhay Gardens, emerging across from Debenham's.

The right side was more likely, he thought, adjusting his trajectory to allow a wider turning angle. As he bounced off the far wall with a raised hand and kept running, he glanced over his shoulder just in case, but there was no sign of the fleeing man in either direction.

He must have gone somewhere though, and these were the only two choices, this the more likely of them. He kept going, not slowing his pace. Southam was built for speed not endurance. Pete thought he could catch the man, given time.

Not that he had much of that. He had no way of knowing what the other Southam – the one suspected of killing a young girl in Bath several years ago - would do to Tommy as soon as he got the chance. He reached the far end of the alley and another T junction. Glanced right and left. Was just in time to see Southam dodging to the right in front of the big department store. He set off after him once more.

Surely, they weren't stupid enough to have parked whatever vehicle they had in a public car park? They had to realise it would be covered by CCTV. And yet they had to have kept it close. How else could they have hoped to get in and out of the court building without being seen?

But these were all questions for later. First, he had to catch them.

There were more people around here. A crowd was gathered around a burger stand a few yards ahead, another in front of an ice-cream van in the middle of the block-paved cross-road in front of the big department store. More individuals and small family groups milled around from shop to shop. As he closed on the crowd around the burger van a small group broke away, straight into his path.

'Police. Coming through,' he shouted.

They froze, heads turning towards him in shock. This wasn't a normal event in a British shopping mall. But thankfully, they stayed still. He went past them, dodged around a woman with both hands laden with store-named shopping bags and made the cross-road. The street ended abruptly only fifty yards away, but he couldn't see Southam. Where had he gone?

Pete hesitated.

He could have entered any of the several shops on either side of the short pedestrianised street or continued through the narrow access path that led through to the tourist information centre and the entrance to the multi-storey car park.

He frowned, thinking again, *they can't be that stupid. Can they?*

Most villains were caught by their own greed or stupidity but the Southam brothers had proven themselves far from stupid. Ruthless, vicious and twisted, but not stupid. A shop, then. But which one? He cast his gaze around. Most of the shops along here were small, single-entrance establishments, easy to trap someone inside. He wasn't the type to take a hostage and try to escape that way. It seldom worked anyway. The department store then. If so, he hadn't gone in the main door. It was right on the corner where Pete would have seen him. So, the next one along. Once inside, would he aim to double back and lose Pete? Pete was on his own. They could go round and round in circles like that until he called in reinforcements, so he'd best do that now. He took out his radio and pressed the transmit button.

'This is DS Gayle. I think the fugitive is in Debenham's, but I need backup before going in. Any available units to my position ASAP.' Then he took out his phone and dialled. 'Ben,' he said when the call was picked up. 'Put me through to Graham, will you? Then get onto security at Debenham's and see if they can confirm Adrian Southam's presence and current location in there. Tell them to track him but not engage, all right? Emphasise that. He's dangerous.'

'Will do, boss. Hang on.' The line went dead for a moment, then a new connection was made. 'CCTV room.'

'Graham, its Pete Gayle. I need you to try and track someone for me.'

'Who and where?'

'Adrian Southam. Big, bulky feller in a dark suit. Short sandy hair. He's run from the combined court house up into the precinct. I know he turned right at the cross roads there, but I've lost him. Also, a similar male with a small boy, a few minutes earlier.'

'You mean you've *just* lost him? Like now?'

'Within the last minute or so.'

'I'll call you back.'

As he hung up, Pete was grateful for Graham's presence in the CCTV room. They had their jokes and banter, but Graham was good at his job and sensitive when it was needed.

He put away his phone and concentrated on carefully watching the several entrances to the department store in front of him.

He heard running footsteps from behind him and glanced around just as his phone rang in his pocket. Jane, Dick and two uniformed officers were hurrying towards him as he turned back towards the department store and took out his phone. 'Yes?'

'Pete, its Graham.' The one you're after went in Debenhams' north door. I haven't got the other one with the boy, though. Nowhere to be seen. Sorry.'

'Nowhere?' Fear was creeping through his veins like liquid ice.

'Not a single frame. Not anywhere.'

'But…' Pete had been convinced that the younger Southam had made it out with Tommy ahead of them: that Adrian had stayed behind to delay them – to give Steven time to get away with Tommy.

That was the main reason for going after him with such determination. To catch him and get him to talk – to reveal where his brother would have taken the boy. Otherwise… 'Where the hell did they go then?'

'I've got no idea, mate. But they didn't go the same way as you just did and there's no sign of them on Southernhay Gardens, as far as I can see, so they must have had a vehicle waiting somewhere in the alleys round there.'

Pete's panicking mind refused to accept that. 'The lanes are too narrow. A parked car would have been noticed. It would have blocked anywhere they left it.'

'There's no wider areas? No garages, parking bays, anything like that?'

Pete tried to think. What had he run past on the way here? But it was all a blur. He'd been moving too fast, been focussed too tightly on his prey to notice much of his surroundings along the way.

He shook his head. There was no use panicking. That would get him no nearer to Tommy. He slowed himself down by force of will, sucking in deep breaths, forcing the fear out with them.

Images flickered in his mind. Images of buildings packed in on either side of the narrow lanes, walls crowding the rough tarmac and cobbles, some painted white, others bare red brick or old stone. A mix of widths and heights. Then he paused.

'There's a row of garages. Four of them, just before a junction, but there's no room to park in front of them without blocking at least three and they wouldn't have done that. They'd have known they'd be in the courthouse for some time and they'd have wanted to stay unnoticed.'

'And all the garages were closed and locked?' Graham asked.

'I dunno.' Pete hesitated again. 'They were all closed, but again – park in someone's actual garage and you're going to get more than noticed if they come home, aren't you?'

'Yes, but if they're out at this time on a week-day, chances are they're at work, right? They'll be gone all day.'

'Maybe,' Pete allowed. 'But it's a hell of a chance to take.'

'Aren't the Southam brothers all about taking chances and opportunities, regardless of other folks?'

'Well, yeah, but...'

'Best check them, I'd have thought,' Graham said. 'It's the only way I can see they'd be able to get away from the area unseen.'

'And we can't...? No.' Pete stopped himself. They couldn't find the vehicle without knowing what it was. But how many vehicles would be coming and going along those narrow roads at this time of day?

'Do me a favour,' he said. 'Check whatever CCTV you've got covering the entrances to those alleys. Go back twenty minutes, max. See what vehicles came out of the area in that timeframe or any that went in after 9.00 am.'

'OK. Four cameras then. I'll call you back.'

CHAPTER THIRTEEN

Pete's phone rang as soon as he broke the connection with Graham. He glanced at the screen and accepted the call. 'Ben?'

'I've been onto the shop security guys. They confirm he went in there a couple of minutes ago. He's gone up to the restaurant and picked up a drink he's currently queueing to pay for.'

'OK, thanks.' He ended the call and turned to Jane, Dick and the two uniformed officers who had joined him. 'Are you two armed?' he asked the two PCs.

The smaller one nodded. 'Taser.'

The other one shook his head. 'Just the baton, Sarge.'

'He's in the restaurant upstairs, getting himself a drink.'

'I bet he needs it after all that running,' Dick said. 'He's not exactly built like Mo Farrer.'

'No,' Pete agreed. 'But, he's amongst a lot of people we can't afford to put in danger. And make no mistake, as soon as he realises we've spotted him, they'll all be in danger. He may or may not be armed but he won't hesitate to hurt somebody if it gets him what he wants. Or even just for the fun of it.'

'So, what do we do, boss?' Jane asked.

'Unfortunately, there's only one way we can play this. Wait for him to come out and take him on the street – hopefully by surprise. Until then, we split up and cover all the exits. Jane, you and I'll take the west entrance. Dick, you take the north, which is where he went in. You two cover the main one – just stroll casually up and down past it every half a minute or so, staying close-up but out of sight between passes. I'll call in some reinforcements.' He took out his phone and dialled. In moments he was through to the duty sergeant.

'Andy, it's Pete.' He explained the situation briefly. 'So we need a couple more Taser officers down here pronto. And it'll be a case of deploying it immediately – forget the niceties.'

'By niceties, you mean protocol?'

'If you want to be pedantic in a situation guaranteed to put the public in danger, yes. That's exactly what I mean.'

'Right. I'll send Nikki French and Justin Davis.'

'Nikki's already at the courthouse,' Pete reminded him.

'So's Justin. I take it that's no longer a priority, though?'

'No, we've cleared it.'

'Right. I'll have them with you in two or three minutes, at a guess.'

'On their way here, can you get them to check the row of garages they'll pass and make sure all of them are actually locked?'

'Why?'

'The Southam brothers might have borrowed one of them. Left a getaway vehicle in there.'

'OK. Will do.'

Pete ended the call. 'Reinforcements are on the way,' he told the others. Let's get into position. I don't know where the restaurant is in there – what view he'd have if he sat by a window.'

'It looks out over the west side up there,' Jane told him, nodding towards the building.

Pete made sure they all knew what their target looked like. 'Right, let's move.'

*

Standing with Jane close to a display window to one side of the department store doorway, Pete had his back to the doors allowing Jane to look over his shoulder – or rather past it, considering her height – as they conversed in low voices. Jane had avoided mentioning Tommy, trying to keep Pete focussed on the job in hand.

'How do you reckon he's planning to get away from here?' she asked. 'I mean they'll meet up somewhere obviously, but how's he getting from here to wherever without being spotted? He'd guess there's cameras round here.'

Pete was about to reply when his phone rang. He took it out and answered it.

'Pete, its Graham. I've got a four by four towing a box trailer – the type burger stands use – and a dark red Ford Focus coming out of there within the timeframe. The Focus turned out onto the ring road and then off towards Topsham Road.'

'Well, they're not going to drag a trailer around so, unless they nicked the whole package from the lanes, the Focus is our...' He paused, about to say 'boy,' but that was too close to the truth for comfort.

'Yeah,' said Graham, glossing over the point. 'That's what I thought.'

'So, do we know where he's going?'

'No. He went up there about five minutes ago, but he hasn't passed the school yet.'

'He must have turned off, then. Can you put an alert out? Do not engage but follow and report.'

'No problem.'

'Cheers, Graham.' He ended the call. 'My guess,' he said to Jane. 'He's swinging around to pick Adrian up. Which means he's got to come out here pretty soon.'

'It would be good if we could pick up both at the same time,' Jane said.

'It would be perfect,' Pete agreed. 'But it ain't going to happen, is it? Too many possibilities to cover discretely in the time we've got.'

'That's the trouble – we need eyes every-bloody-where.'

'The eyes we've got. Graham. It's bodies we need everywhere right now.'

'Talking of which…' She nodded over his shoulder. He turned to see Nikki French and a tall, slender male officer walking towards them. Raising a hand, he indicated the male should join Dick Feeney while Nikki continued towards him and Jane.

They split up without breaking stride and moments later the small dark-haired female officer joined them. 'Hello, Sarge. What's occurring?'

'Did you find anything interesting in the lanes on the way here?'

She shrugged. 'One of the garages was empty, but that's not unusual at this time of day. Oh, and the second body in the court house is confirmed as the chaperone who was with Tommy.'

'Shit.' He'd suspected it, but to have it confirmed was still a blow. The man didn't deserve that, whoever he was. 'Empty empty or just no vehicle in it?'

'The second option.'

'So, tools and so on still there?'

She nodded.

'And unlocked.'

'Well, now you put it that way...'

'We suspect the Southam brothers were using one of those garages to store a get-away vehicle – a dark red Focus to be precise – while they were in the court house.'

'So, why are we hanging about outside a department store?'

'Because one of them's in the café inside.'

'And you want taser officers on each door for when he comes out,' she concluded. 'I've heard their reputation but I've never come across them directly.'

'You don't want to if you can help it,' Pete told her. 'They aren't nice blokes.'

'Boss,' Jane said, something in her tone catching Pete's attention instantly. 'He's here.'

Nikki spun around at the same instant as Pete.

Southam had taken off his jacket and tie while he was in the store. The jacket now hung over his shoulder from his left hand.

'Taser,' Nikki shouted automatically. 'Stop or I'll fire.'

Southam swung round sharply, the jacket coming down off his shoulder, swinging out like a matador's cape. He caught it with the other hand, holding it at arm's length.

Nikki fired the Taser, but its charge wasn't powerful enough to strike through the loose-held jacket. It billowed in front of him and he let it fall, charging them as a shout sounded from behind him. The two officers at the main entrance came into view, but too far away to help as Southam's thick arm shot out like a steel bar, catching Nikki across the throat and driving her down. He shoulder-charged Jane, behind her, knocking her backwards too.

The two women were blocking Pete. He spun, leaping back around Jane, one hand rebounding off the plate glass window as his foot hit the low sill, powering him across behind her. As she fell, her head clipped his trailing foot, but it didn't affect his trajectory. He came at Southam from a high angle, arms wrapping around the man's bull neck as his collar bone hit a meaty shoulder. Southam tried to turn with the impact but his momentum was all wrong. He staggered sideways. Pete swung across his back, pulling him down. He felt the resistance go out of the bigger man as he spun around, feet going out from under him.

Pete hit the ground on his back, still clinging to Southam's neck. Southam came down hard, his spine across Pete's already sore ribs as he drove an elbow hard and fast at Pete's crotch. Only a buck of his hips saved him from an agonising injury but then Southam was twisting, turning in his grip until they faced each other. A big fist drove deep into Pete's gut. He coughed as the air was punched out of him, but still refused to let go. Then Southam changed tack. He bared his teeth in a snarl and slammed his head down, open-jawed at Pete's face. The hard enamel of his front teeth struck Pete's cheek bone and he clamped them shut, nose pushing against Pete's tightly closed eye. Pain seared through Pete's face. He felt warm liquid running into his eye socket and down the side of his face towards his ear. Saliva or blood, he didn't know. And he didn't want to. Either way, he had to get the man off him. Then he heard a meaty impact and Southam's jaws opened as he reared back. Pete turned his head, fearing a head-butt, but it didn't come. Instead, another impact and Southam went rigid on top of him like a man in the throes of climax. Pete's eyes opened. The two uniforms from the main store entrance were standing over them, the smaller one with Taser drawn and fired, his finger still firm on the trigger. As he released it his companion dropped a knee onto Southam's legs, grabbed his arms and snapped on a pair of cuffs.

'Legs too,' Pete gasped.

The man complied, wrapping a leg restraint several times around Southam's calves.

'Another.' Pete slapped the big man's thighs.

'You all right, boss?' Jane asked, sitting up.

'Yes. Nikki?' Pete asked, wiping the fluid from his face. A glance down told him it was at least mostly blood. His own.

With Southam fully trussed they finally rolled him off Pete, allowing him to stand. PC French was clambering to her feet at the same time. 'Sarge?'

Southam groaned on the ground between them and started to struggle but quickly found it was getting him nowhere. As the man with the Taser called for the van to transport the prisoner back to the station, Southam rolled over to face them. 'You think this is going to get your boy back, Gayle?' he snarled. 'No fucking way. All you've done is put him at more risk. Stevie will do whatever it takes to get me out.'

'And you know as well as I do, we don't negotiate,' Pete told him despite the twisting feeling of nausea in his stomach. 'All your brother will do if he hurts Tommy is increase both of your sentences.'

'I hope there's plenty of shelves in that kid's room,' Southam sneered. 'You're going to need a good bit of space and a whole lot of jars to pickle all the bits of him Steve's going to send you until you let me go.'

Pete looked up at the man with the Taser. 'Add threatening a police officer to the charge sheet,' he said. 'Along with resisting arrest, public affray, vehicle theft, arson, kidnapping – three counts, murder – two counts and, best of all: conspiracy to perform acts of terrorism.'

'Hey,' Southam protested. 'What fucking terrorism?'

'I'll let you think on that,' Pete told him. 'And on the fact that you're going to be in my house now, so you better play nice or you might have an accident before you come out again.'

'That's threats,' Southam protested. 'You all heard him.'

'Eh?' said Jane.

'What?' Nikki asked.

The two uniforms shrugged almost as one. 'Can't hear a thing over all this racket round here.'

'Police fucking brutality,' snarled Southam.

'Well, you should know about brutality,' Jane said. 'All you and your brother have done over the years.'

'Allegedly,' he sneered.

'And provably,' she corrected. 'That's why you were in Morpeth, wasn't it?'

'Oh, you been looking me up?' he grinned. 'Like a real man, do you?'

'Yes,' she said. 'That's why I try to avoid the likes of you.'

'You don't know what you're missing till you try it, Ginge.'

Jane looked up at the others. 'Crowd round, folks,' she said. 'I don't want any witnesses to what I'm about to do.'

The others grinned and moved to surround the prone man.

Southam saw what was happening. 'Hey,' he shouted. 'Police brutality. Somebody film this.'

'You're repeating yourself, Adrian,' Jane told him. 'And nobody's interested in a nonce like you anyway.'

She looked up carefully and placed a heel over his crotch, toes on his stomach. She began to apply pressure. 'Aargh,' Southam yelled.

'You pussy,' Jane sneered. 'Don't like it coming back at you, do you?'

'Steady,' Pete warned.

'Oh, thanks, boss.' Jane put out a hand to grasp his upper arm as she pushed down harder with her foot.

'Bastards,' Southam shouted.

'Born and practicing, to quote a mate of mine,' Jane agreed. 'Get used to it. Your life's going to be one long round of suffering from now on. They don't like kiddy-fiddlers in clink. As big as you might be on the streets, you never know when there'll be somebody with a shiv waiting around the next corner in there. You think on that before you open your ugly trap again.' She removed her foot from his crotch and grimaced. 'I need to clean my shoe now.'

*

Minutes later Pete hurried across to a seat a few paces away and dropped onto it, the pain in his cheek now a deep, sickening ache but even that overpowered by his fear for his son. The van had gone, taking Adrian Southam and two of the uniformed officers with it. The other two had dispersed across the precinct. Jane joined Pete on the bench, Dick Feeney standing close by as he leaned forward, head hanging, elbows on his knees and a handkerchief clamped to his face with one hand.

'What do we do now?' He looked up at her with a haunted expression. Saw the concern in her eyes. 'Was he serious, do you think? About what his brother would do to Tommy?'

'Nah,' she said. 'Bluster and bull-shit, that's all. He's a bully. It's what he does. And it looks like what we do now is take you to hospital.'

The pain in Pete's cheek came back into focus. He checked the handkerchief. It was deeply stained with blood. He reapplied it to his face. At least bleeding would flush out any infection from Southam's teeth. 'But what if what he said was true anyway? I wouldn't put it past either of them.'

'We need to catch him ASAP then, don't we?'

'Yeah, I wish.'

'Well, we know what he's driving. We've got an alert out for him. His brother's not going to tell us where they were planning to meet but we know it's got to be close. If we spread out… We've got plenty of bobbies in town right now. I'll put a call in.' She took out her phone and called the station. 'Sarge it's Jane Bennett. Have you recalled your people from the court house yet? Good. We need them to spread out around the city centre ASAP. The Southam brothers were planning to meet up somewhere close to Princesshay. The younger one, with Tommy, is in a dark red Focus.' She paused as Fairweather responded. 'OK. Thanks, Sarge.' She closed the connection. 'It's all in place.'

He nodded. 'I just hope to God they catch him.'

CHAPTER FOURTEEN

Another thought struck Pete even as he spoke.

They'd just arrested Adrian Southam. His younger brother, a paedophile and suspected child killer, was out there somewhere with Tommy. There were three possibilities of what he might do when he found out they'd got Adrian. He might run, but Pete seriously doubted it. It just wasn't their style. He might hurt Tommy as Adrian had threatened. Or he might go after either Annie or Louise.

'Shit,' he breathed.

'What's up?' Jane asked.

'Where are Jill and Dave?'

'Dave's at the RDE. Mrs Turnbull woke up. He's there to interview her.'

'What a thing to wake up to,' Dick said with a grimace.

Pete ignored him. 'And Jill?'

'She went to Hanson's to take over from us.'

Pete calculated quickly. 'OK.' He took out his phone and dialled. Hung on while it rang several times. 'Come on,' he muttered. 'Pick up, for God's sake.'

Finally, the connection was made.

'Boss?'

'Dave. Wind up that interview if you haven't already and get over to CDU. Check on Lou for me. Don't tell her anything's wrong but there's a chance Steve Southam might be on the way there and if he is, he won't be going just to say hello so keep a surreptitious eye on her.'

'Right, boss.'

Pete ended the call and made another. This one was picked up on the second ring.

'Jill. Have you found anything at Hanson's?'

'There's nothing here. He must keep the stuff somewhere else.'

'He's self-employed and the place isn't exactly stuffed. Why would he need somewhere else? Never mind. I need you to get yourself over to Annie's school. We've got Adrian Southam in custody but his brother's still in the wind. I don't want him getting anywhere near her. But nor do I want to scare her so keep an eye from outside the school, OK?'

'Will do.'

Pete ended the call and put his phone away. All they had to do now was find his son and Steve Southam. The trouble with that was that, as soon as the elder brother missed whatever rendezvous they'd arranged, he would know something was wrong and he would at least suspect what it was, which left Tommy's safety very much on the line.

His phone rang again almost before he'd finished the thought. He took it out.

DCI.

'Shit.' Much as he didn't want to, knowing what was probably coming, he had to take the call. He tapped the icon to accept. 'Sir?'

'My office. Now.'

'Sir, I...'

'I don't care. Get here. Now.'

The call was cut off before Pete could say anymore.

'Boss?' asked Jane.

'Silverstone.'

'What the hell does he want at a time like this?' Dick asked.

'I don't know but I can guess,' Pete told him with a grimace.

*

Silverstone looked up as Pete entered his office and drew breath ready to lambast the junior man. Then he saw him and stopped. 'What happened to you?'

Pete reached up automatically to touch the dressing taped over his cheek. It was beginning to ache again now as the local anaesthetic wore off. 'Adrian Southam bit me while we were arresting him. I had to go to Casualty, get a rabies shot. Or at least a tetanus,' he added more seriously.

'But you're OK?'

His concern wasn't personal, Pete thought. It was more about Health and Safety and his own reputation as station chief. 'Sir.'

He nodded. 'Well, you cannot – and you will not – treat this police force as your own private army. You know perfectly well that you cannot be involved in a case involving a family member. It's against every rule and protocol in the book.'

'I was there, sir. On the ground and in position,' Pete argued. 'And my son was in immediate danger. What was I going to do – let a violent criminal get away just to pander to a rule set miles away and years ago by some clueless oik in an office?'

'There are reasons for every rule that we work by, Detective Sergeant, as you well know. And insubordination will not further your cause. If I catch you or your team anywhere near the Steven Southam case, you will be suspended without pay, pending a full and detailed enquiry. And that applies to all of you. Do I make myself clear?'

'Crystal. Sir.' *Just don't even think about giving the case to Simon Phillips,* he thought.

Silverstone was staring at him suspiciously, as if he was looking for an angle, thinking this had been too easy.

Pete couldn't resist it. 'Can I take it you're going to let DI Underhill do his job, sir?'

'Get out of my office before I bloody sack you, Gayle!' Silverstone bellowed.

Pete didn't need telling twice. He turned sharply on his heel, reached for the door and was out of there, despite his aches and bruises, before Silverstone had a chance to call him back.

Ben looked up as he approached his desk in the squad room seconds later. 'Jesus! What happened? Fast-track finally lose the plot?' he asked.

'Kind of. We're off the Southam case.'

'Off it?' Ben protested. 'We've done all the work. How's that any kind of fair?'

'Life with him rarely is. I did have a dig about letting the guvnor do his job, though, in hopes the case would go to Jim or Mark.'

'I thought I heard yelling. Sounded like a bull having his nuts crushed.'

Pete couldn't keep the grin off his face. 'And doesn't that sound like a plan? I'd best call the DI and tell him the good news.' He took out his phone and pressed a speed dial number as Ben's began ringing on his desk.

They ended their calls within seconds of each other.

'That was Northants, boss. The ANPR system picked up Joe Hanson's Peugeot on the A5 at a place called Weedon.'

'Which is exactly how I feel after a visit to Fast-track's office,' Pete commented. 'Weed on. And pissed off. How did he get to somewhere as obscure as that without being picked up before?'

'Must have used back-roads, I suppose. Avoided the cameras. Sat-navs can help you do that.'

Pete grunted. How he'd got there was irrelevant, as opposed to what he was there for, what he might have done on the way and where he was going next. 'They need to give him a tug, make sure it's him driving and, if so, tell him to phone his daughter.'

'I'll ring them back.' Ben picked up his desk phone and began to dial as Pete's mobile began to ring. He checked the screen. *Jane.* He picked up.

'Boss, what's going on? The guvnor just told me and Dick to get back to the office.'

'We're off the Southam case.'

'But... Fast-track got wind, did he?'

'Don't know about wind but a bad case of hot air.' Pete tried not to be disrespectful to his seniors in front of the team, but he was still too frustrated and annoyed with the DCI to give much of a damn at the moment, despite Ben's attempt at distraction.

'We're on the way.'

'Northants said they'll pick him up,' Ben said as Pete laid his mobile phone on his desk.

'Right. Meantime, we need to find out if he's got a lock-up somewhere. Jill said he's got no books, receipts or anything at home.'

Ben thought for a moment then blinked as a memory surfaced. 'He used to use an old brick shed on his uncle's farm, I think. It's a long time ago, but I remember going there with him and Sally. He kept his cement mixer there and some of his other bigger tools. Stone saw, set-squares, acro-props – stuff that wouldn't fit in his garage without being inside his van. I don't remember any papers there, but you never know. I perhaps wasn't paying too much attention to stuff like that.'

He caught Pete's look. 'He was showing me the ropes. Teaching me the job. I thought I might like to get into it at the time.'

Pete grunted and glanced at the squad room around them with its chaos of papers, computer screens and procedural manuals. 'What happened?'

Ben grimaced. 'We uh… Had a bit of a falling out. He caught me and Sally out there one afternoon without him. Wasn't happy about it.'

Pete imagined catching Annie in a quiet spot with a boy in a few years' time. He wouldn't be happy either - even though she was sensible enough not to do anything with consequences that she wasn't prepared for.

'Do you remember where it was?'

'Out along Stoke Hill.'

A narrow country lane off Pennsylvania Road, north of the city, Pete recalled. It wouldn't be too far for Hanson to go from his home on Wreford's Lane. 'Right, let's go.'

'What about this lot?' Ben asked, indicating the large stack of files he'd been working through.

'Make sure you mark them clearly – ones you've checked and ones you haven't. Jane and Dick can take over when they get back. We'll let them know once we're on the move.'

*

Stoke Hill was a perfect example of how isolated and rural a place could be even though Pete knew that the city centre was only two or three miles away. The narrow lane with tall, dense hedges at either side could have been miles from anywhere.

'Just round the next bend on the left,' Ben said from the passenger seat.

Pete let the car slow as they approached the curve in the road. He could hear sheep bleating from somewhere. A blackbird flew, squawking, from the hedge on his right, its wings almost striking the windscreen before it curved away in front of them.

'There.' Ben pointed towards an ancient red-brick and timber cart barn that faced out directly onto the road. It was partly stacked up with split logs, an old-fashioned Land Rover parked in one of the bays. Behind it, he glimpsed a set of farm buildings that looked as if they might have been constructed soon after the Second World War and, at the far side, a large house, again of red brick, set behind a walled front garden.

Pete pulled up on the compacted dirt in front of the wood stack.

The yard behind the cart shed was paved with black flat-topped cobbles strewn with straw and muck. Pete could hear a tractor working in one of the sheds. Then it emerged, a grey-haired man in blue overalls and a flat cap at the wheel. He saw Pete and Ben and stopped the tractor. Leaving it idling, he climbed down and crossed towards them, waiting until he was just a few steps away before speaking.

'Afternoon.'

Pete nodded. 'Are you the owner?' He glanced around the yard.

'Yup. You look like you've got on the wrong side of a pit-bull. Who are you?'

'DS Gayle and DC Myers, Exeter CID.' Pete showed him his warrant card.

'Myers? I knew one of them, years back.'

Ben nodded. 'Yeah, that was me.'

The man nodded lazily. 'Thought there was something about your face. What do you want?'

'Does Jonas Hanson still keep some of his stuff here?' Pete asked, pulling the man's attention away from Ben in case there was any ill-feeling there, though it was hard to tell with this taciturn figure who could have been anywhere between fifty and eighty.

'He does.'

'Can we see it? He's gone missing. There might be something there that'd help us find him.'

The man nodded again. 'Missing, is he? Off on one of his trips, I expect.'

'Except he never told anyone he was going, which he generally does, apparently.'

The man's mouth pulled into a grimace that was as much a shrug. His dark blue eyes returned to Ben. 'Don't see how but it's still where it was.'

'Thanks,' Pete said. 'Do we need a key?'

'No locks round here. No need.'

'Thanks, Arch,' said Ben and turned to Pete, nodding towards one of the low brick buildings at the far left.

Arch nodded and turned back towards his tractor. As they walked along the front edge of the yard, Pete heard the engine noise increase behind him.

'Chatty feller,' he said to Ben, having to speak up over the roar of the tractor.

'Always was, boss,' Ben agreed. 'Could never work out what he thought of me. Or of much else, to be honest.'

'Look on the bright side,' Pete said. 'At least he didn't thump you. The size of his arms, I'm guessing you'd stay down if he did.'

'I've seen him throw an eight-month-old calf on its back. He barely seemed to put any effort into it.'

The shed the farmer had indicated had an ancient wooden door with a rusty iron latch. Ben reached for it and they stepped into a space that was surprising large but lit only by the cracks in the roof and the light that followed them in through the door. Pete looked around. As predicted, a cement mixer took pride of place. Orange and battered, it stood in the middle of the cobbled floor. To one side of it were a stone-cutting saw and a small pneumatic drill, behind them, along the back wall, was a loose stack of scaffold planks and poles. Over to the left, against the wall, stood a variety of shovels, crowbars, pick-axes and sledge-hammers with two or three long, bright yellow spirit levels and a variety of other tools, almost concealing the side of a dark metal filing cabinet.

'Here we go.' Pete stepped forward into the gloom. 'Is there a light in this place?'

'I think so.' Ben felt around near the door for a couple of seconds then found the switch. A single dim yellowish bulb in the bare rafters was not a lot of help but it was all they were going to get.

Pete pulled the top drawer of the filing cabinet. It didn't move. He glanced at Ben. 'What happened to no locks in this place?'

'Well, I don't remember any,' he said. 'I know, when I used to come over here, even the cars in the yard were left with the keys in.'

'Must be something significant in here, then. Have you got your pen-knife?'

Ben reached into his pocket to bring out a small, silvery multi-tool. He handed it over and Pete opened one of the blades and used it to force the lock on the cabinet.

'There. Now then…' The drawer space was filled with dark green hanging files. He reached in and took out a bundle of A5 envelopes from one of them. Started flipping through and opening them at random. Receipts and quotes were mixed together, seemingly at random. He looked for a date. Finally finding one, he read it out. 'May 2015.'

Replacing the papers, he took some from the next envelope. A similar mix of quotes, receipts and other bits and pieces. He rifled through them until again, he found a date. January 2015. He continued searching. 'March '15.' So, each folder amounted to a year's worth of papers.

In the next folder back, he found November 2014. He looked at Ben. 'We're going to have to take this whole bloody lot back to the station and go through it: look for correlations with any missing persons or unsolved deaths. Or with any of that stuff we got from Hanson's house.'

'What about a warrant?' Ben asked.

'We got permission from the landowner. Anything on his property is included in that – his or otherwise.'

Ben nodded. 'What about forcing the lock?'

'The man said there weren't any, so I thought it must be stuck,' Pete shrugged. 'Best get some crates from the car.' He kept a few collapsible ones in the boot for instances like this.

Ben was silent as he stepped outside.

*

They finished emptying the third drawer of the cabinet and Pete pushed it closed with his knee as Ben reached for the handle of the fourth and last one. He pulled it open. 'Whoa. No more files in here.'

Pete turned back from the crate he'd put the last files into. 'What you got?'

'Photos. Loads of them.'

As Pete stepped closer, Ben opened the packet in his hand and pulled out a batch of prints.

'Jesus!' he said as soon as he saw the top one.

'They weren't processed by the local mini-lab.'

Ben checked the packet. It looked like an ordinary commercial one from Boots or some other processing lab. 'There's no negatives. They must be printed off a computer.'

'What, all them? There's a bloody fortune in printing ink and paper there.'

'Well, I never knew him to be into dark-room stuff and they don't smell of photo chemicals.' Ben raised the pack to his nose and sniffed then grimaced as if he'd smelled something unpleasant. 'No. Definitely ink-jet.' He passed the pictures up to Pete and reached for another pack, flipped it open and dropped it back. Tried another and another as Pete flipped through the ones he'd got.

'They're all the same, boss.'

Pete paused at a picture of a young woman with long, dark hair and terrified brown eyes. She was bound, hands behind her back, naked and on her knees in a woodland glade, a gag tight across her mouth. The previous pictures had been a series, tracking through Hanson's observation of her on the street, her abduction then more shots leading up to this one. He was about three quarters of the way through the pack. He could guess where it would end but he would have to look, much as he didn't want to. He looked at Ben. 'How many bloody victims have we got here?'

CHAPTER FIFTEEN

They were loading the crates into the back of the car when Ben's phone rang in his pocket. Pete continued working as he answered it.

'Sal. How are…'

He paused, listening as she interrupted him.

'Yes, we are, but… Sal, I can't. It's an ongoing investigation now.' Another pause. 'I know that and it's not that I don't want to, but I can't talk about it at this stage. To anyone.'

Pete turned to face him, held his hand out for the phone. Ben handed it over without hesitation.

'Sally, this is Pete Gayle.' He pictured her face when they'd met briefly, earlier in the day. 'Ben's right. He can't talk about an on-going investigation. It's regulations, plus it's not his place. As Senior Investigating Officer, it's mine.'

'So, can you tell me what's going on? Why you're out at Uncle Archie's? He's not there. I already checked before I even called Ben.'

'Take a breath, Sally. You don't mind me calling you Sally, I hope?'

'No, just… Whatever. I need to know about my dad, Mr Gayle, that's all.'

'OK. Well, you're right. He's not at his uncle's. We weren't expecting him to be. We came out here to see if he'd left any signs of where he might have gone.'

'And did he?'

'No. But that's OK. We've just heard there's been a sighting of him - or at least of his car - up in the Midlands. Our colleagues up there are following it up as we speak. We'll let you know as soon as we find out if it's him or not, OK?'

'If it's his car, why wouldn't it be?' Her voice faded as she spoke. 'If something had happened to him,' she added, answering her own question.

'We've got to stay positive until we know different, Sally,' Pete said. 'It's no good worrying about something that hasn't happened.'

'Yeah, but... The Midlands? What would he be doing up there?'

'You said he worked all over the country on different occasions,' he reminded her.

'I know, but he's packed all that in,' she argued.

'So maybe he's gone to visit a friend.'

She grunted. 'And not told anyone? I can't see that. And what about all that stuff in his attic? What's that all about?'

'What it's about is simple. Why he's got it is another question entirely and that, we don't know the answer to yet.'

Ben's eyes went wide at the lie.

Pete shrugged.

'But you'll keep me informed, yes?'

'As I said: as soon as we know anything for sure, we'll call you, all right?'

'OK.' She sounded reluctant to let go.

'We'll get to the bottom of it. I promise. In the meantime, is there anything you need? We can send a family liaison officer round if you like. Someone trained in helping people to cope in your kind of situation.'

'I've got family for that,' she said, and Pete could almost hear the curl of her lip.

'All right, then.' Pete didn't want to be the one to end the call. That way she'd be less likely to call back. 'You're OK now, are you?'

'Far from it, truth be told. But I'll have to live with it for now, won't I?'

'We'll have some answers pretty soon, I'm sure.'

'Right. OK, thanks.'

She hung up and Pete handed the phone back to Ben. He raised it to his ear, heard the ring tone and ended the call. 'We don't know the answer?' he said. 'What's all this, then?' He waved towards the boot-full of crates.

'Evidence. It's not proof until we've gone through it and tied it all together with what we've already got back at the station,' Pete reminded him.

'Yeah, but... Really?'

'Really. This lot could have come off the Internet until we prove different.'

Ben reached for the last of the crates. Hefting it up into the car, he shut the boot. 'Best get to it then, eh?'

*

'Mark Bridgman's taking over the Southam case,' Jane announced as Pete and Ben walked into the squad room with a crate of evidence each. 'And we got a call from Northamptonshire a few minutes ago. Blimey, what's that lot?'

'A portion of what we've got in the back of my car.' Relief swept through Pete at the news that Simon Phillips wasn't going to handle his son's case again, after the balls-up he'd made of it before and the tension that had caused between them. 'You've handed over, have you?' he asked as they put the crates down at the end of their workstation.

'Yes.'

Mark was quiet, a plodder, but he got the job done. Give him a bone and he'd gnaw at it until he'd got through to the marrow and he made sure his team were the same. What he might not be as good at was dealing with the volatility of someone like Steven Southam, but time would tell on that. Pete was… Not happy, but willing to give him a chance.

'What did Northants say?'

'He's left their jurisdiction. Gone into Warwickshire. Maybe West Midlands by now. They all come together round there.'

'Sounds like he's aware of what he's doing,' Ben observed. 'Hopping between forces to stay off the radar. Prevent us picking him up if does get spotted.'

'Have they told Warwickshire and West Mids?' Pete asked.

'Yes, but you know what it's like, boss. Resources are limited. There's only so many cars on the roads so, if he's got a way of avoiding the cameras, he could get anywhere in a short time.'

'Depending on where he's headed,' Dick added.

'Which we've got no way of knowing,' Pete cautioned. 'We know he's travelled the country in the past. He could be going anywhere or nowhere.'

'So we've just got to wait and see if they pick him up?' Jane didn't sound impressed.

'No, we've got to go through everything we've already got. One, to prove whether he's a multiple rapist and murderer. And two, to see if he's left any clues to where he might be heading. Dick, come and give us a hand fetching this lot in, will you? The quicker we get started, the sooner we can do either or both of those things.'

It took three more trips up and down the stairs and out to the car park to bring in all the crates of evidence that Pete and Ben had collected.

Finally, the three men all slumped into their chairs.

'Is that it now?' Jane asked.

'No,' Pete gasped. 'That's just the start. We've got to sort through it now. Correlate one set of evidence against the other, check against the missing persons database, see what matches and what doesn't and if we can develop a timeline that matches up. But first, I need a drink. Fetch us a coffee, somebody.'

Jane sighed heavily. 'I'm not a bloody tea-girl, you know,' she said but got up anyway.

'No, but you love us and we're in need,' Ben replied, sagging in his chair as much as the two older men.

'Dream on, Spike,' she said as she headed for the squad room door.

'Miss you already,' he called after her and she stopped, turning to face him with her hands on her hips.

'You could always fetch your own.'

Pete turned on him. 'Shut it, Ben. And learn to know when you're onto a good thing.' He looked back at Jane. 'Ignore him. He's dehydrated.'

'And exhausted,' Dick added.

'That's just your age, Feeney,' Jane told him. 'If I didn't know better, I'd say you were looking grey after all that exercise.' She reached for the door handle and stepped through to the corridor beyond.

'She's right,' Pete said. 'You do look grey.'

'Yeah, yeah,' Dick retorted. 'Tell us a new one.'

His nickname throughout the station was Grey Man for the combination of his hair and the colour of the suits he wore along with his smoker's complexion.

'I think she's wrong,' Ben put in. 'I was sure I saw some colour in your cheeks, coming up the stairs that last time.'

'You want tipping out of that chair, young-un?'

Ben started upright in his seat. 'Don't you start on that.'

Dick chuckled. 'Got you moving, didn't it?'

167

*

A shot of caffeine and a few minutes' rest and recovery saw them starting work on the mountain of evidence they'd accumulated. They hadn't got far into it when Pete's phone rang. He checked the screen and picked up the call.

'Jill?'

'Annie's just left school, boss. She's gone with a friend in the mum's car. Should I stand down?'

'No. Follow them and keep an eye out for suspicious vehicles. Southam may have been in a dark red Ford earlier but that doesn't mean he is now. You know what they're like for nicking cars.'

'Are you sure this is still OK with the chief?'

'You let me worry about him, Jill. Not your problem.'

'OK.' She sounded unsure, but she wouldn't question him further.

'Boss.' Jane had looked up from what she was doing, her expression hard to read.

'Talk later, Jill,' he said and ended the call. 'Jane?'

'I think I've got a match.'

NO MIDDLE GROUND by JACK SLATER

CHAPTER SIXTEEN

'Tell me.'

Pete was all attention, fully focussed on Jane.

'This set of photos.' She held up a bunch of pictures, the white backs towards him. 'Against a misper from 2010. In Norwich.'

Pete was out of his chair and heading around the desks in an instant. 'Let me see.'

Jane turned her screen slightly as he stopped at her shoulder. 'Her. Against her.' She held up one of the pictures. It showed the girl – in her mid-twenties, Pete guessed – at night, walking towards the photographer, who was at a low angle as if seated. In a car, perhaps, he thought, shooting through the windscreen as she approached.

'Looks like her,' he agreed. 'Have you got anything closer on the victim's face?'

'Yes, but it's not pleasant viewing.'

'We're not here to look at holiday snaps.'

'OK.' She flipped through the set of prints until she came to one and plucked it out. 'Don't say you didn't ask for it.'

Pete took the print with some trepidation and looked down at it. The young woman – clearly the same one as in the earlier photo – was now laid out, almost as if in repose except for the wound in her neck. The blood had flowed freely. It was matted in her hair at one side and smeared on her neck and shoulder. She was nude, hands bound in front of her and raised as if in prayer. And between her forearms, tip towards her chin, was what looked like an eight- or nine-inch bone-handled Bowie-style knife with blood smearing the highly polished blade.

Her eyes were open but staring blankly in death.

Pete flicked his gaze back to Jane's screen. 'You're right,' he said. 'It looks like her to me, too.'

'Shall I phone missing persons?'

'No, leave it a while. There might be more yet.'

She grimaced. 'Aren't you the cheerful one?'

'There's a whole lot of girls recorded in these crates, Jane. If most of them aren't on the misper database I'd be surprised, wouldn't you?'

'Well, I'd hope so, I suppose.'

'It'd be a sad old story if they weren't,' Dick agreed.

'Boss.' Ben looked up, looking excited. 'Look here.'

'What have you got?'

He was going through the receipts and invoices rather than the pictures. He held up a small bunch of papers. 'A definite match.'

'Between?' Pete asked as he went back around the closely packed desks.

'Joe Hanson's paperwork and the disappearance of a young woman in Lincolnshire.'

'Show me.'

'Here.' Ben pointed to his screen, which showed a report of the disappearance of a young woman from Grimsby. Then he waved the little bunch of papers again. 'The day after these put him in Louth, which is only just down the road.'

'When you say, "just down the road"…'

Ben tapped his keyboard and the image on his computer screen changed to a map. 'There,' he pointed 'And there.'

Pete leaned in closer, saw the scale of the river running past the old fishing port, compared to the distance between the two towns and nodded. 'Pretty close,' he agreed. 'Save her details. When was this?'

Ben held up the receipts again. 'June 2009.'

'Jesus, how long's this been going on?' Dick demanded. 'And nobody's picked it up until now?'

'I didn't know you were a Phil Collins fan,' Jane said.

'Van Morrison,' Dick retorted.

'We'll find an answer if we shut up and keep working,' Pete glanced at both of them as he said it and was surprised that he got no response, especially from Jane, who he had partnered on the beat for some time before they joined CID.

*

Pete put down the latest batch of photographs that he'd matched with a misper from Greater Manchester in the summer of 2012 and looked up at the others. After two more hours on it, they'd come up with another three definite matches but there was still something missing.

'We keep getting two sides of the triangle here,' he said. 'Either the photos or his receipts match the misper files, but we've got nothing yet that joins all three dots. Nothing that definitively links him to these girls. It's compelling, but it's all circumstantial at the end of the day. We need more, and we need it before he gets pulled in. You guys keep checking, I'll make some calls to the forces involved in the cases we've got links on.'

He cleared his desk and spread the five cases across it. Starting left to right in whatever order they came, he picked up the phone and dialled.

'Police. How can I help?'

'Can you put me through to your CID, please?'

'Who's speaking?'

'DS Gayle, Devon and Cornwall police.'

'One moment.'

The line went dead then was picked up again after a few seconds. 'CID, DC Harper.'

'This is DS Gayle from Exeter. I believe we may have a cross-over with one of your cases.'

'Oh yes? Which one?' Pete listened to the man's accent. It was almost like one from the West-country, but flatter. Must be a local lad, he guessed.

'A misper from Norwich in 2010. Claire Mulligan.'

'2010? Blimey, that's going back a bit. And you've just found a link to her?'

'That's right. I need to speak to the SIO, see if there might be some corroborative evidence.'

'Right. Let me call it up and find out who that was. Hold on a sec.' His phone clattered onto his desk and Pete heard the tap of computer keys. Then a pause. The scrape of the phone being picked up again. 'Right, I'm back. It's DI Travis you want. He's gone off home, I'm afraid, but I can get him to call you in the morning. I don't suppose she'll be going anywhere after all this time, will she?'

Pete felt a flash of anger at his attitude. '*She* won't. But the bloke who killed her might. We've got a lead on him. We don't want him arrested until we've got some firm evidence against him, but we don't want him getting away either.'

'Oh, right. No, I can see that.'

'So maybe you can have a look at the case file. See it there was any physical evidence. If it's not too much trouble.'

'Hey, there's no need for that. I was just saying… After ten years, she's unlikely to be alive, right?'

'It's been known,' Pete said. 'In this case you're right, though. She is dead. Along with a whole lot of others.'

'Uh… Right, here we go. I'm in. Now… Hold on. Just scanning through the file.'

'Better yet, how about you send it over to us? It'll complete our picture of her if nothing else.'

'Yes, I can do that.' He sounded relieved. Time for him to scoot off home, Pete guessed. It was after half-past five, after all.

'Good.' He didn't want the lad rushing the job and missing something.

'I'll do it now. What's your email?'

Pete gave it to him and signed off. Next was the Manchester case. He looked up the number and dialled. A few minutes later he had five case files in his in-box, three of which he'd been told would be dead-ends. No forensic evidence had been found. While he'd been on the phone, he was aware that Jane and Dick had each come up with another matching case. He was about to dig into the first file when Jane interrupted him.

'Boss?'

He looked up.

'Hadn't you better clear off? Lou and Annie will need talking to and Dave will need relieving.'

Pete sighed. 'I suppose you're right.' It wasn't a conversation he was looking forward to. Especially after last year, when Tommy had been missing for several months and Louise had spiralled into a deep, corrosive depression. But Jane was right – it had to be done. He was only surprised that one of them hadn't called him already to ask how the day had gone in the courthouse. Unless they already knew, in which case he'd be in the dog-house for not calling them. He grimaced. That wasn't a conversation to be looked forward to either.

'I'll just forward these files to all of you.'

*

He made the call as he passed the Co-op a couple of streets from his house.

'Boss?'

'I'm thirty seconds out.'

'Right. I'll see you into the drive and stand down, then.'

'Perfect. Thanks, Dave.'

'Of course. What's Fast-track have to say about all this?'

'That Exeter CID isn't my private army.'

'And here I thought they called us the Gayle Force for a reason.'

Pete laughed. 'How long have you been saving that one up?'

'Oh, ages now. Sounds like it worked though.'

'Yes.'

'Ah. I see you turning into the road.'

'That's me.'

'And this is me. Night.'

'Cheers, Dave.' He reached for the comms screen and ended the call as he slowed towards his driveway. He was about to turn in when he saw Dave's pool car pull out from the roadside twenty yards ahead and start towards him, passing as he stopped his silver Ford and switched off the engine. He stepped out and was half way to the front door when it opened and a small figure came flying out, leaping towards him and clinging with narrow arms and legs like a limpet to his hips and neck as he staggered back under the impact.

'Daddy!' She stopped abruptly, a look of horror sweeping over her face. 'What happened?'

'I got damaged making an arrest. I'm OK now. Might have a scar to add to the collection, though.'

She seemed to accept that. 'So, have you testified? Has Tommy? Is he coming home tonight? Are we going to be a family again?'

'We are a family, Button. Always have been,' he said as he tried to recover and step forward again towards the front door. 'I love you enough to burst like an exploding tomato.'

'Ew! That's messy. Have you testified?'

'I have.'

'And has Tommy?'

'He started to, but we ran out of time.' Strictly speaking, it was true. And at the same time, it spared her the details. He was going to have to tell her, but it could wait for a few minutes until he could tell her and Louise together.

'So, he's not coming home?' She hopped down as they reached the hallway.

'Not yet, love.' He kicked the door shut behind him. 'Louise,' he called.

'In here.' Her voice came from the sitting room to his right.

'Oi,' he said to Annie, reaching for her. 'Come here, you. I haven't finished with you yet.' He grabbed her hand and dragged her back. She turned back instead of heading for the kitchen and, no doubt, her homework on the little table in there. He scooped her up again, a forearm under her backside as she wrapped herself around him again.

'What?'

'You're under arrest,' he said playfully, pushing into the sitting room where he found Louise in her usual place on the sofa.

He swung Annie crosswise and sat down next to her. 'How's it going, love?'

Louise's eyes snapped wide as she saw him. 'Christ, what happened to you? You look like you've come off second best against Mike Tyson. I heard what you said to Annie. Why did Tommy run out of time? A bit of poor organisation, wasn't it?'

'They sometimes start testimony like that late on,' he said. 'Lets the jury sleep on it, knowing there'll be more in the morning. But in this case, it wasn't that.' He drew a breath. He knew it would be on the news either tonight or tomorrow, so there was no keeping it from her, but he still felt awkward and reluctant – almost fearful - to continue.

'So, what was it?' Louise pushed.

'That bloke who visited Tommy in Archways the other day. Frightened the living daylights out of him. He's got a brother who we suspect was responsible for that girl's death in Bath a few years ago that Becky Sanderson's dad was involved with. They should both be in jail but neither of them is. Anyway, they raided the court house this afternoon. It'll be in the press later, I expect. On the telly, even. Tommy was testifying at the time. Everything was put on hold while we tried to deal with it all, but they got away from us. We got one of them in the end but, in the process, they killed the judge.'

'Sh... So, it'll all have to start again with a new judge?'

'Yeah. But that's not the only problem.' He sucked air through his teeth, hating the need to tell them both this next part of the story, knowing their reactions, though wildly different, would be equally as distressing – for them and for him. 'The one that got away,' he continued. 'Well... He took Tommy with him.'

'What?'

'No! Daddy…'

Pete reached out to take her in his arms. 'They had a car tucked away in an empty garage behind the court house. He took Tommy with him, made it out somehow and… We tried to track him down. The whole station got involved, one way and another. Until Silverstone got wind of it. Then…'

'He took you off it,' Louise guessed.

Pete nodded. 'But this time Mark took it over. And we'd already made some headway. We knew what car they were in, roughly where they were going to be. We just didn't manage to get close enough.'

'So now there's a child killer out there with his brother in jail and Tommy to do with whatever he pleases,' Louise summarised. 'And you arrested his brother.'

'I know it sounds bad but…'

'But nothing! It is bloody bad. As bad as it gets. My son's out there somewhere. His life's in danger and that stupid prick in charge of the bloody station's too concerned with political correctness and keeping his nose clean to know what common sense is, never mind how to use it. Do something, Pete, for God's sake! Save our son!'

'Dad, please,' Annie joined in, tears streaming down her little face. 'Can't you get Tommy back again?'

'We've got to let Mark Bridgman do his job, love. I promise he's good at it. If anyone can find them, he can.'

'But he's not you,' she insisted.

Pete smiled at her confidence in him, then instantly regretted it as pain dug into his cheek deeper and more intensely than when the injury was created. 'No, he isn't. But he's allowed to do it and I'm not right now. I wish I was, but my boss won't hear of it. It's against protocol.'

'Well, fuck protocol!' Annie declared, hopping off his lap to stand defiantly in front of them, hands on her hips. 'I want my brother back - safe and soon.'

Pete's eyes snapped open in horror. 'Where the hell did you get language like that?'

'Wake up, dad! I'm at school every day. Do you think all kids my age are polite and innocent or something?'

'No, but you should be. And especially in this house. I don't use language like that and I don't expect you to, either.'

'So, how else am I going to wake you up?'

'I'm fully awake, Missy, and don't be so bloody cheeky.'

'I'm not being cheeky, I'm being a sister. And you should be a father.'

'That's enough!' Pete snapped as Louise reached for Annie's arm and puller her in closer.

'Calm down,' she said. 'Your dad's explained the situation. None of us like it, but it is what it is. We've got to wait for Mark to do his job and that's all there is to it.'

'If I did get involved again now, it would compromise any case we had. The man would be free to walk away and do something like this to someone else. Or to us again.' He shook his head. 'We can't risk that.'

'But we can risk Tommy?'

'That's not what I said and not what I meant. You know better than that, young lady.'

'Do I?'

'What's the matter with you tonight?'

'I'm scared! At least last year we knew he was alive, wherever he was. Now he's with a man whose brother you've put in jail and who won't think twice about using Tommy as a pawn to get him back. I know what I'd do for my brother. Why should this man be any different?'

Pete took a breath, once more amazed at how grown-up his young daughter could be. 'He's very different. But, you're right to be scared. I am, too. But we've given Mark all the information we managed to find. What he looks like, where he's from. What car he was driving when he was last seen. Where we were hoping to pick him up. What he's done in the past. So Mark's got as much chance as we had.'

'He hasn't got the same incentive, though, has he? He's not Tommy's dad. It's just another case to him.'

Pete shook his head. 'No. Police are like family to each other, you know that. The things we see, the things we go through together, they create a bond that's stronger than any job outside the emergency services or armed forces. If Tommy's my son, then Mark thinks of him as a nephew.'

'Yeah,' Louise sneered. 'So how do you account for Simon Phillips?'

'There's an exception to every rule. And he's not on the case anymore. His involvement ended when Tommy was brought in.'

'Who cares about Simon Phillips,' Annie broke in. 'If he's not on the case, he doesn't matter. Tommy does. And this man that's got him. Where is he, Dad? And what's he doing to...' Her voice faltered and Louise pulled her in, holding her tight.

'Every resource we've got is out there trying to find them,' Pete told them both. 'Dave said it earlier tonight: for now, it's not the Devon and Cornwall force he's up against, it's the Gayle force. And we will track him down. I promise.'

'Words,' Louise retorted, rocking Annie gently as she sobbed into her shoulder. 'We don't need words, we need actions.'

'And there will be action. There already is: as much as we can throw at it.'

'Then it better be enough.'

CHAPTER SEVENTEEN

Pete was surprised and pleased to see his whole team already at their desks when he got in the next morning after dropping Annie at school. He'd spoken to Colin Underhill the previous evening, arranging for the guard on Annie and Louise to be made official, then spent a troubled night, tossing and turning as his brain refused to shut down and rest.

'Bloody hell,' Dave said. 'You look as rough as a badger's arse.'

'Thank you for those few kind words.' He touched the dressing on his cheek and the stubble around it that he hadn't been able to shave. 'I feel it, too, but there's too much to do, to give in to it. What's the latest?'

'The papers and the local news have got hold of Mrs Turnbull's story and Cathleen Webber's death but they're a couple of pages in and with a lot less copy than the Combined Courts attack. That's gone national and it seems like Fast-track's getting earache from on high about it, especially when it was announced on the ten o'clock news that the son of a police officer was abducted during the commission of the crime. Didn't you see any of this?'

'I've been too busy trying to keep the rest of my family safe to bother with the news.'

'Fair enough. Well, like I say, the chief's not a happy camper. He was spitting bullets first thing. It's all way too much like taking the piss and he seems to be taking it personally. On the plus side, though, the Southams' pictures are out there now. They've been described as wanted men from Wiltshire with a do not approach warning. Call us on sight. And we've been through the five files you got last night. Plus another three that me and Dick came up with. Only one of them had any forensic evidence that could be definitely linked to it, though, and that was a bust.'

'Why?'

'They got DNA. Not semen but a pubic hair. Just the one, mind. They developed a profile from it, but they'd got nothing to match it to - and there's nothing in the database either.'

'That, we can remedy,' he said. *How bloody long had they stayed last night?* He felt a swell of gratitude and had to clear his throat before he could continue. 'We've already got access to his house. A hair brush, a toothbrush, a piece of clothing that's been worn and not washed. A hat, maybe. There's all sorts of places to find his DNA in there.'

'What about getting a warrant, though?' Dick asked. 'He's officially a misper, not a suspect as of now.'

'We've got enough to make him a suspect, even if we haven't got enough to bring charges yet. And we've already got permission to enter from his daughter. I can get a warrant sorted, I reckon.'

As he was speaking, the squad room door opened behind him. He turned to see who'd come in.

'Mark. Any news?'

The slim, dark haired DS grimaced and shook his head. 'It's like they've vanished. Must have gone to ground somewhere.'

'How? A grown man with a boy as hostage – where are they going to hide?'

Mark shrugged. 'If he's prepared to kip in the car, there's endless places. It's not like, with modern cars, there's a button to pull to open a door anymore, is it? He could lock it up, pocket the key and sleep safe in the knowledge that the kid couldn't go anywhere, tied or not.'

'And no sign of the red Focus?'

'Unfortunately, yes. Abandoned in a supermarket car park. Nothing missing from there but two from another one nearby. No idea yet which, if either, they're in.'

'Without getting physically involved, which supermarkets are we talking about?'

Mark hesitated for an instant then seemed to reach a decision. 'Alphington R...'

The door opened behind him and he snapped his head around as one of Simon Phillips' DCs, walked in and headed for his desk, giving them a nod of greeting as he struggled not to react to the glaring white dressing on Pete's face, surrounded by livid bruising.

'So... Sorry, but that's all I can tell you,' said Mark. 'Except that we'll put all we can into it.'

'I know that.' Pete clapped him on the arm. 'I told Louise and Annie last night.'

'All right then.' Mark headed towards his desk on the adjoining block. Pete had just taken his seat again when DS Jim Hancock walked in.

'How you doing, Pete?'

Pete cocked his head. 'I've felt better,' he admitted. Then looked across towards the one member of Simon Phillips' team who was in the room. 'And worse.'

'Take it easy, mate,' Jim said and headed for his desk.

Pete knew the few words were an expression of support. He pressed his lips together, accepting them as such and turned back to his crew.

'I'll have a look,' Jane offered.

Pete was torn. He didn't want to undermine Mark but at the same time, he needed to know he was on-track. 'All right. Just a glance. Then we need to focus on Hanson. Has anybody seen the guvnor yet?'

'No,' said Dick, his tone saying much more – like *Stupid question. You know what time it is.*

'OK. I'll wait for him to come in and see him about the warrant.'

'The Chief's in,' Ben said.

Pete looked at him. 'The less I have to see that… him, the better I'll like it.'

'What, again?' Dick asked.

Pete knew exactly what he meant. 'Yes, again.'

Dick shook his head. 'Whatever happened to discipline in this country, eh? What did you say now?'

'Not a lot,' Pete replied. 'Couldn't get much of a word in.'

'Still,' Jane offered. 'Even he's not awkward enough to refuse a justifiable warrant out of spite. Is he?'

Dave grimaced. 'I wouldn't put anything past the dozy prig.'

'Was that with a "g" or a "ck"?' Jill asked.

'Take your pick,' Dave said. 'Either's appropriate. But, as it happens, it was a "g" on this occasion.'

'That's what I thought. You haven't gone politically correct on us all of a sudden, have you?'

Jane snorted as Dick choked and Ben giggled.

'There.' Dick pointed towards the window behind Jill, Dave and Jane.

'What?' Jill and Ben asked together.

'It's gone.' Dick's shoulders slumped. 'I was sure I saw a pig flying past. Or it might have been a prig.'

Dave nodded slowly. 'Take the piss all you want,' he said. 'I can take it.'

'I can't,' Pete said. 'We haven't got time.' He pushed his chair back with a sigh. 'Oh, well. Into the lion's den, I suppose.'

*

'Ben,' Pete called. 'Have you got anything?'

'Not yet, boss.'

'Bring some evidence bags up here, then.'

Pete was standing in Jonas Hanson's bedroom, staring down at what was lying in the bottom of the wardrobe. He heard the stairs

187

creak a couple of times then Ben stepped in, his hands, like Pete's, already clad in light blue nitrile gloves.

'What have you got, boss?'

'The pillow there. Don't bother stripping it, just take the whole thing. The slippers on the floor and the shoes – especially the trainers - in the wardrobe here.'

'Nice one. Nothing in the bathroom?'

Ben knew that was the first place he'd have looked on coming up here.

'His toothbrush and razor are gone and he's put fresh towels and facecloth out.'

'Downstairs is similar,' Ben said as he stepped forward and crouched to pick out the black trainers and put them carefully in an evidence bag. 'All neat and tidy, ready for him to come home to, whenever he decides to.'

'Unless we track him down first,' Pete replied.

Ben sealed the evidence bag and took another one from the small stack he'd brought for the next pair of shoes. 'I can't make out why he'd have gone off without telling Sally, at least, if he was up to something nasty. It'd be bound to bring her round here looking for him.'

Pete took an evidence bag and picked up the slippers. 'What kind of father was he?'

'Strict, but he loved her.'

'So, she loved him. What was she like as a kid?'

'Happy. Bubbly. Full of fun. But not dippy. She had brains and knew how to use them. It was just, she got pregnant young, I suppose. Took motherhood seriously enough to put her career to one side.'

'What kind of career was she after?' Pete asked as he labelled the bagged slippers.

'Nothing fancy. She was brought up by a builder and a shop-worker. She'd got no university aspirations or anything,' Ben explained. 'She talked about wanting to go into the ambulance service at one time. I think they'd come out to her gran or something. But it never happened, of course.'

Pete slid the pillow into a large paper sack and folded the top over twice before taping it. 'So, he had to expect her to come round looking for him. But he can't have expected her to go up into the loft.'

'Why would he? Anybody who bothered would only give it a glance, see he wasn't up there and come down again. It was just that she'd been looking into the family history – ancestors and that. And her mum hadn't been exactly forthcoming, she said, so she thought he might have something she could use tucked away up there.'

'That must have been a hell of a shock, finding all that stuff in there instead.'

'Yeah.' Ben was writing the label for the last of the pairs of shoes. 'It took some soul-searching before she came to me with it.'

'I bet. It's a good thing she did, though.'

Ben glanced around. 'Anything else in here, do you reckon?'

'I haven't checked the bedside drawers yet. Might be a bin, too. Did you check the one downstairs?'

'Yes. Emptied and a new liner in it.'

Looking around as Ben spoke, Pete spotted the one up here and stepped across. 'Same here.' He reached for the bedside drawer unit as Ben moved towards the one on the other side. Pulling it open, he found the usual detritus in there. A small jar of change, a nail clipper, a pair of scissors, a box of tissues, a small jewellery box which he lifted out and opened. A tie pin and matching cuff-links glinted back at him, old-fashioned and cheap-looking. He snapped it shut and replaced it, continuing to rummage. He found a notebook and pen, a small torch. Then a photo packet like those in the trunk in the loft.

'Hello.' He lifted the packet out, unsure what he was going to find inside.

Flipping it open, he pulled out the contents and relaxed. Family photos. Sally as a youngster, her mum, even a couple with Jonas in them, holding or playing with his daughter.

'Boss?'

Pete looked up.

Ben was holding up a similar but bulkier photo packet. As Pete watched, he opened it and removed the contents. Pete saw his jaw clench. He frowned, flicking through a few, then handed them across.

The top one was of a young woman, bound, gagged, naked and terrified. Pete checked the next one. Different girl, similar pose. The next one again. And the next. He flipped through the pile. There had to be fifty or more pictures there.

Ben was watching him, his expression somewhere between horrified and numb. 'And everybody thought Fred West was an evil bastard,' he said when their eyes met.

'Either this is some pretty sick porn or, if these are all different subjects, as it looks like, then West's got nothing on this bloke,' Pete confirmed. 'We need to go through them and check if they match what we've got from upstairs then let forensics have a go for fingerprints and DNA. It's a bloody shame we haven't got his computer.'

CHAPTER EIGHTEEN

Pete's phone rang as they were climbing into the car outside Hanson's house. He took it out and answered it automatically.

'DS Gayle.'

'Pete, its Bob. I've got a call for you.'

'Who from?' Pete asked the desk sergeant back at Heavitree Road.

'Don't know. He wouldn't say. Just said he wanted to talk to you about yesterday.'

Pete's gut felt suddenly cold and tight, but he couldn't say why so instead, he said, 'Put him through.'

There were a couple of clicks, then a hollow sound on the line.

'This is DS Gayle. How can I help?'

'You could let my brother go, so I don't have to start hurting your son. Or you could keep him and I will hurt the boy. In fact, I'll probably kill him in the end, but he'll suffer long and hard before then. Up to you.'

Pete felt nausea and rage at the same time. He turned away from the car and Ben at the far side of it, speaking in a low tone. 'You harm as much as a single hair on that boy's head and I'll track you down and kill you, regardless of the job. If anyone knows how to get away with it, it's a copper. You remember that, Southam. Now, you'd be best advised to let him go. Because, as long as you've got him, we'll be hunting you down like the rabid dog you are.'

'That your final answer, is it? Don't want to phone a friend? Your wife, maybe? Or your daughter?'

'They can't release your brother, Southam. Come to that, nor can I now. He's in the system.'

'You can drop the charges.'

Pete grunted. 'I wasn't the only copper there when he was nicked. There was a whole team of us. If I dropped the charges against him, they damn sure wouldn't.'

'Just get him out or I'll start sending bits of your boy to your house. One a day until I run out of bits or he runs out of blood.'

The red-hot rage boiled up in Pete's brain, swamping the nausea along with his senses and his reason. 'Listen, you sick fuck...'

'Twenty-four hours,' Southam snapped over him. 'That's when I make the first cut.'

The line clicked dead. Pete heard it and growled, deep in his throat.

'Boss?'

Pete ignored Ben as he tried to regain a modicum of control.

'Boss? Are you OK?'

Pete was concentrating on his breathing, long and deep, in and out through his nose. His eyes were closed. One hand was on the roof of the car, the other down at his side, limply hanging onto the phone.

'What is it?' Ben sounded closer now. Standing in front of him.

Pete opened his eyes. 'Steve Southam,' he grunted. 'Threatening Tommy if we don't release his brother.'

'Jesus. What are we going to do?'

Pete had been telling Southam the truth. He was the arresting officer, but cases of assaulting a police officer were brought by the individual officer, separately to whatever other charges may have led to the encounter. If Pete could drop the main charges against Adrian Southam, the others would stick. And Fast-track wouldn't hear of it anyway. Pete could hear him now, spouting from the book of regulations as if it were part of the Bible – 'Thou shalt not negotiate with criminals or terrorists.'

And Pete knew perfectly well that was one regulation that was right and proper. If Adrian Southam was released it would cost a lot of people a lot of suffering and many of them their lives. But this was Tommy he was talking about. His flesh and blood. His son. His job was to protect and serve the public but his every instinct as a father was to protect his family above all else.

What the hell was he going to do?

'Do you want me to drive?' asked Ben.

'Eh?' Pete blinked.

'Do you want me to drive, boss? You're in no fit state.'

'I'm all right.'

'No, you're not. And that's no criticism. It's only natural. Give me the keys, I'll get us back to the station while you think it through.'

'There's nothing to think through,' Pete snapped. 'There's no choice in the matter, is there?'

'There's one,' Ben said.

'What?'

'Find the evil bastard before he can carry through on his threat.'

'Which we can't do because it's not our case.'

'Sod that. It's your son being threatened. We're behind you all the way. All of us. And that's a promise.'

'No,' Pete shook his head. 'It's one thing my career getting screwed. It's another thing for the rest of you. I can't agree to that.'

'There's nothing to agree to,' Ben stated. 'It's not a choice we're offering. We're in, like it or not.'

'What about the others? Don't they get a say?'

'They've already had it. We talked it through before you came in this morning.'

Pete shook his head again. He appreciated what Ben was saying. At any other moment in his life, it would have brought a lump to his throat, but right then his emotions were in such turmoil he couldn't feel anything but the desperation of Tommy's situation and his own anger and frustration at not being able to react directly to it.

'Keys?' Ben held his hand out and Pete handed them over without resistance. Ben stepped past him and dropped into the driver's seat, forcing him to walk around the car and get in the other side.

Pete sat in numb silence as Ben drove down Pennsylvania Road. They had almost reached the inner ring road before he said with a hollow voice and an empty heart, 'How are we going to find him?'

'I don't know yet. But we will. We have to.'

'Twenty-four hours, he said. Then he'll start cutting Tommy.'

'Shit. No pressure, then.' Ben put his foot down hard on the throttle, flipped on the blue lights and accelerated hard down the short stretch of dual carriageway to the roundabout where he pulled the car hard round into Heavitree Road, tyres squealing as they slid on the warm tarmac. He almost hit an on-coming car, missing it by inches. The driver slammed on his brakes, looking at the same time terrified and enraged, but neither Pete nor Ben cared. Ben accelerated again, gave the siren a brief 'whoop,' as he went up the side of the white-rendered station and pulled around into a parking space. 'Right,' he said as he switched everything off. 'No time to waste.'

Pete's brain still hadn't kicked back in as they went in through the rear door and through the custody suite.

'Nothing for me, this trip?' asked the burly custody sergeant. 'That's not like you.'

Pete followed Ben past the desk without responding, barely aware of the comment.

At the top of the stairs, Ben turned and put a hand on his shoulder. 'Do us a favour, boss?'

'Huh?'

'Get us some coffees?' Ben nodded towards the kitchenette further along the corridor.

'Why?'

'Private conversation needed.'

'Don't you go getting yourselves in trouble on my account,' Pete argued.

'We got where we are on your account, boss. We're all grown-ups. We can make our own informed decisions.'

Pete shook his head. 'No, I can't...'

'Not your choice, boss. Either you get the coffees or the rest of us will. And it'll be kind of snug with five of us in there. You never know who might feel what.'

Pete grunted. 'Try that with Jane and she'll have your arm off, space or no space.'

'Exactly. So, better you in there than us. Health and safety at work and all that.'

'Huh.' Pete knew when he wasn't going to win. 'You'll make someone a good wife, the way you argue.'

'Needs must,' Ben said and opened the door to the squad room.

When Pete arrived with six mugs of coffee his team were waiting for him and so was Mark Bridgman. 'If I'd known, I'd brought an extra one,' he said to his fellow Detective Sergeant.

'Don't worry about it,' Bridgman replied. 'Ben's told us what's going on. You know you've got our full support, don't you? All of us, my team included.'

'I do. And thanks, all of you. But what are we going to actually do? We've got twenty-four hours – more like twenty-three now – until he starts…' His throat clogged.

'We know,' Bridgman stepped in.

'The first thing is to trace that call to your phone. If we can get a number, we can track its location,' Ben said. 'Your smartphone could get us the number if the call had come direct. Seeing as it didn't, it's a bit more complicated, but it's still possible. I'll have to go down to the front office.'

'Go. This will be waiting when you get back.' Pete put down the coffees and started passing them out.

'Give mine to DS Bridgman,' Ben said. 'I might be a while.'

Bridgman took a sip as Ben headed for the door. 'If Ben can do that and we can track Southam down through it, we'll have him.'

As Pete sipped his own drink, he felt the first glimmer of hope since he'd received the call.

*

'There.' Dick pointed to one of the photos Pete and Ben has rescued from Joe Hanson's house. 'She's in one of the sets. I'd swear it.'

Pete was carefully laying the new set of pictures out on his desk and photographing them so they could be input to the computer system, making the task of matching them to what they already had that much easier. And despite his warning about the contents, Dick was watching over one shoulder while Jane had come around the desks to look over his other. He continued laying them out, nine at a time. Then Jane stopped him.

'I recognise her. Don't know if it's from Hanson's other pictures, though.'

'Where, then?' Pete asked.

'Not sure. She might be one of the mispers we were looking through.'

'OK. We'll see when we get them all in the system.'

Pete finished laying out his third batch of nine pictures and picked up his phone to photograph them, one at a time. It looked like he was about a third of the way through the stack. Dick had already asked how many there were.

'I don't know,' Pete had told him. 'I don't want to handle them anymore than I can help.'

Dick had nodded and said no more. Evidence preservation was vital. Any prints or DNA on these would confirm who had handled them in the past, removing any possibility of Hanson claiming they weren't his although they'd been found in his house.

Now he emailed the pictures to himself and picked up the photographs with gloved hands to add them to the smaller stack on his left before continuing the task. The door opened across from him and Ben returned to the squad room.

'Where've you been?' asked Jane. 'Slide off home for some lunch, did you?'

'I wish. I've been in the back office, tracing that call from Southam.'

Pete looked up, his whole body going still. 'And?'

'I did it. He was using an unregistered phone but, having got the number, that made no difference. He called you from within a few yards of your house, boss.'

'Jesus!'

'He's not there now,' Ben added quickly.

Pete stopped himself from throwing down the photos in his hand and running for the door. 'Where is he now, then?' he asked, realising how ridiculous such a move would have been on several levels.

'He must have been there deliberately to add impact in case we managed to trace the call,' Ben said. 'What he doesn't seem to realise is that you've got to actually dismantle a phone to stop us tracking it - not just switch it off. His latest location, as of about seven minutes ago, was four miles north of the city and he'd been there for twenty-three minutes.'

'So, he's found somewhere to hole up.' Pete's whole body itched to get out there after the man, but he knew he couldn't. It was one of the most frustrating feelings he'd ever endured. 'Tell Mark,' he said reluctantly. As Ben stepped across to the next bay of desks, he forced himself to continue laying out the next batch of pictures. Working on something else was the only way he could stop himself from not just getting involved but barging in and taking over the case. And the last minute or so had shown him that, despite his best efforts, the situation had indeed impaired his judgement. And more than his judgement – his self-control. He'd maintained it by the skin of his teeth, but that was only because he was here in the squad room, not out there close to his son and the evil bastard who'd taken him.

'Are you all right, boss?' Jane asked, a small hand resting on his shoulder.

Pete grunted and shook his head quickly. 'No,' he said as, behind him, Bridgman and his team scrambled. 'Far from it.'

'They'll find him,' Jane reassured him.

'I bloody hope so.'

'Have you spoken to the chief?'

'What for?'

Jane's lips pursed. 'I know he can't allow us to get involved, but he could put more resources into it, in the circumstances.'

'Mark will do that.'

'Yeah, but…' She turned away, heading for the door.

'Where are you going?' Pete demanded.

'For a wee.'

He knew damn well she was lying but he couldn't stop her and, deep down, he appreciated what she was doing much more than he could express.

CHAPTER NINETEEN

'If we can track Steven Southam by his mobile, why can't we do the same for Jonas Hanson?' Pete asked.

'Because he hasn't got one,' Ben replied. 'I checked. He took his computer with him. No doubt uses free wi-fi wherever he happens to be. But he hasn't got a mobile phone anymore. Got rid of it when he retired from work. He never liked them anyway, as I recall. Don't know why.'

'And we've had no further sightings of him?'

'Not that I know of. Anyone else?' He looked around the cluster of tables but received no response. He shrugged. 'Just a matter of waiting, I suppose. In the meantime, what about those pictures?'

Pete had finished photographing them, uploading them to his computer and sending them on to the rest of the team. He had replaced the packet in its evidence bag and called forensics to come and collect it. His gloves were off and binned, and he'd split the screen on his computer into two side-by side windows, one of them containing the first of the new set of pictures. 'We need to compare them to everything we've got so far. The pictures from the loft, the misper files – all of it.'

'That's a hell of a job,' Dick said.

'Not the most pleasant, I'll grant you. But if we split them up, ten at a time each, it shouldn't take too long.'

It had turned out that there were seventy-nine pictures in their latest find and no two of them were of the same subject.

'Identification of the victims is the key,' Pete reminded them. 'If we can do that, we can find out when and where they were last seen and compare that to Jonas Hanson's whereabouts at the time. It might be circumstantial, but the weight of circumstantial evidence is evidence in itself: just ask any statistician.'

'Yeah, you know what they say about statistics, boss,' Dave said.

'Lies, damned lies and…' Ben started.

'You can prove any bloody thing you want with them,' Dick put in. 'And I'm damn sure Hanson's brief will use that in court.'

'Maybe, but it doesn't let us off this particular hook,' Pete said.

'I'm not saying it does, boss. Or that it should. I'm just saying we shouldn't rely on it.'

'And we're not going to. We're detectives, not Cluedo players. Let's get this done and we can move on to something less unpleasant like tracing his history.'

'Who's to say that's less unpleasant, given what we think he's been up to?' asked Jill.

Dave snapped his fingers and pointed at her. 'What she said.'

'Nothing, but at least it won't be so in-your-face.'

Dave tilted his head. 'Fair point,' he said as Jane came back into the squad room and headed straight for her chair.

'Better?' asked Pete.

'Huge relief, thanks. And I gather Mark Bridgman's off out with his team and twelve extras.'

Pete pursed his lips. He wasn't going to commend her for ignoring what he'd said, but at the same time, he couldn't complain. She was only doing what she thought was best in the circumstances. 'I see,' he said. 'So, now you're back, you can take ten of these new pictures and see if you can match them to anyone on the files we've already got for the case.'

'Of course. I take it you've already allocated them?'

'Yep. Yours are in your in-box.'

'Right.' She switched on her computer screen and knuckled down, along with everyone else.

*

They were not even half way through their first batch when Mark Bridgman and his team came back in. Pete looked up and met the other man's gaze. He shook his head slightly and crossed the short distance between them.

'He was long gone,' he said, keeping his voice low. 'Left the phone for us to find. We might get something useful off it, but I doubt it. He doesn't appear to be stupid.'

We don't need to admire the bastard, we need to catch him, Pete thought. 'We know that much. He got away with killing that girl in Bath, didn't he?'

'Yeah, but that was years ago and he's desperate now. He wants his brother out of here. That could push him into a mistake.'

'It might, but has Tommy got time to wait for it?'

'If he kills Tommy, he's got no bargaining chip left,' Bridgman argued.

'No, but you know what he said: that could take a while and Tommy would go through a living hell in the meantime.'

Bridgman grimaced, sucking air across his teeth. 'Yeah. I'm going to get onto the phone providers, see if I can find another phone that was in that same vicinity in the last few hours – apart from ours, of course.'

'What about CCTV or traffic cameras leading in and out of there? They might give you a timeline.'

'They might if we knew what he was driving now.' Bridgman said dubiously.

Pete felt a flash of annoyance. 'The point of him going out there was its quiet, wasn't it? How many cars are you expecting to go in and out of the area in the timeframe you're looking at?'

'Not too many, when you put it that way.' He gave Pete a nod and headed for his desk.

Pete turned back to his team, disappointed in Bridgman's attitude. 'Right. We'll come back to this fresh in the morning,' he decided. 'No good getting too tired and missing something.'

'I can't see us missing anything,' Dave said. 'The number of hits so far suggests they're all on record somewhere.'

Pete tipped his head. They had found most of the girls amongst the collection from Hanson's loft. Some had been reported missing, but disappointingly few. 'The thing is, where was he finding these girls? And don't even think about saying, "All over the place,"' he added quickly, his eyes on Dave Miles.

Dave's eyes widened. 'Would I?'

'We all know the answer to that,' Pete said. 'Maybe a better question, given the spread of locations, is, "How was he finding them?"'

'Well, they're a mix of types and… dare I say "conditions"? I mean, some appear to be healthy and well-nourished, others not so much.'

'I'm in shock,' Jill declared. 'Dave Miles asking permission to be politically incorrect? I never dreamed that day would ever dawn.'

'It's bloody near dusk, to be fair,' Dick pointed out. 'Maybe he's tired.'

'There's no need for you to join in,' Dave protested.

'Why not? You would if the shoe were on the other foot.'

Dave pursed his lips then tipped his head. 'Fair enough.'

'So, what you're suggesting,' Pete broke in, trying to get things back on track, 'is they're prostitutes, drug addicts, homeless and so on.'

'Well, yes. They wouldn't be missed, would they? And if they were, they'd be much less likely to be reported as such. Or taken seriously if they were.'

Pete nodded. 'Which gives us at least one other place to search: the PND. But that'll wait for morning. In the meantime, I want to focus on our man himself. We know where he's been living for the past twenty-plus years but where was he before that? Where was he raised? What was he like? How did he treat his family and how did they treat him? And his schoolmates, work colleagues, clients? And what else was he up to that we can find witnesses or records for? Are there any outstanding cases from times and locations we can tie him to? Nobody starts something like this out of the blue. There's got to be a lead-up somewhere. Burglary, rape, assault, indecent exposure: something.'

'Damn!' said Dick. 'Did you draw breath anywhere in there?'

'So much to say and do and so little time,' Pete responded. 'Pass me that stuff we got from his lock-up, whoever's got it. The first thing we need is a time-line.'

'I did that already, boss. I thought I'd emailed it to you.'

Pete checked his emails. 'Ah. That'll be "receipts etc," will it?'

'Yes.'

'Have we all got a copy?'

'I was letting you have a look and send it on if it was OK.'

Pete pursed his lips. 'Just do it. We trust you.'

'Thousands wouldn't,' Jill said, giving Ben a wink.

'Don't do that to him,' Dick protested. 'You'll ruin him for the rest of the day, poor kid.'

'Are you sure that's not you you're talking about, old man?' Ben retorted.

'At my age, I'm too old to care.'

'Well, you need to,' Pete told him. 'At least until we get our hands on Jonas Hanson.'

'I was talking about Jill's flirting.'

'Oh, ah?' Dave joined in, turning to face her. 'How come you never flirt with me?'

'Because flirting's meant to be innocent and you haven't been that for decades.'

Dick laughed. 'She's got you there, mate. Guilty as charged.'

'How come everybody's picking on me?'

'They're not,' Jane told him. 'I haven't had my turn yet.'

Pete was about to intervene when the phone on his desk rang. He let it ring again to confirm it was an outside call and picked it up. 'DS Gayle, Exeter CID.'

'Hello.' The voice had a soft northern accent. 'I gather you've been looking for a green Peugeot estate car, reg ending BBW.'

'That's right.'

'This is Tony Parsons, Lincolnshire traffic squad. Your man's been spotted. Unfortunately, it was mutual. He lost our guys for long enough to ditch the car and get away into a housing estate on the outskirts of Mablethorpe.'

Pete barely managed to hold back a curse. 'So, he's on the loose in – that's a seaside resort, isn't it? While we're busy proving multiple cases of kidnapping, torture and murder against him.'

'Christ. I didn't realise it was anything that serious. Not that it'd have made a difference. At least now he's got no transport, we've got all his stuff and he knows he's being hunted.'

'When you say, "all his stuff," does that include a laptop? Because, if so, we need to see what's on it ASAP. And if he knows we're after him...'

'We've got five more cars on route plus a van and a dog unit,' Parsons interrupted. 'We'll have him. And we'll send you the files from the laptop.'

'I won't say I'll look forward to it, knowing what they're likely to contain,' Pete said. 'But I will look forward to hearing you've caught him.'

'We'll talk soon' Parsons ended the call.

I bloody hope so, if only for the people of Mablethorpe, Pete thought as he put the phone down.

'Yes!'

The shout came from behind Pete. It was Alan Jacobs, one of Mark Bridgman's DC's.

'Got him. He's still in that red Focus. He went in the farm shop at Rowe and bought some supplies. The flag on his credit card came up and they've got a security camera in the car park.'

'I said he'd make a mistake,' Mark announced as Pete turned in his chair. 'Which way did he go?'

'Towards Tiverton.'

'That could be a ploy,' Pete pointed out. 'He could loop back to where Ben traced him to, a mile or so south of there.'

'And at the same time be daft enough to use his debit card?' Mark argued. 'I doubt it. And we can't afford to spread ourselves that thin. I'll give the Tiverton station a buzz, get them mobilised, and Alan can call the traffic squad. Maybe we can box him in.'

An image flashed into Pete's mind: a stand-off, Steven Southam surrounded by police, Tommy held tight against his broad chest with a knife to his throat. Would Southam care enough about evading capture not to kill the boy and throw him at them?

Pete wasn't at all sure and the uncertainty made him feel suddenly queasy.

CHAPTER TWENTY

Pete pushed his chair back. 'We'll come with you, then.'

'No,' Bridgman said firmly. 'If we're going to arrest him we want the charges to stick. We want him in jail for life, not walking the streets on bail in a couple of days.'

But Pete's blood was up. 'That's…'

'Right, boss,' Jane cut him off. 'The rest of us could go, but you can't.'

He rounded on her, was about to snap a sharp reply when a part of his brain realised she was right. He drew a deep breath. 'OK. Do it. I'll stop here and start on this stuff.'

How he'd be able to concentrate, he didn't know, but he had to do something. He couldn't just sit idle and nor could he go home at this point. Louise, especially, would want to know why he was there and not here until there was something he could actually tell her.

Chairs scraped back all around him and bodies trooped out.

Inside, Pete felt as hollow as the half-empty squad room. He allowed himself to dwell on the feeling for a few moments, hating the sense of everything happening remotely and out of his control despite his deep connection to all of it, almost as if he were being punished for something. Then he broke out of the slump and pulled the first of the stack of Joe Hanson's files towards him.

With his radio beside him on the desk, the volume set so that he could hear anything that went on in the search for Southam and

Tommy, he started going through the first of the files for anything with a date on it. He opened the first of the envelopes in there and pulled out receipts, work dockets, delivery notes, bank statements and empty cheque books, sorting them into date order.

While he worked, information was passed back and forth over the radio. Positions, directions of travel, sightings and dismissals. For some time, once the search commenced, he broke off from his paper-sorting to listen every time the radio came to life but finally he reached the point that all police were trained to where he could half-listen while continuing with what he was doing, sure that he'd pick up on anything significant.

Once he'd finished sorting the envelope contents, he took a large piece of paper from his desk drawer and drew a line along the middle of it, long-ways, dividing it into segments for the days of the month. He labelled it at the top: June 2005. Then he started going through the sorted papers again, marking them off on the time-line with date, time, location and a quick note of what they related to: food, fuel, hotel, tools, building materials.

Having done that, he wrote a location summary underneath. Hanson had spent the first two weeks of the month in Exeter, the next in Wisbech. Pete looked it up and found it was in Cambridgeshire. The final week of the month, Hanson had been in Devises, Wiltshire.

Then he checked the missing persons database. There were three young women who had vanished in that month and had still not been found. Two were from London, the third from Daventry, Northamptonshire. She had been last seen while the records showed Hanson was still in Cambridgeshire.

He moved on.

The next envelope he took from the top of the pile turned out to be October. He sorted the contents into order and took another A3 sheet from his desk to compile another timeline. This time, the records showed time spent in Bristol, Taunton and back home in Exeter. He checked the missing persons list. Two women had disappeared that month and had yet to be found: one in Lancashire, the other in Barnstaple, during the week Hanson was working in Bristol.

Still no match.

He was sorting the papers from another randomly picked month when his radio crackled again and this time something within him picked up on what was being said. '... seen him! He's turned left, left, left in Stoke Canon, heading east towards....'

'Huxham,' Dave clarified. 'I'm in Hayes Barton, heading north. I'll try to cut him off.'

Dave would be on that black beast of a motorbike, his radio wired into his helmet. Pete was sorely tempted to pick up his radio and intervene as he pictured the pretty white-painted thatched cottage-style hotel in Huxham – one of the many he'd taken Louise and the kids to over the years to give them an appreciation of country as well as city. But what could he do? Dave knew those lanes and he knew what he was doing. Still, it was a struggle not to get involved.

'I'm just coming up to the cross-roads on Stoke Hill. I'll turn off and come up from there.' That was Jane. Her little green Vauxhall wouldn't be big enough to block even the narrowest of lanes unless she parked across it.

Wasn't there a junction down there somewhere? She'd need to boot it to get past that before blocking him off. Again, Pete almost picked up his radio to tell her so but stopped himself. He had to trust his team. He did trust them. They'd proved their worth on countless occasions over the years. But this time it was his own son's safety or even life at stake. His hand itched to reach for that radio. His jaw clamped, his lips pulling back into a grimace as he fought the almost overpowering urge to interfere. He tried to return to what he was doing, but it was no good. His ears were tuned in, his attention focussed in the wrong direction and there was no stepping back from there. He shifted the radio across to the middle of his desk, both hands clamped around it.

'Anybody up around Rewe?' Dave asked. 'If so, we need you to come across to Columbjohn and south through Brookleigh.'

Yes. Pete had been right. Dave knew those lanes and villages better than anyone who didn't live round there. All Pete knew of them was that they were like a high-hedged maze, some of them only one car wide with passing places at intervals.

'Where the hell's that?' Someone came back.

'Head east at the cross-roads north of the railway crossing in Rewe,' Dave told him. 'When you get to Columbjohn – it's a tiny little place with a couple of left turns close together – stay on the road heading south. Come through Brookleigh – its only three or four houses - and you'll come to a left turn. Take it in case he tries to loop back around.'

'Right Got you.'

Which should box him in nicely as long as he doesn't ram Dave off his bike, Pete thought. And this time he couldn't resist. He pressed the button on the side of the radio. 'Watch yourself on that bike, Dave. He's got a car, remember.'

'If he comes at me he'll know about, boss. Don't you worry.'

I do, though, Pete thought. At least it was light enough for Dave to see who was coming towards him and block the right vehicle. But how he planned to do that, even with his big old 1000cc bike, Pete had no idea.

And what the hell was Southam still doing around there anyway? Had he stopped for tea or something? It seemed crazy when he was on the run. But then, neither of the Southam brothers was anything like anyone else Pete had ever encountered. Which, unfortunately, made them completely unpredictable. For example, if Dave put the blue lights on... He keyed the mike again. 'Dave, don't use your blue lights for God's sake. If you do, he'll be *more* likely to run you off the road, not less.'

'Yeah, I... Here he is.'

Dave cut the radio and all Pete could do was wait.

*

Seconds passed. Tension crackled through Pete's body and mind. Then his desk phone rang, jolting him almost out of his seat. He snatched it up.

'Gayle.'

'Is that DS Gayle of the Devon and Cornwall police?'

'Yes.' *Get on with it or get off the bloody phone!*

'Evening, sir. This is officer Jarvis of the Lincolnshire traffic squad. We've got Jonas Hanson in custody.'

'Yes! How'd you manage that?'

'Officers tracked him down to a garden shed he was hiding in. They had to send the dog in, in the end, but they got him.'

'Thank Christ for that. Can you arrange for transport down here?'

'Already in hand, Sarge. He'll be on his way within the hour.'

'Brilliant. Thanks.' Pete checked his watch. The drive down from Mablethorpe would take six or seven hours, all of which would be taken off the twenty-four they had before they had to charge or release him, once he was in custody. Plus the hour it would take to get him underway. It was going to be tight. Very tight. And the last thing he wanted was to have a man like that freed into the community, knowing that he'd been caught once already. Talk about a flight-risk...

Pete's attention was snatched away by the radio on his desk.

'Officer down, officer down.' It was Jane's voice and she sounded almost in a panic. 'Ambulance needed, and vehicle recovery. Killerton Road north of Ratsloe. Urgent.'

Pete snatched up the radio. 'What's happened, Jane?' Then he returned to the phone. 'Thanks, mate. Got to go,'

'Boss?'

'Yes. Tell me.'

'Dave tried to stop Southam and Tommy. It's a mess.'

'Is he OK?'

'I don't know. That's who the ambulance is for. I found him in the ditch.' She paused. 'Dave? Dave, hold still, mate.' Then she must have realised she'd still got the transmit button depressed. She released it, cutting Pete off abruptly.

'Dammit, Dave Miles, what the bloody hell have you done?' he moaned aloud.

But there was no-one to ask. He couldn't phone Jane at a time like this. He'd be getting in the way of whatever she was doing and that was the last thing he wanted. Again, he just had to wait while fear and frustration twisted up his insides, his fists clenching as he leaned his elbows on the desk and let his head sink onto the cool wood between them.

*

It was twenty minutes before Jane called him back. His brain had been in turmoil the whole time, unable to concentrate on anything useful as it swirled this way and that. What had happened to Dave? Was he all right? And what about Tommy? Had Southam got away with him? Were they also hurt? Jane hadn't mentioned them, but what did that mean? What was he going to tell Louise and Annie?

And if Southam had got away, he now knew that the police were after him despite his warnings about Tommy's safety. What would he do now? Would he take out his fear and anger on the boy?

Was he even capable of fear or would it be just anger, resentment, revenge? The man had to be a seething mass of rage and his obvious psychopathic tendencies made him even more dangerous – not only to Tommy but to anyone else who got in his way. Clearly, he was already dangerous, or Dave Miles wouldn't be waiting for an ambulance out there on that narrow country lane.

He might simply run, at least for now - get as far away as he could from the epicentre of his troubles, give himself room to breathe, to regroup. And if so, would he swap cars yet again? How the hell were they going to find him if he did? They were back to square one: except they weren't – they were further back than that.

217

What had Dave tried to pull on him, that had caused him to react that way? He recalled Dave's own words, spoken just moments before the incident must have taken place: *'If he comes at me he'll know about. Don't you worry.'*

And his own reaction. *I do.* Evidently with good reason.

His phone rang at last. He snatched it up. 'Gayle.'

'The ambulance is here, boss. They're taking Dave to A&E.'

'What happened? Is he OK? Stupid question. How bad is he?'

'He's not as bad as his bike. That's completely wrecked. But it took most of the impact, shielded Dave to some extent. He's got damage to his leg, hip and shoulder. I think the leg may be broken; not sure about the shoulder and the hip. The ambulance crew are worried about internal bleeding but at least he'd got his helmet on so his thick head's not damaged.'

'How the hell did it happen?'

'It seems like his plan was to park up at the roadside, headlight still on, crouch behind the bike and throw a stinger across the road as Southam passed. But either he was too late or he was spotted or both. The stinger was out of his pannier but not deployed. The bike had been knocked back over him and you know what a big bastard it is. No way he was shifting it from underneath like that, especially injured as he was.'

'So Southam must have spotted him. What about the car? Tommy?'

'There some bits on the road from the impact. Headlight glass, bits of metal, but it kept going, There's no sign of it round here. I'd imagine it was pretty well banged up, though. Again, with the weight of the bike, the impact, even if it was a glancing one, would cause a fair bit of damage.'

As she spoke Pete's brain began to regain some semblance of normal function. 'So he'll need to swap it for another one again. We'll need to keep a close watch on stolen vehicles from the area, especially in his last known direction of travel.'

'Yeah, I've put a call out. At least we've got plenty of bodies around here at the moment.'

'True, but they need something solid to aim at. In the meantime, by the way, Joe Hanson's on the way back here in the back of a police van. Or at least I hope he is by now. They caught him up in Lincolnshire.'

'When?'

'About twenty-five minutes ago.'

'Christ, it never rains but it pours, eh? We've got our bloody work cut out, making the charges against him stick in less than twenty-four hours.'

'Especially if we're a man down,' he agreed.

'Are you going to let the others know or should I?'

'I will. But what about Southam and Tommy?'

'We can't be in two places at once, can we?' she said. 'I'll tell Mark Bridgman he'll have to pull in some more crew.'

'No, I should do that.'

'Yeah, but… It's your son we're talking about, boss. Are you sure you're all right with that?'

'Far from it, but what alternative is there? We can't let Hanson walk.'

'No, but we can't let Steve Southam get away either.'

'I know,' he said more sharply than he'd intended. 'I've been struggling with that ever since the last time you called.'

'Sometimes there just isn't a choice, boss. We have to trust other folk to do what we can't.'

CHAPTER TWENTY-ONE

Dick Feeney took his seat and Pete waited a few seconds longer. Then he remembered that Dave wasn't going to be joining them.

'OK. We're one down with a hell of a lot of work to do in not a lot of time,' he summarised. 'Mark's crew's out there with every available mobile unit as well as half of Jim's crew and most of Simon's, looking for Tommy and Steve Southam. We've got to find something – anything – concrete to prove these murders are down to Jonas Hanson. Or that they're not,' he acknowledged with a shrug.

'Well, of course they are,' Jill protested. 'How else is he going to have all that stuff? All those photographs, the jewellery and so forth, all hidden away in his loft like that.'

'You know as well as I do what the CPS are like,' Pete reminded her. 'They're looking for excuses not to prosecute wherever possible. They've always been that way, but especially now, with budget cuts, staff shortages and the costs involved in a trial.'

'Yeah,' Dick grunted. 'Worst bloody thing ever invented, they are. Designed to get in the way as much as possible of both police work and justice.'

'Nevertheless, they're the reality we've got to live with. So, the order of the day – or night, in this case – is to work our way around them as solidly as possible. And to that end, I've started compiling a timeline from his paperwork so we can compare it to the

221

murders we know he's got evidence of. If we can put him in any of the locations at the time of the disappearances, we've got him nailed. Because, of course, the stuff he's got...' he glanced at Jill. '... the CPS will say he could have got off e-bay. To be fair, there are some sick buggers out there who collect that kind of stuff.'

Jane grimaced. 'That's all kinds of...'

'Sick?' Pete suggested.

'Exactly.'

'So, if everyone's up for it, let's get down to work.'

'Have you called Louise, boss?' Jane asked. 'Let her know what's going on?'

It was Pete's turn to grimace. He knew he had to make that call, but he really didn't want to.

'Not yet,' he admitted.

'I think you should.'

'I know, but with Tommy still out there...'

'She knows the score on that,' Jane argued.

'Doesn't mean she likes it.'

'Of course she doesn't, but she'll like it even less if you leave her in the dark,' Jill pointed out.

Pete grunted. He knew they were right. It didn't make the prospect any easier to face, though. 'OK, In a minute. First, let's get this lot allocated.'

Nobody had objected to the extra shift, even though it would probably go unpaid.

'What I've been doing is taking a month at a time, as that's the way he's stored the stuff, and created a time-line from it, then tried to match that to the disappearances.' He handed out one of Hanson's monthly envelopes from the file he'd been working on to each of the team. They could see what he'd done already on the board opposite their block of desks. 'Even one solid connection will help but several will nail him to the wall.'

He sat back, took a deep breath and picked up his phone to dial.

'Hello?' Annie said, picking it up.

'Hello, Button. How are you doing?'

'Daddy! Will you be home soon? Have you got Tommy back yet?'

It would be so easy to answer her questions and let her pass the information onto Louise, but it would also be a cop-out. 'You'd best put your mum on the phone, love.'

'Huh?' she sounded disappointed. 'You haven't, have you? Where is he? Is he all right, at least?'

'As far as we know, yes, love. He is. And there's an awful lot of people out there trying to make sure he stays that way.'

'But you're not.'

'You know as well as I do, I'm not allowed to be,' he said. 'Fetch your mum, eh? I'll see you soon.'

He saw Jane's eyebrows rise at the lie and waited until he heard the clunk of the phone going down on the table before saying, 'It's all relative, isn't it?'

She grunted. Then the phone was picked up. 'Pete?'

223

It was Louise.

'I'm just calling to tell you I probably won't be home tonight. Or if I am, it'll be late. I had to tell Annie we haven't caught Steve Southam yet, so we haven't got Tommy back, but there's a hell of a lot of bodies out there, searching, and they've got it narrowed down to a pretty tight area so I'm waiting for a call anytime to say they've got him.'

'You're waiting for a call?'

'You know I can't be directly involved but the team have been. Dave's at the RDE because of it. And we have got a huge job on here, too, and we're on the clock.'

She knew what that meant.

'What's happened to Dave?'

'Southam knocked him off his bike.' It was an over-simplification, but it would do for now.

'Is he OK?'

'We don't know yet.'

She sighed. 'We'll see you when we do, then.'

'I'm sorry.'

'Just make sure you find him. Or they do.' She was referring to Tommy, he knew.

'You know Mark. He won't give up until he does.'

They both knew from past cases that Mark Bridgman could be as dogged as a Bull Terrier when he got his teeth into something.

'I love you,' he said.

Louise simply grunted and put the phone down.

With another heavy sigh, Pete followed suit. His home life was going to be more difficult than he'd known for a long time until they found Tommy and freed him from Steve Southam's clutches. But he didn't have time to dwell. He picked up the envelope he'd been working on when it all kicked off – was it really still less than an hour ago?

It was more than possible for someone's life to be turned upside down in a matter of seconds – his own had been a little over a year ago when Tommy first went missing - but it still seemed an incredible concept. You plodded along in your little groove and suddenly something hit you like a tsunami out of the blue, knocking you completely off kilter in a way that was both catastrophic and irredeemable.

Still, he had work to do. He tipped out the contents of the envelope in his hand and began sorting them into order, ready to pull them into another solid timeline.

*

'Boss? Look here,' Ben said into the quiet of the early evening.

Pete glanced across. 'What have you got?'

'A link, I think.'

Between the time of day and the number of officers out on the hunt for Steve Southam, they were on their own in the squad room.

'Here we go. A poet who didn't know it,' Dick said. 'Keep going, Spike, you'll have a limerick in a minute.'

'Just 'cause Dave's not here to pick on...'

'Talking of Dave.' Pete cut in over Ben's protest. 'Jill, give the hospital a call, will you? See if there's any news yet.' He stood up to cross behind Dick and see what Ben had found.

It had been a couple of hours or more since Dave would have got to the RDE and they'd heard nothing.

'Let's have a look, then' he said to Ben.

'Here. End of March 2015, he was in Lowestoft. He bought a tank full of petrol there on the 30th. Two days later, he was in Bromsgrove. We've got a ticket for a B&B there. And on the 31st a woman disappeared in Bedford, which is right in line between the two. She was twenty-seven years old, a mother of three and on the dole as well as being, according to Bedfordshire police records, on the game. And she hasn't been seen since. Here's her mug-shot.' He clicked a button on his keyboard and a new window opened with a police photograph of a slim, dark-haired woman who looked significantly older than her years and was dressed in a strappy, low-cut top.

'That's a bit tenuous,' Pete said. 'He happened to be passing when it happened?'

Ben shrugged. 'Given his record, though, and the fact that she matches one of the photo sets he's got...'

'Well, that's better, but it's still not conclusive.'

'How's this?' asked Dick.

'What?'

'He was actually in the town in question at the time for this one.'

'Yes?'

'Bristol. Again, the turn of the month. June to July 2014. A seventeen-year-old vanished from Fishponds on the 30th. He was staying in the area at the time. She hasn't been seen since, either. Wasn't known to be a prostitute, but she did have a drug habit and a limited income. There should be a picture of her in the misper file.' He tapped a few keys and as Pete headed back to his chair. 'Here we go.'

The photo was not an official one but a family portrait. She looked a lot less than her age, despite her drug habit. There was no telling how long she'd had that when the photo was taken, though, he reflected. And appearance-wise, she could have been the younger sister of the one Ben had found.

'Are we beginning to think he's got a type?' Pete reflected. 'Or is it too soon to say? Either way, it's time I ordered some grub.'

Jill put her phone down and looked across. 'Dave's still in surgery, boss. He had internal bleeding from a ruptured spleen. It's been a bit touch-and-go, the nurse said. They're dealing with that before they get to his broken bones, but they've struggled to stop the bleeding.'

'Well, they will, won't they?' said Jane. 'He's on warfarin since he had that triple bypass – what is it, four years now?'

Pete nodded. 'Surely, they knew about that, though. He goes to the RDE, to the clinic.'

'Bloody right hand don't know what the right hand's doing, never mind the left in that place sometimes,' Dick muttered. 'I expect they'll blame the new computer system – even if it is four or five years old now. Best ring them back and tell them, hadn't we?'

'I'll do it,' Jill said. 'Don't want you pissing them off when they've got a mate of ours under the knife.'

'Bloody bingo!' Jane shouted. 'This one, there's no arguing with.'

'What?' Pete demanded.

'End of September 2014, Hanson was in Cardiff. I've got a receipt from the Mount Pleasant Hotel there for five nights overlapping into October. And on the third of October, the morning after he left Cardiff, a young woman was reported missing. Eileen Atkinson, aged 22, last seen with "friends" the previous evening.' She hooked her fingers in the air to emphasise the quotation marks in the comment. 'She wasn't known to the police, but she was a prostitute, as admitted by one of those friends. And last seen means getting into a green Peugeot estate car with a blond-haired man, probably in his fifties. She'd popped round the corner for a pee, was on the way back at the time she was picked up.' She took a breath. 'And get this... The friend in question got a good enough look at the bloke as he drove past her before turning the corner that she was able to provide a sketch.'

Pete's eyes widened. 'Well, don't leave us in suspenders, let's have a look.'

Jane grinned as she turned her screen around and peered over the top of it. 'Remind you of anyone? Ben?'

'If that ain't Joe Hanson I ain't from Devon,' Ben said firmly.

'Nice one,' Pete confirmed. 'You get tonight's gold star. Have we got the witness' details?'

Jane grimaced. 'Yeah, that's where the news isn't so good,' she admitted. 'She was a heroin addict. She's no longer with us.'

'Doesn't that make her evidence inadmissible?' Ben asked.

'Ohhh, no,' Pete denied in a deep voice, imitating a certain dog from a well-known series of TV ads. 'Section 116 of the 2003 criminal justice act allows it at the judge's discretion.'

'So, we've got him,' Jane said.

'Go, girl.' Jill reached across to give her a high five.

'It certainly makes it a strong case,' Pete said. 'Plenty strong enough to take to the CPS. But the more we can find, the stronger it'll be.'

'How about I call them and you call Pizza-Hut, then?' Jane suggested.

Pete aimed a finger at her and depressed the thumb. 'You're on.'

Jill's desk phone rang. She picked it up. 'PC Evans, Exeter CID.'

She didn't need to say anymore, her expression did it for her as she listened briefly and lowered the phone as if in a daze.

'What?' Pete demanded.

'It's Dave,' she murmured. 'They thought they'd stopped the bleeding, so they moved on to try and fix his hip. But the spleen started leaking again.'

'Gimme that,' Dick demanded, holding out a hand for it. Jill passed it to him.

'Hello? This is DC Feeney. Are you people actually aware that he's on warfarin? Attending regular clinics in that hospital where you're standing right now?' He paused. '*No?* What do you mean, no? You have got his notes there, have you? At least a digital version of them? Well then bloody well read them for Christ's sake.' He reached across and slammed the phone down on its cradle. 'Load of clueless bloody arseholes. If we made half the cock-ups they do we'd get fired out of hand.'

CHAPTER TWENTY-TWO

Pete put the last date onto the timeline for February 2013 and slipped the papers he'd been working from back into their envelope. Hanson had ended the month here in Exeter, having started it laying a driveway in Stroud followed by two weeks in a village just north of Swindon.

Returning to his computer, he began to search through missing persons and unsolved murders for that month. It didn't take long – there were only five female missing persons, and, of the several murders, there were only six unsolved from the entire United Kingdom. He discounted the two from Scotland straight away and was left with nine young women to look at more deeply. One of the murders was in north Wales, another in Manchester on a day that he had proof Hanson was in Stroud. There was a misper in Northumberland, another in the Peak District. Then a murder popped up, the victim disappearing on St Valentine's day, the body found three weeks later, after ten days of bad weather. She'd lived in Swindon, her body being discovered in woodland between there and Devises, to the south-west of the city – just where you wouldn't expect Hanson to be. But a witness had reported seeing a green estate car in a parking area adjacent to the dump-site on the night of the15th.

There was no make or model, but Joe Hanson certainly drove a green estate car.

'I just might have trumped your Cardiff case, Jane.'

'Why? What have you got?'

He explained briefly. 'I'll need to check the details, mind. Let's see if I can find the witness…'

He was already logged into the case file. He scrolled down and found the witness' details, picked up the phone and dialled.

Moments later, it was picked up. 'Hello?' The voice sounded groggy. Pete glanced at the clock and grimaced. *Whoops!* He hadn't thought about the time. It was after nine.

'Mr Johnson, sorry for the late call. This is DS Peter Gayle with Exeter CID. I've just come across your witness statement about the green estate car you saw back in 2013. I wonder if you could give me any more details?'

The man hesitated. 'Well, not really. I told the officers up here all I could at the time. It was dark and I'm not much on modern cars.'

'You didn't see the driver?'

'No, just the car parked up with its lights off. It's deep woodland round there so even darker than most places. My headlights picked up the car in a little dirt layby that people use for walking in the woods. I thought it was odd, at that time of year, especially in the snow and it was a bitter night. Must have been well into minus figures.'

'I see. If I could get someone to come round with some vehicle photographs, do you think you'd be able to pick it out? I realise it's a long time ago, but it would really help if you could.'

'Well…' he hedged. 'I don't know. I could try. But, hold on. My wife's a bit of a dab-hand on the old computer. Maybe you could send them to us? It might be quicker.'

'Well, if that's all right with you.'

'Hang on, I'll pass you over. She knows all the details.'

The phone was handed across. A female voice said, 'Hello? You need our email address?'

'Please.'

She must have been listening to the conversation and got the gist of it. She read out the address and Pete wrote it down on his pad. 'Right, I'll compile a bunch of pictures and send them over. It'll take me a few minutes.'

'OK.'

'Thank you.'

Pete ended the call and opened a new on-line window on his computer, not wanting to lose the case file. He called up an array of images of Peugeot estate cars and picked out several, including one of the same model and year as Hanson's. Then, for good measure, he did the same for Citroen, Ford and VW. He compiled a page of them in a publishing program and emailed it across to the Johnsons.

It was only minutes before his email pinged with a reply: *"It was just like picture four."*

'Yes!' He looked over at Jane. 'Confirmed,' he said. 'The car's a match for Hanson's.'

'So, we've got him.'

Pete's phone rang on his desk. He picked it up, expecting it to be Mr Johnson, confirming his identification.

'DS Gayle.'

'Did you really expect to pull a stunt like that and not have any consequences?' asked a voice that he recognised. Steve Southam.

A cold feeling gripped his innards. 'I didn't pull any kind of stunt. I was here.'

'Well, some of your oppos did. And you'll be the one paying for it. Or your boy will.'

'There's no need for that,' Pete said quickly. 'He's done nothing to you.'

'But he's here and handy.'

Then a more distant, higher pitched voice sounded over the line. 'What? No. NO!' A scream.

The phone on the other end of the line was picked up again. 'Look out for the post in the morning.'

'What the hell have you done, you...?'

The line went dead, humming gently in Pete's ear.

'Bastard,' he finished softly.

He sat there, stunned, for several seconds. When he blinked and looked up from his cluttered desk, the rest of his team were all staring at him.

'Are you OK?' Jane asked.

Pete swallowed and worked his tongue around his suddenly dry mouth.

'Not really. Better than Tommy, though, by the...' His throat clogged and he squeezed his eyes shut. Opened them again after a couple of seconds to find them moist and blurry. 'He's...' His voice sounded strangled. He cleared his throat. 'Hurt the boy somehow. He said to look out for the post in the morning.'

'Jesus!'

'Evil son-of-a-bitch,' Dick said.

'To get it here for the morning, he'd have had to drop it directly at the sorting office. Not that we need CCTV to know who's sent it, of course. Where's he sending it, though? Here or your place?' asked Jill.

Pete hadn't thought that far. 'I hope it's not at home. It would destroy Louise. Annie, too, probably.'

'Bastard,' Jane gasped. 'What are you going to tell them?'

Pete drew a breath and let it slowly out, trying to calm his roiling stomach. 'Nothing until I have to.'

'But...'

'It's probably best,' Dick said. 'No sense worrying them until you need to.'

Pete grunted. 'I need to let Mark know, though.' He picked up his desk phone.

'What time's Hanson likely to get here?' asked Dick before he could begin to dial.

Pete paused. 'It'll be after midnight. Maybe even one or half past.'

'We've got a bit of time then. How about you go off home for a bit. We can carry on here for another couple of hours unsupervised, see what else we can find. I'll call Mark Bridgman and the custody desk can call you when Hanson gets here.'

Pete grimaced. 'I'd rather stay here, keep going.'

'You'd rather not face Louise, you mean,' Jane countered with a twinkle in her eye.

'Saves lying to her,' Pete said. 'And I'd have to until they've got Tommy back and Southam in custody. How else am I not going to tell her what's happened?'

'Yeah, never thought of that,' Dick admitted.

'Still, you can't run yourself into the ground,' Jane said. 'Especially with the extra pressure from Tommy's situation. You've got to go home sometime.'

Pete sighed and slumped in his chair. 'What's that about a rock and a hard place?'

*

Pete was glad he'd only had one slice of the pizza he'd ordered, leaving the rest for his crew. If he'd had any more, he'd have thrown it up by now. His stomach heaved repeatedly as he drove home. He'd stayed on for another couple of hours, trying to gain as much ammunition against Jonas Hanson as he could before interviewing him the next day. They'd found another three cases that they could link him to, if only tenuously. Dave had still been in surgery when he left the station, but he couldn't put it off any longer. He had to go home and face whatever Louise was going to throw at him.

At least, by now, Annie would be in bed and hopefully asleep.

It was a cowardly delay in some ways, but at least it would allow her a night's sleep.

As he drove past the Co-op a couple of streets away from his house he was still trying to figure out how he was going to tell Louise what had happened. He'd faced killers, rapists, child-molesters and just about every other kind of vicious, unpredictable and despicable human being you could think of in his time on the force as well as victim's families at the worst moments of their lives, but this was probably going to be the most difficult conversation he'd ever had. And that he hoped he ever would.

How should he handle it?

Just say it? The quick knife cuts cleanest as the saying went.

Or should he be as gentle as possible? Lead up to it with all the kindness and sensitivity he could muster, despite being in the same boat as she was?

His training suggested the former but there was no one-size-fits-all answer and this was his wife. And their son who was the victim.

He got home without reaching a conclusion.

Pushing the car door gently shut, he locked it and walked up to the front door. He opened it quietly, not wanting to wake Annie.

'It's only me,' he said, just loud enough to be heard in the sitting room.

Louise was on the far end of the sofa, one leg tucked up under her. 'I was beginning to wonder if you were ever coming home,' she said without looking away from the TV, which was playing on low volume because of Annie being asleep upstairs.

'Yeah, they caught the bloke we've been after up in Lincolnshire. We had to make as much progress as we could before he gets down here. Don't want him getting bail and doing a runner.'

She looked up at last. 'So, what's up?' she asked, seeing immediately that something was wrong with him.

Shit. She knows me too bloody well.

And that decided it. Sitting beside her, he took a deep breath and reached for her hand.

'We... You know we nearly caught Southam this evening. Dave was knocked off his bike in the process. Broken bones. Internal injuries. They rushed him to hospital, but some idiot didn't manage to join the bloody dots before they opened him up so... They've been struggling to stop him bleeding out.'

'Oh, my God. Is he all right?'

Dave was a friend as well as a colleague.

'They're still trying to stabilize him. But that's not the worst of it. The fact that we *nearly* caught Southam means we didn't. And he's still got Tommy, so... He called me. Threatened him.'

He felt her hand clamping onto his.

'What do you mean, threatened him? With what?'

'I don't know, but... While I was on the phone, there was a bit of shouting. And a scream.'

She snatched her hand away abruptly, her eyes going wide. 'A scream? What does that mean? He's...'

'He said he'd hurt him. That's all I know for now.'

'What the bloody hell does that mean? *That's all I know for now?'* Her voice had got louder and was getting louder still. 'Our son's with a fuckin' psychopath. He's been hurt, maybe even killed, and you come here telling me you don't know?'

Pete reached for her hand again but she pulled away, avoiding it. He put a hand on her leg, desperate for contact, but she stood quickly and moved away across the room, staring at him with an angry, accusatory look that felt like a knife to his heart.

'What are you doing here when you should be out there tracking the evil bastard down? Bringing our son back, regardless of what Steven bloody Southam's done to him?'

'Keep it down, will you, or you'll wake Annie up. Do you think I'd be here, telling you this if I had a choice? If I could be out there looking for the boy, of course I would. Christ, I'd do anything if I thought it'd help.'

'Except jeopardise your precious job,' she retorted.

'Jesus! I'd lose the damn job in an instant if it'd save Tommy. But Mark's got half the county force out there looking already. One more pair of eyes wouldn't make any damn difference. You know that as well as I do.'

'It only takes one pair of eyes to see him and *you* know *that*. You might not be allowed to join in as a police officer, but they can't stop you as a private individual. People join in searches all the time. Members of the public. Even the damn perpetrators, half the time. What's wrong with doing that?'

'What's wrong is that you're talking about cases with a known death, a missing kid – things like that. Not cases where there's a direct risk to the searchers and not cases like this where, if I found them, it would mean any case against Southam would be

239

screwed. I want him in jail. Hell, I want him dead, but that's not going to happen.'

'Accidents do,' she argued. 'And that one bloody well would if I was out there and could do it without harming Tommy.'

'Me, too. And that's exactly why officers aren't allowed to work on cases involving family members.'

'Dammit, screw the rules! This is our son we're talking about. Bloody do something.'

Pete felt like screaming back at her, *I can't!* 'There's…' He started but then a thought struck him. '…one thing I could try. Hold on.' He took out his phone and found the number he needed. It was answered in a couple of rings. 'Ben? Did you manage to unlock the source of that call from Southam and ping it?' He'd asked Ben to do it almost immediately, but it wasn't a quick job. It meant Ben calling the provider, Pete giving his permission for the search and then the search itself which would result in a call back to Ben as the requesting officer with the official aim of making it easier to direct the search.

'Yes, boss. I passed the information onto DS Bridgman.'

'Well, you can pass it onto me as well. The location, at least.'

'Boss, you can't get involved. You…'

'As of this moment, Ben,' Pete cut in over him, 'I'm off-duty and, as such, I'm a private citizen. There's a search going on for my missing son and I need to join it, but I need a place to start.'

'I know you've been over this loads of times with the Chief, boss.'

'And I'll take full responsibility. Just give me the location.'

'I can send it relevant parties and accidentally include your home email. But I didn't say that.'

'Fair enough. Thanks, Ben.' Pete ended the call and headed upstairs to his office in the small room next to Annie's. Closing the door to save disturbing her, he switched on the computer and logged onto the Internet. Calling up the email account, he checked the in-box. A new email from Ben Myers was at the top of the list. He opened it and read, "Weston near Honiton." In small text at the bottom of the page, it said, *Sent from my i-phone.* Which would mean his personal one.

Weston, Pete knew, was a small village just west of Honiton, north of the junction that led off the Roman Road into Honiton itself. There was a mobile phone tower there as well as one in the town. If he could make the stolen car driveable after the impact with Dave's bike, it would be far better for Southam to get to a place the size of Honiton, dump it somewhere quiet and steal a new car in the town, rather than taking one from a remote area where it would be missed faster and identified more easily. But he wouldn't stay still, so where would he have gone from there? He'd stay fairly close to Exeter and his brother, but he'd want to get away from Honiton before the vehicle he'd taken was missed. And he'd want somewhere quiet and out of the way to dig in for the night.

There was a large area of woodland between Honiton and Ottery St Mary with several minor roads running through it. It wasn't an area Pete knew well but he was sure there'd be plenty of places to park up out of sight for the night. Picnic areas and so forth.

Ben had passed the information onto Mark - that was the purpose of finding it, after all - so the search would have moved across to that area.

Would Southam be aware of this possibility or would he rely on having blocked his caller ID to keep him safe?

He could go round and around in circles, second-guessing himself all night but he didn't have time for that. He had to make a decision and act on it. And if it meant being out all night, he'd have to do just that.

He deleted Ben's email and shut down his computer before heading back downstairs. He poked his head into the sitting room. Louise was pacing up and down the room, the tension plain to see in her pinched expression.

'Stay here and stay safe,' Pete told her.

She spun around to face him. 'Where are you going?'

'What you don't know, you can't tell.'

'No, but…'

'I'll see you later.' He stepped back and reached for the front door. Outside, he backed the car out of the drive and headed off into the night.

CHAPTER TWENTY-THREE

His first port of call was the picnic area off Argyll Road on the northern edge of Exeter, not far from where Jonas Hanson lived, but it was deserted. He went from there to Ashclyst Forest, a few miles north of the city. There were two spots up there he thought Southam might take shelter in for the night – an off-road picnic area and a bridleway that led across the open heathland at the top of the hill and down into a narrow valley to the west. If he'd taken a 4x4, then it was perfectly possible to get down there into the trees and hide up, at least until morning.

Pete checked the picnic area first. His Ford saloon car was not designed to go off-road. But there was no-one there so, leaving the easier option, he parked on the roadside, among the bracken and ferns and headed down the track on foot.

About half way down the hill the dirt path was interrupted by a wide patch of muddy ground. Pete stopped and examined the soft dirt with his torch in the moonlight. No wheeled vehicle had been this way in some time. He returned to the car and moved on.

There was another wooded area a short way beyond where Southam had encountered Dave on his motorbike. Pete went there next. It was less likely, but still possible. When he got to the gate that opened onto the only track into the woods he found it locked with no sign of anyone having entered illegally.

Again, he moved on. There were a lot of places to check and not a lot of time to do it in. The only advantage he had was that Southam was not local and wouldn't have had the time to research likely spots. He'd have to choose from the more obvious and easily found ones while at the same time, needing to stay hidden.

Pete pictured the wide, exposed area where the Exmouth road crossed the river at Ebford behind Topsham. He and Louise had parked up there many times to watch the herons fishing below the weir or the pair of rare Marsh Harriers wheeling in the sky above. A location like that was definitely out of the question, as was the lane that led from there down to the Exe, below the ancient little port town. Although it was secluded, narrow and twisty, there were a few large, expensive houses down there, the owners of which would undoubtedly notice a strange vehicle parked up overnight.

On the other hand, the kind of private track that led down to the barn where Malcolm Burton had kept Rosie Whitlock and the other girls he'd abducted would be perfect. But how many of those were there in the area? He had no idea, but he imagined the answer was a lot.

A thought struck him.

Did Southam know about the place? Certainly, his brother did. And after all, with Burton in prison, no-one would be going there. It was too early in the season for the meadow adjoining the barn to be mown and baled. That wouldn't happen for another month or more.

Should he try it? Or was it too obvious?

Pete pursed his lips.

It would be the ultimate irony for all this to end where, as far as he was aware, it had all started. It wasn't that far and if he didn't, he'd be thinking about it all night. Best cross it off the list, he decided, heading back towards the edge of the city before cutting west towards the village of Holcomb Burnell and the farm the barn had belonged to. The glow of his headlights swept along high hedges and through tunnels of overhanging tree branches, oppressive in the night.

When, twenty minutes later, he reached the entrance to the dirt track leading through the trees towards the barn, he turned off his headlights and drove slowly through to the meadow beyond. He could see no vehicle parked in front of the ancient stone building so continued past it.

Nothing.

It had been a wasted journey.

He switched his headlights back on and turned back towards the road with a feeling of deflation that was quickly swamped by the knowledge that he was at a total loss. There were endless farm tracks, dead-end lanes, parking places and bridle ways where Southam could be holed up within a mile or two of the city and Pete was one man alone, the rest of the force concentrated out towards Honiton, several miles away. They might as well have been in a different county.

But he couldn't give up. He had to keep searching. His son's life quite possibly depended on it.

If only he had some clue of where to start.

*

He was still searching when his mobile phone rang in his pocket. He hit the button on the car's Bluetooth. 'Gayle.'

'Pete, it's Karen on the custody desk. Your man Hanson's just arrived.'

'Blimey, that was quick. What time is it?'

245

'Twenty past twelve.'

Pete blinked in surprise. 'Jesus! I hadn't realised. Just book him in, will you? We can let him stew until morning, see what he has to say for himself then.'

'OK. You sound like you're driving? Been out on the razz?'

Pete grunted. 'I wish.' He couldn't tell her the truth. 'Family issues,' he said instead.

'Louise thrown you out, has she?' Karen asked with a laugh.

Pete returned the laugh as best he could. 'Not yet. See you in the morning.'

'Yup.'

He ended the call and kept driving. He was beyond tired, but he had to keep going.

An hour later, though, with several possibilities eliminated but endless more to go, his eyes were so sore and he was feeling so groggy that he was forced to stop or run off the road. He pulled over in a passing place on a narrow, tree-lined lane, set the hand-brake and switched off the engine. He'd take a few minutes to relax and regroup then keep going.

*

The next thing he knew, he was opening his eyes to the predawn glow, birds twittering in the trees around him as the sky began to lighten.

'Shit.'

He checked the dashboard clock. It was three minutes to four.

'Bloody hell,' he muttered, sitting up and starting the engine. He needed to get home, grab a shower and change his clothes before getting back to the station to interview Jonas Hanson.

But first he had to figure out where he was. He'd covered so many miles last night, he'd lost track. Still, if he just drove down the road he was on, he was bound to come to a village or a main road and get his bearings from there.

He switched on the headlights and set off. In minutes, he was driving into the small village of Bickleigh. He headed through to the main road and turned south, towards the city. It was early enough that the roads were almost deserted so, without rushing, he was home in under twenty minutes.

As he walked in, Louise's voice came from the sitting room. 'Where the hell have you been? I've been worried sick.'

He went through. She was sitting in her dressing gown in the near-darkness with a throw wrapped around her like a shawl, legs tucked up under her.

'I've *been* out looking for Tommy. Not because you asked me to, but because it was the right thing to do and what I needed to do.'

'You could have let me know.'

'I had my phone.'

She sighed. 'I'm tired. You look like shit warmed over. Let's just call it a draw. It's too late to bother going to bed. We'd have to be up in another hour or two anyway but come here and sit awhile.' She patted the settee beside her.

Pete complied and reached for her hand. Glancing at the clock on the mantle, he said, 'I've got an hour. Then I'll need a shower and some coffee and to head into the station. I've got an interview to conduct that could make Malcolm Burton look like small-fry.'

'Eh? What's this?'

'The case we've been working on. A friend of Ben's brought it to us. The bloke had done a runner. The one I told you was caught last night up in Lincolnshire and transferred down here.'

'So, what is he, another paedophile?' she asked, taking the cue from his mention of Burton.

'No. Rapist and murderer. Allegedly.'

'I haven't heard about anything like that.'

'You wouldn't have. He was careful. Didn't do any of it locally. He was a jobbing builder, went all over the place, carried out the attacks while he was away and even then, travelled a bit from wherever he was working, according to what we've managed to pull together.'

'So, how... Never mind. Tell me after. For now, let's not talk shop, eh?' She shifted her backside across so that she could lean towards him and settled her head on his shoulder. 'You scared me, going off like that. I thought...' He felt her slump against him. 'I don't know what I thought. Lots of things. But mainly, I can't lose you.'

'You're not going to. But like you said, I had to do something and that was the only thing I could think of. Not that it got me anywhere.'

'You've been driving all that time? You must be knackered.'

'I am. But not quite all the time. I had to stop for a little while. Shut my eyes for a few minutes.'

Which was what he'd intended at the time, even if it wasn't what had happened. It seemed like a small omission to make to keep her calm and relaxed. He couldn't handle any more stress just now. He let his head rest onto hers and they were quiet for a time. He began to nod. Then jerked awake as his phone began to buzz in his pocket.

'Who the hell's that at this time of day?' Louise demanded as she straightened up 'Christ, it's not even six.'

Pete took out the phone and checked the screen. Number withheld. A sinking feeling seeped into his gut, cold and clammy. He touched the green icon. 'Gayle.'

'Tried to find us, didn't you?' A dry chuckle. 'I bet you were out there all night. Along with half the bloody force. Didn't look far enough, though, did you?' Another chuckle. 'Still, we'll be back down there soon enough. Post arrived yet, has it?'

'No.' It didn't arrive until at least ten, most days, and the parcel post was later still. As long as he made it home to collect it before Louise and Annie, he'd be able to save them both the trauma of seeing whatever Southam had sent.

Pete didn't think for a moment he was bluffing. It wasn't his style.

'Oh, well. When it does...'

'You know you're not going to get away with this, don't you?' Pete said.

'Why not? You ain't got far towards stopping me yet.'

249

We've got your brother, though, and he was the brains of the operation, Pete thought, but didn't say. 'You really think you're going to evade every copper in the country? Because that's who's going to be looking for you from this morning.'

'And if they find me, I've got a chip off the old block to bargain with, haven't I? Nothing like it to screw with your head, force you into a mistake.'

'Which is why we don't allow victim's relatives to work cases.'

'No, but you will, won't you? You'll find a way if anyone will.'

How had the Wiltshire man got to know so much about him? Unless… Tommy. He must have been torturing information out of the kid. Pete was sorely tempted to tell him that if he'd hurt Tommy in any way at all, he'd be hunted down like a dog and no court would ever see him alive, regardless of the consequences but, with teeth clamped together and rage boiling inside him, an effort of will that he hadn't realised he was capable of somehow stopped him.

'You think you know me?' he said instead. 'You don't know the half of it.'

Southam laughed. 'I don't need to, Gayle. I know your nightmares – that's enough.'

And before Pete could respond, he cut the call.

Pete drew a deep breath, trying to calm himself.

'What did he mean?' Louise demanded. 'About the post.'

Pete shook his head. 'I don't know.' Which was true, at least technically. 'Mind games, I expect. Trying to scare me into a mistake.'

She shook her head. 'No. It was too specific. He's done something, hasn't he?'

There was no way Pete was going to tell her what he suspected. 'That's the point, love. Make it as plausible as possible. That's what makes it work.'

She pursed her lips, not convinced but unable to argue the point further with no real evidence and the likelihood of playing right into the man's hands.

Pete squeezed her hand and leaned across to kiss her. 'I might as well have that shower, now we're awake.'

CHAPTER TWENTY-FOUR

Pete sat down, put his coffee on the table and reached for the recording system as Dick Feeney settled beside him. On the other side of the table the gaunt, long-haired and grizzled-faced Jonas Hanson was already seated.

'Do want anything, Jonas?' Pete asked him. 'Do you prefer Jonas or Joe?'

'Joe'll do.'

'OK. So, you'll have been told why you're here when they arrested you up in Mablethorpe. On suspicion of rape and causing the deaths of multiple victims. Have you got anything you want to tell us?'

'No comment.' Hanson kept his gaze on the table between them.

'OK. We don't need a confession,' Pete said with more confidence than he felt. 'We've got all the evidence we need. Based on that, you're looking at a full-life term. This is about giving you the chance to put your side of the story. I know there's always at least two sides. Sometimes an explanation that we haven't seen. Maybe you collected all that stuff in your loft in some innocent way?'

'No comment.'

'I mean, they sent your computer down with you. Maybe you got all that stuff off e-bay or something? We can check your purchase history and see if that's the case. Or maybe there's some sort of collectors' organisation for that kind of memorabilia?' He shrugged. 'It's not something I've heard of, but I'm always willing to learn.'

Hanson stayed silent.

'Oh, and we've been out to the farm. Got your records. Very thorough. They put you in several places where young women went missing while you were there.'

'No, they don't.' He looked up briefly at Pete, his pale eyes fierce.

Ah, a response at last, Pete thought. He nodded. ''Fraid they do, old son. The vicinities, at least.'

'Coincidence.' His gaze had returned to the table.

Not that many, it isn't. But he didn't argue. Not yet. 'So, what about the stuff in your attic? Where did that all come from?'

Hanson looked up and connected for the first time, a calculating glint in his eyes. 'Did you have a warrant to go up there? Or into my house, even? 'Cause I can't see how you'd have got one and, without it or my permission, anything you found up there'd be inadmissible, wouldn't it?'

Pete shook his head. 'We didn't need a warrant. You were reported missing. That gave us reasonable cause to enter the property to ascertain your possible condition or whereabouts. Plus, in your absence, we had permission from your next of kin.'

His lip curled into a sneer. 'I haven't...' He stopped, eyes narrowing as realisation dawned. 'Sal. She let you in.' It was a statement, not a question.

Pete nodded. 'She was concerned for your safety. How's that for ironic?'

Hanson's eyes narrowed. 'I've got nothing more to say to you. I want a solicitor.'

Pete tipped his head. 'You'll need a good one, to get you out of this.' He took a sip of his coffee and checked his watch. 'Interview terminated at 08.17.' He switched off the recorder and stood up. Looking down at Hanson, he said, 'You do realise what happens to the likes of you in prison, don't you? It ain't good, I can tell you that.'

Hanson looked up, eyes hooded. 'Solicitor,' he said.

'Come on, DC Feeney. Let's go prepare his bed for him to lie in. For as long as they let him.'

Hanson sneered. 'You've got nothing. Circumstantial, at best. You won't get a conviction on that.'

Pete turned back from the door. 'I thought you wanted a solicitor?'

Hanson shrugged. 'Just saying.'

Pete stepped forward, leaning his fists on the desk between them as he stared down at the smaller man. 'You've got away with this for so long, you think you're clever. Invincible, even.' He nodded. 'And you have been clever about it. But not clever enough.' He winked and straightened up, turning away to follow Dick out of the small room, leaving Hanson to dwell on that while he waited alone for his solicitor.

*

In the corridor, Dick looked at him with a twinkle in his eye. 'His brief won't be here for another hour or more. That's a long time for him to wonder what we've got on him.'

'Exactly,' Pete agreed as they reached the custody desk. 'Bob, you'll need to put Mr Hanson back in his box for a bit.'

'Lawyered up, has he?'

Pete nodded.

'Shame.'

'Yeah, well. We'll have him.'

As they headed back upstairs, Dick said, 'He's right, though. Hanson. The case is basically circumstantial apart from that one hooker's witness statement that the judge might not even admit into evidence.'

'True, but the weight of evidence comes into it. Plus, he doesn't know that. Not now. He might try for a deal when his brief gets here.'

'But if he doesn't? I mean, we've only got half a day or so to charge him and Fast-track won't want to do that without something concrete to support it.'

Pete turned around to face him, annoyance flaring inside him. 'So, we'd best find something, hadn't we?'

'How?' Dick asked. 'All that paper work'll only add to the circumstantial, it's way too late for forensics and we haven't got time to use the press.'

Pete raised an eyebrow. 'Is it?'

'What?'

'Too late for forensics?'

'Have you seen the state of a builder's van? And it's been ages since his last victim that we know of.'

'That we know of, yes. But what if there's been a more recent one? I mean, why was he all of a sudden off on a road-trip?'

Dick's eyes widened. 'What – you think he's done one in the past few days?'

Pete's eyebrows rose. 'It's worth a shot.'

'But the car's up north still.'

'They do have civilization up there. Even electric lights now, so I've heard.'

'Wonders will never cease,' Dick responded. 'Best get onto them then, eh?'

They continued up the stairs and took their seats in the squad room, Pete opening his desk drawer to withdraw a note book.

'How'd it go?' Jane asked as Pete took out his notebook.

She must have arrived while they were downstairs. She seemed to be busy already, though, and with a steaming mug at her elbow.

'He lawyered up,' Dick told her. 'But the boss sowed a seed of doubt before we left him to stew.'

Finding what he was looking for, Pete picked up the phone and dialled.

'Lincolnshire police. How can I help?'

'Can you transfer me to the Mablethorpe station? This is DS Gayle of Devon and Cornwall.'

'One moment, sir.'

There was a pause, then a ring-tone. A click. 'Police. How can I help?'

'Is this the Mablethorpe station?'

'It is.'

'This is DS Gayle from Exeter. You transferred a prisoner down to us last night. Something's just come up in interview.'

'Oh, yes?'

'Can you get forensics done on his car as a matter of urgency? We're looking for fibres that don't belong and, more importantly, for blood. Specifically, blood that doesn't belong to the car's owner. If you didn't take his DNA, it'll be on the steering wheel for exclusion.'

'This is... Blimey, you don't want much, do you? Blood and DNA results in fourteen hours! You'll be lucky.'

'I know, but if you can get them in process, that could get us a further twelve hours, pending the results. Let me know, will you?'

'OK.' The man still sounded dubious but at least he was willing to try. Pete hoped.

He gave him the station's direct number, thanked him and rang off.

'Have we heard anything from the hospital yet?'

The door opened to his right, admitting Ben and Jill.

257

'They managed to stabilize him in the end and fixed him up. He's not out of the woods by a long shot, but he's headed in the right direction, they reckon,' Jane reported as they headed for their seats.

'Is that Dave?' Jill checked.

Jane nodded.

'At least we've got a bit of good news, then. I don't suppose we've got a confession from Jonas Hanson?'

'He's stringing out his five minutes of fame,' Jane told her.

Pete frowned. Then one eyebrow rose. 'Well done, Jane,' he said, getting up.

'What?'

'You've given me an idea.'

'What?'

He headed for the door, ignoring her repetition.

*

'Come.'

Pete opened the door and stepped in. 'Chief.'

'Peter. What can I do for you?'

The question sounded far from genuine, the tone flat and uninterested as DCI Silverstone stared up at him.

'I think we'd benefit from a last-minute appeal to the media in the Hanson case, sir. Get the TV crews down here and make a national appeal for witnesses or victims. He didn't start off with killing these women, did he? They work up to it. Indecent exposure,

258

theft, burglary, rape. Someone must have survived and can tell their story. Or someone must have seen something, at least.'

'That sounds a little desperate, Detective Sergeant.'

'Dotting the I's and crossing the T's, sir. We've got a mountain of circumstantial evidence but only one witness statement so far. More would be helpful.'

'And with the man already in custody, time is of the essence.'

'Exactly. We have got one other iron in the fire, but the more the better.'

'And what exactly is that?'

'Forensics.'

Silverstone's eyes flashed wide in surprise. 'Forensics? How long has it been since his last attack?'

'We're hoping just a few days, sir. Why else has he suddenly upped and offed on an extended road-trip without telling anyone he was going?'

Silverstone tipped his head, lips pursed. 'All right. But we have only a matter of hours, Sergeant.'

'A simple test for blood doesn't take long, sir. And I have asked them to prioritise it.'

'Very well. In the meantime, I should be able to get an urgent press conference organised.'

'Perfect. Thank you, sir.' Pete turned and reached for the door.

'And what of the still un-arrested Southam brother, Detective Sergeant?' Silverstone asked before he got hold of the handle.

Pete stiffened and turned back to face the senior man, who was sitting there with his fingers steepled in front of him, an innocent expression on his face. 'He seems to have taken it into his head to contact me personally, sir. He's done so twice so far.'

'And have you shared the details of those contacts with Detective Sergeant Bridgman?'

'The first one, yes. The second, not yet. I've been interviewing Jonas Hanson.'

'Then you'd better go and do so now, Detective Sergeant.' He eyes hardened. 'And you know my feelings on direct action in a case involving a relative.'

'I do, sir. Is that all, sir?'

'Carry on, Detective Sergeant.' Silverstone looked down at the pad in front of him and began writing.

CHAPTER TWENTY-FIVE

'I've just heard back from North Yorkshire, boss,' Jane told him when he returned to the squad room. 'We knew Hanson was raised in Northallerton. His parents are dead. Road accident when he was a teenager. Their car went off the road one night on the way back from a trip to the cinema. The car appeared to have run out of power steering fluid. Hanson had had a problem with his dad ever since he was young, according to his grandparents at the time. He was an only child. At least an only surviving one. He had a sister about three years younger, died when she was two and a half. Drowned in a paddling pool.' She paused to let the significance of that settle in.

'Any evidence it wasn't an accident?'

'Which one, boss?'

'Either.'

She shook her head. 'Nothing provable. They rode him hard over the parents' deaths, but nothing came of it. In the end, they had to be put down as accidental.'

'Anything else we should know about?'

'As a teen, he was caught in the girls' changing rooms on more than one occasion. Told the teachers it was a bet the first time; the other, he said he was pushed in there by his mates. Maybe an incorrect term. Apparently, he didn't have many mates. Bit of a loner, by all accounts.'

This was sounding more and more promising as she went on. Nothing directly evidential yet, though. 'Are we leading up to anything useful here?' he asked.

'Does pulling a girl's knickers down at the top of the stairs in school count?'

Pete nodded slowly. 'Yeah.'

'Claimed he'd tripped, reached out automatically and this girl was immediately in front of him.'

Pete raised an eyebrow.

'Yeah, the school staff didn't believe him either. Nor did the local police. He only just avoided prosecution that time. He was suspected when the same girl's house got burgled a few weeks later, but there was nothing proven. He was supposedly at home, in bed, when it happened. His parents made a statement to that effect. But two days later he was admitted to the local hospital with a broken arm. Reckoned he'd fallen out of a tree.'

'Yeah, right.'

Jane nodded. 'But again, no-one would say otherwise. His first actual conviction was for burglary when he was seventeen. He was caught red-handed by the house owner. They reckoned he was after the wife's jewellery, but he didn't have anything on him. He got six months' probation.'

Pete shook his head in disgust. 'Makes you wonder why we bother sometimes, doesn't it? When you've got a clear history like that and a strong likelihood of reoffending.'

'Which he fulfilled. It was a few months later that his parents died. He was just a couple of weeks over eighteen, so he was free to do as he pleased, more or less. Insurance gave him the house. He was suspected, soon after, of peeping, but wasn't actually caught so that might have been just local rumour. A few more burglaries in the town and the surrounding villages followed, but again, nothing proven. And that's all they've got on him. They did mention they'd been asked by County Durham police about a couple of rapes in Eaglescliffe, which isn't far from Northallerton, but again, nothing proven. He hadn't exactly got an alibi for either, but there was no forensic evidence to connect him.'

'It sounds like that's where he developed his MO though. Nip into the next county so he's not connected to the crime.'

She nodded. 'I just wish we could use any of it.'

'Yes. Keep working with what we've got though. We might come up with something. I've got to have a word with Mark Bridgman, then nip home.'

'For half a day's kip, by the look of you,' Jane responded.

'I wish I had the chance.'

Mark wasn't in the squad room, so Pete phoned him to report the latest contact from Steve Southam. Then he left the office and headed downstairs. At the bottom, he was lifting his ID card to the reader that would allow him into the back corridor when a voice called him from the front desk.

He turned. 'George. How's it going?'

'Not bad. Here, got a package for you.' He raised a small, paper-wrapped package, about five inches square.

Pete's stomach sank. He felt suddenly faint. He swallowed. Tried to speak but couldn't. Clearing his throat, he stepped forward. 'What's this, then?'

'Don't know, mate. Postmark says Taunton.'

Pete took the package with trembling fingers. He trudged back up to the squad room. He knew he had to open it. In Mark's absence, it was down to him and it was far too late to hold off for forensics. Gloves would help, but its exterior had already been handled by several people.

The last thing in the world he wanted to know was what was inside it, but what choice did he have?

As he stepped back into the squad room Jane looked up, saw him and dropped her pen, staring. Dick saw her reaction, glanced across and froze.

'What is it?' Jane asked as he neared their desks.

'A package. From Taunton. Southam said last night he was going to send one.'

'He called you last night?'

'Yes.' Pete didn't want to think about what had happened during that call and certainly didn't want to talk about it, but he knew he was going to have to. 'He threatened to hurt Tommy if we kept after him.'

'And you reckon this is the result.' She nodded to the small square package in his hand.

He nodded and headed straight for Colin Underhill's office. Colin saw him coming and waved him in. With the door closed behind him, Pete put the package on the senior man's desk and pushed it towards him.

Colin looked up at him. 'What's this?'

'It just arrived downstairs.' Pete briefly explained the history behind it. 'Mark's out and about or it'd be his responsibility. As it is…' He shrugged. 'We can't… I mean *I* can't leave it unopened in case it does contain what Southam threatened.'

'So you want my agreement to open it.'

Pete tipped his head.

'Well, you've already handled it, along with George and Uncle Tom Cobbley in the post office.' He reached into his desk drawer and took out a pair of scissors. 'Here. Carefully.'

Pete compressed his lips. Carefully went without saying. He pulled on a pair of gloves, took the scissors and slid the tip of one blade into a corner of the wrapping. Cutting carefully along one edge, he went along another edge and a third, making a flap that he could fold back and pull the box out through. It was of heavy-grade brown card, like two open-topped boxes, top to top within each other. Pete cut the tape holding it closed at either side, put down the scissors and looked at Colin.

The DI nodded.

Jaw clenched, Pete slid the top off. Inside was a wad of crumpled toilet paper. Tension crackling through his every muscle, he withdrew the paper. He hadn't realised he was holding his breath until it whooshed out of him.

Under the wad was another, similar one. And between them lay a single, small piece of paper, folded across the middle. He took it out, holding it by the very edges, saw there was nothing underneath it and carefully unfolded it.

In red block capitals, were the words: *"Whatever you thought was in here, you're not that lucky. There's another box at home for you.*' 'Shit,' he breathed. 'I can't have Louise or, worse still, Annie finding that and opening it.'

'What time's your post?'

Pete checked his watch. 'Anytime now for letters. Parcels, another hour or so and one like this won't got through the letterbox.'

'We'll give it forty minutes, then go and see.'

Pete paused for just an instant as he absorbed the senior man's response. 'Right.'

'You didn't expect me to let you go on your own, did you?'

Pete tipped his head. 'Hadn't thought that far, to be honest. I just know I've got to pick it up before anyone else sees it, whether they leave it or put a card through to go and collect it.'

'Go on, I'll give you a shout in a bit,' the senior man said, thrusting his chin at the door.

Pete turned without responding and left the small office.

'North Yorks have been on,' Dick told him as he returned to his desk. 'Best they can do on the forensics is getting them in tomorrow morning.'

'Another twenty-four hours?'

Dick nodded. 'They understand the urgency, but they've got a lot else on, apparently.'

'Shit. That means Bob getting permission from the DCI to hold him for the extra time.'

'Well, he can't refuse, surely,' Jane said. 'The bloke's the definition of a flight risk. Plus, he's a danger to the public.'

'Allegedly.'

'OK, but…'

'All we've got so far is circumstantial,' Pete reminded her. 'Apart from that one statement from a dead woman.'

'Yeah, but there's a hell of a lot of it.'

'Don't tell I,' Pete quoted.

Jane grunted. 'It makes you wonder how arse-holes like that get jobs at all, never mind senior ones.'

'Trying to figure that out will drive you round the bend,' Dick told her.

'I think the word you want is nepotism,' Jill said from the far corner of their cluster of desks.

'You make that sound dirty,' Dick said with a grin.

'It is.'

'But it doesn't help our case,' Pete said. 'We need something that does. And pronto.'

'We could do with knowing what vehicles he's owned in the past, to see if we can match any of them with witness statements,' Jane said.

'The DVLA don't hold that kind of thing, though,' Pete pointed out.

'Sally might know,' Ben said. 'Not necessarily licence plates – who would – but makes and models.'

Pete nodded. 'Give her a call.'

Ben picked up his phone and dialled. They all waited with bated breath until he finally spoke. 'Sal, its Ben. Quick question: can you remember what cars or vans your dad owned over the years? I know he had that white Astra van when we were seeing each other, but what else has he had?' A pause. 'We're trying to figure out where he might have been in the past, to see if he might be in any of those places now.'

Good thinking, Pete thought. They hadn't yet told her of his arrest and didn't want to until they could also tell her she'd be safe from retribution from him for allowing – or even causing – his current situation.

'OK, thanks, Sal. We'll let you know as soon as we have any firm news. Bye.'

He put the phone down and looked up at Jill and Jane opposite him, then across to Dick and Pete. As his gaze roamed around the group, his lips twitched and spread slowly into a smile.

'Well, come on, then,' Jane said impatiently.

'He's not had many vehicles over the years. Basically, wears them out and sends them for scrap before he gets a new one and even then, he doesn't buy new. Always second-hand.'

'Get on with it, Ben,' Pete told him.

'OK. He had a white Astra van from 2005 to 2009. Replaced that with the green Peugeot. Before that, Sal remembers him having a VW van. Like a camper but without the windows. It was pale blue, she said. And the only one she remembers him having before that, was a Transit. A white one.'

A groan passed around the team.

'Great. The most common and unidentifiable vehicle on the roads,' Jill observed.

'Except his had a red lightning stripe along the sides,' Ben said with a grin.

'And when did he get that?' Pete asked.

'Don't know. Before she can remember, so prior to '94, at least. And he'd got rid of it by '96, so he'd have had it for a while. Probably got it around 1990, judging by his other ones.'

'When did he meet his wife?' Jane asked. 'Ex-wife, I mean.'

'Don't know. I can ask her.'

'Do that,' Pete said.

Ben picked up his phone again. 'Why didn't we think of this before?' he asked as he dialled.

'Because we were focussing on what we already had,' Dick told him.

'Still,' Pete said. 'We should have. Can't afford to get too locked in on one option in this game.'

'Mrs... Mary, its Ben Myers. Yes, that's right. I've just been talking to her. We were trying to figure out what vehicles Jonas has had over the years. We got back to the Transit. Do you remember what he had before that?' He pulled a wry face at Jill. 'No, I understand that, but anything you can recall might help.' He paused again. 'OK, thanks for that. I'll talk to you soon.'

As he put the phone down, he looked across at Pete. 'She doesn't know much. She's not into cars and that. Not interested at all. But she does remember what he had when they first started seeing each other, back in 1984. It was before he started on the building. He was working in some factory down by the river. Hadn't been in Exeter long. It was a dark blue estate car that you could fold the back seats down flat in. A biggish VW.'

'Passat,' Dick said.

'Bless you,' Jane retorted.

'She said he'd had it a while. Must have brought it down from Yorkshire. He changed it a couple of years later, got his first van. Another Transit, but "shit brown," she called it.'

'Well, at least it wasn't white,' Dick said.

'But we haven't got any of the registrations,' Pete pointed out.

'Two partials,' Ben said. 'The Passat was YAP something. And the van after it was OWL.'

'Well, that's not local,' Dick said. 'Oxfordshire, wasn't it?'

'Why would you even know that?' Jill asked.

'Because I'm old,' Dick told her. 'I know most things. Don't necessarily remember them, mind, but this brain's full of stuff.'

'Wisdom, knowledge is not always, Obi-wan,' Jane said with mock-solemnity.

'Old, I may be, but at least I've got there, young 'un. You might not.'

She raised an eyebrow. 'Are you threatening a police officer, Mr Feeney?'

'He isn't, but I will,' Pete broke in, 'if you don't stop buggering about and get us something useful.'

270

Jane threw him a salute. 'Aye-aye, cap'n.' She picked up her phone. 'Passat estate from Yorkshire, partial reg YAP, changed ownership around… What? 1982?'

'About that,' Ben agreed.

'Right, that's mine. You get the shitty brown Transit, Spike. We'll alternate up the list. Dick, you can check his locations against his vehicles and then against any witness statements.'

'Oi,' Pete said. 'Who's the sergeant here?'

'Me, in your absence. And I'm guessing you're about to be absent?' She nodded over his shoulder. Colin was coming down the middle of the squad room towards them.

'What about me?' asked Jill. 'Don't I get to play?'

'You get to help Dick,' Jane retorted.

Pete checked his watch and stood up. 'Whoever does what, play nice while we're out. And let our beloved lord and master know what you've found as soon as you find it. He can include in his press interview.'

*

They were early.

The post van had not yet arrived in the street when Pete pulled into his drive, Colin Underhill beside him.

They went in, Pete pausing to pick up a couple of envelopes from the doormat. He checked them. One was obviously advertising, the other had a bank logo on the outside. He ripped it open, knowing as he did so what it would be. Heading through to the lounge, he dropped both in the bin and turned to Colin.

271

'Cup of tea?' the senior man suggested.

Pete grunted. It was disconcerting to be on the other end of standard procedure for dealing with victims and their relatives. Calm them. Give them something useful to do, to take their minds off what they were inevitably focussed on. He headed for the kitchen nevertheless and flicked the kettle on.

With the tea made, they leaned against the worktops, mugs in hand.

'Any news on Dave?' Colin asked.

'He's stable,' Pete said, guessing that Colin already knew the answer. 'It took them a while with his anti-coagulants, but they've fixed him up, I'm told. Haven't been to see him yet, but I don't suppose he's awake anyway, after all they were doing to him last night.'

'I'll go later. Give him your best.'

'Ta.'

'Mark was out all bloody night, you know. And his crew. Didn't do any good, mind.'

Pete grunted. He knew - in both respects.

'If that box was posted in Taunton, it wouldn't have, though, would it?' Colin continued.

Still, Pete didn't respond apart from a shrug and a sip of his tea.

'How'd he get up there without triggering an ANPR camera, though?'

'We didn't know what vehicle he was in,' Pete pointed out. 'Still don't, as far as I know.'

'We should do soon, unless the owner's away on holiday or something.'

'Wouldn't that be our bloody luck?'

A knock sounded at the front door. Pete pushed away from the worktop and headed through, mug still in hand. He set it on the table in the hall before opening the door to the blue-shirted figure beyond.

'Parcel for you,' the postman said, handing it over.

'Thanks.' Pete returned his nod and closed the door, turning back to Colin, his tea forgotten, hands trembling as he held the small wrapped box, similar in size and shape to the one he'd received at the station.

'Where's it from?' Colin asked.

Pete glanced down, his mind a blank, emotions swirling. 'Post mark's Taunton again, but that's just the sorting office it went through, isn't it? And there's not as many of those as there used to be.'

'Best bring it through.'

Pete stepped forward, barely aware of his feet moving. It felt like an iceberg had replaced his innards from chest to groin. He couldn't feel his fingers, his face and scalp tingled, the hairs standing up on the back of his neck. The parcel in his hands felt like it was about to explode but he couldn't let go of it.

He stepped into the kitchen. Colin had moved across to the worktop opposite and taken a knife from the block. He nodded for

Pete to sit down at the small table and waited until he had before handing him the knife. 'Got any more gloves?'

Pete blinked and reached into his jacket pocket for another pair. He pulled them on and drew the box towards him again. Carefully, he cut the wrapping open and slid the box free of it. Looked up at Colin with his stomach in knots and his throat clogged as if he might be sick.

'Here, let me,' the senior man said, pulling on a pair of gloves of his own and reaching for the box.

Pete almost waved him off. Almost. But Colin sat down opposite him and began to slide the lid up and off. Pete stared, fascinated. It came free, revealing the same scrunched-up toilet paper as last time. His gaze lifted to Colin's face. Watched as he lifted out the paper wadding and set it aside. The shift in his expression and pause in his movements were slight, but he couldn't hide his reaction entirely.

Pete's eyes were drawn downward, despite himself.

He didn't want to see what was in there. Didn't want to even think about what it could be. But something inside him operated automatically, instinctively.

Colin tilted the box slightly towards himself, but Pete had already glimpsed the pink of flesh and the browning red of blood.

'What...?' He heaved. Swallowed twice. 'What is it?' he whispered.

CHAPTER TWENTY-SIX

Colin looked from Pete down to the box and up again, meeting his gaze.

'It's…' He grimaced. 'It looks life half an ear. A smallish one.'

'Bastard. Fucking evil bastard.' The nausea left Pete as the rage took over. 'He'd better hope Mark catches him before I do.'

'Focus, Pete,' Colin said. 'We need to stop this bugger. Anything you can think of might help. What do we know about these two? They're from Devises, but where do they live now? Apart from in prison, of course. Have they got any family down this way? We know they've got associates, but who, other than Malcolm Burton? And how do we find out?'

'Ask Burton,' Pete growled. 'And he's mine, not Mark's.'

'Right. Next stop, New North Road. And I'm coming with you.'

Pete gave him a look that said, *don't even think about trying to stop me.*

'As observer, not interviewer,' Colin qualified.

Pete grunted and started for the door while Colin gathered up the box and followed.

'We need to get this to forensics as soon as possible,' he said. 'Make sure it is what, and who's, we think it is. Meantime, Mark can check their prison records, see if there's anything useful there.'

Pete grunted as he unlocked the car. 'It will be what he said. Southam's not the sort for bullshit. Not in that sense.'

'I'll deal with that. You just drive. And not like Lewis bloody Hamilton.'

They climbed in. Pete gunned the engine and backed out of the drive as Colin took out his mobile phone and scrolled through the contacts list. They were passing the Co-op before he lifted it to his ear.

Pete tried to focus on his driving, but it was not easy as Colin began to speak.

'Hello. Yes, this is DI Underhill, Heavitree Road station, Exeter. I need a package collected and analysed ASAP.' He paused, listening. 'Right, I'm not there just now, but I can get it brought back to the station. OK, will do. Thanks.'

He ended the call and made another.

'Andy. Yes, this is Colin Underhill. Can you get a squad car round to the prison ASAP? I'm on the way there and I need someone to meet me, collect a piece of evidence and take it back to the station for forensics to pick up. Send someone now, they might beat us there.'

Pete ignored the comment, concentrating on the road ahead. They were about half way between his house and Heavitree Road nick: would pass it in a couple of minutes.

Colin was putting his phone away when it rang in his hand. He grunted and lifted it to his ear. 'Underhill. Yes, that's right.' He listened. 'I see. OK, I'll let my people know. Thanks for the call.'

This time, his phone got into his jacket pocket before he spoke again.

'The court house,' he told Pete. 'The trial's due to re-start next Wednesday. New judge, new jury, from scratch.'

'Which is exactly what the Southam brothers were aiming for.'

'There wasn't really an option, was there? The existing jury couldn't be expected to give Burton a fair trial after what happened.'

Pete didn't respond.

They heard sirens from somewhere in the near distance. Couldn't tell from which direction, despite the new multi-tone sirens supposedly being easier to pinpoint. Pete kept going, unable to see any flashing lights in front or behind.

Reaching the prison with its imposing dark walls a few minutes later, they saw a patrol car already in the small car park. When the occupants saw Colin rising out of the silver Ford, their doors opened and the two uniformed officers stepped forward.

'Guv? You've got something for us?'

Colin handed over the box. 'That needs to go in an evidence bag and be taken back to the station. Forensics will be there soon to collect it and take it to the lab for analysis.'

'What is it, guv?'

Colin looked sternly at the man and spoke in a hushed but firm tone. 'An ear. And that's exactly how it was sent.'

The man who was about to take the box from Colin recoiled slightly. 'An ear,' he said after a second. 'Seriously?'

'Seriously. And you see DS Gayle over there, chomping at the bit to get in? We think it's his son's.'

'Shit. Right, guv. Leave it with us.' The man reached for the box as his partner took out a plastic evidence bag and shook it out.

'Do you want to label it, guv, or should we?'

'You can. Just write on it that I gave it you.'

'Guv.'

Colin left them to it and followed Pete towards the intimidatingly large dark blue gates and the man-sized door cut into the left one.

*

'What are you doing here? My trial's not over yet, you're…'

'Not here about the trial,' Pete cut in over the smallish blond man with his shrewish features and thinning hair. 'We're here about the blokes who stopped it.'

'For which I thank them profusely.'

'You won't when you're charged as an accessory. Unless you help us.'

Burton's eyes narrowed. 'What are you talking about? I had no part in that. And if I did, I wouldn't have expected them to go that far.'

'So, what do you know about what they did?' Pete demanded.

'Just what was on the news last night. That they killed the judge and the man who was with TJ - Tommy.'

'That's all, is it?'

'What do you want me to say? That I was in on it from the start? That would be handy for you, wouldn't it? But it's not true. It was as much of a shock to me as anyone else, I swear.'

Pete was well aware of how manipulative and credible a man like Burton could be, but his whole demeanour was utterly convincing. Reluctantly, he had to admit, he believed the man. 'Well, they didn't do it for you. Trust me. And what you shouldn't know if you weren't involved, because it wasn't reported in the press, is they abducted my son and cut off his ear as a threat to me. So, I need to find out where they'd go round here. Who they'd know. What local contacts they might have, other than you.'

'And Tommy,' Burton said.

Pete's lips pressed together. 'Don't push it.'

'What else have I got left in life, sergeant?'

'That's detective sergeant to you,' Colin cut in. 'And what you've got left *is* your life, as miserable as that may be, looking forward.'

'Miserable and short, unless we like what you've got to tell us,' Pete said. 'General population can be a bitch for someone like you.'

'You can't... I won't be put in gen pop. They can't. It would infringe my human rights. Be a death sentence.'

Pete shrugged. 'Mistakes can be made. Paperwork mix-ups. Prisoners transferred incorrectly.'

'That's... That's...'

'An unfortunate truth,' Colin said.

Pete glanced at him and Colin held up his hands in apology.

'So, what have you got for us?' he asked Burton.

Burton stared at him for several seconds without responding. 'There's one bloke I know they know. He's not that local. Tiverton, I think. But we don't exactly exchange names and addresses. Best for all concerned. We just use Internet handles, even when we meet in person. Steve Southam only used his real name because he thought it would intimidate people, being a murder suspect and a martial arts expert.'

'So, how do you know this one's from Tiverton?'

'I don't for sure. It's just his handle. TiviTim.'

Pete tipped his head. It was suggestive but, even if true, it didn't mean he still lived there. In fact, it could suggest he didn't. That he'd moved. To Taunton, for example.'

'You mentioned meeting. Where would that happen, and did you ever meet TiviTim?'

Burton shrugged. 'It could happen in a variety of places. It depended on the circumstances. Usually somewhere neutral. A service area, a café, a park. Or occasionally a group would meet.' He paused, eyes narrowing suspiciously. 'I'm incriminating myself here.'

'The cameras are off,' Pete said. 'No-one's listening. This won't go towards your case. It's a separate enquiry completely. Focussed on the Southam brothers, not you.'

'So, can I make some sort of deal, here? A reduced sentence for co-operation?'

'As DS Gayle said, don't push it,' Colin interjected. 'We'll see what you can give us first.'

Burton paused, assessing his options, maybe deciding how to put what he was going to say next. Then he sighed. 'Some knew about the barn. Not where it was, but... I'd meet them and bring them to it in the back of the van so they couldn't tell where we were going.'

'And was TiviTim one of them?'

'Yes.'

'And the Southam brothers?'

Burton nodded. 'Although, after the first time, they went there under their own steam. I... They... '

'Got the location out of you by force?' Pete suggested, weighing up the man's reactions.

He gave a single shameful nod. It was the first time, Pete noted, that he'd ever shown any shame over what he'd done. The child-abuse, rape and other perversions hadn't elicited any such response. It just showed what a sick individual he was. Pete said none of this, though. He was here to gain information from the man, which meant keeping him, at least to some extent, on-side.

'I can understand that,' he said. 'So TiviTim's the only one you know who's relatively local. What about the others who turned up? How do you know they weren't?'

'I know a couple came down on the train. Others drove, so they could have come from anywhere, I suppose, but accents tell you a bit, don't they? Two or three were well-spoken. Hard to tell. But others were distinctive. One sounded Bristolian. Another from Cornwall. Two from the Midlands. Not Birmingham, but somewhere in that direction. There was one from Dorset and one from Hampshire – Southampton, Portsmouth, somewhere round there. And a couple of northerners. I imagine they must have moved somewhere closer, rather that coming all that way for a single event, though.' He shrugged. 'That's about all I can tell you.'

'I'll need a list of all the handles for those who attended.' Pete held back from adding, *your little soirees,* as he took out his note book and pen to pass them across the table.

Burton looked dubious.

'It's my note book. No-one has access to it without my permission and this is relevant to another case, not yours. I'm not even going to add your name to it.'

Burton drew a breath, took up the pen and pulled the note book towards himself to begin writing. When he was done he put the pen on top of the note book and pushed them back towards Pete.

Pete glanced down at the open page and looked up at Burton as he closed the little book and returned it and the pen to his pocket. 'And you don't know of any other links the brothers have in this area? Anybody or any places they're familiar with?'

Burton swallowed. 'Now I think of it, there's one place. They wouldn't come into the city, of course. Not to stay, at least. I know of one occasion, though, when they stayed over in the area. There was a place on the far side of the river, down past Powderham. They insisted I bring TJ and one of the girls down there one night. Got some kind of thrill out of setting something up under the owners' noses. An old boat shed, looked like it had been abandoned for years – leaky roof, holes in the walls, everything. The floor of the storage croft even had gaps in it. You could see the water through them. I don't know how they found it. It's not exactly on the tourist map, or any other I can think of. But I remember them saying they were staying close by. I presumed a hotel or B&B. They never struck me as the sort to rough it.'

'And do you remember how to get to this place?'

Burton nodded. 'It's on the Kenn, a little way north of the mill at Kenton. You take the turn-off for the mill and there's a track that goes off on the other side of the bridge, headed upstream. It's up there. So, I imagine they must have stayed somewhere in Kenton or South Town.'

And yet Southam had been roaming the lanes to the north of the city last night and ended up somewhere in the direction of Taunton. Was that him trying to distract them from the truth or was Burton doing the same? He seemed genuine, but then one of the main characteristics of men like him was their plausibility.

He watched the man carefully as he asked his next question. 'So, you don't know of any links they have to the area round Rewe and Brookleigh?'

Burton pulled his lower lip back. 'No.'

'Or anywhere between there and Taunton?'

Burton shook his head. 'As I've said, only TiviTim, although I don't know that they had any connection with him other than the barn.'

'All right. I need one more thing from you then. The exact way you contacted this TiviTim.' Pete took out his note book and pen once more and passed them across.

NO MIDDLE GROUND by JACK SLATER

CHAPTER TWENTY-SEVEN

'Dave's awake,' Jane announced as soon as Pete walked in.

'How is he?'

'Not out of the woods, but he's getting there, apparently.'

'Eyeing up the nurses, I bet,' Jill said.

'One of the perks of being ill,' Dick said, giving her a wink.

'Perv.'

'Ben, I need you to go onto the dark web,' Pete said, tilting his seat back.

'How come?'

Pete glanced over his shoulder at the three junior officers who were now at their desks on Mark Bridgman's work station. 'It's related to Malcolm Burton. Additional information from the man himself. I've got the guvnor's sanction.'

'So, what am I looking for, boss?' Ben asked.

'A subscription forum called Little Ones Play. And within it, a user whose handle is TiviTim. I need his IP address and, from that, his real one along with anything else you can dig up.'

'If it's a subscription site, won't it have his bank details?' Jane asked.

'It depends,' Ben told her. 'Some do, some don't, according to how professionally they're set up. Plus, we're talking about the dark web. Not the most trusting or trustworthy users on there.'

'Could be handy, though,' Pete observed.

'So, where is the guvnor?' Jill asked. 'He went out with you. I haven't seen him come back.'

'Observant as ever,' Pete said. 'He's still out and about. On his way to Kenton mill with a bunch of armed officers, as it happens.'

'I hope they've got telescopic sights if they're after the Powderham deer from there,' Dick said, eyes wide.

'That'd be illegal, wouldn't it?' asked Ben.

'They're not,' Pete said before they could go off on another circuitous ramble. 'They're after something much closer to home and much more dangerous. Specifically, Steve Southam. He'll have informed Mark on the way there, I expect,' he added for the benefit of any ear-wiggers on the neighbouring work station.

'I've got the site,' Ben announced. He grimaced. 'Not something your average member of the public would want to be looking at, that's for sure. Now, then...'

'Talking of average members of the public, where are we on Jonas Hanson?' Pete asked.

'We've got links to three more cases, but nothing concrete still,' Jane reported.

'Here we are. TiviTim,' Ben said. 'Let's see if I can find anything on him.'

'We need to get a move on, then, if we want to keep Hanson in custody.'

'Silly sod,' Ben said. 'He's only gone and put a link to a Twitter account on here!'

'What a mistake-a to make-a,' Dick quoted. 'Let's have a look.'

In a few clicks, Dick had a photo of the man in question and Ben had his actual name and address. 'Found him. He's not a Tim. Kenneth, actually. And he's out of our patch. A place called Ashbrittle in Somerset.'

'Never heard of it,' said Jill.

'Me neither, so I looked it up. It's a tiny little place a few miles west of Taunton.'

'He wouldn't take much finding, then,' Dick said. 'Even for the Somerset lot.'

'Hey,' Pete cautioned. 'They swept up that drug packaging place we told them about.'

'Yes, but only *because* we told them about it. How long had it been there before that?'

'It's the result that counts. I'll give them a ring. Don't want you getting their backs up.'

'Just because Dave's not here...'

'Doesn't mean you can take over from him,' Pete finished.

'Do you want me to look up anyone else on here?' asked Ben.

Pete shook his head. 'Haven't got any more specific details. But you could pass what you've found onto the NCA. Give them something to do.'

It was the job of the London-based National Crime Agency to deal with multi-jurisdictional and large-scale crimes.

'What, again?' Dick asked. 'Give them much more and they won't be able to get their heads through the Scotland Yard doors, they'll be so big, all on the back of our actual work.'

They had referred a huge child-sex case to them the previous year which had come to light during the investigation that led them to Malcolm Burton. There was no doubt in Pete's mind this would be related if not actually part of that.

'As I said a minute ago, its results that count,' Pete reminded him. 'Plus, we haven't got time to be buggering about with a job like that.' He picked up the phone and checked his notebook before dialling.

'Avon and Somerset police. How can I help?'

'This is DS Pete Gayle of Devon and Cornwall, Heavitree Road station in Exeter. We've got a favour to ask and to offer.'

'Sounds complicated.'

'We've come across a member of an on-line paedophile ring living on your patch. A little place near Taunton.' He gave the details. 'We need him picked up ASAP, but there's a potential problem. In fact, you might say two problems. A man called Steven Southam might be there and should, at all times, be considered armed and dangerous. A black-belt in Karate and a vicious bugger with it. He won't come quietly, and we believe he has a hostage – a young boy from here in Exeter who may already be injured. The National Crime Agency is going to have an interest in the main subject and we've got one in Southam and his hostage. Apart from anything else, we want him on a murder charge. And obviously the boy's parents want him back as unharmed as possible.'

He wasn't going to mention that he was one of those parents. It would only lead to complications that he didn't need.

'OK, we'll co-ordinate through the Taunton station. Thanks for the tip. We'll let you know the outcome.'

'Thanks.' He put the phone down and picked it straight back up again. This time he didn't need to look up the number.

'Silverstone.'

'Sir, we've got something we need to refer to the NCA. Information received and confirmed on a national, if not international case.'

*

Pete was searching through rape cases on the Police National Database with a similar MO to Hanson's when his phone rang. An external call. He picked it up. 'DS Gayle. How can I help?'

'It's Colin. No sign of him at Kenton.'

'Shit.'

'Yeah.'

'Thanks, guv.' He put the phone down and saw Jane frowning at him. 'The guvnor. Southam's not there.'

'Damn,' said Dick. Then he paused. 'Hang on. We've got his brother. Can he be persuaded to give up any likely locations, do you think?'

Jane laughed. 'You're joking, aren't you? He'd sit there as smug as a cat with cream all over its chops if he thought his brother had got one up on us.'

'I know, but it depends how we put the question, doesn't it?'

'How would you do it, then, Obi-wan?' Jill asked.

'By not telling him what his brother's up to, for a start. Tell him we've already got him. We're after places they might have stayed or visited down here, other than the barn.'

'He still wouldn't bite,' Jane said. 'He won't answer questions of any kind unless it's to gloat.'

'So, we need to make him look clever?' Jill checked.

Pete nodded. 'And interviewing suspects, lesson one: don't ask questions you don't already know the answers to.'

'Or maybe some of the answers,' Dick suggested. 'Enough to let him know you're onto him but you don't quite know everything yet.'

'He'd still gloat. Why not? He doesn't give a shit about prison time. He's broken out before, he'll figure he can again. And he'll rule the roost in there until he does.'

'Not worth a crack, then,' Dick said.

Pete gave a quick grimace as he shook his head. 'We've got nothing over him.'

'What about his brother? Has he got a weak point?'

'His only weakness is for little girls,' Ben put in, glancing up from his screen.

Pete held up a hand to quieten the team. 'There is one weakness we might be able to exploit.' He got up from his chair. 'Jane, with me.'

'What, he likes red-heads?' she asked as she switched off her computer screen and stood up.

'No, but you're a sight more subtle than Dick.'

'I resent that remark,' Dick protested.

'You're welcome to. As long as you're useful while you're at it.'

*

Adrian Southam had been transferred from the station to Exeter prison. Pete drove there, making a call on the way so they knew he was coming and who he wanted to speak to.

When the gate guard opened the entrance door, he blinked. 'You again? Twice in one morning. Must be a record.' He nodded to Jane. 'DC Bennett.'

As always, they were escorted across the cobbled yard to the main building, where they signed in and were led through to the interview rooms.

'He's in number two,' the guard told them and opened the door when they reached it.

Adrian Southam was seated at the central table, hands manacled to the ring built into it. He grinned as the door clanged shut behind them. 'Morning,' he said. 'This is a pleasant surprise. I do like a pretty lady.'

Pete sensed Jane stiffening beside him but she held her tongue as they sat down across from the big man. 'What the hell possessed you two, to kill a judge?' he asked.

Southam shrugged as if it was nothing out of the ordinary. 'If we couldn't get to Malcolm Burton, the judge would be the next best option, wouldn't he? Theoretically. Anyway, what are you here for, apart from to tease me with what I can't have? Yet.'

Pete's eyebrows rose. 'You wouldn't be threatening a police officer there, would you, Adrian? There's a law against that, you know. Not that you'd care. We're here about the one thing you do care about other than sex,' Pete told him. 'Your brother.'

'Yeah? What's he been up to, then? Still got your boy, has he?'

'What he's been up to is getting the armed response team on his arse,' Pete said, ignoring the second question. 'So, unless my team and I get hold of him first, he's liable to get shot.'

'And you want me to tell you where he is.' He raised his hands as far as the cuffs would allow. 'How am I supposed to do that from here?'

'You know where he's likely to be. Where you've been before around here. Where he might hole up while he waits for what isn't going to happen – your release.'

Southam winked. 'Not officially, it won't. But I've got to go to court tomorrow and all sorts of shit happens on the roads these days.'

Pete laughed. 'Don't hold your breath, matey. You'll have a full royal escort there and back. No way he'll even get close.'

The blond stubble of Southam's crew cut glittered under the fluorescent light as he tipped his head in a shrug. 'C'est la vie.'

Pete waited.

Southam waited.

'So, do you want to save your brother's life or not?' Jane asked.

'She speaks, too,' he said to Pete. 'You've got a live one there, haven't you?'

'You can't even imagine,' Pete said.

'Oh, I can. Trust me,' he leered.

Pete stayed focussed, fully aware of the revulsion that Jane would be feeling, if not displaying. 'Maybe, but that doesn't save your brother's life. Which is more important, eh?'

'One thing I'll say about that: if he dies, he'll make damn sure to take your boy out first. And you'd better be looking over your shoulder every minute of every day until I do, too. Whether I'm inside or not.'

Pete knew he wasn't bluffing: he would put a contract out on anyone he thought deserved it. But he couldn't allow the man to see his fear. 'That's two things. And there's no use threatening me or Tommy. I'm not in command of that firearms squad and they won't listen to a DS trying to call them off. They get out there, they're like a dog with a bone. There's no letting go until the target's down. Us, on the other hand – we'd at least try to bring him in alive and healthy.' He shrugged. 'Up to you, mate.'

Southam's eyes narrowed as he tried to weigh Pete up and determine if he was telling the truth.

Eventually he seemed to reach a decision.

'You'd best make your peace with the idea of losing a son, then. But there's two places we've stayed down here. One's Kingskerswell, near Newton Abbot. The other's Ottery St Mary. Out of the way, small hotels, just big enough to stay off the radar, not be noticed.'

'I'll need details,' Pete told him. 'What do the likes of you two get up to in places like that? I'd have thought you'd get bored out of your brains.'

'You don't know anything about us.'

'You don't seem like the rural rambling types.'

'Well, that just goes to show, dunnit? We don't spend all our time in pubs and clubs, you know.'

Move on, Pete thought. *Maybe the trip up to Taunton was just a decoy, then.* He held his hands up. 'Far be it from me to judge a book by its cover. There's nowhere else you know of he might run to, but stay close to Exeter?'

A sharp frown crossed Southam's brow then he shrugged. 'The place ain't big enough to get lost in the crowds, is it? Torquay might be, I suppose, but he's not the bucket and spade type.' He grinned. 'Mind you… He is partial to some of those who are. So, no. There's nowhere else I know of that he'd stay. Unless he's got a car big enough to kip in, off the road, somewhere quiet.'

Which was a possibility Pete hadn't wanted to think about. Especially as they still didn't know what vehicle he was in.

'Nothing up around Taunton area?' he pressed. 'Ashbrittle, for example?'

Southam's eyes narrowed again. 'What about it?'

'We heard about a friend of yours lives up there. Our Avon and Somerset colleagues are on the way to pick him up as we speak. Probably there by now, I should think.'

The stocky man grunted. A tiny trace of a snarl pulled at his lip before he masked it. 'What friend?'

'TiviTim who isn't a Tim at all.'

Beside Pete, Jane reached into her pocket, took out her phone and checked the screen. 'Excuse me, boss.' She held up the phone and turned away to knock on the door to be let out.

'Steve wouldn't go there.'

'Why?'

'The bloke's a bullshit artist. Likes to confuse folk. Like, you'd assume Tivi would mean Tiverton, but it doesn't. He comes from up near Minehead. And Tim - well, you already know that's not his real name.'

Pete tipped his head. 'We do.'

The door opened behind him.

'Boss?'

He turned. She looked hesitant. 'Jane?'

She held the phone up. Beckoned him out with a tilt of her head.

Pete turned back to Adrian Southam. 'Don't go away. I'll be back in a tick.'

Southam gave him a sarcastic smile as he stood up and stepped out to the corridor, waiting for the guard to close the door behind him before asking Jane, 'What is it?'

'It's Tommy. Ben's got an email alert thing set up to search for anything new coming up on him. Had it since last year. He opened it and found a video clip. We need to find him. Fast.'

CHAPTER TWENTY-EIGHT

'Ben,' Pete said into the car's Bluetooth system as soon as it connected to his mobile. 'What have you got?'

'A video clip, boss. Streamed live, but not long enough to trace its source. I got an alert on it a few seconds after it went up. It had already finished by the time I knew about it.'

'What was it, Ben?' Pete demanded impatiently.

'Tommy. Trussed up and suspended by his ankles from a branch over a river. Couldn't tell where; there wasn't enough background and what there was, was full of trees. His hair was just touching the water and whoever was behind the camera was saying, "The tide's coming in."'

'Sounds like he's been watching too many American movies,' Dick said in the background as Pete almost slammed the brakes on as his stomach writhed, fear clutching at his soul. 'You remember the old B-movies they used to play after the main feature in the flicks when you were a kid, boss?'

Pete didn't have time for reminiscences, especially irrelevant ones. 'Where do we know, relatively local, that's wooded on the side of the water?'

'Powderham?' Ben suggested.

'There's some woods further down from there, too, near Kenton,' Jane said.

'Some on the Otter near Kersbrook,' Dick added in the background.

'That's about it that's tidal, I think,' Jane said.

'There's some on the Teign as well,' Ben said. 'Down from Newton Abbot, near Netherton.'

'How do you know that?' Jane asked.

'I didn't. I'm on Google Maps. I've saved the video clip in case we need it.'

'Shit, that's four locations and we haven't got time to be wrong,' Pete said.

'I'll get the Newton Abbot boys out to Netherton,' Dick said. 'That leaves three.'

'Where's Colin?' Pete asked, unaware of his unusual use of the DI's first name in a professional situation.

'Just got back here five minutes ago, boss,' Ben said.

'In that case, Jane and I are closest to Powderham and Kenton. We'll go to Kenton. Dick, get yourself out to Kersbrook if you know the area and Ben, go to Powderham.'

'What if the big boss asks what's going on?'

'I'll talk to Colin in a minute.'

'Right, we're moving.' Ben cut the call as Pete hit the roundabout at the top end of the New North Road and swung around it to head the other way, back past the university towards the edge of the city. As he passed a modern brick building that looked like a block of flats, he tapped Colin's number into the car's comms system.

'DI Underhill.'

'Colin, its Pete. There wasn't time for protocol. The team are off out to try to find Tommy. Ben got a lead and it's an urgent one. If we don't' get to him in time, he'll drown.'

'OK, I'll square it with the chief and let Mark know. Do you need any help?'

'Air ops might be useful, but we've got four possible locations.'

'I'll get them up if they aren't already.'

Although it was based at Exeter airport, the police helicopter covered the whole of Devon and Cornwall. It couldn't be in two places at once.

'Thanks. You could get the Ottery station to check out the woods overlooking the river near Kersbrook. Dick's on the way but they're closer. The Newton Abbot boys should already be heading out to the second site and we've got the other two at Powderham and Kenton covered unless the helo can get there quicker. They'll want the infra-red to spot him.'

'Right. You're talking riverside woods – what about Dukes Meadow?'

'Shit.' Pete slumped in his seat. 'Hadn't thought of that.'

Like his team, Pete had been thinking further out, more secure from Southam's point of view. But the irony of setting Tommy up in the city, right under their noses, sure they wouldn't suspect it, would definitely appeal to his warped mind.

'I'll send someone.' The ring tone signified that Colin had put his phone down.

Pete hit the Topsham Road with the blues and twos flashing and screaming. Traffic parted, opening the way despite the narrow road. He climbed the hill, slamming up through the gears as the road levelled and straightened ahead of him, roaring out towards the golf club roundabout where he turned right towards the old stone bridge across the broad expanse of the Exe and its accompanying canals and marshes.

He turned south, heading towards Exminter, and was passing the filling station when his phone rang. He glanced at the screen as he slowed the car, braking for the turn into the small industrial estate on the left. *Colin.* He hit the green button on the screen and swung the wheel across.

'Guv?'

'You should see the chopper coming over your head any minute.'

Pete breathed out for the first time in several seconds. 'Thank you.'

Again, Colin rang off without further comment.

Pete kept the blue lights flashing as he accelerated down the little lane that passed the industrial estate and cut out across the marshes towards the riverside road that would take him down past the Powderham castle grounds towards Kenton and Starcross. There was no traffic here, the road rarely used except by the occasional farmer or someone cutting across towards the yacht club. Grass grew up the middle in places, sparse hedges protecting it from cross-winds and rare passing places allowing two-way traffic. At least you would see any on-coming traffic in plenty of time, despite the bends in the road, across the flat, open land.

They hadn't made the riverside road yet when Jane pointed up and ahead. 'There.'

The still distant blue and yellow chopper was cutting across the river, angling to the south of them towards Kenton.

'Get on the radio,' Pete said. 'We don't need to intervene but at least we can hear what's going on.'

Jane reached for the car's communications system and switched it to the police radio, setting the volume so they could hear comfortably.

'Target area in sight. Switching to infra-red.'

'Roger.'

The helicopter swept closer, curving south as Pete neared the junction ahead. Then it began to hover, sinking lower over the river. He knew the infra-red cameras were of limited use through tree-cover so no doubt they were getting low to disturb the branches so they could get flashes of anything warm beneath the leaf canopy.

Slowing, he turned right onto a road that was hardly wider than the one he'd left, but at least was a little better maintained. Water was lapping only a foot or so below the weeds and bushes to his left. He pressed the accelerator, picking up speed in a desperate race to reach his search area before the tide peaked.

As he sped along the narrow road, he couldn't help picturing in his mind a trussed-up Tommy writhing upside down on the end of a rope, his hair brushed by the lapping salt-water, stomach aching and head swimming as he struggled to stay alive, hoping and praying that someone would find him before it was too late.

Something Dick had said finally sank in. This *was* like a bad B-movie. Had Steve Southam been watching too many 1960s American TV shows? Re-runs of Mission Impossible and the like? Or old adventure films?

It didn't matter where he'd found his inspiration for this latest piece of cruelty. What mattered was making sure it didn't succeed.

Then something else struck him.

'Where would he have got the rope?' he asked Jane. It wasn't something the average person randomly carried around with them and Southam didn't have the build to be a climber.

'Does it matter at this moment?' she countered. 'We know he got it. Knowing where from won't help us catch him.'

'It might if he goes back to wherever he spent the night. He wouldn't have gone too far to get hold of it.'

'Unless it was in the car he stole.'

Pete's lips pursed, frustration flaring inside him that he struggled not to release. '*Helpful* suggestions would be appreciated,' he said.

He felt Jane's stare on the side of his face. She was silent for a long count. 'There's limited options round here, I suppose. Farm supplies. Sports places for sailing, paragliding and so forth. I don't know where else.'

'Get on the phone. Get some people searching.'

He reached the outer edge of the Powderham deer park, refused to allow his gaze to go across towards the castle. The helicopter was still hovering over the trees to his left. The urge to stop and search from the ground was almost overpowering but he forced himself to keep driving. Ben was only a couple of minutes behind him at most, and Southam was likely to stretch him as far as he could. The whole plan was clearly designed for maximum impact and stress, pushing the police resources and Pete to the limit and beyond.

Jane began speaking into her phone, leaving the car's comms system to provide them with radio commentary of the helicopter search.

'We need feet on the ground to agricultural and water-sports retailers. Has anyone seen Steven Southam in the last twenty-four hours? Specifically, buying rope or cordage of any kind. Anywhere else that might sell it, too.'

Then her voice was drowned out by the noise of the helicopter as it swept forward overhead, the crew unable to see anything relevant at Powderham. They were moving on to the woods further down the estuary near Kenton. The woods Pete was heading for.

*

'We've got something.'

Pete was still half a minute out from his destination when the call came over the radio. But he didn't recognise the voice. It wasn't the chopper.

'Stand by.'

Where the hell were they?

Pete tensed, ready to put his foot down hard, despite the narrowness of the road.

'It's a body.'

'No,' Pete groaned, his face pulling into a grimace of pain and grief as his hands tensed on the wheel and his stomach knotted. He felt Jane's hand on his leg, squeezing briefly.

'Steady, boss.'

'Correction. He's alive.'

Pete let out a huge sigh as Jane's reassuring hand left his leg.

'Ambulance needed immediately, Netherton woods.'

The north bank of the Teign, a few miles from their current location.

Pete slammed his foot down, ignoring Jane's protest, 'Whoah! Easy, boss. No need to kill us. There's people already there with him.'

They swept under the hovering helicopter, which would keep searching until the target was confirmed. Soon after, they reached the South Town area of Kenton. Pete hit the sirens, barely slowing for the junction with the main road as he turned left towards Starcross.

'Victim not responding.'

This was a main tourist route. There was no telling what bumbling fools would be trundling up and down it at this time of year, acting as if they'd got all week to travel the five miles to the next coffee shop, so he kept the sirens on as they sped south at a pace that was just short of reckless. His police training came to the fore as he passed cars, vans and lorries that braked and pulled over when they caught his approach. Then he came up behind an old Morris Minor that refused to move with a lorry coming towards them, a line of cars behind it.

'Jesus!' he muttered and hit the horn repeatedly.

It still took seconds for the driver of the little car to register their presence on the narrow road with its stone walls up either side. There was nowhere to pull over now if they wanted to.

'Scene photographed, victim recovered,' the report came over the radio. *'We need to untie him to commence CPR. We'll preserve what evidence we can.'*

'Get on with it,' Pete growled.

Finally, the oncoming traffic thinned and Pete pulled out to pass the old car, expecting to see an old man with white hair under a flat cap at the wheel as they passed.

'Jesus!' he muttered, glancing across to see a young woman at the wheel, a pair of bright yellow earphones clamped over her head. 'What the bloody hell goes through these people's brains?'

'You're assuming they've got some,' Jane responded.

He kept driving, reaching the railway town of Starcross and rushing through it. It was about another five miles to their destination. If he could maintain current speed, it would take no more than five minutes to get there, but five minutes could make the difference between life and death if Tommy had stopped breathing. And the ambulance, although coming from Newton Abbot, would be at least as far away as he was.

There was nothing more over the radio until the helicopter crew confirmed, 'Nothing found at Kenton. Returning to base.'

'Roger,' came the reply from control.

Pete and Jane were silent as he concentrated on driving, the road now clear of traffic.

Pete couldn't keep his mind from conjuring images of Tommy. He must have been trussed up like a Christmas turkey, suspended by his ankles over the rising water, able only to wriggle and writhe or use his stomach muscles to bend upwards out of the lapping brine. But they would have quickly weakened. The pain would have been excruciating but desperation would have kept him straining until he couldn't anymore. The blood would have been rushing to his head, pressure building as his whole vascular system tried to adapt to the unnatural state of inversion that it was not designed to cope with. He would have got quickly swimmy-headed so that concentration and even coherent thought was difficult. Then his stomach muscles would have finally admitted defeat, leaving no more that swinging and writhing to keep his head above water. But even that would only have worked for a while. He would have swallowed the salty water. May have been sick, which could be disastrous in his upside-down position, but even if it wasn't, when he could no longer hold his breath, swallowing water would have given way to breathing it.

Pete just hoped the Newton Abbot officers hadn't been too late: could bring him back from the brink.

Minutes stretched out like the road ahead. They seemed to be getting no closer as time ticked past. He itched to put his foot to the floor, but safety still registered at the back of his mind. He wasn't alone in the car. He would never forgive himself if he caused anything to happen to Jane. Yet, at the same time, he wasn't sure he'd be able to handle it if he got there and found Tommy dead.

At last, he reached Teignmouth. The tourist town was busy, roads clogged with traffic and pedestrians. He kept the sirens on, the undulating sound echoing off the buildings. People were slower to react here, unsure of where he was until they saw his flashing lights.

This was where a light bar on the top of the car would have been an advantage. Flashing lights in the grille were much less visible in a closely-packed environment, especially in daylight.

Frustration boiling inside him, he worked his way through the town and finally free of it, heading upstream towards the larger, more urban area of Newton Abbot, the wide expanse of the river close on his left, water rippling and glittering in the sun.

Two minutes at most and he would be there.

Open rolling hills fell gently towards the estuary from his right. A line of trees sheltered the fields from the worst of the salt spray that would be lifted by a southerly wind in the colder months, but Pete had no time for such thoughts now. Above everything, he needed to get to Tommy.

He saw the flash of blue in the distance ahead, dimly heard the tone of a siren other than his own. The ambulance. He could see a bunch of trees ahead. Hardly a spinney, never mind a wood, but it appeared to stretch across the road and right down to the river.

He saw more flashing blue lights, not sure yet whether they were amongst or beyond the trees.

'Ambulance arriving. PC four five niner still performing CPR on the victim.' The words over the radio were followed by two notes of the ambulance's siren, then the broadcast was cut off as the man released the transmit button.

The second constable would be at the roadside to direct the ambulance crew in.

Pete reached the edge of the trees, sunlight giving way to deep, dappled shade so abruptly that, for a second, he could hardly see.

Then the blue lights gave him a direction. He pulled up facing a patrol car, an ambulance parked behind it, lights flashing on both. He jumped out of the car almost before the engine had stopped turning, looked around desperately. They would be down to the left, but he could see nothing. Then he made out a narrow mud path. He didn't even lock the car before setting off at a run, Jane somewhere behind him, her low-heeled shoes not suited to the soft ground.

Still, he could see no sign of the police and ambulance crew attending his son.

Finally, sliding around a muddy bend in the path, he caught a glimpse. A figure in green coming towards him through the trees. Moments later, another glimpse: a better view. Both members of the crew, moving fast, a stretcher between them. They vanished again in the dense trees. A darker figure replaced them briefly. One of the coppers.

Pete kept running, dodging left and right around trees and bushes. A fallen branch blocked the path. He jumped over it. Saw the approaching EMT's again, much closer. No more than a few yards. He saw the blanket draped over the stretcher. They were running.

Oh, God. He felt suddenly weak with fear, but gravity kept him going rapidly downhill.

They were closing fast. Just feet now.

He jumped off the path, took out his warrant card and held it up. 'How is he?'

He saw Tommy's face, lying there. He looked calm. Pale. Pete's heart went out to him, a physical ache in his chest as his son went past, riding the stretcher up towards the ambulance and, hopefully, salvation.

'Not good,' the lead man said briefly. Then they were past. Pete turned, about to follow when the first of the police officers caught sight of him.

'This way, sir.' He stopped, looking grateful for the excuse. It was a steep climb and he was a big man, two or three stones overweight. Plus, modern uniforms included about twenty-five kilos of kit.

Pete glanced back towards his son, desperately ill on that stretcher. He was torn. Professionalism demanded he attend the scene, but his son needed him to be there, up at the roadside, in the ambulance as the crew fought to save him.

But Jane was back there. The boy knew and liked her. And the scene of crime wouldn't keep forever.

He grimaced, sucked a deep breath in through his nose, his body tense as logic and reason fought for dominance against raw emotion. His teeth ground together as the turmoil raged inside him. He didn't know which way he was going to go until, almost without conscious input, he spoke. 'Jane, stay with him,' he shouted back up the hill, then turned back to the uniformed officer. 'Lead on.'

The man turned gratefully just as his partner caught up. He thrust his chin at the older man, telling him to turn back.

He'd seen Pete's warrant card, but only from a distance. 'You know the victim, sir?' he asked as they started back down, Pete following.

Pete's lips tightened. He was tempted to tell him the truth but fought it down. 'Yes.'

*

They led him to a point on the bank of the tidal river that was just like every other place for yards to left and right except for the down-trodden grass and weeds and the big old oak standing just a few feet from the water, several twisted, rough-barked branches extending out like writhing pythons over the lapping flow.

The younger man pointed to a position among the branches. 'There, sir. That's where he was suspended from. How the hell his attacker got up there and back, Christ knows.'

He threw the rope from right where you're standing, Pete thought, shaking his head. *No bloody idea.*

'We retained the bindings,' the second one said, holding up three evidence bags. Pete could see that one of them contained only a piece of crumpled cloth.

A gag.

Which would soak up the water, intensifying the terrifying experience and speeding up the process of drowning as it acted like the towel used in what the Americans called waterboarding.

Pete turned away, trying to hide his distress as his stomach heaved. He coughed, clearing his clogged throat and reached for one of the other bags, holding it high as he examined the contents.

They had cut the rope in such a way as to preserve the knots, showing both their positioning and their technique as well as retaining any forensic evidence they might contain.

Not that he needed to identify the suspect in this case.

'Good,' he said, handing it back. Maybe they weren't completely clueless after all. 'Anything else?' He cast his gaze around the small patch of ground. 'Footprints, cigarette butts, anything he might have dropped?'

'Nothing we've found, guv.'

Pete doubted there would be anything useful. 'OK,' he said. 'I'll go and check on the victim, then, if you want to get that stuff to forensics. DS Gayle, Heavitree Road.' He reached out to shake their hands.

'PC Petersen and PC Tufnell, Newton Abbot,' the older of the two said in response.

Pete gave them a nod of thanks and headed back up the slope. He'd got only a few yards when a siren indicated the ambulance was on the move. A new sense of urgency powered him forward as he took out his phone and dialled Jane.

'Where are you?' he asked when she picked up.

'In the ambulance, on the way to Torbay General. He's… They're trying everything, boss, but it doesn't look good.'

Pete was running up the hill, breathing hard. Jane's tone told him much more than her words. His throat clogged so he could barely breathe. He needed to stop, to hang his head and wail out his grief, but he forced himself onward, the need to be with his son overpowering everything else. He fought to bring his emotions under control enough that he could speak. 'I'll follow. There's nothing here for us.' *Steve bloody Southam, I'm coming for you, you screwed up bastard. And if my boy dies you better hope I don't find you before someone else does.*

NO MIDDLE GROUND by JACK SLATER

CHAPTER TWENTY-NINE

It was probably an abuse of privilege, but Pete didn't even think about it as he pulled up beside the ambulance at Torbay General hospital and followed the crew with the trolley his son was lying on into the building, Jane at his side.

They had called ahead and were met just inside the doors by two doctors and several nurses who rushed the trolley through into the trauma room.

One of the doctors held up a hand to stop Pete and Jane.

'I'm his father,' Pete told him brusquely. 'And a copper.'

The doctor seemed to relent. At least, he gave up the idea of trying to stop them.

A nurse whipped the curtains around while another readied the resuscitation paddles. The machine gave a high-pitched whine as it charged rapidly, a third nurse quickly hooking him up to an ECG monitor. A steady tone was emitted from the machine.

Tommy's heart was not beating. His thin chest was already bare from the ambulance crew's attempts to revive him. It looked remarkably vulnerable and horrifyingly still. Pete saw the red marks of the rope bindings livid against the paleness of his arms, legs and chest and anger swelled again, pushing the fear aside.

The nurse handed the charged paddles to a waiting medic. 'Clear,' he called and pressed the pads to Tommy's chest before triggering them. Tommy jerked violently, rising up from the bed despite his arms and legs remaining limp. The whine of the ECG remained steady, the higher-pitched scream of the recharging paddles underlying it. Again, the doctor called, 'Clear.'

Again, he triggered the paddles.

Again, the ECG trace remained resolutely flat.

'Epinephrine,' the doctor snapped.

'Isn't that…' Jane started as the nurse handed him a pre-prepared syringe. 'Jesus!'

He'd slammed the needle straight into the centre of Tommy's chest like he was hammering on a door. Now he squeezed the contents out of it.

'What the…'

'Adrenaline straight to the heart can sometimes shock it into re-starting,' Pete told her as the doctor withdrew the needle and handed it back to the nurse before starting to pump the boy's chest with the heels of his crossed hands.

The monitor beeped rhythmically in time with the compressions. Unconsciously Pete gripped Jane's shoulder, the tension squeezing his very soul.

'Come on, son,' he said through tight lips.

The doctor kept going. A dozen beats. Twenty.

'Come on, Tommy. Stay with us,' Pete insisted.

The doctor stopped at fifty compressions and the ECG flat-lined immediately. He shook his head. Looked first at the rest of the trauma team then across at Pete.

'No,' Pete moaned. 'No. No!' His denials grew louder. Desperately, he looked from one to another of the hospital staff, but none would meet his gaze. He turned to Jane, but then turned away. She wasn't his wife. To seek comfort from her would be wrong in so many ways.

She reached out to him. 'I'm sorry, boss.'

But Pete wouldn't allow her touch to penetrate the infinite depth of his grief. He felt like he was falling into a dark pit, a bottomless shaft of inky blackness where no light, no touch, no humanity could penetrate. He didn't know whether to go to Tommy or to turn and leave, get out of there, be alone with his grief.

He stepped forward.

'I'm sorry, son,' he murmured. 'I'm so sorry.' *For everything,* he thought, dimly aware of the other people around him – people he didn't want to share his private thoughts with. *For not being a better father. For not finding you last year when you were missing – were with Malcolm Burton. And most of all, for doubting you. For thinking, even for an instant, that you might have been guilty of what he said you were – of what the evidence we had suggested you were.*

If the boy was really dead but was spiritually still here, then would he be able to read Pete's thoughts? He doubted it. He was too much of a realist to believe in such things. Nevertheless, he hoped the boy's spirit, if it was here, could see and sense his grief and sorrow, his regret for not being a better father.

'You did all you could, boss,' Jane said, putting a hand on his shoulder. 'We all did.'

'It wasn't enough, though, was it?' he snapped, turning on her. 'He's gone. And now I've got to tell his mother and his sister.'

His face screwed up as the bitterness welled up inside him. 'Steve bloody Southam's cut him down before he could even get to be a man. I'll kill the evil son-of-a-bitch, so help me, I will if I can get my hands on him,' he snarled.

Jane said nothing, though he could tell she was itching to. *'No, you won't, boss,'* he imagined her saying. *'You're too good a man to stoop to his level, even after this.'*

You don't know what you're talking about, he thought. *I appreciate your faith in me, but I swear, if I catch him, I will finish the bastard.*

'The thing is, how are we going to track him down?' Jane asked.

Do you really expect me to give a flying fuck at this moment? 'I don't know, Jane,' he said. 'But trust me – we will. Now give me a minute, will you? All of you.' He let his gaze roam around the faces of the hospital staff as he said it, coming back finally to rest on Jane's vivid green eyes. 'I need...' His throat clogged with emotion. 'I need to be with my...' he whispered. 'My son.' His eyes closed and he squeezed them tight to hold back the tears that he could feel prickling at the backs of them as his throat bulged and his lip quivered. Then his body began to shake. He withdrew into himself, barely aware of Jane nodding for the others to leave and following them out of the curtained cubicle, pulling the drapes across behind her.

He stepped forward. Rested a hand on Tommy's arm and bent down to kiss his forehead, ignoring the raw and bloody injury to his ear which the nurses had had no time to deal with. Now, he could speak his mind in private. 'I'm so sorry, son,' he murmured. 'I wish I could have been a better dad to you. I did try, even before you went missing, but even more so afterwards. And I wish I could have found you when you were gone, but you know how it works. There's only

315

so much a bloke can do when he's directly involved in the case like I was. We all did all we could, though. Your mum, your sister, the guys at the station. Well,' he grunted. 'Not Simon Phillips, maybe, but he always was a lazy arse-hole.

'I miss you already. I have ever since you went, last May. And I never seriously believed you were guilty of what Burton said you were, despite the evidence. I just hadn't figured out a way of proving it yet, that's all. I'd have got there, given a bit more time. And I was so proud of you in that courtroom. I really was.' He squeezed the thin arm he was holding and drew a deep breath, letting it out in a sigh. 'So now I've got to go and catch the bugger who did this to you. Because, whether I'm officially on the case or not, I'm here and he's out there somewhere, a danger to society. And you're…' he stopped, his throat closing up again as emotion overwhelmed him. Bowing his head, he let his tears drip onto Tommy's bare chest. Sobs began to wrack his body. He tried to hold them back, keep them in, keep his grief to himself, but the feelings were too strong. He sank to his knees beside the bed, both hands clutching Tommy's arm and hand as he gave up the fight and let it all go.

*

He didn't know how long it was until he calmed down and stood up. He kissed Tommy's brow once more. 'Rest easy, son,' he whispered. 'I'll get him, don't you worry.'

He wiped his eyes with a cursory hand and stepped out through the curtain. Jane was waiting a few steps away, near the door on the far side of the long, narrow room. One of the nurses was with her but they weren't speaking. Jane looked across as he emerged and took a step forward. The nurse turned towards him, a large woman with soft strawberry-blonde hair tied up in a bun and a kind face.

'I'm so sorry,' she said.

'Thank you,' Pete returned. 'And thanks, all of you, for trying to save him.'

She reached out with both hands to take one of his briefly as she moved past, towards the cubicle where Tommy lay.

Where Tommy's body lay, he thought firmly.

'You all right, boss?' Jane asked.

He nodded, not trusting himself to speak. Of course he wasn't all right, but he was as near to it as he was going to get for a while. He blinked. Took a deep breath.

CHAPTER THIRTY

Pete was silent for a long time as they drove back towards Exeter, his mind numb and empty.

Jane had asked if he felt he could drive but Pete had decided the concentration would be good for him. He'd drop her off at the station before going on to the RDE, to Louise. He had to tell her about Tommy in person. It was the only way.

They were over half way back when he remembered something. 'You asked earlier how we're going to track down Steve Southam. There's been nothing from Honiton about the stolen vehicle so maybe he got lucky on that, but he must be somewhere. He must have stayed somewhere. Not last night, maybe, but before that. And with his brother when they came down here before. Adrian mentioned two options: Kingskerswell and Ottery St Mary. He'd probably have gone back to one of them. An out-of-town hotel, off the main roads: somewhere remote enough not to overdo the security, where he might be accepted as a familiar face. There can't be that many around those two places. And if he was lying, we widen the search to anywhere in a sensible range of Exeter and Burton's barn. We'll need to get out and about in person with the Southams' mug-shots, see if anyone recognises them – other than from the news reports.'

'I'll call in, get things started. The Newton Abbot boys can help out again with Kingskerswell. Ottery can see to their own patch again, too. I'll have a word with the guvnor if we have to widen it out.'

Pete nodded, not trusting himself to speak again for a moment. He was deeply grateful for Jane's unquestioning acceptance of his need to continue with the case, despite the rules against it.

Then another thought struck him.

'There's two things that Steve Southam's fixated on now. One's getting his brother out of prison, which isn't going to happen, and the other's hurting me. If we could convince him that Tommy's still alive and able to testify against him, he might come out of the woodwork.'

'A baited trap. Yes.' She paused then continued carefully. 'They'll have to bring Tommy back to Exeter. If that was done with an ambulance, blue-lighting it back there as if it had a critical patient on-board, Tommy on a stretcher in the back, a side-room arranged for him to supposedly occupy on ICU.' She looked at him. 'Do you reckon it would work?'

'I don't know, but its one more string to the bow in case the hotel angle doesn't pan out.'

*

Someone was pulling out of a space in the twenty-minute pick-up zone outside the main entrance of the Royal Devon and Exeter hospital as Pete drove up, so he stopped and reversed into the space they'd left, switched off the engine and sat, lost in thought.

His eyes closed and he hung his head as he thought of his son, who he had consistently failed ever since he stepped beyond toddlerhood. He'd been reliably absent whenever he was needed, work consistently taking precedence over family life until, even at the end, he'd failed the boy. Failed to protect him from Malcolm Burton, from the Southam brothers and ultimately failed to find him

319

before Steve Southam could put him through the most horrendous, tortuous death.

It was Pete's fault, he concluded, that Tommy had died in the way he had – agonised, alone and terrified, miles from the comforting presence of his loved ones and knowing that suspicion still hung over him and now would forever. Pete's face screwed up there in his car, shame and grief tearing at his soul.

Then fear nudged in beside them. How was he supposed to tell Louise that she'd lost the son that she'd spent so long waiting to recover - that she'd gone through so much for over the past year or more, even beyond the normal maternal stresses and hardships that had preceded Tommy's disappearance last May - that she'd mostly gone through alone, unsupported by the absentee husband that Pete had become? How would she react to this latest blow? Not so much in the immediate moment, though that would be hard enough, but beyond that.

A sob forced its way out. Even alone in the car, he tried to turn it into a cough, but it didn't work. It was followed by another. He brought his hands up to cover his face as he felt the unwelcome moisture on his cheeks again.

The thought of possibly losing her – of losing both her and Annie, for she certainly wouldn't leave her daughter with him if she went – was more than he could bear. He couldn't lose them too. He just couldn't. His life would be over. Wasted. He'd be left as bereft and terrified, as alone and agonised, albeit emotionally rather than physically, as Tommy had been in his final moments.

Maybe that was Tommy's justice. To destroy the man who had let him down so often throughout his short and blighted life. It would be fitting after all.

But that selfish release couldn't come before he'd at least gained justice for the boy. Revenge of sorts, albeit through the courts rather than the direct personal violence of Charles Bronson's seemingly endless Death Wish movie series. He wouldn't stoop to that. Not now, with the immediate threat to his son over. But he would catch the vicious bastard who'd put the boy through such needless and sadistic cruelty.

Before that, though, he had to face his wife, to tell her that her eldest child was no longer alive and to try to support her through the agony of loss.

In the back of his mind, he was aware that he was soon going to have to tell his daughter the same thing: that she'd lost the older brother that she'd doted on and delighted in almost since she'd been born. But that was for later. Now, he had to get out of this car, go in there and face Louise with the worst news of her life.

Of either of their lives.

He pulled in a breath, wiped his eyes with the heels of his hands and reached for the door handle.

Walking into the hospital was like an out-of-body experience. He felt completely numb and detached, his senses distant and remote, like his brain was somehow disconnected from his body or at least only tenuously linked to it. He was aware of the people around him, but only in the vaguest of ways – as colours and shapes moving past him rather than as sentient, recognisable human beings. If anyone spoke to him, he was unaware of it as he moved through the big reception area, heading for the ward he knew Louise would be working on.

Even as he pushed through the doors onto that ward, he still felt the same remoteness, like he was viewing his surroundings not as immediate reality but through the eyes of a drone he was somehow controlling and directing from a distance.

Vaguely, as if through cotton-wool, he heard his name. It was repeated. He blinked. Turned. Shook his head as if that would dislodge whatever was getting in the way of his connection to the world around him.

'Pete. Are you all right?' It was Louise's friend and colleague, Janet Hedges. Pete had joked and flirted with her countless times over the past few years. Now she looked at him with an expression of deep worry.

'Where's Lou?' he asked.

'Here, sit down. I'll fetch her.' She indicated the door to the tiny space they called a staffroom – hardly bigger than a cupboard, but containing a kettle, a tiny sink and a handful of worn-out seats along with an assortment of mugs and the makings of tea and coffee. 'Do you want a drink?'

Pete shook his head and, still moving as if under remote control, perched on the edge of a low seat as if he didn't belong there and was prepared to run at the briefest notice.

He had no idea of the passage of time. It could have been seconds or hours before he sensed someone walking in to his right.

'Pete? What is it? What's happened?'

He turned and looked up at the woman he loved – that he'd loved since they were barely out of school – and he was lost. He had no idea what to say or how to say it. As a police officer, he was trained how to handle situations like this – how to tell someone that they'd lost a loved one. But all that had deserted him now. He had nothing but the emotion that welled up suddenly like the bursting of a dam inside him. He surged up out of the chair and took her in his arms, squeezing her so tightly that he felt her gasp and tense, but he couldn't let go as his emotions came pouring out in a flood of sobs that he didn't care who heard or saw.

He didn't care about anything at this moment, other than the woman in his arms and the overwhelming need to keep her there, to give her comfort and draw it from her.

He felt her arms around him and it felt as good as anything ever had in his life.

'Pete? What is it? What's wrong?' She sounded scared and... In pain, he realised suddenly and eased the grip of his arms around her.

'I'm sorry,' he said. 'I'm so sorry.'

'Pete?'

One more sob wracked his body. 'It's...' He felt like something had dropped out of him, out of the very core of him, leaving an empty space right in the centre of his body. He couldn't breathe. He could barely stand. Only the fact that he was holding onto Louise kept him from collapsing. 'It's Tommy,' he choked. 'He's... Gone.'

'What do you mean, gone? What...?' She pushed herself back from him, staring up into his face. 'What do you mean, gone?' she repeated more forcefully.

'He's dead, Lou.'

'No!' she wailed. 'No, he can't be. He can't be dead!'

He gathered her into his arms again, but she pushed him back.

'No! You're wrong. You need to get out there and find him.'

323

He shook his head. 'No, Lou. I did find him. It's… Oh, God, I'm sorry. I wish it wasn't true – more than anything, I do. But it is.'

She pushed back again, more forcefully this time, and he saw the glitter of anger in her eyes. 'And you… Where were you when it happened, eh? Where?'

'I was trying to find him. I was…' As the realisation hit him, something broke inside him again. 'I was probably only a few hundred yards away,' he whispered.

'And you didn't save him.' Her small fist struck his chest with the force of anger and grief. 'You didn't save him! How could you! How could you be so close and not save him? God, you make me sick! Your precious bloody job's more important to you than the rest of the world put together – including us!'

Pete was lost. What could he say? What could he tell her? 'That's not true. It never has been, not for an instant. You and the kids, you're everything to me. I'd give up the job, give up everything for this not to have happened. And I tried, Lou. God knows I tried! I just…' He grimaced. 'I just couldn't get there in time.'

'Couldn't or were too busy to?' she snarled. 'Tied up on another bloody case, as usual, were you?' Then something registered in her eyes and Pete felt a new dread creep up inside him. 'Couldn't get where?' Her voice had calmed, deadened, focussed. 'Where was he?'

'He was down by the Teign,' he said.

'And you knew this?'

'Not until the last minute, and it was too late by then.'

'How did you know? How did he die, Pete?'

Oh, Jesus. 'We knew because Southam told us. He sent us a message. Just didn't tell us *where* he was.'

'So… Tommy knew what was happening before it happened? How long before? How did he…?' She stopped, the horror overwhelming her.

Pete slumped, letting his eyes close. He'd known this would happen, however much he'd wanted it not to – wanted to delay the inevitable so that she could absorb one thing before being hit with another. Or so he told himself, knowing as he did so that he wasn't admitting the truth even to himself.

'He drowned,' he whispered.

'Drowned? In the river?'

He nodded, opening his eyes to meet her horrified gaze.

She retched, almost puking. 'Oh, God!' She dropped onto the seat behind her as if the strings holding her upright had been cut.

Pete took one of her hands in his and numbly, she left it there. 'I'm so, so sorry, love,' he said.

She stayed silent and still, as if unaware he'd spoken or that he was even there for what felt like an age. Then she turned her head, her expression firm once more. 'Just get the fucker. Don't be sorry, just get him. Put him in jail for the rest of his miserable, worthless life. Or, better still, kill him. Because if I ever see him, I swear to God, I will.'

CHAPTER THIRTY-ONE

Pete switched on his phone as he left the hospital some time later. He'd expected to have to gently ease his wife through the first stages of grief, but she'd surprised him. She'd regained the strength of character that she'd had until a year ago when she was robbed of it by Tommy's disappearance, so now the tables were turned, the roles reversed, and she had eased him through the worst moments of pain and loss, driving him on with her own determination and resolve.

The phone beeped in his hand before he'd even returned it to his pocket. He checked the screen and saw that he'd missed two messages – one from Jane and one from Ben. Just a few feet from his car, he waited until he'd got in, started the engine and the phone had connected to the Bluetooth system before dialling the station as he drove away.

'DC Bennett, Exeter CID,'

'Jane, its Pete. I just got your message. Ben's too. What's up?'

'Are you OK? How's Louise?'

Emotion welled up in him again. He swallowed but still his voice was thick and hollow when he spoke. 'We're about like you'd expect. But we both know what's got to happen now. For Tommy, even if there wasn't any other reason.'

It was Jane's turn to hesitate as she absorbed what he'd said. She was all business when she finally spoke again, for which Pete was deeply grateful. 'We've got a break in the Jonas Hanson case at last, boss. Two, in fact. We heard back from forensics up north. They've still got their own unit in Lincolnshire, you know.'

Until relatively recently, all forces had had their own forensics units. It was quite a new and unfamiliar phenomenon that some, like Devon and Cornwall, had closed them and employed private contractors instead.

'And?'

'Well, they found blood and hair in his car. From two sources, one of which they've identified. The other is the hair, which was found down between the seat and the backrest on the passenger side.'

'And the blood?'

'Comes back to a young woman who was reported missing eight months ago, boss. From Sidmouth.'

'Sidmouth?' he repeated. 'How come we didn't know about that?'

The small seaside town had its own police station, like Newton Abbot and Ottery St Mary, but they had no CID so anything major would have been referred to Exeter and, initially, to Heavitree Road. Their own department.

'It was never escalated, boss. She had a history of running off. Drugs. Turned out, when the locals looked into it, she also had a history of prostitution although her parents didn't know. There'd been no convictions.'

'And we know that Hanson's preferred target demographic tends towards prostitutes,' Pete said.

'Exactly.'

'A bit close to home, though.'

'Hence this trip, maybe. He was getting antsy.'

Pete grunted agreement. 'So, what about the other evidence they found? You said it was a hair?'

'Yes, in the front seat. They haven't identified it yet, but then any mispers tend to take a while to get onto the database if they do at all. And minor felonies like prostitution often don't have DNA taken anyway, do they?'

Pete pursed his lips, knowing she was right. 'And there's only these two samples detected in the car?'

'That's what they said.'

'If this recent trip was a spree, you'd expect more than that.'

'They did say the car was remarkably clean, boss. Especially for a builder's vehicle.'

'So maybe he's fastidious. Cleans up after each one. Maybe he watched CSI or Silent Witness on the telly.'

'Or one of those true crime channels on Sky.'

'Hmm.' Pete never watched them. Too much like a busman's holiday and he'd got frustrated and angry at the inefficiency and outright laziness of some of the officers involved in the few cases he'd seen on there, when Louise had tried them out, curious as to what he got up to all day, she'd said. Not that he liked CSI or Silent Witness either, as wildly detached from reality as they were. 'Either way, it seems he's forensically aware.'

'In which case, why keep trophies?'

'Because, sadly, in this day and age, he can afford to,' Pete reminded her as he turned into the station. 'Stuff like that doesn't mean as much as it should with sick buggers like him selling it on e-bay and so forth. Especially the arrogant ones who think they've built themselves a reputation.'

'And if we're right about the number he's killed, he would be that arrogant,' she agreed.

'I'm in the car park downstairs,' he told her. 'I'll be up in a minute.'

'Are you sure, boss? You don't want to be at home with Louise and Annie?'

'Annie doesn't know yet and Lou's still at the hospital - said she wants to keep working, let her mind process things while she's got other stuff to concentrate on. Plus, she wants to be there when they bring Tommy in. Wants to see him before they...' He paused, drew a shaky breath and let it out again. 'Before they take him to Doc Chambers,' he whispered.

He pulled into a space and switched off the engine, killing the Blue-tooth system. He sat there for a while, gathering himself, trying to regain control before facing the team.

Finally calmer, he stepped out of the car and went inside.

When he stepped into the squad room, moments later, his whole team stopped what they were doing, their eyes fixed on him, but no-one said anything.

Pete was deeply grateful for their silence. If anyone had spoken, asked him how he was, he didn't know how he would have reacted - if he could have stopped himself from either breaking down or yelling at them.

Instead, he took his seat, looked across at Jane and asked, 'So, what have we got, then? Details.'

'Right. The blood comes back to seventeen-year old Rebecca Newton.'

'And what about the hair? Was it long or short? Brown, red, blonde? Dyed or natural? With or without a root?'

'Dark brown, straight, with a root - hence the DNA although it doesn't match any on record - and about four inches long.'

'Fairly short, then, for a woman. What are we talking about? A bob, a page-boy cut, something like yours?'

Jane shrugged. 'Mine's probably more like six inches. It could be a layer cut or something like that. Any number of styles, really.'

'Was the end split?'

Jane raised an eyebrow at that. 'No, it wasn't.'

'I am married, you know,' he reminded her. 'So relatively recently cut, then. And potentially pulled rather than shed, as it had a root. What about products – dye, shampoo, all that stuff?'

'They said it was clean, boss.'

He nodded. 'So probably not a street girl. Any indication of how long it had been there?'

Jane shook her head. 'No way to tell. The car was clean, so no dust or anything adhering to it.'

Pete pursed his lips. 'Looks like it could be a dead-end, then. We've still got the blood, though. If we can put Hanson there around the time she disappeared, that will corroborate the physical evidence and give us a good case.'

'A confession would do the same,' Dick pointed out.

'Yeah, good luck with that,' Pete said.

Dick shrugged. 'Phone records and receipts it is, then. Shame we can't do anything with the hair though.'

'We can't have everything in life,' Jane said.

'We can pass the details on to the Missing Persons Bureau, though. For whenever they're able to use them. It could help somebody's family.'

'Fair enough,' Jane agreed, side-stepping the connection with Pete's own situation.

'Sidmouth's a bit close to home, isn't it?' Dick said, mirroring Pete's earlier comment. 'What about not shitting on your own doorstep?'

'Ew!' Jill grimaced.

'All criminals make mistakes,' Pete pointed out. 'It's how we catch them, more often than not.'

'Good point, well made,' Dick acknowledged.

'When was it that girl went missing?' Ben asked.

'Eight weeks ago,' Jane told him. '29th of March'

'Got him.' Ben waved a paper in the air. 'His mobile was in Sidmouth on the 29th. Came back to Exeter that night, about 2.00 am.'

'Which way?' Pete asked.

'The main road.'

He'd hoped Hanson would have taken the back roads, giving him more chance to dump the body and them more chance to find it. Otherwise… He picked up the phone and dialled an internal number. 'Bob, can you get me through to Sidmouth nick?'

'Yeah, of course. Hold on.'

The phone went dead, then started ringing again.

'Police, how can I help?'

'Hello. DS Pete Gayle from Heavitree Road. You had a case a couple of months ago. A missing girl. Possible runaway, known prostitute.'

'That's right. Rebecca something… Newton, was it?'

'Yes.' *At least the guy remembered her.*

'What about her?'

'We've got a match for her. A blood sample found in the back of a murder suspect's car.'

'You reckon she's dead, then?'

'It seems likely. Just a matter of finding the body. It'll be round your way somewhere, or between here and there. We know which way he came back that night.'

'We'll get a search under way, then. Thanks, mate.'

'We'll see what we can do from here, too. Meet in the middle somewhere if we don't find her first, eh?'

'If we do, I'll buy you a pint.'

'If we do, I'll need one.' Pete hung up and headed for Colin Underhill's office. There was no need to knock. Colin saw him approach and waved him in and to a seat.

'I'm really sorry about Tommy,' he said. 'But you know that already. What do you need?'

'Thanks. What we need is a search party. A big one. Probable remains between here and Sidmouth. They're getting organised from that end but we're going to need plenty of boots on the ground and cadaver dogs. I know what I'd have done with the victim if I were him: dumped her in the Otter or the Clyst or in the woods at Hawkerland, in a part people don't go into much. If it was one of the rivers, it's unlikely she'll still be there after eight or nine weeks, but you never know. She might have got caught up somewhere.'

Colin nodded. 'Give me the details, I'll pass it on to uniform. Then get yourself off home.'

Pete checked his watch. It was almost 2.30 pm. 'I'll give it another half-hour then go and pick Annie up. I'd rather be working in the meantime. Had enough time off last year and it got me nowhere. I'll see what Lou and Annie are like in the morning but if they don't need me at home, I'd sooner be here. There's too much to do not to be until Hanson's put away and Steve Southam's caught.'

'Which is not your problem.'

Pete drew himself up but managed to remain silent despite the anger and indignance that blazed in his mind. Deep down, he knew Colin was right. Being reminded of it, though, didn't help.

Colin looked at him. 'You know the rules and you know the boss man's got it in for you already. Don't give him an excuse, that's all I'm saying.'

Pete maintained his silence for a few seconds longer. 'You know we've got a time limit on this,' he said at last. 'We can't let him out of here.'

Colin nodded. 'Noon tomorrow. You'd best nail him then, hadn't you?'

CHAPTER THIRTY-TWO

Pete was waiting outside Annie's school when the kids came out at 3.00. She was about to rush past him with her friends when she spotted his car and stopped in her tracks. Swallowing heavily, he waved. She said something to her friends before stepping towards him.

'Dad? What are you doing here?'

'Can't I pick my daughter up from school now and then, when I get the chance?' he asked.

'Yes, but…' She shook her head. 'How come you're not at work?'

'Uncle Colin told me to clear off.'

'You haven't… No. Why would he do that? I thought you had a big case on, apart from finding Tommy.'

'I have. And finding Tommy's something I can't officially get involved in, as you well know. Come on, get in.'

'I don't understand,' she said when she was sitting beside him, pulling on her seat-belt. 'Why would Uncle Colin send you home? What's happened?'

Colin wasn't an uncle, of course, but he was Tommy's God-father as well as Pete's superior officer, mentor and friend.

Was this really the time or place to tell her? Hell, he didn't want to have to tell her at all. He didn't want it to be true, but he knew it was and he knew that, the sooner it was out there, the sooner she'd be able to process it, rather than stringing it out, making her suspicious and nervous before springing it on her, which would only make it worse. He drew a breath.

'Annie, there's something I've got to tell you. Your mum knows already and…' *Never mind the long way around,* he thought. *Get on with it, man.* 'It's Tommy. I'm afraid we didn't get him back in time, love.'

Her eyes widened with horror and dread as the truth began to penetrate her consciousness. 'No.'

'He's not coming back.'

'No,' she repeated, louder this time.

He reached for her hand. 'The man who had him was determined that Tommy wouldn't ever testify against him.'

Tears began to run down her cheeks. 'Dad.'

He leaned across, taking her in his arms. 'I'm sorry, love. Tommy's dead.'

'No,' she wailed. 'No, he can't be. Please!'

Pete rocked her as best he could in the awkward position enforced by the gear-stick and equipment console. He stroked her hair as she howled her grief to the world, not caring who saw or heard. There was no point in saying anything, she wouldn't have heard him anyway. Then, taking him completely by surprise, she wriggled free and snatched at the door handle. The next thing he knew, she was out and running.

'Annie,' he shouted, every instinct driving him out of the car and after her. She was fast and she'd got a good lead on him by the time he'd got his seat-belt off and jumped out and around the open door, slamming it as he set off in pursuit.

'Annie, stop!'

A gaggle of kids filled the pathway, oblivious to all around them as they milled around, laughing and shouting. Pete dodged through and around them, eyes focussed on Annie, but it cost him more precious seconds. He hadn't made it out of the seething crowd when she darted right, straight out across the road without looking. A car coming around the bend towards them stopped abruptly, tyres screeching on the tarmac, horn blaring, but she took no notice, running on blindly.

'No!'

Pete saw the driver gesturing, then setting off again as he finally freed himself from the crowd but, by then, Annie had turned the corner a hundred yards away.

With a quick glance behind, he darted across the road before the oncoming car got too close. As he did so a dark brown four-by-four screeched out of a roadside parking space between him and the bend, engine roaring as it headed rapidly away from him, a logo-printed black cover over the spare wheel on its back door.

Pete didn't need to see the driver to know who it was even before it went around the bend and out of sight.

'No!' This time it was a primal roar from deep within him as he surged forward like an Olympic sprinter out of the blocks,

He heard the big tyres screech again. A scream. A deeper-toned shout.

'Annie!'

He was fifty yards from the bend when the second scream sounded. Then a car door slammed. Still he couldn't see what was happening but his mind conjured images that horrified him to the core.

A shout echoed off the surrounding houses. Feet slapped on pavement. Another shout was followed by a high-pitched yelp.

Pete reached the corner. He leapt at a big horse-chestnut tree, bouncing one foot off the rough bark to help him make the turn even before he looked across at what was happening. He surged ahead once more with barely a break in his stride. Saw the four-by-four stopped at an angle, nose into the pavement. The doors were closed and Annie was struggling in the arms of a tall, heavy-set man in a dark jacket and black beany hat.

He was facing away from Pete, but he knew instantly who he was.

'Southam!'

'Dad!'

The big man roared as her teeth sank into his hand.

'Annie, drop,' he shouted. Then he was on them.

Annie jerked her feet up and forward as Southam turned his head to glance back at Pete, but he was too late. As Annie's backside hit the pavement, Pete careened into him. Annie managed somehow to tangle his legs and he went down hard but instantly rolled to the right.

Pete's momentum carried him over them both. Given the chance, he would have stomped the big man on his way past, but his quick roll sideways saved him as Pete's foot hit the pavement instead. Pete stopped, turning back fast. Annie was rolling away. Southam tried to stop her with a foot but managed only to slam his heel on the pavement. Then he bucked up and over in a backward roll, feet rising to meet Pete with an agility that belied his size. Pete was already dropping towards him, knees aimed at his collar bone while his fist was aiming at his lower belly. Or where it had been. Instead, one of Southam's feet hit Pete in the chest, near his arm-pit, the other narrowly missing him. The impact threw him off, his body twisting awkwardly, a spasm of pain lancing up his back as his knee hit the ground hard, the other one impacting the back of Southam's thigh as the big man pushed up with one arm, twisting his body so that, as he completed the roll, he came down on top of Pete, crushing him onto the unforgiving pavement.

He heard Annie screech.

'Run!' he told her, his body pressed awkwardly beneath the incredible weight of the other man. He tried to use his back muscles to throw Southam off but he was too heavy. Then a ham-like fist crashed into Pete's neck, at the base of his skull. An inch to the left and it would have broken his neck but instead it hit him on the muscle that went down one side of his spine, supporting his head. Agony blazed through his whole shoulder and he yelped as he was driven flat down on the pavement. Southam's massive bulk lifted off him. Pete tried to move but he used the wrong arm and fresh pain made him gasp as his entire body froze. Then a heavy boot slammed into the side of his skull and everything went black.

CHAPTER THIRTY-THREE

Pete woke with a jerk, pain driving spikes through his skull and down into his neck and shoulder. He groaned. He was on his back, softness beneath him. Grass? No, the light was wrong.

Artificial. He was inside. In bed. He could feel a sheet over him. He cracked open his eyes but the brightness sent fresh, even more intense agony spearing into his brain so he closed them immediately with a hiss of air through his teeth, before they could clear the moisture that filled them and allow him to see.

Annie!

He jerked up but was restricted by the sheets. 'A...'

'Pete.' Louise's voice penetrated his consciousness. *Where had she come from? She was at work, wasn't she?* 'He's awake.'

'Am I?' he groaned without opening his eyes, more aches and pains registering through the agony of his head. 'Or is this Hell? Where's Annie?'

'I'm here, dad.' Her voice came from beyond the foot of his bed.

Relief flooded through him, easing the pain. He tried opening his eyes again. It was still painful but blinking several times seemed to clear the moisture and lessen the impact. Louise was standing over him in uniform. The ceiling beyond her, curtains around them and the bright square lights all said Hospital. The man in a white coat at the end of the bed, standing next to Annie, clinched it. 'How'd I get here?'

'Annie saw Evie and her dad and sent him back for you. They saw a man jump into some sort of Land Rover and drive away like he had a rocket up his arse but they didn't get a registration or anything. You were out of it, so he called an ambulance.'

'I need to call in. Get an alert out for him.' He looked around, tried to sit up but failed, gasping as pain lanced through his shoulder. 'Where's my jacket?'

'What's the matter?' Louise frowned.

'I told you, I need...'

'No. Your arm.'

'Shoulder,' he corrected. 'He hit me in the neck. Nothing broken that I know of.'

'Your jacket's over here,' she said, pointing towards a chair at the head of the bed. 'Hang on.'

'More importantly,' the doctor cut in. 'We need to examine that shoulder.'

'Depends on your priorities,' Pete argued. 'The man who did this is a suspected killer and he's out there running free.'

'Here, dad,' Annie said, holding out the phone.

Louise took it from her. 'I'll do that,' she said as the doctor stepped forward along the far side of the bed.

She used the speed-dial function and got almost straight through to the squad room.

'Jane? It's Louise.'

'Ow,' Pete protested as the doctor probed with hard fingers at the base of his neck.

'Yes, he's here in A&E. He was attacked by that Southam bloke. He's driving a...?' She raised a querying eyebrow at Pete, whose arm was being stretched out straight and gently twisted by the doctor.

'Dark brown Discovery,' he gasped. 'Black wheel guard with the Watson's logo on it. Registration unknown.'

Louise repeated what he'd said into the phone.

The doctor continued to manipulate Pete's arm and shoulder.

'Right. Cheers, Jane.' Louise hung up. 'All right?'

Pete grunted, unwilling to nod.

'The shoulder's fine,' the doctor announced. 'There'll be a bruise though, and it'll be sore for a few days. I'd suggest keeping it in a sling for forty-eight hours.'

'Thanks.'

The doctor looked up at Louise. 'We'll keep him in overnight for observation due to the concussion and loss of consciousness, but he should be good to go by morning.'

Pete tried to move again but collapsed back onto his pillows. 'I can't...'

'You can,' she told him. 'And you will. Annie and I'll be OK for tonight.'

'If he knows where her school is, he knows where the house is,' Pete argued.

'So we won't stay there.' She sounded firmly determined but he saw the flash of worry in her eyes.

'We'll get him,' Pete told her, reaching for her hand with his good one. 'He's desperate. He'll make a mistake.'

She nodded to the doctor, who stepped out through the curtain. 'He'd better make it soon.'

'He will. His main reason for sticking around is because his brother's in clink, due in court in the morning. He wants to return the favour and break him out.'

She looked horrified. 'He won't get away with it?'

Pete went to shake his head but stopped with a wince. 'No. He'll have an extra escort. Or two.'

She pursed her lips.

'We know what's coming so we can deal with it,' he reassured her. 'Big brother's going nowhere and little brother – well, younger anyway – will soon be inside where he belongs.'

'With you and Dave Miles both in here?'

Pete smiled at her faith in him. 'We're not the only capable coppers in this city.'

She grunted. 'Don't tell DCI Silverstone that.'

He laughed and another jolt of pain drove deep into his neck. 'I won't if you don't.'

*

'There's good news and bad news,' Jane announced as he walked into the squad room the next morning, having been kept in the hospital until the doctors made their rounds just after nine.

'Give me the good. I need it,' he said, sitting down stiffly. He'd discarded the sling they put his arm into as soon as he left the building. It was painful, but he needed both arms free, if only to drive.

'Someone got a registration on the brown Discovery.'

'Good. And the bad?'

'No-one's seen it since. No ANPR hits, no CCTV – nothing.'

Pete winced. 'Has he dumped it then? Nicked something else?'

'No reports have come in yet, on either count.'

'But none have on the Discovery, have they?'

'True. The owners must be away on holiday or something,' she agreed leaning back in her chair.

'So where does that leave us?'

'Back where we were before he turned up at Annie's school,' she admitted.

'Was a watch put on my place last night?'

'Don't know, boss.'

The phone on Pete's desk rang before he could say anymore. His shoulder protested as he reached for it. He swapped hands and picked it up. 'Gayle.'

'It's Bob downstairs. I've got something for you.'

'I hope to Christ it's something good,' Pete said.

'Someone down here in reception wants to see you.'

'Who?'

'A woman who saw the DCI's bit on telly last night. Wants to talk to the person in charge of the case.'

'OK. I'll be down.' Pete put the phone down and stood up, holding his bad arm against his stomach with the other hand.

'What was that all about?' asked Dick.

'Jonas Hanson.'

'Oh, ah?'

'Seems like our beloved leader's earned his keep for once. There's a woman downstairs wanting a chat. Come on Jane.'

Dick was nodding. 'About time we got a break.'

'Hmm. While we're gone, I need the rest of you to find me something solid on Steve Southam's whereabouts.'

Normally, that would have garnered a sarcastic response from at least one of the team, but there was silence behind him as he headed for the door with Jane close behind him.

'So, what have we got down here, boss?' Jane asked as they descended the stairs.'

'You know as much as I do, Jane.'

They went through the door at the bottom and turned left towards reception. There was only one person waiting there – a woman in her late thirties, Pete guessed. Dark hair cut in a Page-boy style, and a long, loose short-sleeved dress, dark with a pale pattern threading through it. She had an attractive face but wore little make-up, as if she didn't want to attract attention.

He held out his good hand, only too aware of how he looked with a clearly injured arm and the bandage still on his face. 'I'm DS Gayle. This is DC Bennett. How can we help?'

Her hand was limp in his, a cursory touch. It looked marginally more decisive in Jane's.

'I've… I've come to report a rape,' she said, her girlish voice getting weaker as she spoke until it was barely a gasp.

Pete tensed. 'When did this happen?'

'June the second.'

Pete's eyes widened. That was just a few days ago.

'1995,' she added and he felt himself slump.

'You must have been very young,' Jane said, reaching for her hands again.

'Seventeen. I was in the middle of my A-levels. Had to give them up. I couldn't go out of the house afterwards. Not for ages. Couldn't talk about it – not even to my parents.'

'So, what did you tell them had happened?' Pete asked.

'I didn't. I just shut myself away and refused to come out except for the bathroom for… I don't even know how long. We don't talk about it.'

Jane stepped in again. 'But you're willing to talk to us now?'

She nodded meekly. 'I saw the bit on the local news last night and thought I had to. If it's happening again…'

Pete shook himself out of whatever non-thinking state he'd fallen into. 'Do you want to come through and talk somewhere private?'

'Yes, please.'

He led the way through to the back corridor where he found an interview room not in use, showed them in and went on to the custody desk to tell the duty sergeant that he was using it.

Back in the room, he found Jane sitting on the same side of the desk as the woman, the red light showing that the digital recorder was already running. He pulled up a chair across from them. Jane looked at him and nodded.

Leaning forward, elbows on the table, he asked, 'So, what's your name, Miss?'

'Lucy. Lucy Willoughby.'

'And why did you want to speak to us specifically, Lucy? What made you believe your attack was relevant to our case?'

'The van. Your DCI whatever mentioned three or four vehicles the man had had over the years and I recognised the van. White with red stripes down the sides.'

Pete felt the excitement surge up inside him, but he kept himself outwardly calm. 'A white van. What kind of van?'

'A big one. The white-van-man kind. Transit?'

He nodded and glanced at Jane. She tipped her head.

'I didn't see the piece on TV last night, Lucy, but would it be OK if I showed you a picture? Not of the van, but a man. If he's the right one – and I'm not saying he is – it's a recent one so he'll be a lot older than he would have been back then.' He smiled. 'We all are, eh?'

She tensed but nodded once, holding on tighter to Jane's hands. 'OK,' she whispered.

Moving carefully, Pete took out his phone and brought up a photo of Jonas Hanson. Turned the screen towards her.

She gasped and recoiled, turning her head away to look down at her hands in Jane's. After what felt like an age, she nodded without looking up.

'That's him?' Pete checked after putting the phone away. 'The man who attacked you in 1995?'

'Yes,' she gasped.

'And would you be willing to go to court and say so?' He seriously doubted it at this moment and, if she did, the defence would send her sobbing out of the witness box, a traumatised mess.

'Yes,' she said, surprising him with the strength of her voice as her eyes met his.

Pete was surprised not just by the vividness of their blue colour but by the intensity of her gaze. Still, he had to ask: 'You're sure?'

'They can throw whatever they like at me. It's only words.'

Pete sat back in his chair, a deep sigh releasing the tension he'd been bottling up as they spoke. 'We're going to need the details of your attack,' he said. 'Only as much as you're willing to tell us at this stage. I appreciate how difficult this must be. If you want to speak to Jane alone or with another female officer instead of me, that's fine.' *Either Jill or, if necessary, a specialist officer from force HQ at Middlemoor.*

Lucy shook her head. 'I'll be facing men in the court, won't I?'

'Yes,' Pete nodded.

'So, I might as well start now. At least you're on my side.'

He gave her a smile. 'Very much so. Do you want a drink or anything?'

'A cup of tea would be nice.'

'I'll see what I can drum up.' He pushed his chair back and left her alone with Jane again. The more gently he could approach this, the more they'd get out of her, he thought. And the better it would be for her.

He headed along to the custody suite and in minutes was back with a tea and two coffees. Better a shared experience than to drink alone.

'Here we go.' He said, setting the plastic cups on the table and retaking his seat. He let her take a sip, matching her move for move before saying anything more. Only after they'd replaced their cups on the table did he ask, 'Tell us what you can about what happened, Lucy.'

Lucy looked up from her cup, first at Jane, then at Pete. 'It was a Friday. I had a light day at college. There wasn't much going on with the exams and so on. I was walking along Streatham Drive and this van pulled up a few yards in front of me. It was facing me, on my side of the road. The driver got out. He had a map in his hand. He said something about being confused and late for a job and could I direct him to Howell Road? I started to tell him he must have missed the turn and he dropped the map and grabbed me.' She shivered at the memory.

'I tried to fight him off but he was too strong. I screamed but nobody heard me. He threw me in the van and...' She paused, fighting the tears that sparkled in her eyes. One dropped onto her cheek and ran slowly down. 'He did it. Afterwards, he drove off with me still in the back. We didn't go far. Just somewhere on the edge of town. He came back and I thought he was going to do it again. He started to. Then he…' She drew a breath and more tears were freed from her eyes.

'It seemed like he couldn't, so he got angry and began to choke me. I fought but he'd got his hands round my neck, his full weight on my chest. I couldn't breathe. I thought I was going to die,' she sobbed. After a moment she wiped at her eyes and looked up at Pete again. 'I must have blacked out,' she whispered. 'The next thing I knew, I was lying in a ditch. There was grass and stuff all over the place, over the top of me and everything. It was like I was looking up from a grave.' She shuddered. 'I panicked, bolted up out of there. He'd… I was half naked. I don't know the name of the road. It's off the Cowley bridge. There was a cottage not far away. I told them I'd been attacked and they insisted I call the police, but I told them I'd do it from home. My parents were both at work so, when they took me back, I just went in and had a shower and…' She shook her head. 'I couldn't call anyone. I couldn't speak to anyone. When my parents got home I told them I'd been ill.'

She looked haunted, her eyes big and soft and wet and sad. Pete's heart went out to her. It was all he could do not to reach for her hand. Although she must have been a few years older than he was, she seemed so much younger. Almost as if she'd shed all the intervening years as she recalled the terrible events she'd endured.

'You're incredibly lucky to still be alive,' he said gently. 'He must have thought you weren't when he dumped you.'

She blinked, wiped her eyes again and looked at him. 'I know. I've thought about that over and over. I think that's what kept me going afterwards. The fact that I was given a second chance at life.' Her throat convulsed. 'I just couldn't face living it.'

Jane reached out and took her hand. 'But you have. And now you've come to us and told us about it. Whether you manage to get to court or not – and, to be fair, a lot of women don't. Can't face it in the end – speaking about it outside of that situation will help you get your life back.'

Lucy looked at Jane as if she didn't believe a word of it, but Pete nodded. 'It's true. I don't understand why but I know from experience. I haven't been raped, of course, but I...' He hesitated, unwilling to even speak the words, but it was too late. He'd started the sentence. For her sake if not his own, he had to finish it. He swallowed, let the air out of his lungs and tried to draw himself up but failed. 'I lost my son.'

The sympathy that showed instantly in her tearful, stricken eyes almost broke him but he held it together somehow, by the finest of threads. He coughed and took a sip of his coffee. He felt like he was trembling inside. The words had taken so much out of him that he could barely stand to look at her – at anyone. But he forced himself to meet her gaze.

She gave him a tiny smile of thanks.

'I will go to court,' she said, glancing at Jane. 'I know it won't be easy. They'll want to know why I didn't report it years ago. Claim I'm making it up. Or that it was somehow my fault. But...' She took a deep breath. 'I survived the act, I can survive some slimy clever-dick lawyer badgering me.'

Jane still had hold of her hand. 'It would help us a lot, if you're sure. And all the other women out there who'd fall victim to him in the future.'

She looked from Pete to Jane. 'Has he done it again?'

Pete nodded. 'Yes.'

'And...' She swallowed.

Jane this time. 'Yes.'

351

She broke down then. 'And I could have stopped it. Prevented it.'

Pete felt a surge of anger – not at her, but at Hanson for putting her through this. 'None of what he's done is your fault,' he told her. 'None of it. Your own attack or any of those since.'

Lucy looked up, tears still streaming down her face. 'Any of? How many have there been?'

Jane squeezed her hand. 'We don't know. Maybe we never will. But the main thing is to make sure there aren't anymore.'

'By keeping him locked up,' Pete said. 'With your help and that of the people in that cottage out by Cowley bridge.'

CHAPTER THIRTY-FOUR

'You were right, boss. We should have put a watch on your place last night. CCTV from the Co-op round the corner shows that brown Discovery going past just before six and leaving again a bit after midnight.'

The fear that would normally have sparked in Pete's gut on behalf of his wife and daughter was replaced by anger – both at Steve Southam's bare-faced audacity and at the clueless pillock who didn't put a watch on an obvious target for a known fugitive. 'So why the hell didn't we?' he demanded.

Ben shrugged. 'Above my pay-grade, boss. I know Jane suggested it. Don't know why it wasn't done.'

Was this another swipe at him over the arrest and conviction of former colleague Frank Benton? If so, at least one head would roll for it. He'd make damn sure of that. 'Right. I'll be back in a minute.' He marched up the length of the squad room towards Colin Underhill's office, seeing the DCI in there, but barging in anyway.

'Guvnor. Chief. I need a word.'

'We're having a private conversation, Detective Sergeant,' Silverstone snapped.

'And you're welcome to continue it, sir. But first, DC Bennett asked for a watch to be put on my house last night for the fugitive Steven Southam. It wasn't done, despite his being the most wanted man in the county at this point. And we have evidence that puts him exactly where DC Bennett said he would be. I want to know why it wasn't done, sir, and whose decision it was.'

The uniformed man had gone deathly pale, his thin lips almost disappearing as he pressed them together, dark eyes glittering as he stared at Pete.

'What evidence?' His voice was flat and quiet.

'CCTV.' *And if he got close enough, there'll be additional footage from home because I haven't taken our cameras down yet,* He thought. *Thanks, Annie. Maybe I'm keener on urban foxes than I was, after all.* 'But that doesn't answer the question of who made the decision to ignore Jane's request.'

Colin was sitting in his chair, fingers entwined on the desk, watching the exchange without saying a word.

'It was me, Detective Sergeant,' Silverstone said.

'What?' Pete stepped forward, getting right into Silverstone's face, barely able to stop himself from grabbing the useless idiot by the throat and shaking him. 'Why the hell would you even think of doing that? *Sir?* You knew the situation. You knew he killed Tommy and that he was an immediate threat to my wife and daughter. Why the fuck would you knowingly put their lives in danger?'

'That's enough, Detective Sergeant,' Silverstone snapped.

'No, it's not. Not by a long shot. I *will* have an explanation. And not just an excuse but a full, formal, policy-led explanation in writing that'll justify your actions not just to me but to Middlemoor. Because this is one step far too bloody far. And I want it by tonight. Sir.' He turned on his heel and slammed out of the little office, glass rattling in the door as he slammed it, drawing every eye in the squad room as he stalked back towards his desk.

'Where are we on Southam?' he asked, sitting down and taking a gulp of his coffee.

'He's been off-grid since midnight, boss,' Ben told him.

'So, he didn't come this way and he didn't head for the industrial estates or the motorway. He must have stayed around the residential areas. Whipton, Polsoe, Newtown, Pennsylvania.'

'What's the odds the sick bastard parked up in the cemetery for the night?' Dick suggested. 'He certainly wouldn't be seen there if he left before eight or so.'

Pete grunted, calming down now that he had something to focus on. 'Is it open overnight?'

'Dunno, but it can't be hard to find out.' Dick lifted his phone and dialled.

'If he left there before eight this morning, where'd he go?' Pete asked, his gaze roving around the remainder of the team.

'Well, we know what his primary objective is,' Jane pointed out. 'It's not far from there to New North Road.' She opened a drawer in her desk and tossed a blister-pack of tablets to Pete. 'Here. Take a couple of these, boss. They'll ease that shoulder a bit.'

'Thanks.' Pete glanced down at the tablets. They were Ibuprophen. He popped a couple out and swallowed them dry before returning the pack.

'He can't seriously expect to get away with that, though, can he?' Dick said, one hand over the mouthpiece of his phone. 'He knows we know about it.'

'And you don't reckon he's got the brass balls to try anyway?' asked Jill.

Pete grunted. Actually, he did.

'He knows there'll be an increased police presence,' Ben said.

'So maybe he'll try to take them by surprise,' Jane suggested. 'Hit the van before it even leaves the car park.'

Pete checked his watch. 'What time's Adrian's hearing?'

'Eleven.'

'They'll want him there nice and early. Let him stew a bit before it starts. I'll give them a call and warn them.'

He picked up his phone as Dick put his down.

'The cemetery doesn't get locked,' the grey-haired man said as Pete began to dial.

'That's your likeliest answer then,' Jane said.

'Exeter prison,' a voice said brusquely when the connection was made.

'DS Gayle, Heavitree Road CID. We've got credible intel that Adrian Southam's brother's going to try to break him out of custody as he leaves for the Combined Court House.'

'He's on the way out as we speak.'

'Damn it. Stop that van.'

'I can't. It's too late. I can see the gates from here. The van's… Bloody hell!'

'What?'

'A brown four-by-four just broadsided it like a bull at a gate. There's a bloke jumping out of it and…'

Pete dropped the phone before the man could continue his commentary. 'Move. Everyone.' He was out of his seat before he finished speaking and running for the door. As he hurtled down the concrete stairs, his neck and shoulder jarring painfully at every step, he heard feet slapping and clacking behind him. He made the bottom in four big leaps, good hand supporting the bad arm, snatched out his ID card to slap in on the door release. It took only a second to open but it was five seconds too long for Pete. He slammed through and ran down the corridor, past the custody desk, slapping the door release button and the door beyond as he headed as fast as he could for his car.

Jumping in, he saw Jane, Jill, Dick and Ben all running for theirs. He started the engine, not waiting for them to follow before hitting the lights and sirens and peeling out of the car park and down the hill towards the ring-road.

With scant consideration for other road users, he made it to the prison in record time, but was still too late. He jumped out of the car at a scene of mechanical carnage. The prison transport van was a wreck, its whole left side crushed in, every door open and uniformed men milling around it in seeming chaos. The brown four-by-four that Steven Southam had been driving the day before sat at the far side of the van, its front end, crushed by the impact, a good four feet from the side of the van where it had rebounded on impact.

How had they got away?

He grabbed a police constable. 'What did they drive off in?'

The man seemed to be in a daze. 'Huh? A pale blue Nissan.'

'Did anyone get the plate?'

'I dunno, Sarge.'

Pete turned away from him, looked around the scene but could see no-one in obvious charge. He raised his voice and shouted. 'Did anyone get make, model and registration on the getaway vehicle?'

'Stand by,' Jill said into her chest-worn radio, standing at his side.

'Nissan Primera,' someone shouted.

Jill passed the information on.

'Foxtrot Golf six four,' someone shouted. 'Didn't get the rest.'

Again, Jill passed the message along. 'Alert's out, boss.'

'Thanks, Jill.'

There was no telling which direction they would have taken from here so no point leaving until they had a clue from the cameras or road traffic cars. But Pete was chafing at the bit as he paced up and down the little car park, trying to find order in the chaos. Eventually, he could stand it no longer. 'Who's in charge here?'

There was no response.

And no point in calling forensics. They knew who they were dealing with. He turned to the nearest man in uniform. 'Get the owner of that Discovery identified and informed. We need to photograph the scene and get things moved out of the way.'

Jill's radio sparked. 'Information on the light blue Nissan Primera. Two up, headed north on Cowley Bridge Road.'

'Received.'

'Let's go,' Pete said quickly, running for his car, ignoring the pain in his shoulder.

They could have gone south from here and doubled back, hoping to throw off pursuit, or headed straight out. Either way, when they got to the bridge over the Exe they'd have a couple of options. If they even went that far. They could turn off before that, cut across past Jonas Hanson's house and head up to the north of the city to lay low until the heat of the pursuit wore off. There was no way of knowing and no cameras to pick them up again for a good distance in any of the directions they might opt for.

He hit the radio transmit as he sped up the New North Road, heading for Cowley Bridge. 'All available units, suspect vehicle headed north out of the city. Blanket coverage needed ASAP but approach with caution. Occupants to be considered armed and dangerous.'

'Armed with what, Sarge?'

'They're bound to have weapons of some kind but, if not, they're both karate experts and willing to use any means necessary to evade capture so Tasers set to max.'

'Roger.'

'Is the helicopter available to assist?' Pete's lights and sirens were blaring as he joined the Cowley Bridge Road. The old road was narrow and restricted, but traffic parted somehow in front of him.

'Negative,' the response came over the radio. 'Helicopter occupied at Launceston.'

Damn! Why did a force covering the area of Devon and Cornwall only have one bloody helicopter?

He'd just got to the point where the road widened, more modern houses and business premises lining either side, when the radio squawked again.

'Contact, contact. Target vehicle spotted in Cowley. In pursuit.'

That was that decided then. They were heading up towards Crediton.

'Temporary loss. Repeat, temporary loss. Target no longer in sight.' He could hear sirens in the background.

What? They must have been facing the wrong way, had to turn around.

'Continuing pursuit.'

I should bloody think so!

As he hit the bridge and started up the Crediton Road, another message came though. 'Smallbrook. It's a loss, loss, loss.'

'Bugger.' A thought struck Pete. There were lanes winding south across the countryside towards Whitestone and Holcomb Burnell, where Malcolm Burton's father had had his farm. They wouldn't, would they?

He reached for the transmit button. 'Continue on Crediton Road,' he said. 'Dick and Jill, take the lanes to the north. Jane, Ben and I'll go south.'

'Are you thinking what I think you're thinking?' came Dick's response.

'That depends.'

'Surely, it's too obvious.'

'They might think it's appropriate. Or ironic. There's no point counting our chickens, but it's got to be checked.' It hadn't worked out last time, but they'd want to do something different, just in case.

He was getting uncomfortably close to the town of Crediton when he reached the turn he was looking for and swung left, sirens echoing off the trees around him. A few yards later, the woodland faded from his left side, leaving views across open fields. With the road twisting and turning, seemingly at random, he kept the sirens and blue lights on, mindful of the possibility of meeting other traffic on a lane that was rarely wide enough to pass on with, in places, grass and weeds up the middle. But he couldn't afford to slow down – to give the brothers the chance to escape if, indeed, they were ahead of him.

He kept his foot down hard, his only slight advantage over the Southams being his local knowledge. They might have known about the road – would probably have been told of it as a potential escape route in case of unexpected police presence at the barn – but they wouldn't know its twists and turns, nor where to expect villages and junctions.

Tight turns, sweeping curves, junctions, farms and hamlets, woods and fields to either side led him in minutes to the edge of Pathfinder, the only village before the A30. The road skirted the village, letting him keep his speed up. A solar farm flashed past on his left, a few houses on his right and he reached another junction. A quick left and right and he was passing over the main road towards the village he'd been heading for all along.

Holcomb Burnell was a small settlement with pretty stone and white-rendered cottages, its pub festooned with bright hanging baskets and its little church standing proudly on a rise, stone spire glowing in the sunshine. Pete didn't bother with the left and right that would have taken him past Burton's aunt's cottage. Instead, switching off his lights and sirens, he turned right then left, towards the farm and the barn that Malcolm had retained when he rented out the rest of it.

He'd still caught no sight of the pale blue car that he hoped and prayed was somewhere in front of him.

CHAPTER THIRTY-FIVE

Pete swept past the big old farmhouse that Malcolm Burton had grown up in. He would no doubt be seeing the occupants again soon, at Burton's new trial, he thought, picturing them in his mind.

Faintly, he caught a twinkle of red through the leaves and branches at the next bend.

Was it?

Hope flared and he put his foot down hard. Could he catch them before they reached the dirt track that led off through the narrow stretch of woodland to the little meadow with its ancient stone barn?

It didn't really matter so long as he caught sight of them before they did or before he passed the entrance to the track. Pete didn't care where he caught them. He just cared that he did. The symbolism of place was irrelevant.

Rounding a curve, he saw the car ahead clearly for the first time. He couldn't tell the model, but it was certainly pale blue. It had to be them.

He pushed the Ford harder still, blue lights back on as he closed the gap between them. He needed them to see him behind them. If they tried for the track and the car got stuck, they'd decamp and he'd lose at least one of them. He couldn't have that.

They spotted him and, instead of slowing, accelerated.

It was definitely them.

Yes! I'll have you, you bastards. Rage burned fiercely inside him as he pushed the car to its limits, uncaring of the consequences. They flashed past the obscure turn on the left.

Had they remembered the junction by the little ginger-bread cottage?

He'd soon know.

Tyres squealed, brake lights glaring as the blue car slowed abruptly, swinging left at the narrow T-junction. There was a thump as the offside wheels hit the verge. Pete saw the car tip dangerously towards the high hedge. Metal scraped sickeningly on the cut ends of twigs and branches, gouging the car's paintwork. A bang like a grenade going off and the crunch of shattering safety glass sounded as the top corner of the windscreen hit a tree trunk and the back end of the car kicked up, whipping round like a stallion in a rodeo before hitting the ground again, bouncing violently.

Pete hit the brakes in a controlled emergency stop and was out of his seat in an instant, running for the driver's side of the blue Nissan when its stalled engine fired and roared, gearbox whining as it shot backwards down the road.

'Shit.'

He stopped, switched direction and jumped back into his Ford as the sound of the other car's windscreen being kicked out came from behind him.

How the hell they'd survived that unscathed, he'd never know, he thought as he set off after them again, swerving around the shattered windscreen.

They must have spotted the gateway a short distance down on the left before they hit the tree. They swung quickly into it, tyres squealing, and surged out forwards, heading towards the city.

Pete keyed the radio. 'Contact, contact. Suspect vehicle about to join Dunsford Road at the Holcomb Burnell junction. Any available units to intercept urgently.'

He'd lost about four hundred yards on them but had begun to claw back a little by the time they reached the main road. They swung out without slowing, Pete heard the blare of a horn and the screech of tyres over the sound of his own engine. He flicked on the blues and twos, made the junction and swung out around a car the brothers must have narrowly avoided. There was more traffic here. A lorry was trundling up the hill towards him, a couple of cars behind it. He could see the fast-moving car in the near distance, another vehicle already between them and him. As he watched, they overtook again, this time on a blind bend.

'Jesus! You'll kill your bloody selves like that,' he muttered. Not that he cared if they did, but he didn't want an innocent member of the public getting caught up in it. Should he ease off, kill the lights and siren, let them think he'd given up the pursuit?

If he did, he'd lose the ability to gain ground on them with the other vehicles blocking his path and they'd still see him behind them if they looked. He decided against it for now. He keyed the radio again. 'DS Gayle. Any units able to assist with intercept on Dunsford Road, heading inbound to the city, please acknowledge. Suspect vehicle, pale blue Nissan Primera, now without windscreen.'

'Ben Myers to DS Gayle. I'm currently heading into town on the A30. I can try to cut them off at Pocomb Bridge.'

'Received.'

He didn't know if they'd cut across into the city or head down the A30 towards the bottom end of the M5 motorway but either way, they'd have to pass the spot Ben had mentioned. With any luck they'd be able to catch the brothers in a scissor action.

'Traffic car Delta Romeo five two niner, Dan Bridges, currently M5 southbound. Can head up the A30 towards you in two minutes.'

Pete breathed a sigh of relief. If Ben got to Pocomb Bridge in time, that would leave them only one option for escape if they took it: down Dunsford Hill into the city. Other than that, they'd be boxed in with no way out.

Except one.

He keyed the mike. 'Be careful, Dan. They're not known for subtlety. They'll ram you if they're desperate.'

'Received. We can sting them or go for the waltz.'

Pete knew exactly what he meant: park up out of sight and throw a stinger across the road in front of them to burst their tyres or bypass them and swing across to clip their back end, spinning them around. Neither option was ideal with other traffic on the road, but either would be effective in preventing their escape.

'Be safe, guys,' he responded. He wasn't going to order either choice, but he wouldn't complain if they made one of them.

He flashed past a white bungalow on one side of the road, a double entrance on the other. Junctions, farms, the houses getting closer together as he neared the edges of the city though the road was still rural. He passed under the A30. Ben would be coming down there, hopefully going overhead anytime now. The road curved right. Pete was sure he saw, distant though it was, the battered Primera had its side windows down.

Clever.

They were reducing the drag caused by the missing windscreen by releasing the pressure through the sides. It had to be bloody cold in there, though, and hard to breathe at the speeds they were going. It would be like sitting in a wind tunnel.

They approached the junction on the left.

Decision time. In seconds, he would know which way they were going: turn left into town or continue down towards the A30.

Still hurtling along despite the traffic, they didn't slow.

Too late.

They were committed. He keyed the radio. 'Suspects accessing the A30 southbound.'

Now he could gain some ground on them. He overtook two cars at once, leaving only one vehicle – a small lorry – between him and his targets. The long slip road down to the dual carriageway gave him ample time to pass the slower vehicle more safely than the brothers had. It slowed, signalling as the driver saw his blue lights flashing in his mirrors.

Thanks, matey.

The pale blue Nissan was pushing hard towards the dual carriageway. It would have to slow in a moment to join the busier flow of traffic. But it didn't. Horns blared as it cut up at least two vehicles, forcing others to brake behind them.

Pete, at least, had the advantage that people knew he was coming with his sirens wailing and lights flashing in the grille and the back window. He eased over to the outside lane, putting his foot down hard.

His other advantage showed now. They were having to force their way through the traffic, doing all the hard work for him. He could just press on, his lights and sirens keeping people out of his way.

The radio hissed. 'Sorry, boss,' said Ben. 'Didn't make it in time. I'm about a hundred yards behind you.'

Pete glanced in the mirror, saw a set of blues in the distance.

'They're driving like maniacs,' he responded.

Still, they couldn't out-pace him with the problems they had with their vehicle. He gained twenty yards on them. Then thirty. Suddenly, they swung across left under the nose of an articulated lorry.

'Shit,' Pete gasped, cutting across behind the big lorry as its horn blared deep and angry, tyres screaming, back end juddering as the driver tried to avoid jack-knifing his vehicle on the busy road. Somehow, he seemed to pull it through but, by then, Pete was on the off-ramp leading down to Alphington Road.

At the roundabout, whichever brother was driving used the hand-brake to pull the vehicle around to the left. A car coming from the right was slammed sideways into the chevron-painted guard rail as its front wing was clipped by their rear. The impact threw the brothers off-line too, but they fought the car round as Pete braked hard behind them.

Again, the blues and twos helped, traffic slowing to allow him onto the roundabout.

'Suspects off, off, off onto A377 Alphington Road, city-bound,' he reported over the radio as he made the turn, staying behind them although they surged ahead, gaining back most of the ground they'd lost to him on the dual carriageway. A short way up here, he knew, they could cut left and head out of the city, back where they'd come from - not that he imagined they would. Even if they could lose him, they'd know he must have suspected their destination.

They passed the turn. Passed a supermarket on the right, a filling station on the left. Then, without signalling, they swung sharp right, ignoring the slip lane and traffic lights and cutting up cars in every direction as they turned into the big industrial estate.

Pete grinned.

They'd be planning to lose him amid the maze of little roads and off-shoots but there was no way, as non-locals, they could know all the ins and outs of the place like he did.

'Suspects entering Marsh Barton,' he said into the radio as he slowed for the yellow-boxed junction.

'Two hundred yards behind you, boss,' Ben reported.

'Three hundred,' Dan Bridges said from the traffic car.

'Car Charlie Alpha four seven zero coming down Alphington Road from the city,' a third voice reported. 'ETA fifteen seconds.'

Pete made the turn and accelerated after the fleeing car.

'Received,' he replied.

Surging ahead, they were about to pass the drive-through on the left when they surprised him again, braking hard and swinging right into a junction. Pete slowed, made the turn and...

Nothing.

Then movement showed several yards down, beyond the big car showroom on his left. *Mistake, boys.*

369

'Suspects right, right, right into Ashton Road.'

'I'll block the entrance, boss,' Ben offered.

'Roger. Continuing pursuit.'

Pete wondered if the Southams had planned to bail and nick a fresh car from the showroom forecourt, but decided he was too close.

Either way, they'd gone past and on down the dead-end road.

They took the left-hand curve fast. A quick flash of brake lights and they turned left again. Pete grinned, feral and triumphant. They had nowhere to go now and not long to do it in.

Realisation dawned in Pete's mind. They really didn't know where they were. Had they got confused and taken the wrong turn off the main road of the estate?

He saw them round the far end of the last building in a short row. He was now just a few yards behind, braking hard.

Tyres squealed but to no avail.

The impact was like an explosion as the speeding car hit the spiked steel fencing at the end of the short stretch of concrete. The car bucked as it came to an instant stop, the back end kicking up as the front end crumpled. Pete glimpsed something dark and floppy on the bonnet of the wrecked car as he leapt out of the Mondeo almost before it had stopped. He ran forward, barely aware of the sheen of spilled oil or diesel underfoot. Steam was hissing from what was left of the Nissan's engine. The car was a crumpled mess all the way back to the driver's door.

Steve Southam was slumped over the steering wheel. He'd be going nowhere with his legs tangled up and trapped in the mess that had been the foot-well and engine compartment. His brother was lying awkwardly across the remains of the bonnet and the base of the windscreen opening. Blood was smeared on the fence and pouring from his crushed skull, running bright red across the compressed car bonnet and down the far side towards the front wheel. A deep sense of satisfaction and natural justice overtook Pete. He paused a second to take in the scene then, hearing footsteps behind him, he reached over and touched the elder brother's neck to check for a pulse.

There was none.

Pete knew he'd regret this feeling later but, for now, it was all he wanted, and he revelled in it, ignoring the soft exclamations from behind him.

A soft moan came from the younger brother.

Pete didn't know if he was conscious or not, but he leaned down close to him. Reached out as if to check on him or comfort him.

'That's what you get for killing my son, you vicious bastard,' he murmured. 'You've killed your brother now, too. How'd you like them apples?'

A hissing sigh escaped the wounded man's throat.

Leaving the two brothers where they were and ignoring the three wide-eyed men in filthy red overalls at the corner of the building, Pete walked back to his car, sat in and keyed the radio.

'Suspect vehicle stopped,' he said. 'Ambulance. Fire brigade and pathologist required, end of Ashton Road, Marsh Barton.'

CHAPTER THIRTY-SIX

Standing beside the wrecked car as the fire service, pathologist, scenes of crime officers and RTA investigators worked around him in a confusing sea of different get-ups, Pete checked his watch and was shocked to see that the entire chase around the lanes and back into the city had taken little over an hour. It felt like it had started on a completely different day.

The radio in his car brought him crashing back to reality.

'DS Gayle. Report.'

The brusque voice was instantly recognisable. 'Shit,' Pete breathed. How the hell had Silverstone got to hear of this already? 'I haven't got time for this crap.'

He returned to the car, sat in and shut the door. Pressing the transmit button on the radio, he said, 'Suspect Adrian Southam deceased, sir. Suspect Steven Southam seems close to it.'

'You've been told to stay away from that case. Where are you?'

'I got involved, sir, because I was the senior officer present in an emergency situation. And it seems to me that, if you know enough to be on this radio now, you already know where I am.'

'Answer the question, Detective Sergeant. Or I'll have you up on disciplinary charges as well as the Professional Standards investigation.'

'Ashton Road.'

'What?'

'You asked for my location. Ashton Road.'

'Humph. You know perfectly well, that means nothing to me. Ashton Road. Could be in Barnstaple for all I know.'

Which is more of a reflection on your professionalism as head of the local police station than mine, Pete thought, but knew better than to say, especially on an open radio link. 'You asked, sir. I answered. Is there anything else? The pathologist seems to be trying to attract my attention.'

'Is there anything else?' Silverstone squawked. 'Yes, there's something bloody else! This is the second fatal accident you've been involved in, in about a week, man.'

'Yes, sir. And the dash-cam footage will confirm that's exactly what it was – an accident – so it'll give you all the evidence you need to exonerate me of any blame, sir, if that's what you're worried about.'

Silverstone spluttered. He couldn't argue with that over the radio. 'Right. My office as soon as you get back to the station. And that means as soon as, Detective Sergeant.'

'Sir.'

Pete got out of the car and approached the silver-haired Doc Chambers, who was standing beside the mangled blue Nissan, examining the man who had been driving it. Without even glancing up, he said, 'Your second suspect died, I'm afraid, Peter.'

Pete nodded. 'Thanks, doc. I've got to leave you to it. Orders.'

Chambers looked up at him. 'Hm. Trouble in Paradise?'

Pete gave a grunt. 'I've never heard Heavitree Road called paradise before.'

The pathologist smiled and waved him off. Pete threw him a salute in return.

His mind was busy as he drove away. Should he go straight back to the station or to the hospital first? There'd be nineteen dozen kinds of paperwork to deal with over this, interviews with Professional Standards and all kinds of crap. It would easily take the rest of the day and more. Especially when, as Fast-track had pointed out, he'd been involved in a very similar incident only a few days ago. On the other hand, Louise would need to be told what had happened.

He ummed and ahed until he got to the end of the road. Then, decision made, he left the industrial estate behind.

Family came first.

*

Louise was at the ward desk, a phone to her ear when he walked in. She seemed to freeze when she saw him, losing awareness of anything else. There was no expression on her face as she watched his approach and Pete's heart broke that he couldn't offer her any visual clue as to his own feelings.

He had yet to figure out what they were.

It was way too soon to feel elation or triumph – even satisfaction - at the death of the man who'd killed Tommy. Yet, inside, he knew justice had been served, albeit natural justice rather than the legal kind he'd spent the last twenty years upholding on behalf of an often-ungrateful public.

374

He felt no regret at what had happened - what Silverstone would probably try to claim he'd forced the brothers into. But nor could he claim any sense of joy from it. It was what it was. In some sense that really didn't matter and wouldn't until he'd recovered at least a little from the rawness of Tommy's loss, it provided a degree of closure, if only in an eye-for-an-eye kind of way and in the sense that the perpetrators of the horror he and his family were going through wouldn't be able to inflict such pain on anyone else.

Other than that, he could feel nothing for them or their loss to the world.

His lips tightened and he nodded to her.

Louise suddenly realised she was still holding the phone she'd been speaking into. She jolted back to reality, said something brief and hung up. She went to rise but failed and stayed where she was as he covered the final few steps towards her. He didn't go around the high-topped counter. Not yet. Instead, stopped in front of her and spread his hands on the narrow surface.

'What… What is it? Why are you here?'

'I wanted to tell you in person. The Southam brothers are dead. Both of them. I've just come from the scene. There's no question it's them.'

Her eyes had widened, but he couldn't read the expression behind them. Horror, relief, sympathy, loss. They were all there and more. Like him, she was still grieving, still raw, but this was news that she'd never have expected him to bring.

'How?' she breathed.

'Car crash. I was chasing them. They took a wrong turn. It was a dead-end.' He realised what he'd said and gave her a ghost of a smile. 'They hit a steel fence and it didn't give way.'

She looked confused. 'You were chasing them?'

He nodded.

'I thought one of them was in prison?'

'He was. There was an incident at the prison gates this morning. His brother managed to get him out of the prison transport van and get away in a stolen car. Time I got there, they were long gone, but I had an idea of where they might go to hide. It turned out I was right. There was a chase.' He shrugged. 'I thought I ought to come and tell you before I go and get my nuts roasted by His Lordship.'

She frowned.

'I wasn't supposed to have anything to do with them.'

'Well… That bloke's unbelievable,' she frowned.

Pete gave a soft grunt. 'Tell me about it.'

'But, how can he blame you for any of this?'

'Oh, he'll find a way. Trust me.'

'Well, he's an arse-hole and if you let me anywhere near him, I'll tell him so,' she declared. 'And if he drops you in it, I'll tell the bloody world!'

Pete smiled fully for the first time since he'd found Tommy. He stepped around the counter at last as she stood to meet him and took her in his arms. 'God, I love you!'

'And I love you,' she replied. 'And we will get through this. I don't know how, but we will.'

*

'We've got news, boss,' Jill declared as Pete walked into the squad room to drop off his briefcase before going to the DCI's office.

'What about?'

'The Hanson case.'

He frowned. 'We've closed that, haven't we?'

'Yes,' Jane put in. 'And now we've locked the door and thrown away the key.'

'Eh?'

'Two things. One: we've found a photo of Lucy Willoughby in Hanson's collection. Confirms what she said to you and Jane. And two: Lincs phoned. You know they were doing forensics on his car. Found blood and hair. Well, they've now got a match on the hair. It was a misper. One they'd had reported a few days ago, but hadn't done anything about because of her history. A prostitute. Her friends had reported that she hadn't returned from a pick-up. Police just figured she'd either got an all-nighter or gone off somewhere to get high afterwards. She was a druggie.'

'Was?'

Jane nodded.

'They found her body yesterday,' Jill continued. 'In a ditch along the side of a B-road about five miles from where she disappeared from. A farmer smelled something nasty. Thought it was a dead badger or something, but then his dog took an interest, came out of the ditch with a shoe and he had a closer look. In the circumstances, they put a rush on the forensics. The hair matches hers and DNA on her necklace matches Hanson's. She was strangled.'

Pete nodded and set down his briefcase. For the second time that day, he felt that triumph was not an appropriate emotion for the occasion. A woman had lost her life while they'd been pursuing her killer. 'That seals it, then. Murder as well as rape. Good work, everyone.'

'Gayle.'

The voice came from behind him, but he knew instantly who it was. He turned. Silverstone was standing in the doorway of the squad room.

'Sir.'

'I seem to recall I said immediately.'

'I was on the way, sir.'

Silverstone stepped back, letting the door shut between them. Pete grimaced at Jane and went reluctantly after him.

Nothing was said as they walked the short distance to his office door. He went in and left it open. Back in the chair behind his desk, he paused a moment, letting Pete stand there like a school boy before his headmaster's desk. Then he took a deep breath in through his nose, neck thrusting forward, brow tightening. 'Who the hell do you think you are, Gayle? John bloody Wayne? Well, let me be perfectly clear. You're not and this is not the Wild bloody West. We have rules and, if you really want to keep your job here, you will abide by them. At all times and with no excuses.'

'Sir.'

'What is it that makes you think the rules of this police force don't apply to you, Detective Sergeant?'

'I don't, sir,' Pete replied, feeling none of the trepidation that he would have in the headmaster's office.

Silverstone seemed to calm. 'You don't.' Then the illusion was gone. 'Then why am I constantly seeing you in this office after some infraction or other? Are you deaf, defiant or uncaring about your career?'

Pete took a breath. 'For you, this is a career, sir. For me, I have little if any prospect of promotion beyond where I am. That's been the case ever since either of us joined the force. This isn't a career for me, it's a vocation. It's not something I do, it's something I am.' Pete spoke in an even, matter-of-fact tone. 'I don't set out to break rules or ignore regulations. I just occasionally find myself in situations where the most appropriate response doesn't comply with them.'

Silverstone let the silence hang as if he were expecting more. Finally, he spoke, still quiet and calm. 'I see. So you see me as a career man rather than a grass-roots copper, is that it? A man with no vocation or concept of the real world, whose orders can therefore be ignored at will?'

'That's not what I...'

'Well, let me tell you, Detective Sergeant,' Silverstone barked. 'I don't give a flying fuck what you think of me. I am in charge of this station and, as such, in direct control your career, job, vocation – whatever you want to call it. And at this moment, I am suspending it. You are no longer part of this force until Professional Standards have completed their investigation into your conduct. Is that clear enough for you to manage to comply with?'

'Perfectly, sir.' He'd already been told by Colin that he didn't need to be here today. This just reinforced that. 'I've just got one thing to do before I go.'

Silverstone exploded out of his chair like a volcano going off, his face bright red. Pete almost expected steam to erupt from his ears and had difficulty not smiling at the image in his mind as the senior man yelled, 'Give me your warrant card and get out of my bloody office!'

Pete stood his ground. 'I was going to say, sir, that I need to inform Jonas Hanson's daughter that we've found her father and she was fully vindicated in her suspicions. He'll be charged with multiple rapes and murders later this morning.'

'I don't care,' Silverstone snarled.

Pete tossed his warrant card on the desk between them, reached for the door and opened it. He knew what the DCI meant, but he couldn't help taking the opportunity to mis-interpret. 'And that's the real difference between us. Sir.'

He closed the door and walked away, leaving Silverstone apoplectic and speechless behind him and knowing that, while he was under investigation by Professional Standards – as he'd expected to be after what had happened – the DCI would have his own problems to deal with. He recalled Louise's indignant outrage when he'd told her about the lack of anyone outside their house last night. She'd immediately picked up the phone and made an official complaint of reckless endangerment against the DCI for neglecting his duty of care to his own officers and their families as well as the wider public, ensuring that the IPCC, the Independent Police Complaints Commission, would be looking into his conduct and competence.

Pete would do what was right before he went off on enforced leave, regardless of DCI Adam Fast-track Silverstone.

Minutes later, he was in his car with Jane Bennett at his side. He'd taken her rather than Ben for two reasons. One: she was a woman and he was on the way to deal with a woman who could well become highly emotional before they left her; a situation for which protocol demanded the presence of a female officer. And two: he didn't want to put Ben in the position of facing the woman who had come to him as a trusted friend, simply in the hopes of finding her missing father.

*

'How do you think she's going to take it, boss?' Jane asked as he pulled up outside Sally Hanson's 1960's terraced house, not far from her father's off the other of Pennsylvania Road.

'She knew what she was doing when she called Ben.'

'Yeah, but… Her own dad? Surely, she must have been hoping we'd exonerate him, not confirm what she'd found?'

'I don't know, Jane. We'll see, won't we? I'm going to see Dave Miles after this.'

'You'll need to be quick,' she retorted. 'He won't be in there much longer. They'll chuck him out as soon as they can – if not for the bed, for chasing the nurses. You'll charge Hanson first, though?'

'I'll have to let you and Dick do that.' He opened the car door and stepped out.

'Do what?' she demanded across the roof of the car.

'Professional Standards,' he said, setting off across the garden with its mostly bare lawn and uneven slab path. He rang the bell and knocked on the dirty white UPVC door.

It was opened by a young woman who looked like life had worn her down over the few days since he'd first met her. 'Hello.'

He raised a hand to Jane. 'This is DC Bennett. Can we come in? It won't take long.'

She stood back, nodding towards a door on the left.

They went into a through lounge-diner. It was clean and tidy if a little worn, Pete saw. She might not have much, but she made the best of it.

'Have a seat,' Sally offered. She took one of the easy chairs opposite them.

When they were all comfortable, Pete drew a breath. 'We've found your dad, Sally.'

A small whimper escaped her throat. 'Is he... All right?'

Pete nodded. 'He's fine. He's at the station.'

She frowned.

Pete leaned forward, almost reaching out to take her hands. 'You were right, Sally. What you found was the real thing. He...'

'No!' she wailed, her head tipping back. 'No.' She hunched up, her face dropping into her hands. 'All those...' She looked up, her face tear-stained, eyes haunted. 'He can't have, can he? How could...? How could *anyone*...? There's got to be...'

Pete shook his head. 'There's no mistake, Sally, and no doubt. I'm sorry, but he did all the things you found evidence of. He's being charged this morning.'

She hid her face again, sobbing tragically.

'I'm so sorry, Sally,' he repeated.

She sniffed and raised her eyes to look at him, her face tear-stained and mascara-streaked. She drew a breath. 'It's not your fault, is it? It's his. But my life here in Exeter is over, isn't it? Mum's too.'

It was a sad reflection on modern society, but that didn't make it any less true. 'We'll do all we can to protect you. You know that. But honestly? You'd be better off moving. Changing your name.' He recalled her fiancé, Tony. They might not be living an ideal life, but he seemed like a good man. A man who cared about her and their son. 'Although I don't know you as well as Ben, I can tell that whatever you do, wherever you go, you'll make a success of it.'

She reached out to him then, took his hands in hers. 'Thank you,' she said. 'For finding him and for finding the truth. As much as it hurts, he's hurt a lot more people a hell of a lot more. A lot of families whose lives he's ruined. I just wish I'd found that stuff a lot sooner. It might have saved... God knows how many lives.'

'You can't put that on yourself, Sally. None of it's your fault. None of it.'

'No, but... I can't imagine what pain I'd feel if I lost Jem.' She shuddered at the thought. 'And he's put how many people through that?'

Pete couldn't help thinking of Tommy, picturing him hanging in that tree over the river, as still as only a dead body could be.

'Too many,' Jane said. 'Way too many. But it's over now. You need to hold onto that. There'll be no more.'

NO MIDDLE GROUND by JACK SLATER

AUTHOR'S NOTE

First and most importantly, I have to thank a number of people who helped during the writing of this book. As always, Pru was indispensable. Also retired magistrate Maurice Humphries and former traffic warden Lois Richardson who pointed me in the right direction when necessary, a certain desk sergeant at Heavitree Road who wished to remain nameless and the staff of my local police station in north Oxfordshire who provided valuable insight in procedural matters.

As a reader as well as a writer, I have learned that credibility and credulity are essential in fiction. If you lose either, you have lost your reader. So, although these books are an entertainment, an important part of providing that entertainment is to maintain factual accuracy where a reader might know better. I hope and believe that I succeed in that aspect of the writing, as comments received suggest I do, but any inaccuracies that slip in are entirely my fault and I appreciate any comments from readers who spot them, if only so that I can learn and correct them.

Exeter is a vibrant, busy and attractive city with a small-town footprint and a friendly atmosphere. Settled for at least two thousand years, it is an eclectic mix of modern, old and truly ancient and I wanted from the outset to feature is as much as possible in these books, almost as a character in itself.

Nonetheless I sometimes have to take geographical liberties for the sake of security, privacy, commercial considerations or dramatic effect, sometimes creating fictionalised locations within the city or its surroundings. In this book, I have altered certain aspects of the Combined Court House, its immediate environs and the streets and alleys between there and the central shopping area of the city. Other examples throughout the series include the village of Holcomb Burnell, Risingbrook school in book one, the ice rink mentioned in book two and The Old Mill carvery which has featured in more than one book as well as the homes and workplaces of the characters. Otherwise I try to remain as accurate as possible to the true feel and topography of the city, both in order to please those who either live in or have visited Exeter and to do the city itself justice.

I hope you have enjoyed this book and, if so, that you will take the time to post a review on whichever platform you purchased it through.

I hope also that you are looking forward to Pete Gayle's further adventures as much as I am.

You can contact the author either through Facebook at facebook.com/crimewriter2016 or via the Jack Slater web site at http://jackslaterauthor.site123.me/

51270441RQ0236

Made in the USA
Lexington, KY
01 September 2019